IN THE LABYRINTH
OF THE
BISHOP'S PALACE—DEATH

Someone else was in the passage up ahead.

Whoever he was, wherever he was, the stranger moved quietly. Then he stopped.

Perhaps a minute passed before Maurice could hear the stranger move again. There was the sound of cloth on cloth, of metal on stone. He switched the flashlight back on, aiming it into the darkness like a weapon.

A man's face turned to face the glare, his arms laden with objects—a book, a scroll, a golden cross. His eyes were charged with terror as he leapt into the light.

Maurice pulled out his gun just as the cross descended, glittering. The flashlight tumbled from his hand, dragging the darkness down. He pulled the trigger to the sound of breaking glass.

There was a dull thud as the two men came together, and then the cold retreating echo of a cry. . . .

Gospel Truths

J.G. Sandom

BANTAM BOOKS
NEW YORK · TORONTO · LONDON · SYDNEY · AUCKLAND

This novel was inspired by a real death. Readers should not think this is anything other than a work of fiction, however, as all of the characters in the book, whether central or peripheral, are purely the product of the author's imagination. Though a similar death actually occurred, all of the events surrounding it, as well as the actions, motivations, thoughts, and conversations of the characters, are solely the author's creation, and neither the characters nor the situations which were invented are intended to depict real people or real events.

This edition contains the complete text
of the original hardcover edition.
NOT ONE WORD HAS BEEN OMITTED

GOSPEL TRUTHS
A Bantam Crime Line Book

PUBLISHING HISTORY
Doubleday edition published March 1992
Bantam edition / January 1993

CRIME LINE and the portrayal of a boxed "cl" are trademarks of Bantam Books, a division of Bantam Doubleday Dell Publishing Group, Inc.

Grateful acknowledgment is made for permission to reprint an excerpt from "The Ultimate Atrocity," from *Collected Poems* by Siegfried Sassoon. Copyright © 1918, 1920 by E. P. Dutton. Copyright © 1936, 1946, 1947, 1948 by Siegfried Sassoon. Used by permission of Viking Penguin, a division of Penguin Books USA Inc.

All rights reserved.
Copyright © 1992 by J. G. Sandom.
Cover art copyright © 1992 by Tim Jessell.
Library of Congress Catalog Card Number 91-26067.
No part of this book may be reproduced or transmitted in any form or by any means, electronic or mechanical, including photocopying, recording, or by any information storage and retrieval system, without permission in writing from the publisher. For information address: Bantam Books, 666 Fifth Avenue, New York, NY 10103.

If you purchased this book without a cover you should be aware that this book is stolen property. It was reported as "unsold and destroyed" to the publisher and neither the author nor the publisher has received any payment for this "stripped book."

ISBN 0-553-29629-9

Published simultaneously in the United States and Canada

Bantam Books are published by Bantam Books, a division of Bantam Doubleday Dell Publishing Group, Inc. Its trademark, consisting of the words "Bantam Books" and the portrayal of a rooster, is Registered in U.S. Patent and Trademark Office and in other countries. Marca Registrada. Bantam Books, 666 Fifth Avenue, New York, New York 10103.

PRINTED IN THE UNITED STATES OF AMERICA

RAD   0 9 8 7 6 5 4 3 2 1

FOR ZANE AND ELSE

Even the most matter-of-fact contents of consciousness have a penumbra of uncertainty around them. Even the most carefully defined philosophical or mathematical concept, which we are sure does not contain more than we have put into it, is nevertheless more than we assume. It is a psychic event and as such partly unknowable. The very numbers you use in counting are more than you take them to be.

CARL G. JUNG
Man and His Symbols

Gospel Truths

Prologue

RAIN STARTED TO FALL AS MAURICE
Duval drove his battered blue Peugeot through the
gate behind Place Saint Michel, onto the crackling
gravel drive which skirted the cathedral and the ancient
Bishop's Palace. As he neared the palace, he dropped
his cigarette through the open window and turned the
car lights off. The rain fell fiercely. The white stone
window frames glimmered dimly between muddy brick,
the wet slate roof shimmered through the trees. Maurice cut the engine and the car crawled to a stop.

Behind the falling rain, the sound of organ music
swelled the evening air. Someone was practicing late,
he thought. The night watchman was nowhere to be
seen. Maurice slipped his porkpie hat on and took the
pistol out again, to check the ammunition, to calm himself.

Above the southern wing of the palace, the rose of
the cathedral's transept window glowed red and cobalt
blue. In a year or more the renovation of the palace
would be finished, and a trade school would replace

the emptiness. The École Supérieure was a flagship
project of the new socialist government, but Maurice
knew that to the farmers and fishermen of the province
the building would always remain the Bishop's Palace.
The emblem of Picardie was a snail, after all, and despite its name a bishop had not slept within the resi-
dence for a hundred years. The windows were boarded
shut, the walls emblazoned with graffiti. He closed the
car door noiselessly and headed for the southern wing.

A cement mixer stood by the door leading down
into the basement. Maurice hesitated. Was he too late?
He pulled a flashlight from his jacket and turned it on.
The basement door was closed but he could clearly see
a piece of paper wadding stuffed beside the bolt. The
organ music had stopped. Cold rain washed the palace
walls. He pressed his elbow to his side to feel the gun
again. Then he opened the door and stepped inside.

The air in the basement was sweet with Noviganth
and other chemicals. Empty Kronenbourg beer bottles
lay strewn across the floor and on the dusty windowsills
which faced the outer palace square. Maurice moved
through the room, illuminating the corners with his
flashlight. He had almost reached the door leading up
into the palace when he saw the hole. It had been
neatly concealed behind a pile of earth, cut in the
ground right at the foot of the southern wall. He
walked slowly across the basement wing and shone the
flashlight down into the opening. A piece of corrugated
iron partially blocked the shaft, but he could still make
out a kind of tunnel, hemmed in by stones. He tossed
his hat on the ground and began to kick the dirt
roughly to the side.

It took him only a few minutes to lift the corrugated iron high enough for him to slip down into the
opening. He moved head first, the flashlight bouncing
in his hand as he dragged himself along on his belly.
Suddenly the organ music echoed up the passage, and

he realized he was moving underneath the cobbled road between the palace and the great cathedral.

He crawled forward for another fifteen meters in this fashion when he sensed the air grow fresher about his face. The stone tunnel turned abruptly to the left. Then, just as suddenly, it opened onto a larger corridor below him. He shone the flashlight through the darkness. The floor of the corridor was a good two-meter drop from the mouth of the tunnel.

Maurice lowered himself carefully down into the corridor. As he turned, he saw the lintel of a narrow doorway to his left. It led into a small room, a closet really, around which ran a low stone bench.

Beyond the closet the corridor curved sharply to the right. Maurice started slowly up the darkened passage. The music seemed louder now, and for the first time he realized that it was not particularly good, just a patternless series of notes, an endless repetition.

He turned the flashlight off and crouched clumsily against the wall. Someone else was in the passage up ahead.

Whoever he was, wherever he was, the stranger moved quietly. Then he stopped.

Perhaps a minute passed before Maurice could hear the stranger move again. There was the sound of cloth on cloth, of metal on stone. He switched the flashlight on, aiming it into the darkness like a weapon.

A man's face turned to face the glare, his arms laden with objects—a book, a scroll, a golden cross. His eyes were charged with terror as he leapt into the light.

Maurice pulled out his gun just as the cross descended, glittering. The flashlight tumbled from his hand, dragging the darkness down. He pulled the trigger to the sound of breaking glass.

There was a dull thud as the two men came together, and then the cold retreating echo of a cry.

·   ·   ·

"That was close." Father Marchelidon lifted his hands from the keyboard. He glanced through the opening in the wall of the organ room to the cathedral floor below. The sound of thunder followed. "Did you hear that?"

The bearded man beside him shrugged. "The wind," he suggested. "Thunder and wind."

"It sounded like a scream," the priest said.

"Someone heard your playing." The bearded man laughed and clamped an arm about his companion's narrow shoulders. "The ghost of Antoine Avernier, no doubt. Have I told you the story of his death? It's one of my best. He carved the choir stalls, you know."

"Save it for the tourists, Guy." The priest looked down again into the dark basilica. Nothing stirred and yet the shadows seemed a little longer, the cathedral colder.

The night watchman shone his flashlight through the windshield of the blue Peugeot. He had not noticed it pull in, and this worried him. It was his boss's car.

"Maurice?" The rain fell heavily from the darkness above, stinging his eyes. There was no answer. "Maurice." He shone his flashlight round the square and sighed. It was a lonely job, night watchman, not suited to his friendly temperament, his unfashionable sense of camaraderie.

He turned from the car and began to walk back toward the Bishop's Palace. The basement door was slightly ajar. He ran his fingernails along the gap. This was unusual. This was wrong.

With another sigh he leaned down, careful to support his back, and picked up a piece of rain-soaked scrap wood from the ground. If it was the Flichy boys again he would need it. They had evil temperaments, he thought, unsuited to anything but petty crime and pimping. They would end up dead someday, not just dead but casual dead, in an alley, in an oily harbor with their pockets empty. He opened the door.

Perhaps he had had too much again. But it was cold for May, he told himself as he moved across the room. And besides, his bottle was his only stalwart friend these days, the only ally left.

The light bounced off the far wall and returned. He scanned the basement carefully, the corners and the windowsills. Then he smiled and called out loudly once again, "Maurice." There was no answer. He checked the door to the main part of the palace. It was locked. He turned away and in that movement he resolved, as he had done already twice that month, that he would leave the bottle home next time. He was too old to rely upon his reflexes alone, to think his instincts would preserve him as they had done in Vietnam and in Algeria. The breaking of a twig had saved him once, the splinter of a palm across the path. But the Flichy boys would never give him that. They were too cautious, and providence had left his life a droplet at a time.

The night watchman moved back through the basement room, not once aware of the two hands which pushed the dirt up slowly from below, until the hole in which Maurice had vanished only thirty minutes earlier had disappeared from view, until the ground was smooth and featureless and almost all was as it had been.

Part I

Chapter I

LONDON
August 10th, 1983

HE WAS LATE, OR EVERYONE ELSE WAS early once again. Nigel Lyman dug his elbows in his sides and leaned into the morning, moving with the cadence of a military parade. He was not a particularly tall man, but there was a solidity about his body, a tightness of the neck and shoulders, that lent itself by nature to this kind of grim, determined walk. He moved as if to prove the definition of a line.

A fierce breeze played against the rain, and as Lyman walked he pointed his umbrella at a dozen different clouds, jabbing at the fickle wind. The sidewalk was almost empty. Most of the city was at work already, save for a few resilient shoppers, the tardy secretaries, the intentionally lost. The street coursed dreamily along, the shop walls rising to the rain, the gray slate roofs and grayer sky of London.

Lyman turned off the street and entered the police station. A small crowd waited by the elevator. He passed them with a terse hello, and noticed as he headed for the stairwell at the back that a line of water trailed his wet umbrella down the hall. It was going to be one of those days, again.

He took the steps two at a time, trying to ignore the dark familiar landmarks of the first few floors, the sergeant constable on duty, the holding cells, the paperwork policemen, where Dotty Taylor worked with rows and rows of numbers in accounting.

When he reached the fourth floor, he stopped and took his scarf and coat off, dropping them delicately across a battery of pipes near the door. Then he hung up his umbrella, the bent spoke closest to the wall.

No one gave him much more than a passing glance as he entered the office, but Lyman knew they registered his presence. It was almost ten A.M. Some were just too polite, he thought, too bloody shy, or too embarrassed to say anything. Some really didn't care. And then there were the rest, who hoped that one day his apparent lack of gumption would be noticed upstairs, but who refused to drag his failings from the shadows by themselves, afraid perhaps that adding peccadillos to his already damning sins might seem vindictive.

He walked between the rows of desks. Eight policemen shared the office, and most sat with their faces turned away, trying not to look at Lyman. Some read reports with studied concentration. Some talked in whispers on the telephone.

Lyman sat down at his metal desk. It was the tidiest in the room, the surface empty save for an old black telephone, an ashtray, and a well-oiled manual typewriter.

"Starting early," Inspector Blackwell said beside him.

Lyman turned, facing Blackwell and the open window. It was always open, sun or snow. He reached into his pocket, removed a tin of licorice, and popped one in his mouth.

"By the by," continued Blackwell, "Chief Superintendent Cocksedge wants to see you. As soon as you come in. Hello. Are you there?"

Lyman frowned. "When did Cocksedge poke around?"

"Poke?" Blackwell's eyebrows seemed to skate across his forehead. "The detective chief superintendent does not poke. His representatives may poke. He delegates. He confers."

"Just answer the question, Blackwell."

"Very well. Although I'm not exactly fond of your interrogation methods. Positively rural. He sent the Lemur down at nine."

"Thanks," Lyman answered in a kind of cough. His head hurt. It had hurt since late last night, or even longer. He pushed his chair away from the desk.

"I won fifty pounds in the football pool yesterday," Blackwell crowed.

Lyman ran his fingers through his hair. It was still thick, just grayer round the edges, like burnt paper. "Good for bloody you."

"Now I can pay you back that twenty quid."

Lyman straightened his suit jacket. "Wrong again, Blackwell. It's I owe you."

Inspector Blackwell smiled. "There you go," he said. "Clever lad. And when exactly, if I may ask, are you going to pay me?"

Lyman glanced down at his shoes. They were soaked through. He turned and headed for the door.

"Give him our best," Blackwell called after him. "And don't forget my money."

Detective Chief Superintendent of Police Brian R. Cocksedge, late of the Royal Navy, was fond of quoting Siegfried Sassoon in a dramatic baritone whenever he was struck by the oppressive realization that Man was, comparatively speaking, barely out of the trees of Africa. At times, especially when he had been upstaged again by Scotland Yard, he would stand firmly in the doorway of his office, pitching his voice at no one in particular. " 'When the first man,' " he'd cry, " 'who wasn't quite an ape/ Felt magnanimity and prayed for more,/ The world's redemption stood, in human shape,/ With darkness done and betterment before.' "

Nigel Lyman reflected on this as he waited for the elevator. He had never really cared for Siegfried Sassoon. To him redemption was a pointless exercise, an almost Arthurian quest, one which had little to do with real human motivation, and therefore even less to do with crime.

He pressed the elevator button for the third time and uttered a faithless prayer that the chief superintendent was not in one of his discoursing moods again. Indeed, he thought, given a choice between a grim oration and a short farewell, he would prefer the door. What else could it mean? he asked himself. It was amazing he had lasted quite this long. The elevator doors creaked open.

The chief superintendent's secretary, Mrs. Clanger, eyed him with a codlike, blinkless stare. "Ah, Mr. Lyman," she said. "Are you absolutely sure you have the time? I mean, after all." She looked at her wide-faced watch.

Lyman tried to usher up the smile of a conspirator. "Sorry I'm late. I had an early meeting across the river."

Mrs. Clanger did not soften. A moment passed, and finally she poked her vintage intercom and announced his presence.

"Right. Send him through," the chief superintendent bellowed in response.

Lyman walked briskly across the room and opened the door. The chief superintendent's office was cluttered and ill lit, but Lyman took in the details with a single practiced glance: an overfull metal file cabinet; a faded rose-and-foliage shade atop a standing lamp;

several photographs in neat walnut frames, mostly old
navy friends and famous personages; a sizable portrait
of Her Majesty, Queen Elizabeth II, artist unknown; a
rugger ribbon; an honorary degree from Bristol University; green curtains, standard issue; and a massive
coatrack and umbrella stand, barely visible beneath
several coats of various weights and textures.

Detective Chief Superintendent Cocksedge stood at
the window behind his desk, staring out into the wet
gray street. Lollipop crosswalk lights blinked on and off
below, lending his already waxy countenance an orange
patina. "Nasty, isn't it," he said, pulling at his narrow
mustache.

"All week," Lyman answered.

"Yes. All week." Suddenly Cocksedge turned fully
round. His face was long and pale, with a pair of
creases running up and down both sides of his forehead, like poorly sewn seams. "Good for pike fishing
though, eh, Lyman?" He took a reluctant step toward
his desk. "It says here you're a . . ." His hand flipped
through a file. "A 'fisherman of some experience,'
whatever that means. Surely every boy in England over
five years old is a fisherman of 'some experience.' What
do those people in personnel do all day? It's beyond
me, I'm sure."

Lyman remained silent.

Chief Superintendent Cocksedge sighed loudly. He
pulled his chair out and sat formally behind his desk.
"I'll be honest with you, Lyman. You're in a bloody
mess."

"I know, sir."

The chief superintendent raised a hand. "Don't in-
terrupt me, dammit. I'm trying to help you, Lyman. I'm
on your side." He turned to the beginning of what
Lyman gathered was his file.

There was that picture of his ex-wife, Jackie, on her
old bicycle, Lyman noticed. It was stapled to a set of
crinkled yellow pages. Personnel always used yellow for

dependents. Lyman wondered if there was some logic to the color.

"Now," the chief superintendent continued. "There are certain gentlemen here at City of London and at Metropolitan who are of the opinion that Nigel Lyman's talents are on the wane, that after a promising beginning he has fiddled away his career." He scanned Lyman's face. "I am *not* one of them," he added gravely. "Of course, I won't pretend to understand your personal feelings concerning that ghastly business last summer in the Falklands. Frankly, and I say this as a father as well as a former officer in Her Majesty's Navy, I don't believe it should have anything to do with the business at hand, with getting the job done. I lost half my brothers at Tobruk. Two at one time. Your son's death, tragic as it was, was but one part of the price we all pay for decency in this country."

"Yes, sir." Inspector Lyman looked beyond the window. He had never even known where the Falklands were before Peter had enlisted. He had only known the name from reading it on those little plastic tags clipped to the lamb his butcher sold in Golders Green. One of Jackie's cousins had once visited the South Atlantic islands. She had even sent some picture postcards back, but Lyman could not remember if they were still down in the cellar, in that box, or if his ex-wife had removed them with the rest of her belongings.

The flat was empty now. Jackie had gone back to Winchester after the divorce. And all that remained of Peter were his obligations, his gambling debts, his unpaid loans. To this day, Lyman continued to pick up after his son, as he had done throughout his life. Even Peter's little mongrel, George, had found his roundabout way back to Lyman. Jackie hadn't wanted him. He shed too much. He ruined her clothes. He too was now superfluous.

"On the other hand," the chief superintendent added, chopping a hand through the air, "if the personal life of one of my men interferes with his work, then I am forced to take a position. And believe you me, when I take a position, I do so with vigor. Am I making myself clear?"

"Yes, sir," Lyman said.

"I took a risk with you, Lyman. I did your uncle a favor. A lot of people thought that I was being bloody silly, taking in a country constable, despite your success with that so-called College Killer. What am I meant to tell them now?"

"That they were right, perhaps."

"Don't be an ass, Lyman. Buck up. Pull yourself together."

Lyman realized with a start that the chief superintendent was a desperate man. He scowled behind his desk, meshing his narrow fingers like a pair of combs, then pulling them apart. If Cocksedge fell, it would be from greater heights, and this is what concerned him.

The City of London Police were traditionally an indigenous brood. Cocksedge had been somewhat daring in his hiring of Lyman, although it had really been the public and the press who had authorized the move.

For Lyman had once enjoyed a fortnight in the sun, after the daring capture of a history teacher who had systematically dismembered several young boys at a prestigious public school in Hampshire. The "Case of the College Killer," as the *Daily Mail* had called it, had thrown the young inspector live into the hungry crowd. With his newfound notoriety and Jackie's passion for the city, he had moved to London, forever silencing the editorials and all the righteous politicians who had growled, "Why aren't there any Nigel Lymans solving crimes here in London?" He had come and been forgotten, his flirtation with the people but a summer romance after all. "I'm sorry, sir," Lyman answered finally. "Of course you can't say that."

The chief superintendent settled back in his chair, a faint smile pulling at his lips. "Now, about this Crosley matter," he added softly. "Why don't you tell me, in your own words, exactly what happened, so that we can settle this thing once and for all. Sit down. Take your time."

Lyman pulled a chair up beside the desk. "Thank you, sir," he said. He reached into his jacket and removed a pack of Players cigarettes. "May I?" The chief superintendent nodded. Lyman picked a cigarette with care and placed it gently in the corner of his mouth.

"It wasn't just an ordinary case," he said, striking a match and lighting up. "That's why we were armed, according to the directive." A blue sigh of smoke rolled across the desk. "First there was that blond girl with the gardening trowel in her chest. And then all those others."

Cocksedge grunted an acknowledgment.

Lyman told him of the investigation. His voice was calm, devoid of emphasis.

"We thought it was Spendlove all along—Crosley especially. There was something about him neither of us felt quite right about."

He took a long drag off his cigarette, remembering. "We went to pick him up on Friday morning."

"Who's we? Be specific, man."

"Constable Crosley and I, Detective Sergeant Thompson, and Constable John Sykes. Thompson and Sykes stayed downstairs, watching the window, while Crosley and I went upstairs. At first everything went smoothly. Spendlove appeared as if he'd been expecting us. We showed him the warrant and he just fell apart, crying and pulling at his hair. He looked spent."

"Why wasn't he handcuffed?"

"We were about to when he bolted for the door. Crosley ran after him."

"What did you do?"

"First I shouted down to Sykes and told him what had happened. Then I followed Geoffrey—Constable Crosley, I mean. He had tackled Spendlove on the landing. It was then I saw the knife. Spendlove must have had it hidden in his jacket. I was too far away to help, so I drew my gun and shouted out the warning."

Lyman paused. He took a final puff from his cigarette and snapped the burning head off in the ashtray on the desk.

The chief superintendent swiveled in his chair. "Go on," he said.

"Then they both got up. Spendlove was on the far side of the landing, with Crosley caught between us. That's when Spendlove stabbed him."

"Is that all? Wasn't Crosley armed? The suspect was clearly dangerous."

Lyman nodded. "Yes, he was armed," he answered dreamily. "But the directive is still so new. Crosley wasn't used to guns." He turned and looked away. "I had my weapon trained on Spendlove. I remember that. I was just about to squeeze the trigger when Sergeant Thompson fired. People had already started looking out their doors. It was a bit of a riot after that, sir, I'm afraid."

"I see," Cocksedge said. "I understand." He nodded firmly. "You never had a clear shot, is that it? You couldn't pick him off while they were struggling."

Lyman nodded. "Yes, that was it. I couldn't really see. He was a good lad, Crosley. Too young to die like that."

"Of course he was," Cocksedge answered angrily. "But he knew what his job was. He knew the risks. Don't go blaming yourself now." The chief superintendent shook his head. "He was about your son's age, wasn't he? Yes, I thought so. It wasn't your fault, Lyman. It was just bad luck. The question is, of course, what now?"

"Sir? A review, I suppose."

"Do you? Well, don't suppose. Let me do the supposing. That's my job. I don't think we need a review. It seems pretty clear to me. Crosley didn't use his gun, did he? That mistake cost him his life. Good God! After all the time and effort it took to get you people firearms, you'd think you'd bloody use them." He reached unceremoniously across his desk and pushed a button on the intercom. "Where's Randall, Mrs. Clanger?"

"He's waiting out here, sir," crackled the reply.

"Well, send him in. I haven't got all day."

The chief superintendent stared at Lyman with a flat, mishandled smile. Lyman felt he should respond, but he wasn't sure what to say. He had expected a dismissal, or a suspension at the very least. Now Cocksedge did not even want to open a review.

Lyman heard the door behind him open, and then the almost soundless, precious patter of familiar footsteps. It was the Lemur, Superintendent Terry Randall. Lyman stood.

Superintendent Randall was a tiny compact man with curly light brown hair and a pronounced jaw. It was this almost simian aspect of his countenance that had earned him his nickname; that and his quick ascent of the police department's hierarchy. Just as the lemur had survived the age of dinosaurs, so Randall had succeeded where his senior but ungainly competition had succumbed.

"Right," Cocksedge added, waving Randall to the side. "I think the best thing in a case like this is to push on. There'll be some ugly talk for a while. That's only natural. But I'm sure you'll manage. Won't he, Terry?"

The Lemur nodded. "Yes, sir. Like riding a horse."

"Exactly," Cocksedge said. "You have to get back on and forge ahead. All this mooning about will only serve to raise more questions."

"And nobody wants that," the Lemur said. "Do they, Lyman?"

"No, sir."

"Good. Then we're all agreed," Cocksedge said. "The first thing to do is put you on another case. You were on that Pontevecchio suicide last year, weren't you? That Italian banker who hanged himself off Blackfriars Bridge."

"Not exactly, sir. I heard that I might be assigned, but the inquest was closed by the time the official word came through."

"Of course. Well, some silly judge has reopened the case and he's given us another inning. Apparently he thinks the inquest was closed too soon. Terry has the details. He'll give you the files. And you might want to have a chat with Hadley too, if you can pry him loose from his damn garden. Hadley was the one in charge. Did a fine job, if you ask me. But of course, no one does."

"Yes, sir." Lyman began to move back toward the door.

"By the way," Cocksedge added. "You speak Italian, don't you?"

Lyman looked surprised. "No, sir. Some French. My mother was from Brittany."

"Quite. I knew it was a Romance. Well, brush up on your damned Italian. You may need it. That'll be all."

The Lemur opened the door and Lyman started out, his head in a spin. He barely saw the sour face Mrs. Clanger made as he walked by. The elevator arrived and he stepped in like a sleepwalker, the Lemur pulling up the rear.

"Saved again, eh, Nigel?" the Lemur said.

"Don't tell me I have you to thank."

"Not likely. If there's anyone to thank, I suppose it's the famous College Killer. Without him you'd have never made the telly."

"What are you driving at, Randall?"

The Lemur leaned against the elevator wall. His hands were knotted in the pockets of his brown wool suit. "You're a bit thick these days, aren't you, Lyman? That's the odd thing about the telly. When you've been on once, you bloody near belong to it. But it wouldn't

do if this Crosley scandal got about. The whole department would go on trial—not just you. You're a symbol,
Lyman. God help us, but you are. The people picked
you. And the people never make mistakes."

The elevator opened with a creak and the Lemur
started toward his office, his narrow shoulders bouncing as he walked.

Lyman moved slowly in his wake, trying to raise
some passionate conviction, some righteous indigna-
tion, but his anger languished deep inside him, coun-
tered by the fear he felt, the certainty that the Lemur's
sharp appraisal had been absolutely true. He had become a symbol. But of what? The dubious detective
inspector? The coward who had failed to listen when a
fellow constable but half his age had cried out for the
shot, had shrieked for it? "Shoot, Nigel. Bloody
shoot!" Yet what if he had missed?

He hastened down the corridor and as he stepped
into the Lemur's tiny office, all he could think of was
the ending of another poem Chief Superintendent
Cocksedge often quoted. It was by Wilfred Owen, a
writer Lyman favored to Sassoon, and it concerned the
meeting of two foot soldiers in hell, two symbols of the
First World War.

> "I am the enemy you killed, my friend.
> I knew you in this dark; for so you frowned
> Yesterday through me as you jabbed and
>   killed.
> I parried; but my hands were loath and cold.
> Let us sleep now . . ."

Chapter II

THE LEMUR'S OFFICE WAS ONLY HALF the size of the chief superintendent's, yet to Lyman it appeared much larger. The walls were barren except for one small window and a blackboard made of light gray plastic on which the superintendent had imposed a cobweb of black lines, columns of names and numbers inscrutably attached to projects and assignments. A personal computer purred quietly on his desk. A telephone kept it company. There was nothing else, except for two tan imitation leather chairs, one just the slightest bit more padded than the other. The Lemur was already slipping into it.

"What do you know about banking?" the superintendent asked.

"I generally use postal orders myself."

"I don't mean banks. I mean banking, finance."

Lyman did not answer. The Lemur was barking through the telephone. "Pontevecchio, yes," he said, covering the mouthpiece and raising his eyebrows. "Yes, all of them." He hung up.

"Precious little, I'm afraid."

A moment passed and a chubby girl with an armful of files appeared at the door. The Lemur motioned her forward and she slipped them carefully onto his desk. Lyman recognized her. She was one of Dotty Taylor's friends. He had seen them sharing lunch in the Wimpy's down the road.

The Lemur plucked a file of photographs from the pile on his desk, and tossed it to Lyman. "I'll make this simple for you," he said. "There were three central players in this clever little game." He pointed to the foremost snapshot in the file. "That first fellow with the rope about his neck is Salvatore Pontevecchio."

Lyman stared down at the photograph, wondering at the way the head was squeezed off to the side. "I remember the newspaper stories."

"Yes, but one can't always believe what one reads in the press."

In the beginning, Lyman had thought the Lemur's little barbs were cast for his exclusive pleasure. They weren't, of course. Randall made a religion of alienation. He did it to everyone who could not help him by the way. He always had.

"I personally believe the blighter hanged himself," the Lemur added with uncharacteristic candor. "In my opinion, the man was done for and he knew it. The file is comprehensive. I looked it over again this morning.

"Suffice it to say, Salvatore Pontevecchio was the chairman of one of the largest private banks in Italy, Banco Fabiano. By using his position at Fabiano, he was able to misappropriate vast sums of money from the numerous financial institutions he controlled in Italy, and then transfer them illegally to a motley collection of paper companies in such tax havens as Luxembourg and the Bahamas. Chinese boxes, really. For added secrecy and protection he often used the Istituto per le Opere di Religione, commonly called the IOR or Vatican Bank, as a financial conduit to smuggle the cash out of the country. The Vatican is considered an independent state within Italy, you see, with its own laws and regulations.

"The head of the Vatican Bank at that time was —and still is, presumably through divine intervention— gentleman number two: Archbishop Kazimierz Grabowski. The banker Pontevecchio acted as economic advisor to Archbishop Grabowski. In exchange for providing the Church with financial insights and spectacular profits, Pontevecchio obtained the secrecy of the *sottane nere,* the black cassocks of the Vatican."

"A blind eye," Lyman volunteered. He looked down at the photograph of the Archbishop. Grabowski was a big man. He was standing in the street before a crowd, wearing a dark business suit and clerical collar, his arms extended as if to hold the people back, his head bowed, his eyes glaring at the camera.

"Eventually," the Lemur continued, "the money which Salvatore Pontevecchio had transferred illegally through the Vatican Bank made its circuitous way back to Italy. Usually it was then spent in speculation on the Milan stock market, or invested in arms and narcotics. Pontevecchio and Archbishop Grabowski both made money, at least in the beginning. It was easy for them to predict when a company's shares were on the rise because they were the ones driving the prices up, through their shell firms overseas. Of course they had some help. To secure his position on the Banco Fabiano board, and to protect himself politically, Pontevecchio sought the assistance of the third and final player on our list: Marco Scarcella." The Lemur glanced at his watch. "Christ," he said. "Look at the time."

Lyman stared at the puffy round face of the balding gentleman in the photograph before him. Marco Scarcella wore a pair of black plastic spectacles. His eyes were small but full of life, twinkling, like the eyes they always gave to Father Christmas on those family cartoons.

The Lemur fiddled with his papers. "Let's see," he said. "Marco Scarcella. Born in Pritoie, Italy. In 1936 he went to Spain as one of Mussolini's Black Shirts. Saw some action in Albania. Then he fought against the Allies in Italy, 1943, as an SS oberleutnant. After the war, he made his way to Argentina, where he resurfaced as a senior executive of the Perma Mattress Company. In addition to selling mattresses, Scarcella also formed a rat line for escaped Nazis and eventually became a kind of freelance national security consultant." The Lemur looked up and smiled. "Not your average Soho slasher, eh, Lyman?"

"No, sir," Inspector Lyman answered glumly.

"Worse, I daresay. Are you following all this? Stop me if I go too fast."

"I'll manage," Lyman said. "Marco Scarcella. Born in Pritoie, Italy. Fought in Albania. Smuggled Nazis to Argentina."

"Very good." The Lemur thrust his jaw out further. "Scarcella was soon befriended by the great Juan Perón himself. The Argentine dictator was so impressed that he later granted the mattress salesman citizenship, and in '72 made him one of the country's official economic advisors."

"What year did you say?"

"In 1972."

"What were his duties?"

"Import—export. Balance of trade. You know. Guns and butter."

Lyman sat up in his chair. The dull fatigue which had settled on him at the beginning of the briefing suddenly fell away. 1972, he thought. Before the Falklands' war. Guns and butter.

The Lemur continued his narration. "Eventually Scarcella returned to Italy, buying a villa in Tuscany with his savings. According to Interpol, he appeared to have settled down. But it was precisely at this time that he began to construct a political and financial organization which eventually amounted to a kind of state-within-a-state. Working under the guise of a secret Masonic Lodge, Scarcella recruited members from the Italian military and industry, journalists and politicians, anyone of power he could influence. The lodge was called the I Four, or—ironically—the IQ. It stood for Informazione Quattro.

"Every country has its Freemasons," Randall added with disdain. "Even this one, I'm afraid. Of course they're usually fairly social things, business clubs with a little mumbo jumbo in between to make everyone feel like they belong to something."

"I had an uncle who was one."

"Indeed. I'm not surprised. But the I Four, Lyman, was quite unique. Although the Italian postwar constitution specifically prohibits secret societies, Scarcella took this dormant pseudo-lodge and resurrected it. According to former members, he dispensed with most of the normal, arcane rites and bestowed upon himself extraordinary powers as the lodge's Venerable Master. Until it was exposed, Scarcella alone knew the entire membership. Very exclusive. One was asked to join. In exchange for the shortcut to money and power it provided, Scarcella demanded information—something so delicate that it would ensure the member's loyalty, his silence."

"Very neat."

"Yes, very. Of course, not everyone cooperated. There's one report in the file which concerns a Roman magistrate who was persuaded by his local priest to abandon the I Four and testify against Scarcella and the rest. Two days before the trial, the magistrate's youngest daughter—only twelve years old—was kidnapped by a group of Scarcella's men, one of whom we later arrested. That's how we got the story." The Lemur folded his fingers together under his chin, and leaned closer to Lyman.

"According to the informant, they took the girl to a house which they had rented near a town called Terracina, halfway between Naples and Rome, on the coast. Not just any house, mind you. Scarcella was very particular about these kinds of things. It had to be in the suburbs. It could never be too close to a neighbor, in case they heard the screams. But the walls had to be thin enough to hear through." The Lemur sighed. "Well, they found the perfect place, apparently. As was his practice, Scarcella went upstairs and locked himself in a bedroom. He usually preferred a small room; never the master bedroom. His men, meanwhile, took the girl into the bedroom next door, where they proceeded to rape and sodomize her repeatedly for over an hour until she lost consciousness. I'll spare you the grim details. I'm sure it will suffice if I tell you that the leader of this crew had a peculiar talent with a razor.

"No one ever knew what Scarcella did by himself in the room next door. Somehow or other, he always heard or sensed when his victims were hovering near death, for he would suddenly appear in the doorway. The report states he was always impeccably dressed on these occasions, and this night was no exception. Everyone stood aside when he came in. Scarcella walked over to the bed where the girl lay. She was barely conscious by this time. Conscious enough to be afraid, though. Conscious enough to cry out, apparently, as Scarcella pulled the pin out of the rose he was sporting on his lapel. He just stood there over her, the flower in one hand and that bloody straight pin in the other, watching her cower on the bedsheets. Then he leaned forward, turned the rose round in his fingers, and stuffed it into her mouth, stem first, as if he were planting it inside her. That's all he did. He left immediately thereafter, and drove straight back to Rome."

The Lemur leaned back in his chair. "Needless to

say, the girl's father, the magistrate, never testified, and Scarcella was acquitted.

"It was just about this time that Scarcella recruited Pontevecchio. Despite their different backgrounds, both men shared a fascist sensibility, an inordinate fear of communism, and a respect for secret power. In some ways, it was almost inevitable that they should have become partners. They offered each other so much."

"What happened to the girl?"

"What's that?"

"The girl, the one you were just talking about."

"As I recall, she bled to death within the hour." He shook his head. "Are you listening, Lyman? Pay attention, please! Marco Scarcella delivered the I Four, his political protection, and his close connection to several Latin American regimes. And in return Pontevecchio supplied the money from Banco Fabiano, and the cover of the IOR—the discreet banking services and protecting arms of the good Archbishop Grabowski. Together the three men made millions, secretly controlling both the Italian government and much of the press, bribing or killing anyone who got in their way. It was a marriage made in heaven, or almost, anyway."

The Lemur began to stare out of the window. It was as if he thought that Lyman needed just a few more seconds to compile the information, like the computer on his desk.

"Two events," the Lemur added suddenly, "brought this unholy alliance to an end. The first was the exposure of Scarcella's I Four. And the second, the collapse of Pontevecchio's Banco Fabiano.

"In the spring of 1981," he explained, "a French suspect revealed that Scarcella had helped finance a heroin factory near Florence, Italy. A detachment of guardia di finanza was ordered to investigate, but by the time they arrived Scarcella had already disappeared. Tipped off, I'm sure. They found nothing in his Tuscan villa. But at the offices of the local Perma Mattress factory, just a few miles away, they unearthed a list of almost one thousand I Four members. In one day the secret Masonic Lodge was stripped of its most powerful attraction—it wasn't secret any longer. Scarcella escaped to South America."

"Is that where he is now?" Lyman asked.

The Lemur raised an eyebrow. "No, thank God. He was spotted in May last year, in France, one month before Pontevecchio was found hanging from Blackfriars Bridge. But the French gendarmerie let him get away. Then last September he flew to Switzerland, where he was arrested trying to withdraw some fifty-five million dollars from a bank account suspected of being connected to the Banco Fabiano scandal. He's tucked away in Champ Dollon prison now, near Geneva. The chief superintendent wants you to try and arrange an interview, but as far as I'm concerned, it probably isn't worth the ticket. Scarcella won't talk to anyone."

"Is that so?"

"The collapse of Fabiano happened almost simultaneously," the Lemur added peevishly, "resulting in the largest financial scandal in banking history. I don't remember all of the details. There are précis in the files, newspaper clippings and the like. That's your job, anyway."

He looked up. "But it was really just a matter of time for Salvatore Pontevecchio. The financial hole at his Banco Fabiano grew larger and larger, until one day there was no more money left to transfer. Archbishop Grabowski pleaded ignorance, denying the IOR's responsibility, despite the fact that the companies in which Pontevecchio had invested were owned primarily by the Church. When the statements and bank papers were finally unraveled, it appeared that the hundreds of millions of dollars embezzled from Fabiano had simply disappeared." The Lemur smiled darkly. "Pontevecchio had already been to jail during an earlier scandal. It was there he tried to kill himself the first time. He knew what it was like."

Lyman looked down once again at the photograph of the Italian banker, the bulging eyes, the skin puffed up around the nylon noose. "So Pontevecchio fled to London, is that it?"

"That's right. In June, last year," the Lemur said.

"Where he tried to kill himself again, except that this time he succeeded?"

"That's what the inquest ruled, and I happen to agree. For a change. It's your job to see if it was something else."

"But why?"

"Why what?"

Lyman leaned forward in his chair, hunching his shoulders like the pincers of a crab. "I mean, why not Brazil or Argentina? What did Pontevecchio hope to gain in London?"

"Really, Lyman. Shall I lead you by the nose through all of this? According to another Mason named Angelo Balducci—who was his escort into London—Pontevecchio was trying to arrange a meeting with the Opus Dei, a wealthy right-wing Catholic group."

"What for?"

"To save himself, presumably. To ask for absolution, for money, for another chance. How should I know? Balducci was arrested last year on charges of smuggling. But he claims he only helped Pontevecchio get into the country, and he has a perfect alibi."

The superintendent began to reassemble the files before him. "Pontevecchio's wife, who's now living in America, reported that he telephoned her just before his death and told her everything would be all right, that he had found something wonderful and that Archbishop Grabowski would finally have to honor his financial responsibilities. Pontevecchio was clearly on the edge, and tilting. His bank had collapsed into that hole, now one point three billion dollars wide. Scarcella would no longer protect him. Pontevecchio was a public failure, exposed. They'd dug him up, like a grub in a spadeful of earth, and he couldn't take the light." The Lemur slapped the top file loudly. "Justice, Lyman. What we're paid to mete out, hard and true."

"I thought that was the courts' prerogative."

"Don't get cheeky, Lyman. This is our second go on this one, the second inning."

Isn't that what Cocksedge had called it, Lyman thought—a second inning?

"Just do your standard plodding job of it and we'll all be friends again. We'll leave young Crosley in the customary files. Welcome aboard."

The Lemur pushed the rest of the papers across the desk. Then he picked up the telephone and swiveled his chair away. The briefing was over.

Lyman eyed the superintendent closely. He did not feel offended by the briefing's sudden termination, but he was nettled by the Lemur's gracelessness. It would take little imagination to force a conversation on his secretary, yet the superintendent sat there without speaking, the receiver poised a fraction of an inch from his perfect, tiny ear.

Lyman gathered up the files and headed out the door. The corridor was filling up. It would be lunchtime soon and the world was washing up, or making plans, or working through it once again.

If Pontevecchio had died in some hotel, Lyman thought, in another part of London, the case would have gone to Scotland Yard, to the Metropolitan Police. But instead he'd hanged himself, or been the victim of a murder, beneath Blackfriars Bridge. In the public view, in that one square mile which marked the province of the City of London Police. And yet the job seemed like a task best left to Interpol. Lyman sighed. What did he know about Italian Masonry, or finance for that matter? Why wasn't the chief inspector in on this one? The job demanded special skills.

Lyman pushed the button for the elevator and wished himself back to the Brass Monkey, the slow thick shadows of the pub which he had frequented so often as a young policeman back in Hampshire. He tried to visualize the glassy chalk stream of the River Itchen out the window, balanced precariously on the backs of trout, the female bulging of St. Catherine's Hill, its Saxon ditch and rampart gathering the errant trees into a single copse of green, the ancient oaks and poplars rocking him to sleep a hundred feet above the ground, curled like a question mark about the moving branches. Sometimes he thought of going back to Winchester. But they had built a motorway around the Hill, and half his family and friends had died or moved away. There was little point in going back, almost as little as in reminiscing.

The elevator arrived and Lyman stepped in. It was nearly full. He turned his back to the crowd. Someone was wearing a florid perfume. It smelt like jasmine and Lyman thought about Dotty Taylor, the way her thighs had come together at the top and formed a triangle of light as she had walked away from him into the bathroom to wash up. It had only been twelve nights, twelve nights and thirteen days.

The doors creaked open once again, this time preceded by the clapping of a hidden bell. A young woman bundled in a scarf and raincoat stared expectantly into the elevator. "Going down?" she asked.

No one answered, and for a moment Lyman heard the question as if it had been meant for him alone, a grim indictment of the last year of his life. The doors closed just as suddenly and the woman in the raincoat disappeared.

Dotty Taylor wasn't what he needed, Lyman thought. Cocksedge had been right. Work was the answer. He had to climb back on again, but his hands were loath and cold.

Chapter III

THE DARK BLUE TR4 LUNGED ACROSS the crowded motorway, trying to force a space between a Jaguar and a two-ton lorry. Inside the car, Lyman kept one hand on the wheel and the other on a tattered road map in his lap. He had never been to this part of Surrey before, but he knew the turn to Haslemere was fast approaching. Beside him, his dog George stood with his nose half out the window, barking and chomping at the wind.

"Oh, for Christ's sake, George, shut up." Lyman nudged him with his elbow but the animal remained transfixed. His fur was knotted and thick, the color of day-old snow, and he had a corgi's head with indecisive ears which drooped and stood erect and drooped again as he sniffed the air outside the window.

The road curved. Lyman passed another car, and found himself within the current of a roundabout. The road signs seemed unnaturally small, pointing at the oddest angles as if they had been turned by vandals in the night. He glimpsed the one for Haslemere too late.

The tires of the Triumph squealed, George barked, and Lyman swung the car round the roundabout again.

It took him another twenty minutes before he reached the country road which, according to his map, would bring him to the house of former Superintendent Hadley. The sun had disappeared behind a bank of clouds. A wind blew from the west across the fields, bending the hedgerows, tilting the trees. He passed a dairy farm and suddenly there it was, the lane which Hadley had described that morning with punctilious detail.

The house was nestled in a little valley lush with rhododendron bushes. It was a large, neo-Tudor structure with bright white plaster walls and heavy wooden crossbeams. Lyman pulled his car up to the front and turned the motor off. At the rear of the house he could see a conservatory, and beyond that a kind of sunken garden full of rosebushes. He opened the door, mindful not to let the dog out in his wake, and headed for the entrance.

The former superintendent appeared in the open doorway, his hand extended in a greeting. "Nigel," he said. "It's good to see you again. I was expecting you much earlier."

Lyman frowned. "Sorry, sir," he said. "The roads are absolutely jammed."

"None of that now."

"Pardon?"

"No more sirs and superintendents left for me. Given all that up. It's Squire Hadley now." He laughed indifferently.

Lyman tried to smile.

"Just call me Tim. I was only joking, Lyman."

"Yes, sir. Tim." George barked from the car and Lyman rolled his eyes. "Damn dog."

"Well, let him out, man," Hadley said as he bounded from the entrance. He was a tall, broad-shouldered man with thinning black hair and cavernous green eyes. He had been in an auto accident as a child, and still carried the scars along his cheeks, deep-set and knotted purple lines which made his face seem more dramatic than grotesque. Perhaps it was the emerald eyes. Or perhaps it was the smile, so china perfect. Hadley opened the car door and George escaped with a growl.

"I was afraid he'd muck up your garden," Lyman said.

"Don't be ridiculous. Good for the soil. You should see how much I pay for dung each year." Hadley looked up at the sky. "Why don't we walk for a bit," he said. "I'd invite you in but the Mrs. isn't feeling up to visitors."

"Of course."

Hadley grinned again and Lyman thought that it had been a long time since he'd seen him smile that way. And there it was again, twice in a day, in a moment.

There had been a time once, Lyman remembered, soon after his arrival on the force, when he and Hadley had almost become friends. Hadley—then only a chief inspector—had taken the country constable under his wing, at first no doubt to share in the warm glow of the reporters' cameras whenever they came to interview the man who had caught the infamous College Killer.

But after a while, the more they worked together, the more they found they had in common. Hadley frequently assigned the young inspector to his cases, tutoring him with care, introducing him to his most reliable informers. And so it was that in the first year of his tenure with the City of London Police, Lyman solved more crimes than anyone of his rank in the history of the department.

Then something happened that Lyman had never really understood. Hadley was promoted to superintendent, and almost overnight he withdrew from everyone with whom he had hitherto shared his life, including

Lyman. It was as if the previous years had only been a preparation for this inevitable ascension. He joined a different set of clubs. He bought a bigger car. He moved into another flat, in a different part of town. He met the woman who would soon be Mrs. Hadley. "Butterflies don't mix with caterpillars," they said round the office.

Five months later Hadley was assigned to the Pontevecchio case. And then, upon completion of the inquest, the brand-new Superintendent astounded everyone with the news that he was going to retire, ten years before his time. His wife had come into some money, it was said, and he planned to buy a house in Surrey and raise flowers.

Others were less kind, insisting that the superintendent had been sacked, the victim of a power play with Cocksedge. Informal parties were arranged to bid him bon voyage. Lyman had attended these religiously, but each time he had tried to tell the superintendent what a debt of gratitude he felt, Hadley had only shaken his head and pulled away.

In a few weeks, before he had even cleared his desk out, Hadley was practically forgotten. It was his job now that concerned the crowd, the struggle to fill the impending vacuum. Some said the Lemur was the obvious replacement. After all, Randall had seniority, and a fine record of arrests. But he was not well liked. Others insisted Lyman had a chance.

In truth, Lyman had never really cared about the race. He liked his job just as it was, and he did not fancy the idea of spending his career behind a desk on the fifth floor. So when he finally heard the news of Randall's imminent promotion, he felt relieved that he had not been chosen. Only one thing still distressed him. They said that the deciding vote against him had been cast by Superintendent Hadley; it was his last official act.

•   •   •

Lyman and Hadley crossed the driveway and headed round the house toward the conservatory. Neither of them had spoken for several minutes when suddenly Hadley said, "So what exactly do you want to know, about the case I mean?"

Lyman was looking at a bed of heather. The lavender branches were thick with tiny spines. "I thought perhaps that you might . . . I don't know, fill in the empty spaces."

"What did Brian tell you?"

"Not very much. Randall briefed me."

"And?"

"And what?"

"Your findings. Your results, man. Your analysis. Was it a suicide or wasn't it?"

"I have no idea. I've only just begun."

Hadley nodded grimly. "I see. Yes, well, I suppose that's sensible. You'd want to go in with an open mind and all that. Only natural. Who are your prime suspects then, if I may ask?"

Lyman shrugged. "Archbishop Kazimierz Grabowski, I suppose. And Marco Scarcella too."

"Scarcella's in jail, in Switzerland."

"Yes, so I heard. But he wasn't when Pontevecchio died, in June last year. The Lemur told me Scarcella was spotted in France in May, right before Pontevecchio's death, but it wasn't until September that they arrested him in Switzerland."

"Here, let me show you something," Hadley said abruptly. He drew his hands together behind his back and hastened down the path toward the conservatory. Lyman followed.

"Are you a collector, Lyman?" Hadley said, as he fiddled with the door.

"Sir?"

"Stamps, coins—that sort of thing."

"Oh, I see." The glass door opened and Lyman felt a wall of warm moist air surround him. "Not really."

"Pity," Hadley said. "I think it gives a man something, especially when he retires. Don't delay, Lyman. You'll soon be on the ash heap too. Find something, anything. Something to do. Something to hold on to." He strode forward. Lyman could see the racks and racks of vegetation on the walls around them, thick flowers hanging down, a drape of color on the heavy air. "Something to look after," Hadley continued. "Shut the door."

Lyman stepped in.

"Orchids have always been my fancy," Hadley said. "I think it's because they're so vital, so organic. Not like the job, eh?" He picked up a leafless spray. The flowers were creamy white, suspended from a piece of cork board on the wall. "Ghost orchids," he said.

Lyman examined a clot of leaves and petals near the door. The flowers looked like open wounds, fleshy and exposed. Where was the soil, he wondered, or did they simply grow that way? "Very nice, yes."

"Take a look at this one." The superintendent pointed at another plant with verdant, palmlike leaves. A spike of flowers hung down to one side. The plant was festooned with two-inch blossoms, pale green with light brown tips, spoon-shaped and hooded like a line of monks on their way to morning prayers. "It's a *Catasetum trulla*," Hadley said. "A friend of mine imports them from South America. Isn't it lovely? They have the oddest reproductive cycle." He poked a fingertip into a blossom. "See? Their stamens are buried so deep within them that over the millenia they've developed a kind of alkaloid which makes the bees that pollinate them drowsy. The bees fall in, you see, drunk on the nectar, and cover themselves with pollen. Some orchidologists believe the insects actually remember, returning again and again just for the drug."

"Fascinating," Lyman said. "About the case . . ."

"Yes, yes, the case. Well, if it wasn't suicide," Hadley said, "then I'd put my money on Grabowski."

"The archbishop? Why?"

"I met His Excellency in Rome. It was during the first inquest."

"What was he like?"

"Canadian. Big bloke. Six foot three at least. Sixteen stone. He used to play ice hockey as a boy. I suppose that's why Pope Paul employed him as a kind of unofficial bodyguard. But he didn't have any time for us. He kept on saying how busy he was, how he was doing us such a big bloody favor just by seeing me. Meanwhile, all I could think of was how I knew he was born in this hovel in Toronto, on the wrong side of town. His parents were Polish, right off the bloody boat. I mean real wogs. The only reason he even went to university was because he was a priest."

"Why would he have killed Pontevecchio?"

"It's obvious, isn't it? He wanted to cover up the Vatican Bank's connection with Banco Fabiano after the scandal broke. Don't think—just because he's a priest—that he couldn't have done it. Believe you me. He may be an archbishop, but Grabowski is no saint. He's a banker through and through."

Lyman nodded glumly, remembering the file on the archbishop. But at some point, he considered, at some time Grabowski must have honestly believed. In seminary perhaps, or as a parish priest in west Ontario. How strange, Lyman thought, that a man of God should have become a banker in the end, trading as much in numbers, in proven formulae, as in the intangibles of faith. "I suppose so," he said at last. "Then you think he knew Pontevecchio was embezzling from Banco Fabiano."

"He must have. They were using the Vatican Bank to get the money from Fabiano out of Italy. The government was cracking down on taxes and the Church was desperate to account for the missing funds. *He* was desperate."

Suddenly George began to bark. Lyman looked up. The dog was playing in the sunken garden, chasing birds.

"Of course," Hadley added softly, "that's only my opinion. It's your case now, and I wouldn't want to influence you one way or the other."

"Of course." George barked again and Lyman watched in horror as the dog began to dig around a rosebush. "Sorry," he said, dashing toward the door. He swung it open, shouting, "George. George, stop that." The dog looked up momentarily, his paws half buried in the ground.

Lyman shut the door behind him and walked around the conservatory. "Come here," he said. "Come here this instant."

The dog trotted over. Lyman raised a hand to strike him, but at the last moment he felt his anger falter.

"That's no way," Hadley said behind him. "You've got to discipline them. You've got to let them know who's the master."

"Yes, I know," Lyman said. "It's just that when he looks up at me . . ." He could not finish.

"Spare the rod. You know what they say."

"He's really my son's dog. Or was. I'm not very good with animals."

They both glanced down at George. Then Hadley said, "I was sorry to hear about young Crosley, Nigel. He was a good policeman."

Lyman nodded.

"Try not to take it personally. I'm sure it wasn't your fault. I'm sure you did everything you could, by the book."

"By the book," Lyman repeated.

"Let me give you a piece of advice, Nigel. You've had a hard time of it lately. I'd take this Pontevecchio case slowly, if I were you. Work back into things. Don't push yourself. It's really only a formality anyway." He looked back at the conservatory. "Was there anything else you wanted?"

"Actually, I did have some questions about Scarcella."

"Yes, of course. Scarcella. I only ask because I have to drive the Mrs. up to Guildford. It's the music festival next week and—well, you know—she just *has* to have her hair done." Hadley looked down at his watch. "You should come out again sometime. Soon."

"Thank you, I will. But, about Scarcella—"

"The bastard's already in prison, where he belongs. I doubt if I can tell you anything you haven't read in the files. Sorry I couldn't be of any further help. Strange, isn't it? It's only been a year since Pontevecchio's suicide and yet it seems so far away. Another lifetime. I hope we get to see you again. I mean that, Nigel."

"Thanks very much. Another time then. I'll ring you." Lyman patted George on the head. "It was good to see you again."

They shook hands, and started toward the driveway at the front of the house. When they reached the car, Lyman opened the passenger door and George jumped in without a fuss. "Well, thanks again," Lyman said, searching for his keys. "I liked your flowers."

"Think about what I said. Find a hobby. Don't put it off. None of us are getting any younger."

"Yes. Yes, I know," Lyman said, ducking into the car.

"And Nigel . . ."

Lyman looked up through the window.

"Yes, sir?"

"I wasn't sacked, you know. Just to set the record straight."

"I never thought you were."

"No, you wouldn't, would you. Not Nigel Lyman." Hadley smiled sadly. "I made a lot of mistakes in my career, Nigel, but leaving the department wasn't one of them."

Hadley backed off toward the entrance of the house. Lyman turned the ignition key. The motor coughed like a sleeping child, and caught.

It had been a pointless exercise, Lyman thought, a waste of time. He had learned precious little about Pontevecchio, and even less about Scarcella. He headed down the drive, turning only once to catch a glimpse of Hadley in the rearview mirror throwing a heartless wave into the air. Then he was gone.

Lyman drove along the country road, trying to think of something other than his case, trying to forget himself within the constant uniformity of the dividing line. Black, white, black. He thought about Tim Hadley, about his orchids and the way their slender roots had dangled in the air, thirsty for moisture.

Hadley had done all right for himself with his collecting, especially for a policeman. A posh house and a garden, a wife with a taste for music festivals. No wonder he'd retired early.

The road narrowed up ahead and George began to bark once again, lunging at the window. "Quiet," Lyman said. "Please, George." He slowed the car. They were crossing a bridge. On the river far below, a solitary sculler cut the waterway in half, pulling at his wooden blades, gliding on the surface through the reeds.

Chapter IV

LYMAN SAT IN HIS OFFICE, LEANING forward on his elbows, peering at the photograph before him on his desk. It was well past eight o'clock. The rest of the day inspectors had departed, and he was finally alone. A fluorescent lightbulb popped and crackled overhead. The harsh light glazed the photograph, so that the nylon line around Pontevecchio's neck shimmered like a length of barbed wire. The bulging eyes. The blue-gray pallor of the Italian banker's skin. All these details had set themselves inside of Lyman. He couldn't shake them. There was a grisly beauty in the way Pontevecchio's head was squeezed off to the side. It was a tragic pose, as if a great transgressor had finally met his fate, a mythic setting with the dark Thames spilling underneath him, the perfect backdrop for a suicide. Lyman glanced at his watch. Or was it?

He reached across his desk, picked up the phone, and dialed the number scribbled on a scrap of paper in the file before him. A few moments passed before he heard the satellite connect him with New York. Lyman could barely understand the operator at the Treasury Department. He asked for Special Investigator Tony Augenstein.

"Who's calling?" came the reply.

Lyman identified himself and was immediately put on hold. A full minute passed. It was so typical, Lyman thought. Money meant nothing to the Americans. They probably called long distance every day. Suddenly he heard the roaring echo of a man's voice on the line.

"Inspector Lyman?" the American said. "I'm putting you on the speaker phone so we can all hear you."

"Right, thanks," said Lyman with suspicion.

"Mrs. Pontevecchio, this is Inspector Lyman of the City of London Police. The man I was telling you about."

"How do you do, Mrs. Pontevecchio," Lyman said. His own voice sounded like distant thunder, always a few seconds behind. "I appreciate your speaking with me."

"If I can help you, I am happy," he heard a woman reply. "Mr. Green and Mr. Augenstein have been very nice to me since I come to America. What can I do? What can I tell you? Salvatore never talked about money with me. That was business. Do you know what it is like to lose your husband? What happened at Fabiano, I do not care any more. Now I hate Fabiano. The bank killed Salvatore. I hate all of them."

"Who, Mrs. Pontevecchio? The bankers? Whom do you hate?"

"Scarcella. And Grabowski too, the Lord protect me."

"Inspector Lyman," another man cut in. "Would you kindly restrict yourself to those parts of the investigation that pertain directly to your case."

"I beg your pardon."

"What my colleague—Mr. Green here—is trying to

say, is that you shouldn't worry too much about the financial side of this thing. You know what I mean?"

Lyman did. Men woke up every day and drew lines about themselves, borders to their wives, their family, their jobs, their countries. Keep out, keep off the grass, don't stand so close to me. Lyman smiled. There had been a time once when he too had guarded his work so jealously. A long time ago, he thought. But it was the Americans' party. Their game. Their rules.

"I only have a few questions, Mrs. Pontevecchio," Lyman said, "if you don't mind."

"Go right ahead, Mrs. Pontevecchio," answered Augenstein.

Lyman ignored him. "You testified earlier that you didn't think your husband killed himself. Do you still feel that way?"

"Of course I do. Despite everything, my husband was a good Catholic. Do you know what that means, Mr. Lyman? Suicide is a mortal sin."

"And yet, didn't he try and kill himself once before, in prison?"

"People say such things, but I do not believe them. The last time I talk to my husband, he tell me everything will be okay. Okay, he said. His Excellency, Archbishop Grabowski, will have to help me, he said, because I have found a wonderful thing. Even the Pope will kiss my face, he said."

"What had he found?"

"He would never tell me. He said it was better I did not know."

Lyman heard her sigh. He imagined her sitting on a corner of a couch, surrounded by Investigators Green and Augenstein, talking into a little metal box on the table beside her. He imagined the cramped office, the glass partition looking out onto the typing pool, the tattered calendars and notices on the wall, the grimy window, the distant skyline of Manhattan like a piece of torn sheet metal.

"Sometimes it is better not to ask things," she continued. Lyman looked down at the photograph of Pontevecchio on his desk.

"Why did your husband go to London, Mrs. Pontevecchio?"

"He told me he had friends there. Friends in high places, he said. He said that they would buy the wonderful thing he had found, and that the archbishop would have to protect him."

"Grabowski? Protect him from whom?"

"From the Informazione Quattro. From Scarcella." She paused, and he could hear her clear her throat. She had started to cry. He could hear the tears weigh down her words. "And from himself, I think," she added soberly.

"What do you mean?"

"Scarcella is not like an ordinary man, Mr. Lyman. He is *pestilenziale* . . . like a disease. There is something about him, something of the devil, I think. Something evil. It was never what he did to my husband. It was what he made my husband do. You see. It is better not to look sometimes, it is better not to know."

"I think that's quite enough, Inspector Lyman. I don't think there's much percentage in pursuing this any further, do you?" Augenstein's voice was clipped.

"I only have a few more questions."

"I don't think so. Let's just call it quits, shall we? We'll let you know if anything turns up. Okay, Lyman?"

"If you insist."

"Hell, we're all on the same team, aren't we, Bob?"

"That's right."

"I'd like to thank you, Mrs. Pontevecchio," Lyman said.

"Please, be careful, Mr. Lyman. Beware of Scarcella."

"I will. Thanks. Good-bye." Lyman rang off.

He leaned back in his chair. Something was wrong,

he thought. The entire world called it a suicide, except Mrs. Pontevecchio. And she was the one telling the truth. Lyman was convinced of it.

He removed the snapshot of Scarcella from the file. He seemed so innocent in his crisp white polo neck and raincoat. That jolly round face, those twinkling eyes.

Lyman examined the features carefully. Then, sensing another presence in the room, he looked up. Dotty Taylor was leaning up against the door frame, her left hand planted on her hip.

"You'll see him soon enough," she said.

Lyman smiled. "I thought you'd gone home ages ago."

Dotty closed the door and made her way across the room. She was a tall girl of twenty-eight, fair-skinned and angular. She moved awkwardly, as if she'd never passed her adolescence, and yet there was a grace about the way she set each step that Lyman had always found compelling. "It's that time of the month," she said.

"I hadn't noticed."

"I mean report time, silly man. Foster's having a cow. He made everyone work late."

She leaned across the desk and kissed him on the forehead. Her long brown hair fell about his face. It smelled of jasmine.

"As usual," Lyman said. He pulled her close to him. Her hips were slim, which made her appear more youthful than she really was, but her eyes gave her away. They were large and dark, with a hint of disappointment in each corner.

"Aren't you ever going home?" she said. "It's your last night. And you'll be gone for ages."

He felt her reaching for him. "A week at the most."

Dotty sat down on the desk. "Forever," she replied. "You'll meet some girl in *Lederhosen,* and that will be the end of Dotty Taylor." She glanced down at the photograph of Marco Scarcella. "And all for that horrid little man."

"Do you really think he's horrid?"

Dotty picked up the photograph and studied it.

"I think he looks rather jolly," Lyman continued. "Look at that smile. You can hardly say he's menacing."

"You must be mad," she said. "He's probably watching some old lady fall under a bus." She dropped the snapshot on the desk. "Heaven knows how you ever became an inspector. You wouldn't know a clue if it stared you in the face."

She leaned against him softly. Lyman watched her as she slowly undid a button on her blouse. Then, carefully, she pulled the material apart. She wasn't wearing a bra, and he could see the white skin of her breast, the curve and then a tiny swollen nipple.

"Just a hint," she said with a laugh, "of things to come." She pulled away.

"I won't be long," Lyman said. "I promise."

"Promises, promises." She fastened the button on her blouse and started toward the door. "But I'm warning you. If you're not back by midnight, I may be forced to throw open the window and shout for help." She opened the door. "You're not the only policeman in London."

"You're such a little bitch, Dotty."

She smoothed her hair and smiled. "I know. That's why you love me." Then she was gone.

Lyman looked around the room. He was alone again, and yet he had the strange sensation that he was being watched. It was that photograph of Marco Scarcella on his desk.

After two weeks of fruitless effort, the former Venerable Master had finally acceded to an interview. Lyman was booked on the morning flight to Geneva. It was a piece of fortune that had descended on him out of nowhere, and so suddenly that Lyman thought it

seemed to contradict his definition of policework as a
series of planned accidents.

And yet he still felt frustrated and defeated. Despite what Mrs. Pontevecchio had just told him, everything pointed to a suicide. Pontevecchio's body had
revealed no hidden contusions, nothing at all to indicate the banker had been forced into that noose beneath Blackfriars Bridge. They had scanned his blood
and organs. They had checked his fingernails. They had
even analyzed his hair, in case he had been drugged
before and then transported to the scene. Nothing unusual had been found.

And yet . . . Lyman picked up the photograph of
Scarcella. Perhaps he was beginning to understand
what Mrs. Pontevecchio had tried to tell him earlier.

The files revealed Scarcella had returned to Europe
two more times after the exposure of his infamous I
Four in the spring of 1981. The first time, in May of
1982, British Intelligence reports had placed him on
Cap Ferrat in the south of France. Apparently he had
returned at the request of Argentina to purchase additional arms for use against the British in the Falklands'
war. The Exocet missiles which he had arranged for
earlier had already proved to be effective. "Effective."
Lyman wondered at this word. It was the one which
they had used in the report. It was so practical an ad-
jective, so accurate a symbol.

He tried not to visualize the missile swinging low
across the waves, the flash of the explosion, the face of
his son Peter taking one last desperate breath as the
water washed around him.

Lyman focused on the photograph before him. And
then, in September 1982, Scarcella had returned to Europe one more time, where he was promptly arrested
in Geneva for trying to withdraw fifty-five million dollars from a bank account suspected of being connected
to the Fabiano scandal. They had locked him away in

Champ Dollon, and there he had been languishing for nearly a year.

Lyman tucked the snapshot back into the folder on his desk. In less than twenty-four hours he and Scarcella would be sitting face to face, within the same four walls, breathing the same prison air.

He pushed his chair out and rose slowly to his feet. He was tired. He had not slept well for weeks, and his flight to Switzerland was in the early morning. He slipped the files into his briefcase. Then he turned his back to the desk and headed out the door.

When he reached the ground floor of the station, he paused for a moment to check the bulletin board for messages. No one had called. No one wanted anything, and this relieved him. But just as he was walking down the corridor to leave, young Constable Tony Frazier appeared from nowhere and waved at him to stop.

"Is it important?" Lyman asked halfheartedly, without even slowing down.

"There's some bloke downstairs who claims he saw that Italian banker on the night he hanged himself."

Lyman stopped. "What, another one? What's he look like?"

"A vagabond. We just arrested him for bashing up a chemist over on Fleet Street. Anyway, I thought you'd want to know. You're on that Pontevecchio case, aren't you?"

"Yes, I suppose so," Lyman said. "Do you believe him?"

Frazier shrugged. "You should see what he did to that chemist, though. Made a right mess of him, he did."

Lyman sighed. "All right, let's take a look."

They made their way toward the stairway leading to the holding cells. As they walked, Frazier told Lyman about the case.

It had started a week earlier, Frazier said, when the vagabond had taken to sleeping in the alleyway beside the chemist's. At first the chemist had simply shouted him away, threatening the ragged figure with furious reprisals. But as the days wore on, and the vagabond refused to forfeit his new sleeping spot, the chemist had resorted to more stringent methods.

He had tried washing down the area with ammonia. The vagabond ignored it. He had tried leaving out his rubbish in the alley, but the vagabond only moved it to the side, forming a little nest between the empty cardboard boxes and the plastic bags.

That very night, in desperation, the chemist had filled a bucket full of ice-cold water mixed with a little iodine. Then he had crept to the rear of the shop and cracked the side door open. The vagabond had come. He was curled inside a playhouse of old boxes. The chemist moved into the alley stealthily, and tossed the cold solution on the beggar's face.

Despite his well-planned access to the door, the chemist had badly underestimated both the speed and fury of the vagabond. The mound of clothes burst open. A shape emerged out of the shadows and the chemist found himself down on the alley floor, his eyes half covered by a heavy hand, and his left cheek stinging from a hail of blows. It was as if the anger of a lifetime had been suddenly released, he told Constable Frazier later. Only the strength of three strangers attracted by his screams had managed to pull the vagabond away.

The vagabond, it turned out, was a bricklayer and machinist named David Ellison. They had seen him at the station several times before. He had the record of a thousand other workmen from the north, the drifters blown like winter thistles from the hills and empty one-mill towns of Yorkshire. He had made the run down to the city on the backs of lorries, watching the country change round him, the houses grow more frequent and more grand. He had looked for work for months, reading the papers every evening in his tiny rented room near Windmill Street, waiting his days away at the Exchange, watching the fold of bills he always kept upon him slowly vanish, waiting for it to end.

When his landlord finally chucked him out, he had tried living in the shelters for a while. At least he had a bed there, and a plate of warm food every night. But apparently the social workers had always made him feel as if it were his fault, as if he liked to live as he did, as if he really had a choice.

Lyman and Frazier signed in at the entrance to the holding cells and the night guard let them through. Ellison was in the interrogation room at the end of the corridor. Lyman could see his face through the little window in the door. Someone had been at his nose and it looked broken and raw in the icy light.

"Let's have it, then," Lyman said to Frazier as they entered the room. "What's the bastard claiming?"

Ellison lifted himself up in his chair. He had coal black hair and the massive shoulders of a workman. He had not shaved in days. "I'm not claiming anything," he said. "I saw it with my own two eyes."

"What did you see?"

"I saw what they did to him. To your Italian friend. Not that he didn't deserve it, mind you. Now me, I'd rather be poor and alive than a dead banker any day. What's the point of money if you have to die getting it."

"Who said anything about money?"

"All bankers have money. That's why they're bankers. We're the poor ones. We're the ones they piss on."

"Christ," Lyman said. "A bloody socialist." He drew a chair up from the corner of the room and sat down facing Ellison. "And what about you, eh? What about Ellison and his broken nose? Who's going to take care of him—the state?"

"I can take care of myself."

Lyman laughed softly. "So I see." He turned toward Constable Frazier and said, "Why don't you leave us for a bit."

The young policeman cast an angry look at Ellison. "I'll be outside if you need me, sir."

"We'll manage. Thank you."

The door closed loudly. Ellison leaned back in his chair.

"Who broke your nose?" Lyman asked. "Was it Frazier or the shopkeeper?"

Ellison smiled, poking gently at the swollen purple flesh with his fingers. "Neither. What do you care, anyway?"

"I want to know."

Ellison sat up. There was something in the tone of Lyman's voice, a barbed foreboding, an edge, which did not brook debate. "It happened in the alleyway. I knocked it up against the wall. That's the truth."

"I see," Lyman said, after a pause. "I just wanted to be sure." He studied Ellison's face, taking in the thick black hair, the agate circles at the centers of his eyes. Then he pulled a pack of Players from the inside pocket of his worn tweed jacket and offered one to Ellison.

"I have a theory," Lyman said, shaking the pack invitingly. Ellison took one. "The way I see it, you don't need the state. I mean, look what the state's given you already. Bloody all." He lit the cigarettes and slumped back in his chair. "The way I see it, it's because we're all so bloody worried about the state, or the union, or the bloody family that we end up thinking they're the ones we should be taking care of, instead of us." He shook his head. "But you, Ellison. You're all alone. You broke the rules. And now there's only one person who can take care of you." He paused, taking a drag off his cigarette. "And that's me."

Ellison smiled again and for the first time Lyman realized that at one point in his life he must have been a handsome man. Those dark North Country eyes. That strong jaw. He must have been the bane of York-shire women for a few short summers.

Ellison took another pensive drag. "What about the chemist?"

"You tell me what you know," Lyman answered. "You tell me everything you saw, everything, and I'll take care of the chemist. Otherwise you go upstairs. Understand? Assault. Attempted murder."

Ellison looked at the cigarette in his hand. "I was sleeping in the bushes," he said carefully, as if the words were difficult to pronounce. "Just above the em-bankment path, between Blackfriars and the railway bridge. I was bloody tired of the hostels. Full of drunks and thieves anyway. But I had no money. It was warm for June. Anyway, I like sleeping outside. I used to do it all the time up-country."

"Go on."

"Well," he continued. "I woke up and saw this gaf-fer standing on the embankment by the water, just be-side the bridge. He was a toff all right. I could tell from his clothes. So I wondered what he was doing there, all alone in the middle of the night."

"What did he look like?"

Ellison frowned. "I only got a good look at him once, when he crossed beneath the light. It was your banker, I'm sure of that. I saw his picture in every gut-ter for the next two weeks."

"Then what happened?"

"For a while, nothing. He just kept looking up at the bridge and then back at his watch. Then after a few minutes these two blokes come out from the under-pass, where the bridge crosses over the embankment. That's when he started to move away, when I could see his face in the light. He was bloody terrified. But he couldn't run, you see, because just then two other blokes come down the embankment from the other side. He was trapped proper, right between them. Then he tried to smile and put on a bold face, especially for the two men near the underpass."

"He knew them?"

"Oh, I'm sure of it. He was talking to them but I couldn't understand it. Then . . ." Ellison paused, flicking the ashes of his cigarette onto the floor.

"Then what?"

"Then they all came forward, all except one. Your banker tried to stay in the center of the light. Two of them grabbed him from behind, but he didn't really struggle. He kept on saying, 'Nonchello, nonchello,' or something like that, over and over. The bloke in the shadows did all the talking back. He had a deep voice, I remember. The voice of a big man. Then, suddenly, they just pulled him to the ground. One of them took a box out of his coat. It must have been a knife or something because while the other two were holding him, the third one pulled his trousers part way down and stuck it in him, right there, in the groin. Bloody savages."

"Go on."

Ellison smiled grimly. "Doesn't bother you, does it? All in a day's work." He let his cigarette fall to the floor and crushed it with his boot.

"I've seen worse. Just tell me what happened."

"Then they pulled his trousers back up and one of them looked over the railing, down at the river. The fellow in the shadows seemed to be giving the orders again. It was like he knew I was there watching, as if he knew I'd see him if he went beneath the light. They lifted the banker up and hoisted him over the railing. He'd gone all limp, flopping about in their arms. I thought they were going to dump him in the river. Then I heard the sound of a small motor and I realized someone else had come up in a boat. They all climbed over the railing and disappeared, all except the fourth man. I could just barely see him looking over the railing. I suppose he was watching them hang the banker under the bridge. Big bloke."

"What about his face? Would you recognize him again?"

"Too dark," Ellison answered, shaking his head. "All I can say is that he wore a long black coat, and a white shirt. He wasn't wearing a tie." He paused.

"What is it?" Lyman said. "What else?"

"I know you'll think I'm daft," he said uncertainly, "but it looked a little like a vicar's collar."

"Like a priest, you mean?"

"Right. A clergyman. But it was really very dark. Then he walked back up the embankment, up the stairs, and across Blackfriars."

Lyman offered Ellison another cigarette. The vagabond's large hand was trembling. He looked suspiciously at the open box and finally slipped one behind his ear. "For later," he said.

Lyman took one for himself. "Why didn't you tell anyone about this earlier?"

Ellison shrugged. "None of my business. Besides, who would have believed me. I mean, look at me. Would you?"

"I didn't say I believed you."

"Oh, Christ." Ellison pulled the cigarette from behind his ear and dropped it between his teeth.

"You didn't brag about it to your friends?" Lyman insisted. "In a pub, I mean. A story for a pint. And what about the reward? If you saw his picture in the papers for the next two weeks, why didn't you notice the reward?"

"What reward?"

"For information, Ellison. For something on the hanging."

"I didn't see anything about a reward. I must have missed it." He looked away. "Never went to school much. Can I have a light?"

"Unless," Lyman added slowly.

"Unless what?"

"Unless you thought you might get even more if you kept quiet."

"Look, I was afraid. That's all. You can't trust a copper. You and them bankers always work together."

Lyman smiled, shaking his head. "It's no good, Ellison. Constable Frazier was right." He stood wearily, stretching his back. "Pity. You'll miss sleeping outside."

"Wait a minute," Ellison said, grabbing at Lyman's sleeve. "I thought we had a bargain."

Lyman leaned forward suddenly and popped Ellison's head back with the palm of his hand. The vagabond cried out. "Not anymore," Lyman said tightly, turning toward the door.

Ellison started to his feet. "Look, all right, I did know about it. The reward, and all that."

Lyman stopped.

Ellison was rocking back and forth, struggling inside, like a hooked fish underwater. "Christ, all I wanted was a chance. Don't you see? It's got to be worth money. Big money. Why else would he have tossed it? I'm only asking for what's due me."

Lyman walked back to the center of the room. "I see," he answered, carefully. He pulled a box of matches from his jacket and lit their cigarettes. "If that's the way it is." Then he smiled sadly and said, "But what do I get, Ellison? What's my due?"

Ellison grinned. "Half."

"Half of what?"

"Half of whatever we find. I promise. Half of whatever the key leads into. I'm going to need help anyway."

"What key?"

"The little red key. The key the banker tossed away. Half of whatever it brings. All you have to do is let me go. That's it."

Lyman exhaled deeply, the blue smoke rising wave on wave against the naked incandescent bulb above. "I'm sorry, Ellison," he said at last. "But I'm going to have to ask you for it." He seemed genuinely sad, as if he had refused reflexively, as if his honesty were just another habit he had picked up on the way, like smoking. "Tell me about the key."

Ellison sat down. He looked more disappointed than angry. He puffed on his cigarette slowly, meditatively. Then he wiped his forehead with his sleeve and said, "It happened when he leaned against the railing. Your banker. He had his back to the river, and then I saw him put his right hand in his pocket."

"For the key, you mean?"

"Well, that's it," Ellison replied. "I've been over it a hundred times in my head. First he was leaning back against the railing with one hand in his pocket. Then he turned around to face the river—as if he was going to jump for it—and as he did, he put his hands out on the railing. Both of them. Like this." He thrust his own hands out before him. They trembled in the air, huge and callused, mottled with dirt and blood from his fight with the chemist. "That's when he took it out. He must have. It was the only time he turned his back on them. And then they grabbed him."

"Where is this key?"

Ellison took another drag and looked away.

"Forget it, Ellison. Don't start playing about with me now, not when you're almost home."

"The shopkeeper."

"What about him? Does he have it?"

"It's in my bundle. In the alley."

Lyman nodded. "All right, let's take a look." He moved back toward the door. "Come on, Ellison. Doesn't the truth make you feel better, getting it off your chest?"

Ellison dropped his cigarette on the floor and stamped it out with his boot.

• • •

It took Constable Frazier only a few minutes to fetch a
car and drive them back to Fleet Street. The shopkeeper was home recuperating, but his assistant was
still there and he watched them sullenly from the rear
door of the shop as they poked about in the half light.
Ellison found the bundle without trouble. It had been
stuffed into a box marked cotton wool. Lyman unraveled it himself, afraid that Ellison might have a knife
inside. He dumped it on the alley floor, the pathetic
contents spilling out. So little, Lyman thought. A ragged, empty billfold. A comb. A packet of fine tools
such as a clockmaker might use. A penknife. And at
the bottom of the pile, half concealed, a little three-
edged key with the numbers 02 stamped on its bright
red plastic head.

"Inspector Lyman," Frazier shouted from the car.

Lyman picked the key up.

"Inspector, it's a call from central. Something's
come up."

Lyman sighed and walked back to the car. Frazier
handed him the microphone through the window.
"Lyman here," he said.

"Inspector, this is central. We just received a call
from Chief Superintendent Cocksedge. He says you're
to report back here immediately."

"Why, what's happened?"

"I'm not exactly sure. But apparently it has something to do with a fellow named Marco Scarcella."

"What about him?"

There was a pause on the radio. Lyman could feel
the key in his hand, the three serrated edges pressed
against his flesh. "What about Scarcella?" he repeated.

"There was a report. They say he's broken out of
prison. Bribed some guard, it seems. Does that mean
anything to you?"

Lyman did not answer. He looked up at the night sky. It had started to rain lightly, and he could see the drops appear out of the darkness far above, falling through the streetlight to the ground.

"Yes," Lyman said at last. "Yes, I suppose it does."

Chapter V

LONDON
September 2nd, 1983

LYMAN LOOKED BOTH WAYS BEFORE he crossed the road and headed for the row of red brick houses near the Golders Green tube station. The neighborhood had changed so much in the last few years. The buildings were no longer middle-aged, with that air of solid self-reliance which pervaded most of London's nearer suburbs, the stuff of England's civil servants home from the Raj or Africa for good. Now they sagged and crumbled under newer visions. Now synagogues were violated and the elderly robbed at knifepoint. Only the night before a flat in his own building had been robbed. Lyman had been living in the area for almost fourteen years and yet it was these criminal acts which always brought him closest to the city, as if, like many women Lyman knew, she shared her darker intimacies more easily with strangers.

It had been five days since Marco Scarcella's escape from Champ Dollon, five days of almost constant coordination with Interpol, and yet the whereabouts of the I Four's Venerable Master remained a mystery. To

make matters worse, in all that time the lab downstairs
had failed to reveal much of anything about the key
which Ellison had discovered near Blackfriars Bridge.
"Who would have believed me," the vagabond had
said, and indeed despite the key, the rest of the department had dismissed the story as improbable. Ellison
had made it up, they said, to sell it for his freedom. He
had built it from the newspaper accounts. And even if
a part of it were true, the vagabond had never really
seen Pontevecchio throw the key away. He had found it
afterward, on the side of the embankment. He had assumed it was the banker's.

Despite his colleagues' lack of confidence, Lyman
interviewed a dozen other vagrants to check on Ellison's report. He reread every file. He pressed and
pressed the sentences together until one night, in a
sudden fit of temper, he found himself shouting at the
Lemur that the only reason he thought Ellison was lying was because he was a Yorkshireman, a simple
bricklayer from up-country. "Really, Lyman," Randall
had replied. "Don't be so sensitive. Perhaps that's why
you think he's telling you the truth."

In the end, after days of effort all the lab could say
was that it was probably not a safe key, but it might
unlock a locker. It was definitely foreign, but it would
take another week or so before they could tell him any
more. The staff had other pressing matters to attend
to. They would get to it eventually. He would just have
to wait his turn.

In desperation Lyman ignored the standing orders
and pocketed the evidence himself. He knew a locksmith of his own near Hendon, someone who had
worked for him before. If anyone could tell him what
the key meant, it was Stephen Feldman.

A lorry bearing window glass droned by. Lyman ma-
neuvered into the flow of Friday shoppers on the pave-

ment. Stephen Feldman's shop was nestled in between a hair salon and a bakery. Two competing smells always seemed to gather out the door, the scent of scones and the rancid odor of burnt hair. A bell chimed cheerily as he stepped in.

Feldman's shop was the accumulation of a thousand preconceived depictions, the dreaming of eight years of captive solitude. Lyman had caught him in the epilogue of one of his first London murder cases. Feldman, by chance more than design, had been an accessory to murder, and Lyman had helped reduce his sentence in exchange for an address. The full-time locksmith, part-time burglar had served the years with the desperate singlemindedness of an animal plunging through a bog. He had festooned his cell with imaginary shelves and small machines, the sound of cutting keys, the smell of oil. The years converged, like the sand grains in an hourglass, and on the day of his release, it had been Lyman once again who had told him of the little vacant shop in Hendon.

Lyman closed the door and let the heat of the small room surround him. All in all, it was not particularly grand. A narrow counter ran the length of the room. Behind it Stephen Feldman was fitting a template key into a lathe. He was hunched over the machine like a kestrel. His bald pate glistened in the light. His long white fingers moved efficiently, clamping the blank key into place against the cutting edge.

"Stephen."

The locksmith looked up with a smile. "Nigel," he said. "Sick again or just home early?"

Lyman leaned against the counter. "Working, actually. I need a favor."

"Just ask." Feldman took a rag out from behind his apron and began to wipe his hands.

Lyman reached into his coat pocket. "What do you make of this?"

The locksmith dropped the rag onto the counter

and took the little red key up in his fingers. "Looks like a locker key," he said. "But you don't often see them with four edges. And there's a number—oh-two."

"I thought it had three edges."

"Well, the flat edge on the back, the fourth one, is a guide. And sixteen pins. Most keys have five to seven. I'd say it fits a Papaiz, a Brazilian lock."

"Brazilian?"

"That's where it was made, I'll wager. But that doesn't mean the cylinder's in Brazil. Papaiz locks are shipped all over the world. It could come from anywhere. Where did you get it?"

Lyman frowned. "What about the numbers on the head, and those letters on the stem itself?"

Feldman shook his head. "The letters look like they were stamped. A locksmith's mark perhaps. Or maybe it's a company impression. I'd have to look them up."

"Thanks, Stephen."

Feldman slipped from behind the counter and disappeared into a small doorway at the rear of the shop. Lyman examined the walls. Almost every inch of space was covered by keys, row upon row, hanging together from spindly metal brackets jutting from the walls. Some gold, some silver, they stood like silent sentinels on parade, awaiting an impression. They were the patient counterparts to doors and boxes still unopened, and suddenly Lyman thought about the labyrinth of corridors and countless portals of the Vatican.

"I know you'll think I'm daft," Ellison had said. "But it looked a little like a vicar's collar." There had been enough time for the flight from Rome to London, Lyman knew, to Blackfriars Bridge and back. Archbishop Grabowski, normally a late riser, had been seen in the Via Veneto early on the morning of Pontevecchio's death. Indeed, the archbishop had been the first official at the Vatican to hear about it. Yet Lyman was suspicious of this ready answer. Each case had its individual rhythm and another image shook his memory, the photograph of Marco Scarcella on his desk, wearing a white polo neck and raincoat.

Had Chief Inspector Hadley been correct? Had Archbishop Grabowski really been so anxious to conceal the Vatican's association with Banco Fabiano that he had killed Pontevecchio? Or had Scarcella been involved, and why? Why London? Whom had the banker come to meet, and what had he brought to trade for his exoneration, the "wonderful thing" his wife had talked about, the impetus to make the Vatican observe its obligations and cover Fabiano's enormous debts? His questions, like the uncut keys, led nowhere.

Stephen Feldman emerged from the rear of the shop, shaking his head. "Sorry, mate. I think the letters are a company impression, but I don't know the name. SAFA, or something like that. Part of it is missing. One thing though. You might try contacting Papaiz directly. Ask them if they have any clients who either make or distribute lockers."

"Why lockers?"

"It's just a guess," Feldman said. "You know. Like at Victoria Station. The numbers would probably be oh-one, oh-two, oh-three and so on. And the bright red color's for identification." He handed the key back to Lyman.

"Thanks anyway," Lyman said.

"Sorry I couldn't do more."

"Can I use your telephone?"

Feldman pointed to the rear of the shop. "Is it me you're speaking to? How about some tea? I was just about to make some."

Lyman smiled. "I'd love some," he said, crossing behind the counter.

The rear room was jammed with boxes full of keys, a little wooden desk, and a grimy kitchen area. A circular fluorescent light hummed above. The telephone was on the desk. Lyman picked it up and dialed the station house. There was a little electric fire glowing in one wall and he raised one shoe, then the other, turning them slowly in the air to catch the warmth.

The switchboard answered and he collected all his messages. "Nothing pressing," the young receptionist replied. "But Superintendent Randall wants to speak with you."

Lyman heard a series of clicks and then the Lemur's high, familiar voice. "Lyman, where the hell are you?"

"Following up the key, sir."

"Where, I said."

"In Golders Green."

"At home, or did you stop off on the way?"

Lyman sighed. "I'm asking someone else about that key."

There was a pause. "Not that again," Randall said. "Look, I want you to meet me at Dorret's Wine and Ale at eight o'clock. Chief Superintendent Cocksedge and the home secretary's liaison will be there, so look smart."

"Yes, sir," Lyman said. "I was wondering, sir, if you might have Frazier make a call for me. It's to a Brazilian lock company named Papaiz."

"Brazilian. Bloody hell, Lyman. This better be worth it."

"Do you have a pen, sir?"

"Of course I have a pen. Get on with it."

"Yes, sir. Would you ask Frazier to see if Papaiz services a firm called SAFA, or something like that. They either make or distribute storage lockers. Brazil should be at least three hours behind us."

"At least," the Lemur said. "Very well, I'll tell him. But be there by eight, Lyman. I'm not making any more excuses for you."

"Yes, sir. You can count on me. Eight o'clock."

"And Lyman . . ."

"Yes, sir?"

"If you take the tube from Hendon Central, you won't be tempted on the way."

The Lemur rang off. Lyman heard the click and then the hollow echo of the winding subterranean miles between them. "Sorry about the tea," he said, as Feldman reappeared. "I can't stay."

The first thing Lyman noticed as he made his way across the street to Dorret's Wine & Ale was the large emblem just above the entrance, a gray horse rearing and the word "Liberty" in a string of letters underneath. It was a new pub with pretensions of old glamour, but it served a fine mixed grill and looked from its imposing vantage point on the Southwark side of the Thames, across the leaden river to the very span of Blackfriars Bridge where Pontevecchio had been found hanging the year before.

The maître d' led Lyman to a table at the back. Chief Superintendent Cocksedge and the Lemur were already seated. They were chatting with another man who was, Lyman realized, the minister's liaison, Sir Giles Richards. He was a portly man with strands of sandy hair combed delicately across his head, and gold wire-rimmed glasses.

"Sorry I'm late," Lyman said, pulling at his coat. "The traffic's terrible."

The three men at the table barely glanced up. They were talking about the likelihood of cutbacks in the police department's budget, given the Conservative government's new austerity measures. Lyman stood beside the only empty seat, wondering if he should just sit down or wait to be formally introduced. Finally the Lemur pointed at the chair. "Ah, Detective Inspector Lyman," he said, smiling broadly. "I'm glad you could come."

Lyman dropped his coat across the back of the chair and sat down.

"I don't believe you know Sir Giles, do you?" Chief Superintendent Cocksedge asked.

Lyman shook his head. "I've never had the pleasure."

The minister's liaison smiled like a Buddha across the table. They had already ordered and he was busy cutting up a chop. "Cocksedge tells me that you may have found a lead," he said between bites. "Damn good work, after all this time."

"Actually," Cocksedge interjected smoothly, "it may be a bit premature to call it a lead. It may be nothing at all. It may simply be the ravings of a drunkard, for all we know."

"May be, may be." Sir Giles put his knife and fork down on his plate. "It may be nothing to you, but it means a great deal to the minister. This Pontevecchio matter is of the utmost importance, gentlemen. I can't stress that enough. The minister is awfully tired of hearing about conspiracies and mismanagement. Especially now that Scarcella has escaped from Champ Dollon. Trust the Swiss to muck it up. If the last inquest was closed too soon, then by God this one will continue, gentlemen, until all the questions have been answered. Including, Chief Superintendent, the questions raised here by that key of yours."

"Well, Lyman," Cocksedge said.

"Sir?" Lyman glanced from face to face.

"The key, man. Show it to Sir Giles."

Lyman looked to Terry Randall for a sign but he was staring oddly at the chief superintendent. "I'm sorry, sir," he said. "I don't have it on me. Standing orders."

"Yes, of course," Cocksedge answered peevishly, turning back to face Sir Giles.

Lyman had never seen the chief superintendent act so solicitous before, and it seemed out of place and forced. He was not a natural politician. A silence descended on the table. Lyman noticed Cocksedge had a whiskey. Sir Giles continued to whittle away at his chop and stewed tomatoes. Finally the minister's liaison laid his knife and fork down on his plate and wiped the corners of his mouth with his napkin.

"Hambro's, gentlemen," he pronounced, shaking his head. "Even Hambro's, whose ties to Italy date back to Queen Victoria, was caught up in this ghastly business. Hambro's, one of London's finest merchant banks. My God! In Whitehall they ask me why Pontevecchio had twelve pounds of stones stuffed in his pockets, why he would travel all the way to Blackfriars from his rooms at Chelsea Cloisters just to string himself up. Only yesterday a respected MP from Durham, whom I won't name, asked me in all seriousness if I didn't think the banker's death was a kind of ritual Masonic killing; something to do with his feet washing in the tide. Do you understand, gentlemen? Things are getting out of hand. I want it settled once and for all. The minister wants it settled."

"We understand, sir," Cocksedge said. "Inspector Lyman's doing everything he can. Aren't you, Lyman?"

"Yes, sir."

"Well, what about this key, Lyman?" Sir Giles said. "Do you really think this vagabond is telling you the truth?"

"Yes, sir. I do."

"Why?"

Lyman hesitated for a moment. "Because he didn't have to tell me anything. It was unnecessary."

"And the key. Randall tells me it belongs to some locker company in France."

"What's that? You found the company?"

"Didn't I tell you?" the Lemur answered with surprise. "While you were in Golders Green this afternoon, I put the call through to Papaiz. It was a bit of an effort but I managed to get them to look back through their files. Someone actually remembered the SAFAA deal. It seems there was some romance going on between the SAFAA agent and a woman who worked at Papaiz three years ago. They ran off together, to Bahia. Frightfully romantic. That's why they remembered. SAFAA's a Parisian firm. They manufacture lockers for coach and railway terminals."

Lyman leaned back in his chair.

"Sir Giles believes," said Cocksedge, "that you should follow this lead up personally, Lyman. And I agree, of course."

Lyman nodded. "As you say, sir."

"Perhaps," the Lemur said, "it might be better to hand it over to the local authorities, at least until we know if the key means anything. I'm not entirely convinced it bears upon the case. Lyman would be in completely unfamiliar territory. And remember what happened during the last inquest. The Italians only ended up resenting us."

"No, let Lyman handle it," Cocksedge said. "He's done a damned good job so far. Besides, he's been to France before, haven't you, Lyman?"

"Yes, sir. Not for some time though, I'm afraid."

"That doesn't matter. It all comes back, I'm told. Besides, it would be damned unfair to pull it away from him now. I mean, it's his case, after all."

"And in the meantime," Sir Giles said, slightly bored, "I assume that Randall here will follow up the home leads."

"Yes, sir. We'll have to coordinate from London."

"Good. That's settled then. Here's to some speedy answers, gentlemen."

Sir Giles lifted his glass. Cocksedge and Terry Randall followed suit, but Lyman hesitated. He watched them bring their cocktails up together.

"How about it, Lyman," Sir Giles said, noticing his empty hand. "Aren't you going to join us?"

Lyman looked across the table at their faces. They were all smiling at him. They were toasting him. He lifted the empty water glass before him and tapped it gently up against the Lemur's beer. "I'd better not," he said. "I should go home and pack."

Lyman left the pub and walked along the riverfront, trying to clear his head, trying to suppress the thought of stopping somewhere else along the way, just one to help him get to sleep. But the Lemur's narrow face kept swimming into view, the delicate, protruding jaw.

Eventually, when the cold began to creep into his joints, he found a bus and headed home toward Hendon. The bus was almost empty. It was Friday, after all, and the crowds were going into London, not out to Golders Green. An elderly couple sat in the back seat holding hands. Lyman kept thinking about his case, about Scarcella and the locker key, about his pending trip to France, and he almost missed his stop, stepping off into the shadows at the last minute. Gooseberry Close was a modest apartment complex consisting of three brick buildings of dubious architectural value, the smallest and oldest being Thurston Croft where Lyman lived.

He stopped outside the entrance to his building. His hands were in his coat pockets. He could feel the hardness of the little red key even through his glove. Then he looked up, slowly, as if he didn't want to catch it all at once, leaning back, taking in the tent of stars and blackness high above. There was Orion's Belt, and Gemini, but where were the Pleiades? Lyman had not seen a night like this one since the year before, when he and Crosley had gone fishing in the Lake District.

He climbed wearily up the steps into the building. William Harris wasn't in the hall and Lyman missed him, the cheery hello he could almost always count on when he met the caretaker's son. Lyman pressed the button for the lift. Normally he would have walked, but tonight he only wanted to throw some water on his face and fall asleep.

The lift descended into view, a vintage platform, a cage of brass and black enameled bars. Lyman stepped in and closed the accordion door behind him. Someone was cooking fish and he remembered it was Friday. The lift groaned upwards. As it ascended he could see the floors unroll one by one through the grillwork. He had almost reached his floor, the fourth, when the lift suddenly lurched to a stop, the wheezing of the metal sounding even louder in the darkness which pursued it like an echo. Lyman cursed.

Blackout!

He groped for the buttons on the panel to see if anything would happen. They were useless. Someone was shouting. Lyman paused, his back straightening instinctively against the grillwork of the elevator. It wasn't a shout. It was a whine of sorts, a cry.

He reached up through the door. The lift was trapped between storeys, but at the top of the metal frame he could feel the cold stone of the fourth floor, his floor. It was absolutely dark. He took a breath to shout for help when something checked it in his throat. There was that whine again, a kind of muted howl, and it was then that Lyman realized it was George.

He pulled himself up as high as he could, trying to see through the bars. People were starting to mill about on the floors above. He could hear their voices echoing down the shaft. Someone was shining a torch up from below. The whining stopped. Lyman heard a door click open on his landing. He squeezed his face against the bars, trying to see. A wedge of light cut through the darkness. A pair of slippers trimmed with maribou feathers appeared in an open doorway. It was Mrs. Wilson, Lyman's neighbor, with a candle. A pair of black work shoes followed right behind. Then the soft glow of another candle blended with the first, the nimbus growing larger, taking in the bare feet of John Pollock from next door. Mrs. Wilson began to complain about the outage, about all that bloody noise. Pollock's feet retreated into darkness. Lyman was about to call out once again when the door to his own flat opened. Mrs. Wilson moved away. Her husband wanted the candle. The dim reflected light bobbed up and down, then vanished.

Lyman heard the sound of footsteps to his left. A torch flashed on, and he saw a pair of dark brown wing-tipped shoes move steadily away from his apartment door, so close that he could have reached up through the metal grate and touched them. They hesitated for a moment, and then started down the stairwell.

Lyman dropped to the floor of the lift. He tried to make out the landing below, but it was just too dark. No one had come out into the hallway as they had above. It remained pitch black, even as the figure came around the stairwell. Whoever he was, the man with the wing-tipped shoes had turned his torch off on the stairs. Lyman tried to make his face out in the shadows but it was useless. Then the silhouette was gone, an echo in the stairwell, and no more.

The lights came on as suddenly as they had dimmed. The lift wheezed upward and stopped at the fourth floor. He opened the metal door and moved cautiously across the landing. It was too bright now, too ordinary. The door to his apartment was locked.

The first thing that he noticed when he swung it open was the thin red streak which ran along the off-white carpeting the whole length of the corridor. Books and pictures and magazines were strewn across the floor. He stepped across them crouched and ready, although he knew with a dull, uncompromising certainty that he had come too late. Each room he passed was the same. The dining table had been split across the middle, its back broken. The tiles in the bathroom were shattered. They had unscrewed all the piping. They had pulled the outlets from the walls.

He picked a knife up from the floor beside the

kitchen door and stepped across the wreckage, trying
to ignore the side rooms, trying to fix his eyes on that
thin red thread which wound its way across the broken
crockery, the books burst open, from one room to the
next, until he finally saw the body of the dog half covered by the bureau in his bedroom. George was still
moving, licking at himself. Lyman kneeled beside him
and it was only then that he saw the way the dog's jaw
hung off to the side, the flesh stripped from the teeth
and the red tongue trying to lick away the flow of
blood. A puddle of vomit and blood and broken glass
circled his head.

There was a sudden sound and Lyman swung
about, the long knife gleaming in his hand. William
Harris stood in the doorway. Lyman lowered the knife.
"You should know better, William," he said. "I could
have hurt you."

"Christ!" The caretaker's son stepped uncertainly
into the room. "What happened to George?"

Lyman held a hand out to keep him from the dog.
"They fed him something," he said. "It's too late, William. There's nothing we can do."

The boy knelt on the ground, looking from the dog
to Lyman and then back again. "I heard him howling,"
he said. "I was coming to have a look when the lights
went out. I was on my way."

"Of course you were," said Lyman gently. "The
blackout was probably a signal."

"Just like Mrs. Van der Meer's. Except she didn't
have a dog. Two robberies in two nights. They must be
balmy, Inspector Lyman." The boy moved back from
the dog, pushing himself to his feet. There were blood-
stains on his knees. "But you'll catch them. Won't you?
You'll find them."

"William," Lyman said. "Why don't you go down to
your father's and ring the police."

The boy could not tear his eyes away.

"You'll be fine, William," Lyman urged him soothingly. "Leave me alone for a minute. Tell your father."

Finally the boy turned away and headed out the door. Lyman could hear him scrambling over the fallen books and paintings.

When he was finally alone, Lyman reached his hands out and began to scratch George gently about the neck and head. The dog was barely conscious. He kept licking at his mouth, trying to keep the blood which trickled from the small cuts in his gums from flowing back and choking him. Lyman cradled his head. "Oh, George," he said, almost inaudibly. Then he ran his hands about the dog's neck, twisting it with a sudden downward motion, until with a snap, the animal jerked once and settled.

Lyman stood, wiping his hands on his haunches. He walked over to the window overlooking the little garden which the residents of Thurston Croft had planted the year before. Through the darkness he could see a few great poplars swaying near the schoolyard, the thick hedge by the roadside, the flash of taillights as they passed by openings in the foliage. Above, the same stars swung about the house. He could feel that small nub in his pocket, now familiar. He could visualize its shape, the three serrated edges and the final guide. He leaned through the window, looking for the impossible figure in the shadows, like a hungry owl, his fingers squeezed about the sill. It hadn't been just another robbery. They had come for Pontevecchio's key.

"You bloody bastards," he shouted suddenly, the anger welling up inside him. "Fuck you, you bloody bastards." Then he turned away, embarrassed.

One thing at least, he realized, looking down. He wouldn't have to find a kennel now, before his trip to France.

Part II

The dodecahedron was used to embroider the universe with constellations.

PLATO
The Sicelica by Timaeus

Chapter VI

AMIENS, FRANCE
September 3rd, 1983

THE CATHEDRAL OF AMIENS WAS LIKE a crystal growing all around him and Joseph Koster realized, as he let his eyes climb up the arcade and triforium, that through it he could see the constant elemental clash between the vertical and horizontal, the scramble upward to the heavens, the fall to dissolution. At Beauvais just north of Paris, the vault of the cathedral had collapsed in the thirteenth century, its height so great, so arrogant perhaps, that some had called the accident a Gothic flight of Icarus. But here at Amiens the vault soared more than a hundred feet, lifting the people with it, stretching the walls until they folded paper thin into the sky.

Koster moved into the nave. He was a lean man in his early thirties, with long blond hair and a stiff, uncertain stride. His face was narrow, his eyes deep set. He wore an ice blue anorak which hung about his body, and a pair of tight black jeans. As he walked, he noticed that the floor of the cathedral was an arabesque of lines, black and white knots and Indian swastikas of stone. There was an octagonal labyrinth at the center of the nave. It was a whirlpool of black tiles against white granite, broken into quadrants, revolving to a central copper plate. Everywhere was light—within the aisles, in the crossing transept arms, and in the distant choir. He paused for a moment and stared down at the labyrinth. A dozen names were inscribed in the copper plate, or was it brass? He couldn't tell. He felt his eyes drawn up again, directed skyward by the strings of stone which climbed beyond the arcade piers, beyond the arched triforium to form the vault itself.

"No flash," a guard in blue called out.

Near the southern entrance a tourist with three cameras slung about his neck glanced sheepishly at his wife. Americans, Koster guessed, as he started toward them. It seemed to be a tour of some sort. There was another middle-aged couple, probably English, and a barrel-chested bearded man. "Wait a few more minutes," the bearded man advised. "The guards all take their morning nap about this time." Then he began to laugh, as if he had some object in his chest which he were trying vainly to dislodge.

"Excuse me," Koster said. "Is this a private tour?"

The large man with the beard twirled suddenly, his hands aflutter. "Private?" he said. "Exclusive, perhaps. But never private. I am only the unofficial guide, alas. Not sanctioned by the state. My name is Guy Soury-Fontaine." He thrust a stubby hand at Koster. "You are welcome to join us. It is my first and only English tour today."

Koster felt his hand jerked up and down. The American with the cameras was smiling. No doubt he recognized a fellow countryman, an ally who could help him stare down any foreign guard. The English couple kept their distance.

"We shall start outside," the guide said as he shuffled off. "Where Man did."

They headed through the double doors of the west facade and out into the open. Soury-Fontaine drove Koster and the tourists down the steps like sheep, while he remained above them with his back to the cathedral. "This last and perhaps greatest of the High Gothic cathedrals," he boomed, "was begun in 1220 by Robert de Luzarches, when the little town of Amiens had but twelve thousand poor inhabitants. She was the skyscraper of the Middle Ages, so eminent that each and every person in the town could fit within her walls."

Koster knew much of the material already, but he could not share the guide's unbridled adulation of the west facade. To him it lacked proportion somehow. Two galleries had been thrown up on top of one another, a stained glass rose squeezed badly between tiers, jammed in below the cornice at the top. It simply didn't work.

The big guide spoke English fluently, his accent thick enough to charm the tourists, but finally a background hum, a natural pitch. He was dressed in a light brown cardigan which was badly pilled and stretched drum-tight along his shoulders and the ample arching of his stomach. His beard needed a trim. The collar of his shirt was popping up a little in the back. In all a rather shabby guide, thought Koster, and yet there was an animation in Soury-Fontaine's hands and face which seemed to radiate about him, almost in spite of how he looked.

He jabbed a finger toward the sumptuous facade. Mrs. James Dawson, who proved to be Australian, and not English after all, began to pepper him with questions. Soury-Fontaine only smiled with greater forcefulness. Here was an eager student. It did not matter to him that in twenty minutes she would probably be sitting in an air-conditioned bus, a dozen chateaux left to see, the cathedral far behind. His hacking laugh became a mark of punctuation. His eyes, the color of

mutton gravy, pitched side to side as he vainly sought
an entrance.

"Not at all," he said at last. "You must remember
who these people were. Imagine being a pilgrim. You
have been traveling for weeks, perhaps months or even
years. Finally you arrive—tired, covered in lice, foot-
sore. Perhaps you are sick, which is why you came on
this pilgrimage in the first place. Perhaps you are dying.
But it doesn't matter because you have finally arrived.
The cathedral stands before you. Clean, not like it is
now, but new. The portal statues tell you stories as you
climb the steps. You open the door and, suddenly, the
dancing lightbeams stream about you from the stained
glass windows. It is like heaven on earth, a mirror of
the heavenly Jerusalem." His right hand curled into a
fist.

Mrs. Dawson was unconvinced. "Whatever do you
mean? What stories?"

"The cathedral is a book in stone," Soury-Fontaine
replied. "Most of the people of the Middle Ages
couldn't read. They relied instead on the statuary, on
the glass. All of these figures are symbols. The way they
are placed means something. The clothes they wear.
The number in each grouping."

He pointed at a line of figures by the central door.
"Six men on either side of Christ," he said. "A dozen
altogether. Would you care to hazard a guess, Mrs.
Dawson, as to who they are?"

"The twelve apostles, I suppose," she answered ca-
gily. Her husband rocked on his heels. He was enjoying
this.

"You see, you knew already. Even what they carry
has significance. That third one on the left, the fellow
with the T square in his hand, is Thomas. How do I
know? Because Thomas is the patron saint of builders.
That one over there is Peter."

Soury-Fontaine boomed on. Koster took in the can-
opy of stone, the figures on the tympanum and lintel.

He wondered what they had looked like in their painted youth, before the elements and time had stripped them of their brilliant colors. The guide had called the church a book in stone, but Koster thought she must have seemed a comic book of sorts back in the Middle Ages, all gilded and dissembled, the stone cheeks rouged, the eyebrows penciled.

He looked up. The tympanum gave way to arches, more statues tucked in granite envelopes, that rose of hopeless complication, more arches still, and from the cornice, strung like a web between two tiers, a solitary figure peering down. Koster wondered what the little crowd of tourists looked like from that height, and it was only then that he finally understood what he had only glimpsed out of the window of the airplane three days earlier, the distance in between two worlds, the mile on empty mile of gray-blue North Atlantic—he had arrived. He was in France, in Amiens. The months of dreaming and delay were over. The cathedral was no longer framed by printed words, nor by the neat white borders of the Kodak slides which he had borrowed from his architectural firm's extensive library. She was right there before him. Live, and in color.

"Oy." Someone was poking at his ribs. It was Mr. Dawson. "We're off to see the stalls now," he said, rolling his eyes. "You could circle Queensland with the choir stalls I've seen this month. It's a wonder they have any forests left in France. Aren't you with us anymore?"

"Right." Koster followed him up the steps and into the cathedral.

The tourists huddled together at the center of the nave, just beyond the outer border of the labyrinth in the floor. The words of the guide echoed in the vastness of the cool cathedral. Votive candles burned, each flame a spark of expectation. The stone rose steadily.

"Well," Mrs. Dawson sighed. "According to my

book, it's only because most of the windows have been shot out by cannonfire that we can even see the maze."

The guide's broad shoulders sagged. He ran a hand through his beard and stared up at the ceiling. The pause lengthened to a silence. Then he dropped his hands and began to rub them in the air, as if washing them in a sink. "It is a labyrinth, Mrs. Dawson," he said precisely. "Not a maze. A labyrinth has but one passage, convoluted though it may be. A maze has several."

"Well, what's it for?"

"Some say it was used by pilgrims in the Middle Ages. If they were too sick or too old to make the journey to the Holy Lands, they simply acted it out here, by following the labyrinth in the floor. A symbolic pilgrimage. No one really knows for certain. Some say it depicts the passage to a heavenly city, the heavenly Jerusalem."

Mrs. Dawson tightened like a spring. "Well, I suppose it was a long time ago. You've done very well on everything else."

She was a woman who liked to forgive, Koster thought.

"Who were those people?" the American with the cameras chimed in. He was pointing at the copper plaque at the center of the labyrinth.

"Those are the names of the architects, the master masons who built the cathedral. Their guild claimed they could trace their science back to Daedalus, the legendary architect of Crete who built the original labyrinth for King Minos."

"What a wonderful story," Mrs. Dawson added with transparent disbelief.

Soury-Fontaine turned suddenly on his heels and strode away, his hands locked tightly at his back, his head bent and his deep voice coughing out, "The stalls, the stalls."

Mr. Dawson looked at Koster with a desperate ex-

pression on his face. His mouth hung open. His head
wagged from side to side. Then, with a final gesture of
disgust, he followed Mrs. Dawson, who was already
dashing in pursuit. The file assembled. They sidled toward the south aisle quietly, embarrassed by the loud-
ness of their shoes and the pensive shoulders which
appeared quite suddenly as they approached—like
targets in a shooting gallery—from in between the
pews. How could anyone pray, thought Koster, with all
these tourists everywhere?

They spent the rest of the lecture admiring the or-
nate carvings of the choir stalls which rose up nearly
twenty feet around the altar. Soury-Fontaine explained
the Biblical stories which they depicted, but his heart
was no longer in his work. Mrs. Dawson had usurped
him. He simply repeated the words which he had said
ten thousand times before. Even his plea for money at
the end lacked luster. He told them in a flat, uncompromising voice that the state was not his master, and
that he hoped that they would look upon him as the
people of the Middle Ages had looked upon their traveling scholars—with generosity. Then he held his blunt
hands out before him like a living cup, and turned his
head away.

Faced with this final gesture of humility, Mrs. Dawson came undone. She probed her purse, trilling like a
wood dove, and withdrew a one-hundred-franc note.
The Americans were already filing past, pressing their
coins against his fingertips noiselessly. Mrs. Dawson
folded the bill twice, then another time, and dropped it
in his hands.

Koster stood a few steps away, waiting for the band
of tourists to leave. When they had finally shuffled off,
Soury-Fontaine closed his hands and stuffed the money
in his pockets without even looking at it. Then he noticed Koster by the stalls. "A frightening woman," he
said sadly.

"But generous."

The big man laughed. "And you? Did you enjoy the tour?"

"Very much so. In fact, I'd like to see some more . . . if I could."

The guide glanced at his watch. "I'm sorry, I have a luncheon engagement. But perhaps a few more minutes. What exactly would you like to see?"

Koster leaned back against the carved oak stalls. He wound his hand around the head of Israel who was worrying about his son, the dreamer Joseph, thrown in a cistern by his brothers two seats down. At his head the Magi watched the wooden skies, and at his feet a monk prayed with one word carved firmly on his mouth throughout eternity. Who had the unknown carvers of these choir stalls been? thought Koster. Were these their faces? "Actually," he said, glancing up. "I'd like to make a separate arrangement. I plan to be in Amiens for several weeks."

The guide looked delighted. "Really?" he said. "You are a student, a scholar?"

"In a manner of speaking. I'm doing a book on the cathedrals of Notre Dame. High Gothic, really. Chartres and Reims as well."

Soury-Fontaine closed the distance between them with one giant stride, snatched Koster's hands together in his own, and shook them vigorously. "Felicitations," he croaked in French, his long, bearded face intently serious. "It is a great honor indeed. I am at your complete disposal."

Koster looked up at him helplessly. The Frenchman's massive head and shoulders had pinned him up against the stalls. "Thank you," Koster said. He slapped him firmly on the shoulder and the guide stepped back.

"Naturally," Koster continued, "I'll be happy to pay you for your time and assistance."

Soury-Fontaine laughed gruffly. Then his face began to change, a fixed expression at a time, from happiness to indecision, from doubt to resignation, as if he were removing one mask from another, one extra turn along the labyrinth. The almost oafish grin was gone. Instead, a child's fear clutched the corners of his eyes. He shook his head. He turned away. "As you wish," he added, like an afterthought.

Koster leaned forward, his hand still holding the carved head which jutted from the choir stall. There was something odd about Soury-Fontaine, something not altogether right, and Koster felt himself thrown back to Soho in New York. He was having coffee with Priscilla, at a small Greene Street cafe. A station wagon pulled up outside the window, panting at the stoplight. There were two children in the rear of the car. It was autumn and the sun cut through the window at the back, illuminating the children's faces, flooding them with a light of near unnatural brightness. Koster noticed they were girls. They were laughing and throwing their hands against the glass when one of them just stopped, all of a sudden, and looked up at the sky. Koster knew then, in that one brief moment, that there was something terribly wrong with her, but hidden, a slowness of the mind perhaps, a retardation. Even Priscilla knew. The other girl reached forward and pulled her back into the game. And then the car moved on.

Koster tried to smile. The guide seemed perfectly normal. He had remembered all those dates and names —no mean task—and yet Koster could not shake the feeling.

Soury-Fontaine ran his eyes along the stalls, as if searching for another detail to unravel. Then he pointed at the lacy wooden spires at the entrance to the choir and abruptly waved.

Koster followed his gaze. A woman was approaching up the southern aisle. She seemed to hover through the shadows. Only her face was clearly visible, revealed by random lightbeams from the clerestory above. Her eyes were large, her lips almost too full. She had a strong demanding forehead which caught the warm glow of the votive candles as she stepped inside the presbytery gate.

"My luncheon, I'm afraid," Soury-Fontaine said cheerily.

She seemed much younger now, Koster thought. Maybe twenty-five. She was wearing a short-sleeved, blue cotton dress. Her long dark hair was held back by a patterned silk scarf. He watched her rise up on her toes and kiss the guide firmly on both cheeks. "Hungry?" she said in French. Then she reached her hand out slowly, and Koster realized it was meant for him.

"How do you do," she said quite formally.

Koster shook her hand gently, bowing as his father had once taught him years before in Rome. He always did it out of habit, and it always made him feel uncomfortable. "Very well, thank you," he answered. His French was precise, inelegant but perfect.

"My sister, Mariane," the guide said.

Koster leaned against these words, buoyed by them. So he was only her brother, he thought.

They stared at him blankly and Koster realized that he hadn't introduced himself. "Oh, I'm sorry. My name's Joseph Koster. Your brother here has just agreed to help me on a book I'm writing."

"On the cathedral," Soury-Fontaine threw in. "Imagine."

Koster watched the girl closely. The more she smiled, the more genuine she seemed—and the more he felt a fraud. "I'm really more of an architect than a writer," he admitted. "Although the book is quite professional, I assure you." Neither Soury-Fontaine nor Mariane replied. "I will, of course, credit any assistance you might give me."

Soury-Fontaine began to laugh deliciously, but the girl looked unimpressed. Her smile faded. She cocked her head a little to the side and said, "Mr. Koster. I'm

sure that Guy will help you, with or without acknowl-
edgement. Won't you, Guy?"

Soury-Fontaine nodded.

Koster leaned against the stalls. "I'm sorry. I didn't
mean it like that. I'd be very grateful for your help."

Mariane smiled. "You Americans," she said. "I suppose you'd like to buy us lunch as well."

Koster shrugged. "I wouldn't want to impose."

"I only have a picnic," the girl added. "Nothing
very grand by American standards. But you're welcome
to join us."

Koster noticed that the short sleeves of her dress
were a little tight above the elbow, creasing the skin of
her arms. "We'll get more," he said.

Mariane laughed quietly. It made her seem older.
Her hands reached up to pull the scarf more tightly
round her face. "Well, come on, Mr. Koster."

They sat under an oak tree only a few hundred yards
from the cathedral. It was strange, thought Koster, how
the cathedral's flying buttresses seemed less to anchor
the stone structure to the ground—like the roots of a
giant mangrove—than to contain the walls, to keep
them from rushing upward to the heavens. The church
was like a natural force, with the presence of a moun-
tain or a butte, dominating the landscape, watching
over them patiently, constrained yet waiting for release.

Mariane had spread a blanket out on the grass and
she was kneeling on one corner, emptying a picnic basket. Soury-Fontaine sat next to her, opening bottles of
Belgian beer with a key. "Here," he said, handing one
to Koster.

"Thanks."

"Have you been to France before, Mr. Koster?"
Mariane asked casually.

"Yes, several times. I lived in Italy when I was

younger, and then in Switzerland for a while. My father played with the Roman Philharmonic. You may have heard of him. Peter Koster."

Mariane shook her head.

"First oboe," Koster said. "He's retired now." He took a sip of the beer. It was cold and sweet. "How about you? Have you always lived in Amiens?"

"No, not always," she said. "Our family comes from the Channel Islands originally. But we've lived in Picardie for three hundred years now, so the locals are finally beginning to accept us. I spent some time in Paris too, when I was younger, in school."

"Really. Where?"

"The Sorbonne." She laughed quietly. "I studied philosophy and literature. It seems like a long time ago now."

She began to slice a loaf of bread. Koster could not take his eyes off her hands, the way her fingers curled about the knife, the way she held the loaf in place, squeezing it slightly. "Is that what you do now, Mariane? Philosophy?" It was the first time that he had spoken her name.

She stopped slicing the bread and looked up. "No, I left all that behind me years ago. I work at the Cartier Photo Shop. On the other side of the cathedral."

"Why did you leave Paris?"

"I never really liked the city, Mr. Koster."

"Please call me Joseph."

Mariane laid the knife on the blanket beside her. Then she said, "When you're from the country, as I am, Mr. Koster, you're taught to have a certain image of Paris. From films and television. From books. You know. Paris is meant to be the center of everything: fashion, business, the intellectual wellspring." She smiled sadly. "I suppose it is in some ways. Of course by the time I'd finished school, few things still lived up to my expectations." She passed a piece of bread to her brother. "Why did you decide to write a book about the cathedrals?"

Koster smiled. "That's easy. I've always found them fascinating, ever since I was a kid. Their proportion. Balance. I remember my parents took me on a train trip once, from London to Rome. We stopped off for a day in Amiens. I was eleven years old at the time. I remember being in a taxi, riding through the streets not far from here, seeing the spires of the cathedral for the first time across the roofs. There was something about it, something almost magical. It's hard to explain. I was very interested in mathematics then. There's a kind of beauty in numbers, in their powerful simplicity, their order, that I'd never experienced anywhere else. They seemed to belong to a secret world, separate from the everyday, a special place that I could see and play in, but that was invisible to everyone else around me. When we got out of the cab, I saw the cathedral looming over me, just as it is now. It was as if my secret world had come suddenly to life, slipped from some other realm and then made physical before me."

"The heavenly Jerusalem," said Guy Soury-Fontaine. "The church of faith. You're not the first, you know."

"I can't describe it. I remember walking over and touching the stone walls, looking up. I remember entering the cathedral for the first time, seeing the arches unfold above me, over a hundred feet up. The great windows. The breach in the tympanum. The triforium and clerestory rushing together to form that wall of light. It was, I don't know . . . perfect." Koster tore his gaze away from the cathedral. "When I got older I got my graduate degree in mathematics."

"My best subject in school," said Guy. "Remember, Mariane? I won that book."

"I remember," she said. *"Tintin on the Moon.* What kind of mathematics, Mr. Koster?"

"Oh, I struggled with a whole bunch of things. The

null set. Group theory and symmetry. It's a strange career being a mathematician. You're basically an academic, always living at the mercy of the university, trapped in some tiny subsidized apartment. You struggle for grants. You write papers for obscure journals that only a handful of people bother to read. I did my greatest work on something called the Goldbach Conjecture."

"What's that?"

"It's a mathematical hypothesis that's extralogically true, but that defies being proved with logic. Gödel, the great Viennese mathematician, used to call them unprovable verities. Anyway, in 1742 this German mathematician named Goldbach conjectured that every even number can be written as the sum of two prime numbers."

"A prime number," Soury-Fontaine said eagerly. "Wait a minute, I know that one." He screwed up his face in concentration. "A prime number is a number that can only be divided by itself—and one."

"That's right. But it's only a conjecture, because although it's been explicitly verified to around two million or so, no one's ever been able to prove it."

"Not even you?" said Mariane. "But you tried, after all. That's what counts."

Koster smiled. "I guess so. Anyway, my career as a mathematician didn't last too long. Most people do their best work in their twenties." He shrugged. "So I went to the Ecole Polytechnique in Geneva, and got my degree in architecture. Do you know Switzerland? It's been years now since I was there. We were hoping to go next spring." He took another sip of beer. "Then last year a friend of mine suggested I do the book. He's a publisher in New York. I wanted to get away and my company said fine. So I came."

"Would you like some cheese, Mr. Koster?"

"Call me Joseph, please."

"Who is we?" Soury-Fontaine said.

"What's that?"

The guide took another sip of beer. "You said 'We were hoping.' "

"Did I?" Koster smiled tightly. "I meant my wife and I. My ex-wife. I'm divorced."

"Please don't mind Guy, Mr. Koster."

"It's all right. I have nothing to hide."

"But you must have," Soury-Fontaine continued. "That's why everybody comes to Amiens. I remember only last year how a man named Gerard Frank, a postal worker, came all the way from Dinard just to confess he'd killed his brother's wife. Every pilgrim has something to hide. That's why he's a pilgrim."

"I'm sorry to disappoint you," Koster said. He leaned back across the blanket on his elbows. "Do you tell that story to all the tourists, Guy? It's a bit lurid, isn't it?"

Soury-Fontaine began to laugh. "You should hear the one about Antoine Avernier. He's the fellow who carved the choir stalls."

"Perhaps another time." Koster glanced round at Mariane and smiled. She was staring at him, and her eyes looked dark and unfathomable despite the mottled sunlight filtering through the tree. There was something about her, Koster thought. Something vulnerable and strong at the same time. Something wounded. "And what are you hiding, Mariane?"

She handed him a piece of bread and cheese. "I'm not hiding anything," she said, and the words comforted Koster.

She was just like him.

He took the slice of bread from her hand and their fingers brushed together.

They were both wounded. And both of them were liars.

Chapter VII

LYMAN DROPPED FROM THE RAILWAY carriage onto the rain-soaked platform of the Amiens train station. He wore an old felt fishing hat from Ireland, which he had pulled down low across his face, and with his green wool coat hanging heavily from his shoulders, and an old overstuffed tartan suitcase in his right hand, he looked almost like a pilgrim shuffling through the rain.

The terminal was crowded with commuters. Lyman threaded his way slowly through the lines, past a newsstand and a woman selling postcards of the Amiens cathedral. Then he noticed a sign up ahead jutting from the station wall. LOCKERS, it announced, with a small red arrow pointing down. There they were.

He crossed the room and began to study the numbers on the locker doors. 10. 11. 12. It was no use. He scanned them several times but he couldn't find 02, the number on the key which the vagabond had given him in London. Had he been misinformed?

He walked over to the lost-and-found booth near

the ticket counter. Through the opening in the wall, Lyman could see boxes and old suitcases stacked on top of one another, and on one side a teenage boy in baggy overalls checking through a notebook.

"Hello," he said. "Hello, can you help me, please?" Lyman's French was effortless and quick, with barely a trace of English accent.

"What do you want?"

"I'm looking for a locker." He reached into his coat pocket and removed the little red key.

The teenager shuffled over. "Bus station," he said. "Through those doors."

"Thanks." Lyman tipped his hat and headed out across the room.

The doors to which the boy had pointed opened onto a narrow concrete bridge which spanned a vast garage half full of city buses. The air was sweet and cloying from their fumes. Lyman hurried across the bridge and through a door on the other side. The bus station was virtually deserted. A solitary pair of businessmen sat together smoking cigarettes. Posters of faraway places only made the room seem more colorless and drab. There was a thick glass ticket booth in one corner, and on the far side at the back, almost out of sight, a line of lockers flush against one wall.

Lyman crossed the room casually. It took him only a moment to find the familiar number: 02. He put his tartan overnight case on the floor and reached into his pocket. The key looked too big at first. But it slipped easily into the lock, and turned without the slightest hesitation. The cylinder clicked once. The door swung open. It was empty.

Lyman stood quietly for a few moments, staring into the vacant locker, remembering the glint of glasses as Sir Giles and Cocksedge and the Lemur had all toasted him at Dorret's Wine & Ale, slamming the metal door shut on the gnawing fear he nursed that something wasn't right. And now to find it empty. But

what had he expected after all this time? He strode
across the terminal toward the ticket booth.

"Excuse me," he said sharply.

"Wait in line."

Lyman turned. He had neglected to notice two old
women pulling baskets. They looked appalled and
Lyman apologized, stepping in behind them. It was
only a moment before he was by the ticket window
once again.

"Excuse me. Those lockers," he said, hooking his
thumb across his shoulder. "What happens if I forgot
something in them?"

"That depends."

"On what?"

The girl in the window was chewing bubble gum.
"How long ago did you leave it?"

Lyman considered for a moment. Pontevecchio had
been killed in June of 1982. "A little over a year."

The girl began to laugh. "A year!" She threw her
head back and Lyman could see the pink bubble gum
in her mouth like a pearl. "I'm sorry," she said, and
began to laugh again. "If someone forgets a bag," she
added soberly, "we send it over to the police station."

"I see. How do I get to the police station?"

The girl gave Lyman a map of Amiens, marking a
section with a tiny x. "There," she answered, pushing
the map toward him through a slit in the bullet-proof
glass. "Next."

Lyman picked up his bag and angled toward the
front door of the terminal. It opened onto the Place
Fiquet. A monstrous stone tower dominated the cobbled square like a misplaced American skyscraper.
More buses idled in the streets. School children milled
about. Commuters hurried off to work, their faces hidden by umbrellas.

Lyman hailed a taxi and jumped in. The car swung
out into the thoroughfare toward the police station,
and the further they drove, the more convinced Lyman

became that Amiens was, sadly, a rather ugly little town. He had read in his guidebook that through the city to the north ran the River Somme, a battleground for two world wars, and he realized that this was probably why the town was so much 1950s brick and concrete. The rest of Amiens had been destroyed in bombings, rebuilt to dispossess the past, like that giant watchtower off the Place Fiquet.

The streets began to narrow and a few old houses cried out from between the fast food restaurants, hinting of the ghostly tiers which suddenly appeared before the cab—the cathedral portico, and high above, the gargoyles shimmying up the stonework through the rain.

The police station was located only a few hundred yards from the cathedral, across a small park. Lyman paid the driver and trundled up the steps.

It was dark and cool inside the police station. He took his hat off and began to shake the wetness from the brim.

"May I help you?"

Lyman turned. A young policewoman was staring out at him from behind a window in the wall.

"I've come about something left in the lockers, at the coach terminal."

"I see." She picked up a receiver. "Name?"

"Nigel Lyman."

"Inspector Lyman?" She hesitated. "From England?"

"That's right."

The woman began to talk excitedly into the receiver and suddenly Lyman heard the door behind him open and his name called out. A middle-aged policeman with short legs and a round belly approached him from across the room. "Detective Inspector Lyman? City of London Police?"

"Correct."

"A pleasure, sir." They shook hands. "Your office

called this morning and told us you were coming. I am Captain Musel. Yes. Please follow me."

Musel snapped his fingers and a young corporal appeared from nowhere to snatch up Lyman's overnight case. They made their way up a flight of wooden stairs to a large corner office overlooking the park, across which Lyman could see the transept of the great cathedral. Black-and-white photographs covered the white walls. They all featured Musel shaking hands with a variety of men. Musel with the mayor, Lyman guessed. Musel with the veterans' delegation. Musel with the local bishop. A single tatty French flag stood in the corner by a brown file cabinet. The captain pointed to a wooden chair in front of his desk. Lyman sat down.

Musel's desk was at least eight feet long and four feet wide. It dominated the room, serving more to trivialize the French policeman than to enlarge him. "I had begun to think that you were never coming," he said.

Lyman was surprised. "I thought SAFAA was extremely helpful. They're the ones who connected the key to Amiens."

"The key? What does the key matter? You already know the contents of the locker."

"I'm sorry." Lyman shook his head. "I'm afraid I'm not following you."

Musel hunched over his desk. "Our report . . . on the locker. Let's see, it's been almost a year now. Normally we don't bother much with lost property, at least not until two months or so have passed. But then we're forced to open it, to see if there's some identifying clue inside, a wallet or address book. We don't have much room around here for storage, as you can see. The baggage piles up."

He walked over to the file cabinet and began to rummage through a drawer. "I know it's in here somewhere. I reviewed it personally when London called this morning. Voilà!" Musel moved back behind his desk, flipping a file open in his pudgy hands. "A year almost to the day. As soon as I saw Pontevecchio's name I thought it might be useful. That's why I called. I'm sorry," he said. "Am I going too fast for you? I was told you spoke French."

"It's not that, Captain Musel. It's just that I was not aware of any report sent up a year ago, or at any other time for that matter."

"But I don't understand. Why are you here then? Why did I bother calling England all those times if they never even told you?" He dropped the file onto his desk. "I suggest you look this through," he added crisply. "Corporal Berry outside can help you find an office for an hour or so. Please excuse me. I have work to do."

The interview was over. Musel held out his hand and Lyman shook it slowly. The young corporal reappeared from nowhere. Lyman picked up the case file, thanked the captain once more, and followed the corporal out the door.

They walked in silence down the hall until they came upon a little office at the rear of the building which Lyman guessed had not been used in years. The corporal opened it with his passkey, assuring him that he would not be disturbed. Then he turned his back on Lyman and left.

The office was pitch dark, despite a little window set high in the rear wall. Lyman flicked on a fluorescent desk lamp and waited for it to settle before he laid the case file on the desk before him.

The first thing that he noticed was a letter, handwritten on blue airmail paper, and signed Jacques Tellier in a tiny, almost illegible scrawl.

"Dear Mr. Pontevecchio," the letter began. "If you are reading this, then you need only call the number at the bottom of the page and I will guide you through the drawings. I am sorry for this final inconvenience.

But I have known Angelo Balducci many years, and he has taught me to be cautious."

Lyman sighed and began to take his coat off, unhooking the plastic bone toggles one by one. He had never heard of Jacques Tellier, the author of the letter, but Angelo Balducci was another matter. Lyman thought back to his first briefing with the Lemur in London. Balducci had been the smuggler responsible for secreting Pontevecchio into London, just before the Italian banker's death.

"But if this letter reaches other hands," the scrawl continued, "then let the world know that Pontevecchio and the Church have murdered me. Balducci just arranged for us to meet in Klagenfurt. It was Pontevecchio who agreed to buy the Book of Thomas the Contender, and the old Masonic missal. I have only had time to translate a small part. I am a poor scholar, without experience, and now there is no time. But this I know with certainty—the labyrinth is the real door. The entrance that I found is just a secondary shaft, for ventilation. And if you understand Amiens, then Chartres will surely follow. The Gnostic Gospel of Thomas will be yours."

The letter ended abruptly. At the bottom of the page Lyman noticed a telephone number with an exchange he did not recognize. He turned the letter over.

Underneath, bound by a thick elastic band, appeared to be a photocopy of a small book, with the words NUMBER 2-MASONIC MISSAL neatly marked in red on the top page. Lyman slipped the elastic band off and began to flip through the pages.

The missal was handwritten in a curious florid script, in a kind of Latin which Lyman had never seen before, and the pages had been badly marked in copying, with three lines bisecting the same corner throughout the entire stack.

Upon closer inspection, he noticed that someone had inscribed a few additional lines directly in the mar-

gins of the missal's first four pages. And not only were
they written in a different hand, but they were in an
entirely different language—a kind of archaic French,
Lyman guessed. Just after them, scribbled on a few
separate sheets of white paper, someone had added
what appeared to be a translation.

Lyman labored through the tiny words, confused
less by the modern French translation than by the devi-
ous scrawl which marked it as the writing of Jacques
Tellier once again. The more Lyman read, the more he
realized that the lines which ran across the top of the
missal's first four pages were a kind of salutation, as if
the ancient book had been given to a friend.

> Read from your Book of Thomas the Con-
> tender, the twin who knows himself, and think
> of me in your new Temple, a plumb line to your
> sides for these last years. Accept this missal as a
> token of my love. Remember all that Bernard
> and I have taught you, and return one day to the
> bosom of our Lady.

The language became more and more arcane, ending in a sweep of black ink. Tellier had circled a group
of words, just as they were circled in the missal itself.

> The School will suffer in your absence. Now is
> the time that you should be in Chartres. Ber-
> nard has proven that the manuscript the Count
> of Dreux bought from the Levanter comes origi-
> nally from Edessa. Its pages bear the oldest
> Logoi we have seen in Aramaic, predating those
> in Luke and Matthew, with a reference added
> later to the plot which Piso, legate of Syria,
> launched against the Emperor before the perse-
> cution. It is even older than your Thomas the
> Contender which Papias, bless him, copied from
> the sayings of Maththaios. For it calls the Logoi

"devarim" in the incipit like the book of Sirach, while it honors gnosis and the many paths to the Grand Architect. The manuscript was preserved inside a wondrous golden cup with a hinged top which the Levanter called Chaldean, with all manner of precious stone and inlay on its twelve sides, lapis lazuli and rubies, diamonds from the East, an object of inestimable value. It is the original Book of Jude, called Thomas the Twin, the brother of James and of our Savior, the Apostle of Edessa to whom the Lord gave gnosis. It is the Gospel of Thomas.

The note was signed Thierry of Chartres, Lent, anno Domini 1138.

Lyman dropped the papers onto the table and glanced once more through the missal itself. The salutation by the mysterious Thierry of Chartres had been written directly in the margins of the first few pages, immediately above the Latin text. Thierry had even drawn some sketches of his Chaldean cup. Parchment must have been scarce in the twelfth century, and this little act of conservation somehow legitimized the missal to Lyman. Yet it was just a photocopy, Lyman realized, and badly marked at that. Where was the original? And who was Jacques Tellier? What was his connection to Balducci, the man who had smuggled Pontevecchio into London? And what did either of them have to do with this medieval missal?

He replaced the elastic band around the sheaf of papers. There were only two objects left in the file: a slim report, and a kind of map. No, it wasn't a map, Lyman realized. Despite the roughness of the drawing, it was clearly the floor plan of a building. And not just any building. It was the Amiens cathedral. At the center of the drawing was a perfect replica of the cathedral's maze. Lyman had seen the same shape printed on a dozen different postcards at the Amiens train station—a black path between white borders, the quadrants rolling in a perfect octagon. Someone had scribbled numbers all along the drawing, measurements of lengths and angles, and Lyman realized from the stunted shapes of the numerals that they were probably the handiwork of Jacques Tellier. But what had Tellier been calculating, and why?

Lyman removed the last piece in the file. It was indeed a report, tattered yet legible. He scanned the pages quickly.

According to the file, in June of 1982, a small picnic basket had been abandoned in the locker marked 02 at the Amiens coach terminal. When no one came to collect it, it was transported to the Amiens police station for safekeeping. There it remained untouched until September of that year, despite the usual policy of inspecting abandoned property after eight weeks. When opened it was discovered that the picnic basket contained a bizarre collection of documents: a kind of medieval missal, replaced in this file by a copy, due to its delicate condition; the floor plan of the Amiens cathedral; and Jacques Tellier's unusual letter, with its pointed reference to Pontevecchio.

Captain Musel had recognized his obligations, and placed a call to England. The Pontevecchio hanging in London was still a featured story in the local press, and perhaps, Lyman thought, Musel had fantasized that he would solve the case from Amiens and rise, as Lyman himself had done, from regional obscurity to national attention. Whatever his motives, Musel was told by the City of London Police that the matter was already under investigation, and that he should send copies of the documents from the picnic basket to England and await instructions. The captain did just that, but no instructions followed. The original missal remained in his private safe. He called twice more over the next few months, each time conversing with the same man, and each time receiving the identical reply. The matter was already under investigation. He would be notified.

Lyman closed his eyes and pushed his chair away from the desk. The hairs on the nape of his neck rose up, and it came to him out of the darkness that there was only one thing that policemen really feared, even more than dreams of death, or the faces of their wives and children grieving. As rooted as a child's fear of unanswered cries, the power of this fear was like the power of the faith which had resulted in the building of the Amiens cathedral just across the park. You believed. You trusted. You relied on someone else to watch your back. And it had to be implicit, or it was valueless. It had to be a thing of faith.

Lyman had broken that faith, at least in the minds of most of his division, when he had let young Crosley die. He had betrayed it, and deep inside he hoped that it was only this which had prevented him from seeing clearly all that now seemed obvious indeed, and all that he had only sensed before: the key; the ransacking of his flat; his own assignment to the case after the Crosley incident. Lyman knew now, with a keen-edged certainty, that the faith had been betrayed in London long before.

He rose slowly, slipping the file under his left arm. Then he turned the desk lamp off. It was still raining. He could hear it up against the little window, tapping.

Captain Musel did not even rise this time as Lyman was announced. He simply pointed to the wooden chair across his desk and fiddled with his pen cap. Lyman sat down, the green file hanging from his hand.

"Captain Musel, I know how this must seem to you," Lyman said. "But I wonder if I might take you into my confidence. Somehow I feel that I can trust you."

Musel shrugged.

"For some time now," Lyman continued, "I have suspected a certain officer in my division of incompetence. Perhaps I should say we, Captain Musel, because this feeling is something which many of us in London share. I'm sure you understand. You're a man of responsibility. You must know how one man can upset what otherwise would be an exemplary department."

"I suppose so."

"In the past, his failings have not dramatically intruded on his work. You could say that even his incompetence has been ineffectual. But now, thanks to you, I feel that I can act." He paused. "There's just one thing still troubling me."

"What's that?"

"I must be absolutely sure that he's the one responsible for the error, for failing to follow up on your calls. After all, I wouldn't want to rush in on this thing half-cocked."

Musel began to swivel in his chair. "Inspector Lyman, your department's housekeeping is not my responsibility. I have my own problems."

"Yes, of course you do," Lyman answered sadly, nodding his head. He had to be careful not to overplay his hand. He would need Captain Musel. "Still, I would appreciate it if you could think back for a moment to the time when you first opened the abandoned picnic basket and found Jacques Tellier's letter, the drawing and this so-called missal. It must have been quite a shock when you read Pontevecchio's name."

"Yes. Yes, it was."

"That's why you called London, I suppose."

"Of course."

"And to whom did you speak, in London I mean?"

"Isn't it in the file?" Captain Musel said. "Someone named Hadley, I believe. Superintendent Hadley."

For a moment Lyman felt himself drawn back to England, to that little valley full of rhododendron bushes, to the heat and humidity of Hadley's greenhouse. He could see George digging in the garden, his front paws covered in mud. "Are you absolutely sure?"

"Of course I am," Musel replied shortly. "What are you driving at?"

"Did you ask for him by name?"

"Well, no. Not exactly. I asked for your division. But he was the one who always authorized my calls."

"What do you mean, he authorized them?"

Musel looked embarrassed. "Inspector Lyman," he said. "Amiens is only a small city. We're not London or Paris. We don't have the resources to call overseas any time we feel like it. Besides, we were doing you a favor."

Lyman felt his heart skip. "You mean it was a trunk call? You reversed the charges?"

"Yes, of course. And then when Superintendent Hadley never called . . . Well, I did my part. And besides, I didn't put much stock in Tellier's letter. If he hadn't mentioned Pontevecchio, I never would have telephoned at all."

"You know Jacques Tellier?"

Captain Musel laughed. "Everyone here does. He used to run a small antique shop on the rue Dupuis. But he disappeared from Amiens some time ago. His nephew has it now. Listen, I'm glad. Tellier was no good. He spent several years in prison for smuggling and forgery." Captain Musel shook his head. "I think he came from La Tremblade originally, just south of Rochefort on the Charente River."

"When exactly did he leave Amiens?"

"Oh, about two years ago, maybe less. Look, I know what you're thinking. But what would a small-time forger like Tellier be doing with a millionaire like Salvatore Pontevecchio? It doesn't make sense. He used to call us up and complain about prowlers, for God's sake. A nervous man. You understand. Not someone likely to associate with international bankers. So I gave up calling London. You didn't seem to care, so why should I?"

"No, of course not," Lyman said. "And the missal," he continued. "What do you make of that?"

Musel shrugged. "I don't know. Pierre Clermont— the curator of the Amiens museum here—believes that it's legitimate. He told me Thierry was the brother of Bernard of Chartres, someone who ran the famous school there, back in the Middle Ages. Clermont described it as a Masonic book of rites. I used to keep it in my safe, but Clermont insisted that I send it on to Paris, to some expert on this sort of thing. The Countess de Rochambaud, or Rochembord, or something like that. I don't remember. You'll have to ask Clermont. As for the reference to the Book of the Contender . . . well, that's an old legend. Maybe Guy can help you there. He's a guide over at the cathedral. Guy Soury-Fontaine."

"I see. Thank you, Captain," Lyman said. It was clear by the way he was swiveling in his chair that Musel had other things to do. "You've been very helpful. Really." Lyman stood up. "Oh, one more thing, before I forget," he continued. "I would appreciate it if you might treat me, at least on the surface, as if I were just another English tourist. I'm not exactly sure if this Jacques Tellier or the missal are important, but while I'm here I might as well be as inconspicuous as possible. Perhaps something will shake loose."

"Inspector Lyman, you may pretend to be anyone you wish. That is your affair. If I can help you, I shall try. But remember," Musel added. "You are not in London anymore. Paris may have authorized you to carry a gun—against my wishes, I might add—but Amiens is my responsibility. We are country people here. Amiens is a quiet city. Do you understand me?"

"Perfectly."

Musel smiled. "I'm glad," he said. "Then welcome. Welcome to Amiens."

Chapter VIII

AMIENS
September 14th, 1983

LYMAN SAT ON HIS HOTEL BED SMOK-
ing a cigarette, listening to the rain fall dreamily outside the window, staring at the telephone on the table
beside him. He had been sitting there in the same position for at least an hour, ever since his return from the
police station. The room was dark. His coat lay on the
floor next to his tartan overnight bag. The curtains
were half drawn. He reached for his pack of Players
and lit another cigarette from the one still burning in
his hand. Then he blew the smoke out slowly, and
watched it waft across the room across the telephone
and vanish.

What was the point of putting it off? he thought.
He would have to confront Hadley eventually. He
picked up the telephone and dialed the number.

The phone rang at least a dozen times before he
finally hung up. Perhaps Hadley was in his greenhouse.
Lyman tried the London station house instead. The
receptionist switched him to Dotty Taylor's desk, and in

a moment he could hear her soft familiar voice. "Hello, Dotty," he said. "It's me."

"Who's me?" she answered peevishly.

"Nigel."

"Nigel? I don't know any Nigels. In fact I've always rather avoided Nigels."

"Dotty, I need your help."

"Why didn't you call me from Paris? You promised you would."

"I'm sorry," Lyman said. "I meant to. Really, I did."

"I don't know why I stay with you, Nigel. You don't give a fig for me."

"That's not true. You know it isn't."

"What do you want anyway? I'm sure you didn't call long distance just to chat me up."

"Is the Lemur about?"

"No."

"What about Cocksedge?"

"They're all at the funeral. Didn't anyone ring you?"

"What funeral?"

There was a pause and Lyman took another drag off his cigarette. "Dotty, are you there?"

"Tim Hadley and his wife. You'd think someone would have told you."

Lyman stiffened. "What are you talking about?"

"They were in a car accident. The night after you left. Apparently some animal dashed out across the road in front of them. Hadley tried to avoid it and the car flipped over."

"Good God! Did anyone see it happen?"

"I don't think so. Why?"

Lyman stubbed his cigarette out in the ashtray by the bed. Hadley had been the one who had taken all of Captain Musel's calls, and then failed to pass the information down the line. He'd been responsible for closing the Pontevecchio case when only half the evidence was in.

Lyman ran a hand along his face, rubbing his eyes. He had nothing left for Hadley. Nothing at all.

"I'm sorry, Nigel. I know you liked him." Dotty sighed. "I thought you knew. Didn't you send him those flowers?"

"What flowers?"

"They arrived yesterday. I saw them when I dropped a message off for Blackwell. They were just sitting there, dying on your desk, so I brought them back here to look after them. I thought they were for the Hadleys. Everyone's been sending flowers."

"I didn't send any flowers." Lyman swung his legs off the bed, his mind racing. "Is there a note on them, a letter? Check to see." He reached down for another cigarette. In the distance he could hear Dotty tearing open an envelope, removing a card. He could even hear her catch her breath. "What is it?" he said. "What's it say?"

"They're from Superintendent Hadley. The flowers. How ghastly, Nigel. He must have sent them right before he died."

"What does the note say?"

" 'For old times sake.' And then his signature."

"Is that all?"

"That's all, Nigel."

Lyman lit his cigarette. It didn't make any sense, he thought. Hadley had been a good driver. The accident seemed too convenient, the timing too perfect. Had Hadley killed himself? No, not Hadley. And not with his wife in the car. Then, perhaps, it hadn't been an accident. Perhaps it had only been staged to look like one. In that case, why had Hadley sent those flowers, unless they carried some kind of message? It didn't make any sense.

"Are you sure that's all it says?"

"Of course I'm sure."

"What do the flowers look like?"

"There's a whole strand of them. Green with brown tips. The leaves look like little palms. And there isn't any soil, just a kind of cork board at the bottom."

"Cork board?" Lyman remembered the afternoon when he had driven out to visit Hadley in the country.

And what do you think of this one, Nigel? Hadley had said. That's right. Lyman tried to visualize the moment. *A friend of mine imports them from South America. They have the oddest reproductive cycle.* And verdant, palmlike leaves.

"I've seen that plant before," Lyman said.

"You have?"

"Listen to me carefully, Dotty. There's no need to bother anyone else about this. It's probably nothing, but I wonder if you'd take those flowers over to the Yard for me. I have an old friend there in pharmacology. His name's Smythe. Have him run a test for alkaloids."

"Scotland Yard? Why can't I just drop them off downstairs?"

"I trust Smythe."

"What do you mean you trust him? What's going on, Nigel? Are you in some sort of trouble?"

Lyman turned and faced the window. It was still raining but he could see the towers of the great cathedral in the distance, gray against gray sky. "Don't worry," he said without conviction. "Everything's just fine."

Lyman stooped out of the rain into the vestibule of the Amiens cathedral. Distant echoes shook the stillness of the air: a voice here buying postcards; another shouting to a child to stop; and every footfall blending into yet another still until the sounds rose past the arches to the sky.

He had just come from the hotel and he could still

hear Dotty Taylor's voice. "You'd think someone would have told you," she had said. But who? Chief Superintendent Cocksedge? The Lemur—Terry Randall? Both had been with Lyman on the evening his flat had been ransacked. And hadn't it been their idea to assign him to the case in the first place? For good reason, Lyman thought as he started up the cool basilica. Who better to assign than someone who had failed already, with Crosley, with his whole career? It was so easy to be disappointed by Inspector Lyman. He was the one who was always popping licorice between his teeth so that you couldn't smell the whiskey on his breath, the one with all the unrealized potential.

But it could have been an accident, Lyman thought, a rabbit in the headlamps, a deer. Hadley could have simply been unlucky. And the flowers could have been a gift, a kind of peace offering.

He stopped. A man was measuring the maze of flagstones in the central aisle. Lyman put his hands in his coat pockets and sidled up beside him.

The stranger was crawling between the benches, laying his yard-long ruler length to length along the black path of the labyrinth. He wore an ice-blue anorak with a hood, and tight black dungarees. Every few feet, he stopped and removed a little black notebook from an inside pocket to record a figure. Lyman guessed he was in his early thirties, with a thin, pleasant face, and sandy blond hair. "Excuse me," Lyman said. "Excuse me, may I ask what you're doing?"

The man looked up. "I'm measuring the labyrinth."

"Oh, I see." Lyman thought he heard a foreign accent but he couldn't really place it. "Do you work here?"

"No, sorry, I don't." The stranger stood up slowly, dusting his knees. "Why, do you need some help?"

"I'm looking for a fellow named Soury-Fontaine. I think he's a guide here."

"Oh, sure, Guy. I know him. But he won't be back

until tomorrow, I'm afraid." Then he paused. "You're British, aren't you?"

"How did you know? Is my French that bad?"

The stranger laughed. "No, you're just easier to understand," he said in English. Then he extended his hand. "My name's Joseph Koster. American. How do you do?"

Lyman shook it. "Nigel Lyman. A pleasure." They stared at one another for a moment without speaking.

"I know Guy pretty well, you know," Koster finally said. "I'd be glad to set up a tour for you, if you want."

"A tour? Yes. That would be splendid."

"How long are you in Amiens?"

"Oh, I don't know. I rather hate making plans when I'm on holiday. Have to do that all year long."

Koster nodded. "Sure, I know what you mean." He looked back down at the labyrinth.

"What exactly were you measuring, if I may ask?"

"I have a theory," Koster said, "that the labyrinth is a kind of two-dimensional model of the whole cathedral."

"Really? Sounds complicated."

"No, it's not. It's just that the location of the labyrinth, and the number of lines and angles which define it, reflect certain basic mathematical characteristics equivalent to those found in the cathedral's architecture. That's my interest, you see. I'm an architect."

"Oh, I see." Lyman smiled. "To tell you the truth, I was never much good at maths. But you don't need a head for numbers to sell a Royal Coachman. That's what I do. I run a fishing tackle shop in Winchester, just south of London. Dry fly, mostly." He swung his right arm back in a graceful arc. "You here on holiday?"

"I'm working on a book, on the cathedrals of France dedicated to Our Lady, Notre Dame." Koster pointed at the ground with his ruler. "That's why I was crawling around."

"A book. How fascinating. It must have been awfully difficult to get permission. They told me at the hotel that you can't even go up into that middle section there. What's it called again? I was hoping to poke around a bit myself."

"The triforium. Yeah, I know. I tried writing a cousin I have at the Vatican. What a nightmare. In the end my publisher was forced to petition the Minister of Culture in Paris, a friend of his named Charles Langelier."

"Is that so?" said Lyman, turning to look up toward the metal choir gate. "It certainly helps having family in high places, doesn't it?"

"Not really. Most of the cathedrals are state-owned today. It's the politicians who hold the purse strings now—not the bishops."

"What exactly does your cousin do at the Vatican?"

"I'm sorry?"

"Your cousin. I went to Rome once, years ago. On holiday. Damned nice people, the Italians."

"He works with the IOR. It's a kind of Church bank."

Lyman studied Koster's eyes. They were a maritime teal blue, warm waters merging into cold. They did not even blink. "Convenient if you ever need a loan, eh?" Lyman tried to smile. "Hello," he said. "Is that your guide friend watching us? Over there."

A tall man in a dark brown suit was standing in the shadow of a pier across the nave. He looked up at the windows in the clerestory and then suddenly turned away. A second man approached him from the southern aisle. They moved together through the dappled light, pointing here and there at the carvings on the walls.

"No, that's not him. Guy has a beard."

"You know, I wonder if you could help me," Lyman said. "I've landed in a proper hole. You seem to know your way about. Perhaps you could recommend a hotel for me."

"I'm staying at the Hôtel de la Paix. It's all right, I guess. Nothing to write home about."

"Thanks." Lyman looked at his wristwatch. "Well, it's getting on. What time tomorrow did you say Guy would be here?"

"About ten-thirty, usually."

"I love these continentals. They keep such civilized hours." Lyman smiled flatly. "I haven't spoken much English these last few days. Even American makes me homesick." He looked away for a moment, then added suddenly, "Are you busy this evening? Perhaps we could have dinner later on, if you're free?"

"Not tonight, I'm afraid. I've got a date."

"Well, perhaps another time. I'm sure we'll bump into each other."

Lyman shifted his weight from one foot to the other, trying to assume a guise of helplessness.

The American hesitated. "You do know where the Hôtel de la Paix is, don't you? On the rue de la République?"

"No, but if you're heading back that way, I could always send for my kit later."

Koster looked across the aisle. The flagstone lines were fading with the sun. "Why not," he said. "It's been here seven hundred years. I guess it can wait another day."

He put the ruler and notebook back into his anorak, his movements precise, economical. Then he smiled, raising his eyebrows. If he was disturbed by the prospect of Lyman's company, he did not show it. Yet Lyman felt the coincidences tugging at him, just as they had when he had heard of Hadley's death.

A few hours earlier at the police station he had been studying Jacques Tellier's drawing of the labyrinth, and now here was a stranger measuring its lengths. And not just any stranger—an American with a cousin at the IOR itself.

What had he gotten himself into this time? Lyman thought. First the ransacking and George, then Hadley, and now this Joseph Koster. He glanced back down at the labyrinth. It looked like a whirlpool of black stones, and for a moment he felt as if he were revolving slowly toward its center, drawn inexorably between the flagstone cracks and down into the earth.

Lyman spent the balance of the day checking into the Hôtel de la Paix, and relocating his gear. After a private conversation with the concierge, he was given the room next door to Joseph Koster's. It was simple but clean: two beds, a balcony, one dresser, and a shower in the corner. Lyman washed up a little. Then he unpacked and headed down for dinner.

The hotel was not very crowded. Koster had gone out to visit a girlfriend, so Lyman ate a poor meal by himself and read about the cathedral in his Baedeker. After dinner he sat in what the concierge's wife referred to as the "reading room," flanked by a salesman from St. Malo and the owner of a local shoe store, and watched the interview of a famous rock star on the television.

He tried not to think about the case, but he found that his mind kept wandering back to Hadley and his orchids, to George lying on the bedroom floor beside that pool of blood and glass, of Pontevecchio swaying in the current of the Thames. When the interview was finally over, he bid his companions good night and went to bed.

That night he dreamt that he was floating on a subterranean stream, the sound of rushing water whispering about him, the darkness broken only by a distant light. It was as if he had been drifting through this passageway forever.

Occasionally he tried to reach out for the sides, but either his fingers slipped against the surface, or the surface wasn't there. He closed his eyes and let the current spin him gently. There was a groan of twisting metal in the distance. The water lapped against his chin, splashed against his lips; he felt his hands caress the soft side of a body floating next to him. The skin gave way to bone beneath his fingers. The face rolled over through the water into view and Lyman saw it was his son's face, pale as a new moon, bloated and distorted by the brine. Lyman kicked to free himself, to swim away, and bones gave way beneath him. There was another groan of metal and the water bore him to the ceiling as the destroyer slipped down through the cold Atlantic, until there wasn't any ceiling left, no room to breathe, no air and no way out.

Lyman woke to the sound of movement on his balcony. He opened his eyes. The hotel room was lit by streetlights, cool and exact, revealing the twin beds with their threadbare bedspreads. On the other side, beyond a little card table, stood the French doors leading out onto the balcony. Lyman pulled his blankets up, trying to ignore the pounding of his heart.

Perhaps he had just imagined it. Perhaps it was just a footfall on the street below. He dropped his head back on his pillow. A shadow wavered on the wall. He heard the distant clicking of a moped, the sudden frequency transition. He lifted his head once more and turned to see the outline of a man's face pressed up against the window, his two hands cupped about his eyes on either side, his shoulders pushing at the glass.

In an instant Lyman was on his feet. He rolled across the floor to his suitcase and felt inside for the butt end of his Walther PPK. Then the shadow was gone.

Lyman lowered his gun. Someone was shouting. Glass shattered. The noise was coming from next door, from Joseph Koster's room.

Lyman opened his door slightly, to check the hallway. It was clear. He stepped outside, keeping his back against the wall. The shouting was louder now. He held his gun up with both hands before his face, the muzzle pointed at the ceiling. Then he took a deep breath, trying to concentrate on the gun sight. It was a trick his uncle had once taught him years ago, and it still helped to steel his nerves. He took another breath, turned to the side and lunged against Koster's door.

The wooden frame gave way with a crash. Lyman almost lost his balance, steadying himself at the last moment with his left hand. A man was standing at the foot of Koster's bed. He was dragging the American by his neck across the floor. It was the man in the brown suit, the tall man who had been watching them at the cathedral.

Lyman shouted out a warning. The stranger released his grip, and the American fell to the floor. Lyman aimed his weapon at the stranger's face. It was lean and handsome, the eyebrows plucked perfectly like two cuts above his eyes, the thick dark hair combed back. He could have been a Spanish businessman, a Brazilian doctor. Then he was gone.

Lyman jumped after him. The stranger had vanished through the French doors onto the balcony, but now the balcony was empty. Someone was honking a car horn in the street below. Lyman saw a pair of black Mercedes-Benzes and then, only inches from his face, the fingers of the stranger wrapped about the railing.

Lyman reached over and pointed his gun down at the stranger's face. "Don't be a bloody fool," he said. "The game's up."

For a moment the stranger remained motionless. Then he suddenly released his grip and lunged at Lyman's hands, trying to pull him down across the railing. Lyman fired but the shot went wild. The stranger scrambled for another hold. Lyman tried to grab him by the collar of his shirt. He felt the material in his hands, and then the weight was gone.

The stranger almost seemed to smile as he flattened out against the darkness and fell without a sound two stories to the street below. There was a sickening thud.

Lyman leaned against the railing, feeling the weight of the night across his back. His heart was pounding. He looked down at the gun in his hand, and noticed that he had jammed one of his fingers up against the railing; it was bleeding. He closed his eyes, trying to shake his fear, trying to push back the memory of Spendlove in that hallway so many months before in London, the knife and young Geoffrey Crossley's screams . . . *Shoot, Nigel, bloody shoot!*

He heard a noise behind him. It was Koster trying to rise. "Are you all right?" said Lyman.

He helped the American to his feet. Koster brought a hand up to his throat and coughed. His face looked pale as a reflected moon in the fluorescent streetlight. Finally he nodded and said, "I guess so."

"He didn't even scream," said Lyman. "Come on, let's find out who he was."

"I don't think I can make it."

"Of course you can. Let me help you."

Lyman dropped his gun off in his room. Then they walked together down the steps and out through the lobby, which was bursting now with people. The gunshot must have woken every guest, thought Lyman, and he suddenly felt naked in his pyjamas. The concierge and his wife stood near the body of the stranger, trying in vain to push away the crowd of guests that had assembled in the street. It was a cold night and the condensation of their breathing rose up in a great cloud just above their heads. The concierge's wife was shouting but Lyman couldn't understand a word she said. The French seemed garbled, meaningless.

"Let me through," said Lyman simply, and the crowd opened up before him.

The stranger seemed hardly changed by the fall. He lay face up, looking only slightly disconcerted. Lyman knelt down beside the body and began to search his pockets one by one, turning them carefully inside out. Nothing. He checked his belt. He ran his hands along his trouser legs. There was no identification of any kind. Lyman wasn't surprised. The man had been a professional. Only a professional would not have screamed.

He moved beside the dead man's feet, and stopped. The shoes. He saw them now as clearly as if he were still trapped inside the elevator in his apartment building back in England, as if he were still trying to reach up through the grillwork to the floor above.

They were the same, he thought. The same.

Chapter IX

AMIENS
September 15th, 1983

LYMAN REMEMBERED THAT AFTER-
noon in fall, beside the River Itchen with a hatch of
gnats about his head and St. Catherine's in the distance. He was fishing the shoreline of the chalk stream
with a "governor," a ground bee look-alike made from
a woodcock wing with short red hackle legs and a body
of peacock-herl. The morning had been lively. He had
already bagged a brace of grayling and a sullen trout
when with a cast he found his line pulled from the reel
behind him, as if he had snagged the fly on a tree
branch or a bush. But when he turned to trace the line
he saw it rise up like a kite string through the air, and
at the top a swallow with the false bee pinned to its
breast like a badge. Lyman worked it down as gently as
he could, but whether from the final rush to earth or
from its struggle with the line, the bird was dead when
he pulled it from the grass. Its neck had been broken.

As he and Joseph Koster walked from the police
station toward the Amiens cathedral, Lyman reminded
himself that each man faces death his own way just a

little bit each day. Once he had kept vigil over a
shoebox for a week, guarding a dead sparrow from
something he had thought he understood then, but
which now he could not even recollect. Death had kept
pace with him. After all, it was a part of his job. It was
something that happened. But he had never managed
to keep pace with death.

Lyman had always scorned the weekly speeches
made by Chief Superintendent Cocksedge, the way
they coaxed, the way they characterized the department as a rampart of society. Yet he knew that once he
too had traced an even line between the men they
brought in every week and the men who brought them
in. The villains were the ones who killed, while he uncovered. That was his job. The courts brought them to
justice. Except that the longer he traveled by it, the
fainter the line grew, until now it had vanished altogether.

There was no one he could trust in London now.
Now those who killed and those who uncovered were
the same. Now death no longer had the buoy of moral-
ity. It carried with it no distinction. It was at best convenient, or as aimless as his son's death in the visceral
darkness of that sinking battleship; as aimless as Crosley's death, or the man with the wing-tipped shoes.

They reached the end of the park which stretched
from the police station to the cathedral. Lyman paused
for a moment and stared up at the towers of the western portico. It was ironic, he thought. After all that
hatred welling up in him in London, after all that welcome long-lost anger, the man with the wing-tipped
shoes had simply fallen from a balcony. Lyman had
wanted time to suckle him on pain, the way that
George had suffered crawling room to room, the glass
shards churning in his stomach. But the man was gone
now, and the worst part of the stranger's death was not
the theft of Lyman's vengeance but the stark sincerity

of Joseph Koster's gratitude, the aspect which most
marked it as a thing of truth.

Captain Musel had called it an attempted robbery
and it had taken Lyman a pathetically short amount of
time to persuade the American architect that, if safety
were his watchword, then of all the places he should be
in Amiens, the Hotel de la Paix was by far the most
secure. The concierge had begged them to remain, despite his wife's alarms. Their rooms were complimen-
tary, of course, and they were given little books of
tickets worth substantial discounts at a host of local
restaurants and nearby points of interest. Joseph Koster had tossed his book of coupons in the lobby
dustbin, indignant and complaining, but Lyman had
pulled it out immediately. It was this act, Lyman knew,
that had finally turned the young American's fear, that
had trivialized the incident enough to make him smile.
And that was all that Lyman needed, even more than
the gratitude which followed in a rush, the debt of life.
For with that smile Lyman knew that Koster could be
bought, his trust acquired, and that the currency of
greatest value lay not in acts of bravery, but in the
simplest show of human weakness.

Now it would be easy to stay close to Koster, to find
out why exactly he was measuring the labyrinth and
why he had so readily revealed his cousin at the IOR.
Koster had already invited Lyman to luncheon with
Soury-Fontaine. "It's the least I can do," the American
had said. "The very least." Lyman had accepted with a
show of great reluctance, reassuring Koster that he
need not feel obliged in any way. Lyman had done
nothing. He had merely scared the burglar off with his
old army gun. It was a bad lie, Lyman knew, but one
the American would believe.

They made their way beside the great cathedral until they reached the rue Robert de Luzarches, where
Koster suddenly turned off. Lyman followed close behind. The cathedral's southern transept rose up at their

backs, the gray stone of the portico blending into cobbled streets and flint, into the wooden beams which
seemed to reach out from a single ancient root to hold
the houses of the street together. The wars of men and
vagaries of time had somehow overlooked this section
of the city. Except for a few yards of plumbing and a
length of wire cable, nothing had changed here for five
hundred years.

Joseph Koster paused for a moment by a doorway,
and checked the number on the glazed ceramic tile
above the lintel. "I always get mixed up," the American
said. "The houses all look the same. Come on, Nigel.
We're already late."

Koster knocked on the door and Lyman soon heard
footsteps from inside. A woman's voice called out, "Joseph, is that you?" The door flew open and a girl with
dark brown hair and a white blouse threw her arms
round the American. She kissed him on both cheeks
and then reluctantly pulled away.

"I'm sorry," Koster finally said. "Nigel Lyman—let
me introduce you to Mariane Soury-Fontaine, Guy's
sister."

Lyman took her hand. "The pleasure's mine."

"You're the man who saved Joseph's life." She
studied him and said, "He was right. You are remarkable."

Lyman watched her watching him and tried to answer, but he felt tongue-tied as a schoolboy. What was
happening to him? The girl turned back into the house.
"Come on," she said over her shoulder. "Xavier and
Guy are waiting."

They made their way up a wooden staircase to the
second floor. At the rear of the landing Lyman could
see the wink of a small window overlooking a garden,
and then more houses further on. Mariane opened a
narrow door and motioned them to follow.

Two men sat beside a table at the rear of the room.
Behind them Lyman noticed three tall windows

trimmed with curtains. The table had been set for lunch. The men stood up as Lyman closed the door. The larger of the two, a strapping bearded fellow in a faded tweed jacket, strode toward Koster as if he meant to attack him. But at the last moment, he stopped and shook the American by the shoulders, laughing like a child.

"Guy!" Mariane said curtly. "He's been through enough, hasn't he?"

The bearded man turned toward Lyman. "You are the Englishman," he said.

Lyman nodded.

"I'm Guy Soury-Fontaine, Mariane's brother, and this is Father Xavier Marchelidon."

The second man moved forward, proffering his hand. He was dark and very thin, a paring of a man, with a high domed forehead and a drooping, fragile jaw. "I'm only the assistant priest," he said contritely. "Weekday masses and midday Sunday." They shook hands. "Welcome to the rectory."

Lyman was a little surprised. He had thought that they were going to Soury-Fontaine's, but as he glanced about he realized that the room somehow suited Father Marchelidon. It was simple and stark, with plain white walls and a wooden floor. A few books had been piled up in one corner. Except for the table and chairs, and a small wooden cot, the room was barren of furniture. A crucifix hung above the table between the windows, and Lyman noticed a gooseneck reading lamp poised on a typewriter case beside the cot.

"Pronto a tavola," Father Marchelidon said. "Let's eat."

They all squeezed in around the little table. Guy began to tear a baguette into large pieces as Father Marchelidon said grace. There were goat cheeses and cold meats, cooked vegetables and a plate of tiny pickles.

"Well, tell us what happened," Guy said at last. "What did Musel say?"

Koster shrugged. "First he told us not to worry. Then he told us not to leave. Unbelievable. Some guy tries to rob me and when he falls off the damn balcony, we're the guilty ones, we're the ones who have to stick around. You should have seen how he treated Nigel. And then he tells us not to worry, that it's simply a formality."

"Show them your neck," Lyman said.

The American pulled his shirt collar down with care. Mariane caught her breath. A purple line ran across his Adam's apple like a coral necklace. Koster smiled. "Telephone line. I'm sure it looks worse than it is," he said to Mariane. "It wasn't like he was trying to kill me."

"What's that?" Lyman cut in. "What do you mean?"

"Maybe I'm wrong. It's just that I got the feeling he was after something else. Money, I guess."

"Anyway, it's over now," Father Marchelidon said, lifting his glass of Bordeaux. "Let's hope the rest of your stay in Amiens is boring and uneventful. There is a lot to be said for boredom."

They toasted one another and for a moment no one spoke. Lyman noticed that Father Marchelidon had hardly touched his food.

Finally Guy broke the silence once again. "Mariane tells me you're interested in the cathedral, Mr. Lyman."

"Who wouldn't be while they're here? We have one in Winchester too, you know."

"I know," Guy said. "It's one of my favorites. They even wrote a song about it."

Lyman put his glass down. "To be honest with you, I think yours is grander. The pilgrims and the stories. The architecture. I think it's absolutely incredible that people used to walk hundreds of miles just to see it."

"They still do," Guy said, "but now they come for the cathedral. In the Middle Ages they came for the relics. It meant a great deal then if you could say that you'd seen John the Baptist's head. It's here, you know. Walon de Sarton brought it back from the Holy Lands in 1206."

"And Chartres has the Virgin Mary's shawl," Koster added with a wink.

"Don't laugh. Relic worship is what the Middle Ages were all about—the relics as symbols, of course."

"What about the Book of Thomas the Contender?" asked Lyman, as he reached for a piece of bread. "Isn't that another legend?"

"There are always legends," Guy replied. "That's my business, to tell them, to give them life. The Contender story is much as any other. They say that one of the Amiens cathedral's earliest master masons—we don't know his name for certain—either bought or was given a Gnostic gospel called the Book of Thomas the Contender for the cathedral treasury. The story dates back to the early eleven hundreds, but it's never been substantiated.

"The Book of Thomas the Contender, like the Gospel of Thomas and other early Gnostic texts, was said to contain the Logoi or sayings of Christ. Unfortunately, there was a fire in 1137 which destroyed most of the cathedral. The same thing happened at Chartres, when the old Carolingian cathedral burnt down in the eleventh century, and they had to build a new one up around her."

He paused, staring off into space. "Someone else mentioned something about the Book of Thomas the Contender just a few months ago. I think it was Clermont. He's the curator of the Amiens museum. But the real expert, if you're interested, is the Countess Irene Chantal de Rochambaud. She lives in Paris."

Lyman nodded. Hadn't Captain Musel sent the Masonic missal to a countess in Paris? He made a mental note to call the museum curator, Monsieur Clermont, that afternoon. Then he took another sip of wine and said, "What would happen if it were found—this Gospel of Thomas? Would it be valuable today?"

"No, no," Guy said reprovingly. "The Gospel of Thomas is another thing altogether. You mean the Book of Thomas the Contender." He smiled impishly. "I'm afraid the value would be in the hunt, not in the prize. Gnostic gospels are rare, but not unknown. Copies of the Book of Thomas the Contender, as well as other Gnostic gospels, already exist in ancient Greek and Coptic. But I imagine they might fetch a few thousand pounds. One legend has it that a copy of the Gospel of Thomas was hidden in a golden cup, underneath the Chartres cathedral."

"Really?" Lyman said. "Who exactly were the Gnostics?"

This time it was Father Marchelidon who answered. He leaned on his pointed elbows, cupping his chin in his hands. "No one is absolutely sure," he replied. "We know what they came to believe, at least to a certain extent, but the roots of Gnosticism are difficult to follow, to separate. The Gnostics were a religious movement, not a people. And you have to bear in mind that in the first three centuries A.D. there were a lot of competing Christian groups. Look at Paul's letters to the Corinthians. Everybody had a different interpretation of what Christ had said.

"The Gnostics didn't believe in the three-tiered hierarchy of the Church: the bishops, priests, and deacons. They didn't really believe in centralized power. Instead, they elected a priest from their group by lot, someone to read the Scriptures, and a bishop to offer the sacrament. Each week it was someone different. Even women were invited to participate."

He laughed thinly. "But what really marked them as heretics in the eyes of the Church fathers was their belief that to have gnosis, a kind of mystical secret knowledge, also meant that you didn't need the Church, the organization. The more gnosis you had, the more you knew yourself. And the more you knew yourself, your own human nature, the more you were in touch with God. Obviously the centralized Church in Rome felt threatened. To them Peter and his fellow apostles were the only real authority." He sighed and Lyman noticed his fingers tighten around his wine glass. "Eventually all the Gnostic gospels were burned or edited or hidden away. Many Gnostics were killed for their beliefs, while the rest of their communities, for the most part, simply died out."

"Their philosophy sounds almost Eastern," Koster said.

Marchelidon nodded. "Some people see a Buddhist influence. Others claim that the roots are more Persian than Indian. But you're right—it does have an Eastern flavor to it."

"You're certainly well informed," Lyman said. "Are you a historian too, Father Marchelidon?"

The priest smiled faintly. "No, not really. Most priests know something about the Gnostics, simply because they once posed such a tremendous threat to the early Church. I've always found them interesting."

"That's because they were so democratic," Guy added with a laugh. "Go on, tell him. Xavier here is a bit of a heretic himself, aren't you?"

"I don't think so. Unless a heretic is one who works against poverty and social inequality. Then I welcome the title, Guy. Nothing has changed."

Lyman leaned across the table toward the priest. Now he knew the reason for the burr which had been pricking at him. The priest was much thinner and older of course, but there was something about his face that reminded him of David Ellison, the Yorkshire vagabond.

The priest returned Lyman's stare with a sudden

grin. "You know what I'm talking about, don't you, Mr. Lyman."

Lyman shrugged.

"Perhaps I'm wrong," Marchelidon continued. "What exactly do you do, if I may ask?"

"I run a fishing tackle shop in Winchester, outside London."

"You don't seem like a shopkeeper." Marchelidon tilted the wrist of his right hand and his long narrow fingers closed like a fan.

"I don't?" Lyman smiled flatly. "And what about you, Father? Are you from Amiens?"

"Originally, yes."

"Xavier was a *fidei donum* in Brazil," Guy said. "A kind of freelance missionary. Twenty years, wasn't it?"

"Eighteen. Close enough."

"That's when he became a heretic."

"Guy," Mariane interrupted, pointing at the shopping basket at her feet. "Why don't you see if there's anything for dessert."

Father Marchelidon smiled at Mariane. "Yes, it was in Brazil," he said. "But you make it sound much more interesting than it was. After Gutiérrez in Peru, it was easy to embrace the new theology. It became a fashion almost, a hemline. Gutiérrez made it respectable. He articulated. So did Assmann in Brazil. We just understood."

"Gnosis?" Koster asked.

"If you will." Father Marchelidon laughed and Lyman noticed that his jaw had once been broken, then badly set. An accident, perhaps.

"Yes, why not?" the priest continued. "Liberation theology is a theology of the people after all, a people crying to be free from the dominance of the few—the rich, the powerful, the elite. We believe in a more democratic Church, a South American Church to address those problems that are peculiar to the continent, that they know nothing of in Rome." He looked embarrassed. "Well," he said, trying to laugh. "You see. Confessed but unforgiven. I'm sorry." He glanced up at Guy who was standing over him with his arms crossed.

"No dessert," the big man said.

"Oh, well."

"So you returned home to Amiens," Lyman prompted.

"I was recalled—let's put it that way. And when I didn't come they threatened to withdraw their funding of a school which I had been working with up in São Luís. But I wouldn't call it home exactly. Home now will always be Brazil." He paused, looking around the table. "And what about you, Mr. Lyman? What brings you to Amiens?"

"On holiday. The Continent by rail. Switzerland's next, I think."

"Are you Catholic?"

Lyman frowned. "Not much of anything, really. My mother was Catholic. From Dinard, in Brittany. My father was Church of England."

"Ah," Father Marchelidon said, nodding sagely. "Are you married?"

"Divorced." Lyman looked down at the table.

"Any children?"

"One. A boy. We lost him in the Falklands."

"Oh, I'm sorry," the priest said quietly, but Lyman knew that he was lying. It was as if he had known about his son already, about the way in which the Exocet had come in low across the waves and ripped into the battleship.

Father Marchelidon leaned back in his chair and it dawned on Lyman that it was not a knowledge of the facts but a kind of kinship with the circumstances that had led the priest to poke this corner out of all the others Lyman had so carefully concealed. The priest had had this conversation many times before. He had already met his life's allotment of inquisitive policemen. He had already been interrogated. And more, it

was his job to sense the weak points of the human
heart, to press against them gently like a blind man
fingering a stranger's face, searching for recognition.

It was this empathy which gave him strength, as it
gave strength to a policeman. It was this knowledge too
which made him dangerous, and which had already
made his theology of liberation such a spear in the side
of the Church.

Marchelidon had done his job too well. He had understood the peasants of Brazil, their basic needs and
fears, and put them above the needs and fears of the
Church. No wonder he had been recalled, Lyman
thought. And for the first time he began to understand
the power of this latest heresy, and the threat it posed
to Rome. It was the same power for which the Gnostic
Book of Thomas the Contender had been banned so
long ago. And, somehow, it was the power which had
slipped a nylon rope around Pontevecchio's neck.

He looked at Father Marchelidon and recalled the
words which Jacques Tellier had written in his cryptic
note: *But this I know with certainty—the labyrinth is the
real door . . . And if you understand Amiens, then
Chartres will follow. The Gnostic Gospel of Thomas will
be yours.*

Somehow, the gospels were the answer, the gospels
and that cup of gold and precious stones which Thierry
had described. But surely, Lyman thought, the cup
alone couldn't be the "wonderful thing" which
Pontevecchio had mentioned to his wife before his
death. No, it was the gospels which were important.
And more than that, it had to be the Gospel of Thomas
alone. After all, the Book of Thomas the Contender
had already been unearthed by Tellier in Amiens and,
according to his note, sold to Pontevecchio. Yet Guy
had said the gospels had no value, except as rare curi-
osities. There were already other copies in both Greek
and Coptic.

Lyman took another sip of wine. It tasted dusty and complex. It had aged well.

Father Marchelidon was watching him. Lyman put his glass down, and as his hand came to a stop he suddenly remembered another line which Thierry had written in his prologue to the missal: *Its pages bear the oldest Logoi we have seen in Aramaic, predating those in Luke and Matthew.*

The oldest Logoi, Lyman thought. After two thousand years, the words were still killing. Two men had died already: Pontevecchio, and the man with the wing-tipped shoes. How many others had fallen before them? And how many more to come?

He looked out through the windows at the rooftops of Amiens, the slick wet slate, the dark gray clouds gathering like bulls in the sky above.

Chapter X

ROME
September 16th, 1983

ARCHBISHOP KAZIMIERZ GRABOWSKI woke to the sound of church bells ringing in St. Peter's Square. He opened his eyes and the burden of memory descended on him from the ceiling, from the half-light streaming through the shutters, from the sounds and smells of Rome which every morning set him in the world. He sighed and propped his large frame up on one elbow. Sometimes he felt as if the bells would drive him mad.

The archbishop swung his feet off the bed. It had been another bad night. His pyjamas were sticking to his back, wet with perspiration. He crossed into the bathroom and peeled them off. As he did so he caught sight of his reflection in the mirror. He still looked pretty good for his age. His golf games helped him there. And he'd lost a lot of weight over the last few months. He smiled grimly, and turned on the hot water in the sink. In the end, he thought, his trimmer figure had been the only good thing to have come out of the Banco Fabiano scandal.

It was then, as he was reaching for his shaving cream, that he first saw the words on the mirror. He stopped midmovement, trying to sense if he was alone in the apartment. Then he watched the words grow more distinct as the steam from the hot water filled the bathroom. The words read *Dottore Vincenze Marone— Rare Books and Manuscripts.*

The archbishop wiped his hand across the mirror, smearing the soap with which the words had been written. The steam vanished underneath his fingers, revealing his own face in the glass, pale and softened by the condensation, desperate.

A moment later and the steam had covered it again.

That afternoon, Archbishop Grabowski sat working in his office near St. Peter's Square. It was a large airy room, typical of that part of the Holy City, with an eleven-foot ceiling and four tall windows overlooking the piazza below. The walls were dotted with paintings depicting scenes from the Old Testament—the flood, the flight of Lot from Sodom, the test of Isaac.

A bust of Pope Boniface IX stood in one corner. It had been sent to the archbishop as a gift from Cardinal Giovanni Spinelli of Florence at the height of the Fabiano scandal. In truth, Grabowski had never really cared for it. Not only were the features thick and lifeless, but the whole idea had been a bad joke from the very start.

Cardinal Spinelli was a descendant of Niccolò Spinelli, the fourteenth-century advisor to the Visconti court who had written a bitter polemic history of papal power during the pontificate of Boniface IX. Though nominally successful as a history, Spinelli's work had really been a warning to the Church against the perils of material wealth, and even after six hundred years it was still speaking out, however indirectly, through this artless statue. For some reason the archbishop had never seen fit to remove it. Indeed, in some ways he enjoyed the reminder.

There was a knock on the door, the archbishop grunted an acknowledgment, and a young priest entered quietly.

Grabowski looked up over his glasses. "What now?" he said. "More supplicants?"

The priest approached, his right hand extended with the white line of a business card straight as a razor blade between his fingers. "I told him you were busy, your Excellency, but he insisted."

The archbishop took the card and placed it on his desk. It read, *Dottore Vincenze Marone—Rare Books and Manuscripts.* "How long has he been waiting?" he said.

"Only a few minutes, Your Excellency."

"I see." Grabowski looked out through the window. St. Peter's Square was almost empty, but it had been a cold week and the tourist rate had fallen off. Then he turned back and smiled. "Well, Charles," he said. "'Remember ye not the former things, neither consider the things of old.' Send Dottore Marone in."

As soon as the priest had disappeared, Grabowski reached forward slowly and opened a small drawer in his desk. So Marone had come already, he thought, a stranger for the strange name he had read that morning on his bathroom mirror. How the name had come to be there was of less concern to him than what it meant, for Grabowski had found such messages before. They belonged to a part of his life that he had only just begun to put behind him. They meant that the weeks and months which had slipped by without event had only been a false spring after all. He pulled a pocket tape recorder from the open drawer and checked the cassette. Then he pushed the red recording button and replaced the machine in his desk, closing the drawer just as the antechamber doors swung open.

The man who called himself Marone was dressed in a gray, double-breasted suit with a navy blue silk tie. He was well over six feet tall, with an unusually high forehead which would have made his eyes seem small and insignificant were it not for their cold, almost reptilian gaze. He walked boldly across the room, without the customary deference which most expressed when entering the office of the chairman of the IOR. Grabowski moved around his desk to meet him, and Marone bowed, snatching up the hand of the archbishop and pressing the heavy ring seal to his lips. "Your Excellency," he said without expression. "You do me a great honor."

There were two small chairs before the archbishop's desk and Grabowski pointed to them. "Please sit down," he said, as he stepped back behind his desk. "Thank you, Father. That will be all."

Archbishop Grabowski waited for the priest to close the doors behind him before he sat down himself, hooking his fingers together and dropping them at the very center of his desk. Marone smiled.

"I have come, Your Excellency," he said, "because I have heard you are a man of discriminating taste and judgment."

"Cut the crap, Marone," the archbishop answered, leaning forward. "If that's your name, which I doubt. You've got the heel of Scarcella's boot stamped all over your face. It didn't take him long to bribe his way out of Switzerland, did it?"

Marone ignored him. "I have come about a certain manuscript which a client of mine is planning to put up for auction."

Grabowski remained silent, simply appraising Marone's face. This one was articulate compared to most of Scarcella's messengers. He didn't just talk with his hands.

"Understanding your natural interests in this affair,

my client is willing—generously, I believe—to let you make the first offer."

"What manuscript are you talking about, Marone?"

The stranger shifted in his chair. "Surely your cousin, Joseph Koster, has kept you abreast of his latest findings."

"My cousin?" The archbishop unlocked his fingers. "What findings? What does Joseph Koster have to do with anything? I haven't seen him in twenty years."

Marone nodded. "As you wish," he said after a pause. "Then I must assume you are not aware of his work in France for Signor Robinson."

It was only with these words that Grabowski remembered the letters he had recently received from his young cousin in New York. They had mentioned something about France, about a book, but the archbishop received so many letters and he had barely glanced at them. Joseph was his Aunt Martha's grandson. The archbishop had never really known him, except as a boy during the early 60's, when Joseph's father had played with the Roman Philharmonic. But even then he had only seen him once or twice. Grabowski barely knew Aunt Martha's sons, let alone her grandsons.

He smiled at Marone cryptically. Perhaps it did not matter. Marone did not seem to know a great deal either, or else he would have never broached the subject as he had. "What about his work?" Grabowski said.

"A prudent man, Your Excellency, would realize the importance of this manuscript, and that it would be extremely uncomfortable for the Church should it prove to be as old as it appears." Marone shifted forward, reaching for an Alitalia bag which he had placed on the floor before him. He removed a package wrapped in Christmas paper and placed it on the desk.

"As an act of good faith, and as a display of authenticity, my client has entrusted me to leave this package here with you. In it you will find an early Hebrew version of the Gnostic Book of Thomas the Contender which dates back to approximately A.D. 100. It was discovered at the Amiens cathedral some months ago. We received it from a dealer named Jacques Tellier, an acquaintance of your friend Salvatore Pontevecchio." He paused, scanning the archbishop's face. But Grabowski displayed no emotion. "The package also contains," Marone continued, "a copy of another document discovered at the same time. It is a kind of prayer book or missal used in certain proto-Masonic rituals during the Middle Ages." Marone pushed the little package across the desk. "Go ahead, Your Excellency. Please, open it."

Grabowski remained impassive. "I'm sure it's all there," he said. "Get to the point."

"Very well, let me be frank, Your Excellency. My client would like to propose a kind of pooling of information. In exchange for telling us exactly what your cousin discovers about the labyrinth at Amiens, we will permit you to purchase the Gospel of Thomas when it's found. And don't misunderstand me, your Excellency. My client will find it—one way or another, with or without your help."

"What makes you think, after all that happened with Pontevecchio, that I would ever consider dealing with Scarcella again?"

"Frankly—and I'm sorry to be so blunt, Your Excellency—you really have little choice. If you cannot accept my client's terms, and if you refuse to restrict your own half-baked investigations through your cousin, then my client will be forced to put the manuscript on the open market. Consider, for a moment, this event."

"I told you before, Marone. I know nothing about my cousin's activities."

"Then I suggest you reacquaint yourselves. As for the price," he added, "I would not be overly concerned. It is one you have paid already, many times before. All that my client asks is that you continue to extend the banking privileges he enjoyed while your friend Pontevecchio was alive. With more discretion to be sure, but nothing more."

The archbishop stiffened, the darkened passage-ways of memory unfolding like a labyrinth within him, and at each turn the same face with that same smile leaning over that same table at the Hotel Excelsior, stirring his cappuccino with that tiny silver spoon clamped tight between his thumb and little finger. What could be so special about an ancient manuscript that made the former Venerable Master believe he would ever work with him again? Not after Pontevecchio. Not since that bridge in London. Marone was right about one thing—he had already paid.

For months Grabowski had not even ventured into Rome for fear of being arrested on civil charges stemming from the scandal at Fabiano. He had become a prisoner, as if the borders of the Vatican marked the borders of his conscience too. But now, at last, a compromise had been drawn up between the Italian and Vatican authorities. The IOR had never admitted its culpability, but it had recognized its obligations to alleviate the damage done to all those innocent financial bystanders connected to the scandal. After all, Salvatore Pontevecchio had borrowed many millions, from countless other banks, to prop up his illegal ventures overseas, and those ventures had been owned in many cases by the Church. The very least the Vatican could do, insisted the Italian magistrates, was repay a percentage of the missing funds—around two hundred million dollars.

The compromise had been agreed upon in principle only the day before, although it would probably not be finalized and signed for several months. Grabowski was free to travel once again, and he had only just decided to go on a short vacation where he could think without the pressures of his job and the ubiquitous paparazzi.

But now all this had changed. The trip would have to wait. The past had slipped into the present once again.

"Dottore Marone," the archbishop said softly, taking his glasses off and rubbing his eyes. "The banking privileges which you claim your client enjoyed were not dispensed by me, but by Pontevecchio. Of course Scarcella could renegotiate, but even he might find the price of dialogue a little steep. As for me," he added with a shrug, "I can't dispense a box of paper clips these days without some monsignor noting it down."

Marone laughed heavily, like sea stones rubbing in the tide. "I'm sure that you will find a surprising unanimity concerning this issue. Even the pope will praise you. Of course, His Holiness will have to have the manuscript reviewed, by experts, and without the unnecessary tribulation which a premature exposure would undoubtedly produce. But he will pay the price, and he will not forget your part in finding it. You will be wearing crimson in a month, Your Eminence, I guarantee it."

So here's the carrot, thought Grabowski. He's already used his stick. "I have no interest in becoming a cardinal. Not any more."

"Perhaps," Marone answered peevishly. Then, with another laugh he said, "But Church history will record you with a smoother face if you agree. And after all, Your Eminence. Isn't that why all of us work so hard— for posterity, for our children."

"For the Church, Marone," Grabowski said. He stood clumsily, leaning his knuckles against the desk.

"Of course," Marone answered. "Let's not forget the Church."

Archbishop Grabowski was still in his office when the call came in from Monsignor Frank Wovyetski. It was dusk, the gloaming light held off by street lamps and the pitiless illumination of the statues mounted high

above the square. "I'll be right there," he said, and
hung up.

Grabowski took the shortcut to the library, winding
through corridors and through forgotten doors, up narrow stone and wooden stairs which plunged at angles
through walls and under streets and stone piazzas. Occasionally he passed another figure wandering through
the halls and they would greet each other silently, with
nods and quiet movements of the hands.

As he walked, Grabowski tried to think of other
things, but his thoughts kept turning to that package
wrapped in Christmas paper which Marone had delivered to him that morning, and which he in turn had
sent on to the library for analysis that afternoon. He
had played the recorded conversation over and over
again, and still he could not understand it. Marone had
been cautious. But in the end it was not the threats,
nor the vague descriptions of the ancient manuscript
which Grabowski found most disturbing. Instead it was
his own voice rushing through his head, so drawn and
desperate, strung out for exculpation. *"For the
Church,"* the words chimed like a string of bells. *"For
the Church, Marone."*

At first, yes, long before, there had once been a
time when he had marveled at Pontevecchio. He had
been younger then. And more, he had been hungry and
ambitious too, floundering in the shadow of the legendary Bernardino Nogaro, who from a paltry eighty million dollars in 1929 had raised the assets of the Vatican
to more than two billion dollars by his death in 1958.
They were large shoes to fill, and in retrospect Grabowski knew why it had taken him so long to pose the
questions which eventually the fall of Banco Fabiano
had forced him to confront.

There had never really been a single moment of
revelation when he'd finally understood the game that
Scarcella and Pontevecchio had been playing. On some
level he had suspected for a long time, and when the

proof gradually revealed itself, it was more a confirmation than a grim surprise. But something fundamental did change with the knowledge, something at the root of who he was, and he found that what he could never have justified from personal ambition, he now felt obligated to conceal for the security of the Church. He was but one man after all, a single soul, while the money which he earned touched millions in the world. It was the end that mattered. It was always for the Church.

Grabowski stood in the darkened corridor for several minutes before he finally slipped the key into the door and turned the knob. It opened onto a narrow aisle hemmed in by walls of books. A harsh fluorescent light slit the ceiling above. He closed the door quietly and locked it behind him. Then he moved up the aisle between the bookcases until he came onto a larger corridor. Here he paused. Row upon row of bookcases stretched as far as the eye could see in one direction, but in the other he could just make out a desk upon which glowed a soft green light. Monsignor Frank Wovyetski sat behind it, his spectacles glaring like half moons.

"Kazimierz," the monsignor said as Grabowski approached the desk. "You scared me creeping up like that." Monsignor Wovyetski tilted his head to the side, and his thick glasses slipped down the bridge of his nose, revealing tiny blue eyes.

"What have you found, Frank?" the archbishop said in English. He pulled a chair up from beside the desk and sat down facing the monsignor.

"Where did you get these documents?"

"Never mind that. Just tell me if they're valuable."

Wovyetski pushed his glasses back up the ridge of his nose. He had thin gray hair and Grabowski could see tiny balls of sweat shimmering on the pink scalp. "Valuable!" Wovyetski muttered. "Listen to this."

His voice carried the thick inflections of his native Poland. It was a heritage he shared with the archbishop, but unlike Grabowski who had been born and raised in Toronto, Wovyetski had grown up near the city of Kaliningrad, known as Konigsberg before the Soviet annexation. He had come to Rome on pilgrimage in 1948, and never left.

"It's in Eusebius," Wovyetski said, pointing to a weathered text. "You see."

"In who?"

"Eusebius. He was the Bishop of Caesarea in the fourth century. He wrote a history of the Church and here," he said, leaning forward to read the yellowed pages, "here is where he quotes Papias. 'So Matthew collected in the Hebrew language the Logoi, but each person interpreted them as he was able.' That's what Thierry was referring to in his dedication at the beginning of the missal. And this Hebrew version of the Book of Thomas the Contender is what Papias thought were Matthew's Logoi, the sayings Matthew heard from Christ himself."

"What sayings? I thought that all these heretic gospels were discovered a long time ago. What's so valuable about this one?"

Wovyetski shook his head. "It's true that copies of the Book of Thomas the Contender and even the Gospel of Thomas were found at Nag Hammadi in nineteen forty-five. But none is as old or primitive as this one." He reached over and patted the manuscript with a bony hand.

"Is that important?"

"Kazimierz, you're not listening to me. It used to be that the Church thought the New Testament gospels were actually written by Luke and Matthew and the rest. But today we know that they were written only 'in the spirit' of Luke and Matthew, sometime within the first hundred years or so after Christ was crucified. We know this from physical evidence—carbon dating and the like—and from a technique of literary analysis called form criticism which studies the themes and literary forms of early manuscripts. One such theme or *Gattung* is the use of sayings. That's what Logoi means —sayings, proverbs.

"The Logoi *Gattung* is extremely primitive, dating back to the Logoi Sophon of the Jews, and even earlier. Long before anyone began to write anything down, groups of these sayings were passed from generation to generation. Eventually they were put into a narrative framework, like the Sermons on the Mount and on the Plain. In fact both the Gospels of Luke and Matthew are the result of blending certain Logoi from the source Q with the narrative Kerygma framework found in Mark."

"For God's sake, Frank," Grabowski interrupted. "I'm not a Biblical scholar. Can't you simply tell me what it means?"

Wovyetski reached over and lifted the heavy manuscript in his hands. The pages were yellowed with age, cracked like slate along their brittle edges. "Okay, I believe this version of the Book of Thomas the Contender is what scholars have been calling Q for decades," he answered softly. "It stands for *Quelle,* which means source or spring in German. It was written by the followers of Maththaios, which I read as Matthew, sometime between A.D. fifty and seventy-five. And it's probably the same group of sayings which Papias referred to in Eusebius's history."

"You mean it's older than the gospels?"

"More than that. I believe it was used as a kind of source in the construction of the gospels."

"Is that important?"

"Of course it's important. It lends credence to what Thierry says about the Gospel of Thomas. Thierry was the brother of Bernard of Chartres, the chancellor of the Chartres cathedral school from 1119 until 1124. According to his dedication in the missal, there appear to be two separate manuscripts." He pointed to the document on his desk. "The one we have here, from

Amiens—the Book of Thomas the Contender. And the one presumably still hidden somewhere underneath the Chartres Cathedral—a version of the Gospel of Thomas. But it's not just any version, not by a long stretch."

"What do you mean?"

Wovyetski glanced nervously around the corridor, as if to make sure they were alone. "To understand that, you have to first understand the Church's policy on studying the gospels. You probably don't remember," he continued, "but back in 1964 the Pontifical Biblical Commission officially defined three basic stages through which the teachings of Jesus have come down to us. The first stage is represented by the actual words and deeds of Christ. The second is that of the Apostolic Church, when the apostles gave testimony to Christ, and in their preaching they used various 'modes of speaking' or *Gattung*. And the third stage is recorded for us by the evangelists 'in a way suited to the peculiar purpose each one set for himself.' These are the exact words the commission used, and they imply that the 'gospel truth' is not to be found in a naive, literal interpretation of the Bible. What we have in the synoptic gospels of the Bible is not a tradition of the first or second stage, but only of the third—the words and deeds of Christ colored by the early Church's experience of Easter, after several decades of apostolic preaching, the words which the Holy Spirit guided them to keep. Are you following me?"

Grabowski nodded sullenly.

"This particular version of the Book of Thomas the Contender is a group of sayings or Logoi that probably dates back to the second stage of the tradition, to the Apostolic Church, the words handed down by Matthew and his followers which Christ allegedly told his apostle Thomas. It doesn't have the whole narrative structure which we see in later versions of the book, like the one found at Nag Hammadi. That's why I think it's the missing source, the Q."

Grabowski had never seen the monsignor so excited. He was rocking in his seat, spiking the air with his fingers, pulling first one set of papers into view and then another.

So this Book of Thomas the Contender was a missing source, the archbishop thought. But why would Marone have delivered it to him if it were so important? What did Scarcella hope to gain?

"Listen, Frank," he said. "I don't care about the Book of Thomas the Contender. We already have it anyway. I only care about the Gospel of Thomas, the one you say is still buried somewhere at Chartres. How valuable would it be, if someone were to find it?"

"You don't understand. It doesn't have any intrinsic value, or relatively little. But it would be of inestimable value to suppress it."

"What are you saying? Why?"

"Because it would mean the end, Kazimierz." He closed the book before him tenderly. "The end of the Church as we know it," he said. "Don't you see? If this version of the Book of Thomas the Contender is what I think it is, then Thierry may have been right about the Gospel of Thomas too, the one he says 'The Count of Dreux bought from the Levanter.'

"It was written in Aramaic, instead of Greek or Coptic, which was used later. You see? It calls the Logoi 'devarim' in the incipit, which is the more primitive Hebrew term. And if that isn't enough, it bears a reference—which was 'added later'—to the plot which Piso of Syria 'launched against the Emperor.' That's Nero, and the plot he's talking about happened in A.D. 65! If Thierry was right, his version of the Gospel of Thomas is even older than the Book of Thomas the Contender here, perhaps the oldest set of Logoi in existence, Kazimierz. Instead of coming from the third stage like the synoptic Gospels, or from the second as this Book of Thomas the Contender seems to do, it could come from the first stage itself, from the hand of Jude called Thomas the Twin who was very probably, like James, the brother of Jesus himself.

"Think of it, Kazimierz. The very words Christ spoke!" Wovyetski reached out and grabbed the archbishop by the arm. The light reflecting in his glasses made his eyes appear as if they were on fire. "Think what it would mean if we had a historically valid collection of His sayings. And then think what would happen if those sayings happened to be Gnostic, as Thierry claims they are, if the ideas which Christ espoused were not at all the same as those the Church has come to stand for. Can you see the headlines now: Christ Found To Be A Heretic! It would mean anarchy, Kazimierz. The New Testament would no longer be viewed as the Word of God, but only as one set of gospel truths out of many. Can you imagine? Who could possibly be a more powerful spokesman against Christianity than Jesus Christ Himself?" The monsignor caught himself and refocused his attention on Grabowski. "Do you have the gospel, Kazimierz? Tell me if you do."

The archbishop shook his head. "No, Frank, I don't." He reached across the desk and closed the missal with a simple movement of the wrist. "Not yet."

Chapter XI

AMIENS
September 17th, 1983

KOSTER SAT IN THE BACK OF THE TAXI
next to Mariane, thinking as the night whirled by the
window that for the first time in a long, long while
everything in his life was going right. It had been a
faultless evening. First the walk along the river in the
afternoon, watching the sparrows thread the bridge and
water underneath them. Then they had gone to Le
Mermoz, a charming two-star restaurant by the Gare
du Nord. Mariane had ordered duck and he had
watched her pull the dark meat off the bones with her
teeth, and she had seen him watching her and hadn't
cared. It had finally stopped raining. They had left the
restaurant and found a cab to take them back to the
rue Pinsard where Mariane and Guy shared an apartment. Mariane was laughing at nothing in particular,
tilting her head back, staring at the sky through the
rear window when Joseph caught her eye and the look
which he had longed for finally passed between them.
She hesitated for just a moment and fell against him.

They arrived at last. Mariane struggled with the

lock to the front door while Koster paid the cab. He had been to her apartment several times over the last few weeks, but never at this hour, and never when the pink haze of a champagne magnum hovered all about them. The cab droned off, distant. The front door closed and there was a moment in the darkened corridor as Mariane fumbled for the light switch. Koster pulled her toward him, wrapping his arms about her from behind. He could feel the warmth of her skin through her coat. The light came on and she pulled away.

Mariane's apartment was on the second floor. They climbed the last few steps as if they had just ended a long journey. She began to unlock the door. Then the light went out again and Koster heard her click her tongue impatiently. The lights were tied to timers in a conservation effort, and they had dawdled on the stairs.

Koster took hold of her again. She laughed, freeing her key from the lock, and kicked the door open. The apartment was empty. Mariane said that Guy was playing chess that night with Father Marchelidon. They were alone, caught in the doorway in the dark, pressed together like a shipwrecked pair at sea.

She shivered in his arms and Koster kissed her lightly on the eyelids. Her skin felt cool and moist. He pushed her gently through the entrance and closed the door.

After a moment his eyes grew accustomed to the dark and he could follow Mariane's outline as she walked slowly toward the sitting room, taking her coat off on the way and dropping it on the floor. He followed her, reached out, and slipped his arms about her as he had done before. She leaned her head against his shoulder. Her hair smelled of the evening rain. She was wearing a necklace. Then Koster let his hands slip down her sides only to pull them up again slowly, massaging her skin beneath the dress, cupping the full breasts. He pressed himself against her. He reached his fingers back around her neck to find the zipper of her dress. It glided down her back like butter. She shook the material from her hips and kicked it to the side.

"Joseph," she whispered as he slipped his fingers slowly inside her bra, forcing it up. Her breasts felt so soft, so much fuller in his hands than they had ever looked in her simple clothes. "Joseph," she repeated.

"What is it?" She was breathing heavily now. He ran his right hand slowly over her stomach, down, probing with his fingers, drawing a shallow line along her inner thigh with his nails. The material of her panties was soaked through.

"What about Guy, Joseph? What if he comes home?" She began to pull away but Koster held her tight.

"He won't be back for hours."

"But it's already late. And this is wrong," she added, slipping from his arms. She was gone, lost in the darkness. The warmth of her body faded from his skin. A light flashed on.

Mariane stood in the far corner of the room, wearing nothing but her bra and panties and a simple necklace. Her arms were crossed above her breasts.

"Oh, great," Koster said. "It's always Guy, isn't it?"

"Don't say it, Joseph. Please."

She picked her purse up from the floor and walked over to the window. Other than an old overstuffed couch and a small coffee table, the sitting room was empty of furniture. But the walls were covered with photographs, dozens of black-and-whites in identical wooden frames, portraits and places.

"Guy isn't like you and me," she said. "You know he isn't. Someone has to be there for him. Someone has to look after him. He's my brother. And he'll still be here, long after you've gone back to New York. So don't make me choose between you, Joseph."

"That's not what I meant."

"I know what you meant," she said quietly. "Besides, I wasn't talking about Guy. I was talking about us. This is just wrong, Joseph."

She pulled a pack of cigarettes from her purse and Koster watched her light up, the way she put the filter in her mouth, the way she shook the match like a thermometer. Then she opened the window beside her and blew the smoke into the night. "I'm sorry, Joseph," she said. "I thought I could, but I can't."

Koster unbuttoned his coat and took it off. "What's so wrong with this? I'm in love with you, Mariane. What's wrong with that?"

"You don't even know me." She shivered as the wind blew through the open window.

Koster walked over to wrap his arms about her, but she pushed him away again. "You seemed to enjoy my touch before," he said sourly.

"That's not fair. Don't you think I want to sleep with you?" she said. "Sometimes I think your idea of a relationship is just a series of tests to see how quickly, how easily you'll be betrayed. I won't betray you, Joseph. You have to know that. But at the same time, I can't sleep with you. Even if it means losing you. Not yet, anyway. Don't you understand? Not again."

She clutched at her necklace and Koster saw it clearly for the first time. It looked like a small stone medallion, strangely carved. "He gave that to you, didn't he?"

"Who?"

"You know who," Koster said glumly, loosening his tie. He sat down on the couch. "Your lover, Maurice. Guy told me all about him, how he left you cold. He was a fool."

"I loved him, Joseph."

"Then he was doubly foolish."

"It wasn't his fault. He had bad friends."

"What about me? Am I a bad friend too?"

Mariane took another drag off her cigarette. "Why do you say such things, Joseph? You know how I feel."

"No, I don't. All I know is you're always pulling away from me." He leaned forward, his elbows on his knees.

"Joseph, please." She flung the stub of her cigarette through the open window, into the street. "It's just that I feel like this has all happened before, the dinner and the stars, the same drive home, the same stairs. With him, you're right. With Maurice. And when it was all over, instead of having something, instead of getting something from it as I thought I would, all I felt was a loss. And for what, Joseph? He didn't write me once after he left. Not a word. And now it's too late."

She walked over to the little pile of clothes beside the couch and began to dress. "And sometimes, Joseph, when you touch me . . ." She paused for a moment. "I don't know. It's like you're doing what you think is right, what works, instead of what you feel. You're so—detached."

Koster laughed bitterly. "I thought so," he replied. "You sound just like Priscilla."

"I do? Am I really like your wife?"

"My ex-wife. We're not married anymore, Mariane. I'm not married."

"Why do I sound like her?"

"I'd rather not talk about her."

"Did she say that too, that you're detached?"

Koster shifted to the edge of the couch. Mariane had finished dressing and his excitement was suddenly gone, replaced by a dull pain. "In the end," he said. "It's funny, I always thought that sex was the best part of our relationship. It was for me anyway. But one day she told me she was tired of my fantasies. We used to— you know—plan things out. She was good at it. Then something happened. She began to sleep around. You know the story. The bitter, unstable wife. The insipid husband with the surprised, almost comical expression on his face as he stops short at the bedroom door. It's as old as the hills."

Mariane walked around the couch. "You don't have to plan things out with me," she said. "Things will happen. I know they will." She reached out and stroked his hair. "But you can't plan the human heart." She kissed him softly on the head and he looked up, to the side, askew. He would not look at her.

"I'm sorry about before," he said. "What I said about Guy. Maybe I ought to go." He stood up and reached for his coat. It was badly wrinkled, he noticed. It would have to be pressed. He dropped it across one arm and started for the door. Then he stopped, and with his back to her said, "I know I don't seem spontaneous sometimes. I know that. But that's just who I am, Mariane. I've always been that way. But you have to be sure. You have to know what's out there before you can respond. There are so many variables, so many unknowns."

He paused for a moment, his hand on the doorknob. "You know, Mariane, after the robbery at the hotel, I really felt like leaving Amiens, just abandoning the book and getting out. But I didn't."

"I'm glad you didn't."

"But I don't know why I didn't." He finally turned to look at her again. "I mean did I do it because I love you, or because to have left you would have been like leaving love behind, the chance for love, my chance?"

She laughed softly. "I don't care why you stayed," she said. "Honestly, I don't. You make it sound like an algebra problem. All I care about is what I feel."

He tried to answer but the words eluded him. Finally, after a long while, he said, "Thanks for the dinner. Really. I'm sorry if I upset you. I guess I'll see you at the store tomorrow." With that he opened the door and ducked into the outer hall.

There was a skylight in the ceiling. It had started to rain once more, the gentle patter like the drumming of impatient fingers on a table. The champagne haze was all but gone now. He walked down the stairs in the

dark, guided by the rectangle of light which marked the
front door leading to the street. The rain was very cold,
but it was too late to call a cab, and he didn't care. He
walked on through the deserted streets, only the puddles glistening, saucers of street light. No one was
about. They were all inside their living rooms watching
television, or fast asleep. He could hear a main road
humming in the distance.

Mariane was right, he thought. He was a fool, and
love was an impossible equation.

The black Solara GLS rumbled up the country road,
cutting through a copse of trees and the falling rain.
The narrow valley with its spinal stream meandered
mile on mile until Le Blanc, the only town of any size
in the province. But the Solara did not even slow down
as the houses grew more frequent. It was a cruel night.
There was no one on the road in this foul weather.
Soon the town was passed and the car plunged on
through greater forests still, the amber headlights probing at the darkness.

Inside the car, pressed into the puffy, honey brown
leather of the contoured rear seat, Archbishop Grabowski watched the landscape stutter past the window.
Mile ran on to rain-swept mile; the forests were replaced by plains of heather and stunted pine. This was
the Pays des Milles Etangs, the Land of a Thousand
Ponds, and periodically the shallow lakes appeared
across a hedge or round a hill, black and forbidding.
The car hummed, churning up the road. Grabowski
saw a small chateau rise up between two trees a few
kilometers from the road on a hill, the windows glazed
with light. Then it was gone. He saw the scattered forest undulate, watched it scurry across the landscape
past the ponds, alive with thick carp sleeping, past rain-
soaked branches pointing down, past chanterelles and
black oak mushrooms waiting to be picked. But every

image that he gathered from the woods, each new detail served only to return him to his office once again, back to St. Peter's Square in Rome, to Marone and his compact proposition. A good business deal is like a rose, Scarcella had once told him years before—a thing of beauty, with a thorn for every compromise.

The archbishop closed his eyes, remembering Marone's meaty lips against his ring, remembering his own words of agreement at their second meeting. "As long as there is no more violence, no more," he had said with rigid emphasis, thinking even then how substanceless his words were, how meaningless the condition. "Then I'll find the Gospel of Thomas for you." The car turned sharply to the right and Grabowski opened his eyes.

The Benedictine monastery of Fontgombault was almost invisible in the dark. A stand of fruit trees lined the drive on one side, while a field stretched into blackness on the other. He reached for his briefcase and pulled it up onto his lap. Yet he had really had no choice, he told himself. If Wovyetski was correct, if the gospel was truly that dangerous, no price could be too high, no act unjustified. In the distance the lights of the Romanesque church burned hypnotically. After all, who could have faith in a Church which was founded on a lie? Faith was the keystone in the arch. If it were shaken, all would fall, one stone against the other: the image of Christ; the Church; the IOR. Grabowski felt the car slow down. He felt the brake pads rubbing. He felt his own mind veer away, shunning the conclusion of his fears, like a man who cannot see the spot on his own X ray. There was nothing without faith, nothing but a lifetime of thorns, five decades dedicated to a lie, two thousand years . . .

It had been a long, hard drive from Paris and when the Solara finally pulled up at the curb, the hood began to throw off little clouds of condensation like a sweating horse. The door of the monastery swung open and a monk carrying an umbrella ran up to the car. Grabowski thanked the driver. Then he stepped out through the open door and dashed across the courtyard to the entrance of the monastery.

The abbot, Huvelin, stood just inside the main hall by a rack of tourist pamphlets. "Welcome to Fontgombault, Your Excellency," he said.

Grabowski wiped the water from his head.

The abbot looked briefly at the monk with the umbrella. It was dripping all over the floor. "Please," he added. "Follow me."

Huvelin's office was on the far side of the monastery, near the sleeping quarters. Grabowski followed him through the passageways, barely glancing at the tapestries on the walls, the plaster saints, a gilded cross, an ebony Madonna.

When they reached the office, the abbot pointed to a set of chairs before a sandstone fireplace, but the archbishop ignored them.

"I'm sorry this is so sudden," Grabowski said. "I had been planning to go to Colorado on retreat."

"We're honored to have you, Your Excellency. How long do you plan to stay, if I may ask?"

Grabowski walked over to the fireplace and began to rub his hands together above the dull flames in the brazier. The room was frigid despite the fire. "Officially, for two weeks. But I'm here on business, delicate business. In fact I plan to leave day after tomorrow."

"I'm sorry. Day after tomorrow?"

"That's right. Of course, as far as the world is concerned, I'll still be here on retreat. I'm sure you understand. One has to keep working, and there are times when the business of the Church simply cannot be disturbed, especially by the press. Now, if you don't mind. I've been on the go since early morning." With that he turned and headed out the door.

Chapter XII

AMIENS
September 19th, 1983

THE ANTIQUE SHOP WHICH JACQUES
Tellier had operated before his disappearance was
situated on the rue Dupuis, just east of the cathedral
and the Bishop's Palace. It was a crumbling stone structure, wedged in between two other houses, and it reminded Lyman of a weary hooker between props,
waiting for the final whistle of the game. Two stories at
the edges, it was but a story and three quarters at the
center. For the years had weighed it down, bending the
facade, and even the swallows no longer made their
nests under the eaves, sensing perhaps the imminent
collapse. Lyman crossed the cobbled street and entered.

There was a fusty smell about the shop. Despite the
window looking out onto the street and a dim desk
lamp in the back, the room was full of shadows. Lyman
paused by the door until his eyes had adjusted to the
dark. Then there were inlaid desks and bureaus, carved
figures from the East beside medieval hauberks, paintings, hairpins. All the objects seemed to have been

thrown together as if by chance rather than design, like the remnants of a mud slide. A stuffed eagle, missing one eye, posed at Lyman's elbow. A hidden clock ticked softly to his left. There were maps and model ships, a French Revolutionary flag, and bows and arrows from Guiana.

"Monsieur Lyman?"

Lyman turned around and found himself looking down on a shrunken little man wearing a dark wool suit and a tiny red bow tie. "I'm Paul Tellier," the man continued. "We talked on the telephone."

Lyman stepped forward and they shook hands. "A pleasure to meet you," he said, pulling his hand away. Tellier's fingers were ice cold and soft as cooked asparagus. Lyman tried to guess his age. He wasn't exactly old. He just appeared to be because of his crouched, diminished form.

"As I told you on the phone," Paul Tellier continued, "Uncle Jacques is the one who actually owns the store. We only came up here to keep it going in his absence. You know. Until he can be found. We have no designs on it ourselves, believe me." He rolled his eyes.

"Quite. About the room . . ."

"Yes, yes." Tellier turned and started for a wooden staircase at the back. "My wife and I have a new house over in the Henri Ville section. Frankly, I don't understand how Uncle Jacques could stand living here. The place is falling apart. I mean, look at it. I'd sell it in a minute if someone were to make me a decent offer." He stopped at the foot of the stairs and glanced sheepishly at Lyman. "On behalf of my uncle, of course."

"Of course."

They climbed the stairs and Tellier took a key chain from his bulging pocket, shaking it to order. "Captain Musel told us not to disturb the room. But sometimes Anna—that's my wife—sends the girl over to clean up a little." He selected a key and opened the door closest to the stairwell. It was dark inside. The curtains had been drawn. Tellier crossed through the shadows and flung them open. Billows of dust clouds welled up and curled through the sudden sunlight. Tellier waved a white hand. "I'm afraid it's been a while," he added with a frown.

"I'm sure it's fine," said Lyman. "You needn't stay. I'll manage. And thank you, you've been very helpful."

Tellier smiled skeptically. "Always happy to be of service to the police. Call me if you need anything else."

"I'll do that." Lyman looked pointedly at the door and Tellier scurried out.

It was odd, thought Lyman, how with a glance you could tell the room belonged to someone who had once spent time in jail. It had the economy of a prison cell, the same diversity of small conveniences so close at hand, like the room of an invalid. One wall angled in and Lyman had to duck a little as he made his way toward the desk at the back.

He began his search in a natural fashion, opening the drawers immediately below the writing surface first. They contained little odds and ends such as cigarettes and paper clips, scissors, and a box of silver coins. Then he tried the very bottom drawer on the right side. It caught for a moment before finally slipping out. Lyman noticed that the bolt was partly visible. Someone had already been there. Captain Musel perhaps? There were scratches in the wood around the lock. The drawer was empty.

The next drawer was a different matter. Nestled in the back, behind a stack of legal documents and tax forms, Lyman came across a passbook from a local bank with Jacques Tellier's name and address printed in black computer type across the front. Lyman skipped to the last entry. Apparently Tellier had made a small deposit on the nineteenth of May, 1982. One hundred and twenty francs to be exact. He had written the words "Pen Set" in the space beside the figure. Not much of a sale, thought Lyman. And not even a withdrawal. The total account was worth almost eight hundred pounds. He scanned the pages. Yet Tellier had gone to Klagenfurt on something, Lyman realized. A ticket to Austria wasn't cheap. Perhaps he had kept a little tucked away here at the shop, a few francs for emergencies. It was certainly not uncommon. Or perhaps he had had a friend to help him on the way, an accomplice with a pair of tickets waiting in the wings.

His finger hesitated beside an entry dated April 23rd, 1982. This was odd. Unlike the five or six hundred-franc deposits scattered throughout the pages of the passbook, this entry was valued at more than fifteen thousand. Three initials trailed the figure, etched in pencil—*G.L.F.*

Lyman looked around reflexively. The door was still closed. He slipped the passbook into the inside pocket of his coat. Who would know anyway? Then he started for the door. But as he walked across the room, careful to duck his head below the slanted roof, he caught a movement in the corner of his eye and stopped to see his own face staring back at him from the surface of a mirror.

He looked terrible. His eyes were puffy and red, drooping at the corners. His skin was pale as milk. He needed a trim. He looked, he realized, as he always did after a night of heavy drinking. Except that he hadn't been drinking. Not since England. Not since the ransacking of his flat in Golders Green. And it struck him that this was a terrible injustice, a betrayal of the body somehow. He was getting old and soft, he thought, and age had come upon him suddenly, without him looking. He had simply waked one day and realized that the pinch of extra flesh about his kidneys was something he would have to live with for the rest of his life.

He walked back over to the desk. It really didn't matter, he thought, dropping the passbook in the drawer. He would remember it all anyway.

He turned and headed for the door. As he moved beside the mirror once again, he glimpsed a small round leather jewelry box on a chest of drawers and picked it up, absentmindedly, aware of the figure staring back, the movements of his own hands in reverse. G.L.F., he thought. G.L.F. What could it mean? Nothing but a few more coins, a pair of plastic collar stays, a garnet ring. He poked the contents with a fingertip. And on its side, beneath a pair of tarnished cuff links, a tiepin made of gold shaped as a mason's square. It looked exactly like one he'd seen his Uncle Jack wear years before in Winchester.

Lyman smiled. So Tellier was a Mason too. Like Marco Scarcella. Like Pontevecchio.

Paul Tellier was sitting on a stool at the rear of the shop when Lyman came downstairs. The shopkeeper was directing the movements of two teenagers in the midst of unpacking a bust of Napoleon Bonaparte from a crate. The boys were dressed in navy overalls. One was smoking a cigarette even as he heaved and pulled at the general's marble hat.

"Ah, Monsieur Lyman," Tellier said, hopping off his stool. "I hope you found what you were after."

"Not really. But perhaps you wouldn't mind answering a few questions for me."

Tellier sat back on the stool. "Of course," he said.

The boys had finally unpacked the bust and it lay in a heap of straw on the floor. "I've never had the pleasure of meeting your uncle," Lyman said. "Tell me. What kind of man is he? What's he like?"

Tellier lowered his eyes. "Like any other man."

"What about friends? A girlfriend, perhaps."

"Goodness, no. He's not like that. I don't think he's ever had a girlfriend. My father always used to say that he forgot about women when he went to prison, and then never bothered to remember them again when he got out." Tellier laughed thinly, his little eyes shining for the first time.

"What about the shop?" said Lyman. He took a pack of cigarettes from his coat and offered one to Tellier. The little man shook his head. Lyman helped himself.

"What about it?"

"Is it successful?"

"Success, as I'm sure you know, is a relative term. I suppose my uncle would say it is. After all, he started from almost nothing after prison. But personally . . ." He shook his head. "I'm afraid not. To be honest with you, we practically lose money. It's the Socialists, you know. It's Mitterrand and his clique. At least Giscard was a real intellectual."

Lyman lit his cigarette. "Did your uncle keep any financial records? For the shop, I mean. Records of transactions. Receipts. That sort of thing."

"Some."

"May I see them?"

Tellier popped off his stool. "If it's absolutely necessary." He reached across a stack of paintings and pulled a pair of ledgers from a dusty shelf. "These are for '81 and '82. If you need anything earlier, I'll have to look upstairs."

"I'm sure these will be fine. Thank you." Lyman took the ledger marked 1982 and sat down on a chair nearby.

He had never really liked this kind of legwork, perhaps because he had never been much good at it. He preferred to search for answers in the faces of his suspects, in their actions and inactions, in the cadence of their words. He had no instinct for the printed page, for numbers, and yet he knew this was the future of his trade. Pontevecchio had stolen hundreds of millions with the simple movement of a number from one column to another. Computer criminals now accounted for more money lost each year than all the petty thieves and pickpockets of Great Britain. It had all changed since Winchester. It was all different now. Crime had become like war, like the Falkland Islands conflict with its missiles—something waged at a distance.

He finally found the right page, and began to run his finger down from one number to the next. There was nothing unusual, certainly no sales entry worth fifteen thousand francs—almost a thousand pounds. Yet Jacques Tellier had found the money somewhere. "Monsieur Tellier," he said at last. "Do you recall your uncle selling something particularly valuable before he left?"

"Valuable?"

"Yes. Something in the range of fifteen thousand francs."

Tellier looked shocked. "I don't think so." He hesitated for a moment. "That is," he continued, "I suppose it's possible. But frankly, Monsieur Lyman, I doubt it. Not from this shop."

"I see. What about the initials G.L.F.? Do they mean anything to you?"

"G.L.F.? I don't think so."

"And you say you don't recall any of his friends."

Tellier's expression soured. "I'm sorry, but you have to understand. We were never particularly close. Most of our family lives in Rochefort, or nearby in the town of La Tremblade. Jacques was the one who chose to come and live up here. I suppose he wanted a fresh start after prison."

"He had no friends," the teenager with the cigarette said suddenly.

"How do you know?"

The boy shrugged. "I used to work for him. Almost three years."

"What about steady customers?"

The boy laughed. He was tall and stiff with a pocked face and black hair which hung down almost to his eyes. "What customers? Are you kidding?" he said. "The only people who ever used to come here were lost on their way to the cathedral. Tourists. You know." He hesitated for a moment.

"What is it?"

"There was one guy though. He used to come around."

"What was his name?"

"How would I know? Every time he came, Jacques —I mean Monsieur Tellier—used to kick me out. But I've seen him around town. At least I used to. It's been a while."

"What's he look like?"

The boy shrugged. "Dark. Not too tall, not too short. About your height. But younger, maybe thirty."

Lyman frowned. "Thanks," he said. "Anything else?"

The teenager looked around as if the answers to Lyman's questions had been hidden somewhere in the room. "He drove a blue Peugeot," he said at last. "Yeah, that's right. And there was some kind of writing on the side. What do you call it?"

"Like a stencil?" Lyman volunteered.

"Yeah. The name of a store. Like a company car."

Lyman nodded. "Right," he said. "Thanks again." He stood and shook Tellier's hand. "Here," he added, pulling out his pack of Players and tossing them to the boy. "Try these. Those Gauloises will kill you."

"Any time," said Tellier. "And give my best to Captain Musel."

Lyman did not answer. The door opened and closed and he found himself out in the street, the chill of the morning nuzzling up against him. He missed England. He missed the frantic streets of Hendon, the rush to catch the tube, that morning cup of tea at his little desk in front of Blackwell's open window. London seemed so far away now.

He thrust his hands deep into his pockets and

started back toward the hotel. The street was empty now except for a solitary figure in a distant doorway, and an old woman sweeping the pavement near her house. He walked on, remembering his ragged countenance in Tellier's looking glass, a shabby center to the countless clues and dark suggestions which made up the Pontevecchio case. It was his task to reveal the thread that linked them all together, but every time he seemed to glimpse a pattern, it unraveled in his hands.

Where had Jacques Tellier discovered the Book of Thomas the Contender, and how? How had he earned those fifteen thousand francs, and why hadn't he withdrawn them before his trip to Klagenfurt? Who was the man with the blue Peugeot, and who or what was G.L.F.? All at once, all of these questions cried out from within him to be answered, so that he did not notice the solitary figure that had left his distant doorway for the street, that followed through the shadows with his chin down and the collar of his olive-colored raincoat pulled up about his face.

Joseph Koster sat in the brasserie of the Gritti Hotel, stirring a cup of weak espresso, looking through the window at the buses in the Place Fiquet. The cold sun pulled the shadows through the afternoon: the giant tower, a plea for secular vanity over the cathedral; the bald pate of the Gare du Nord, glistening; the gathering crowd of grim commuters, more predetermined than determined, walking in their bat-colored raincoats finally for home. Koster sipped his coffee. The train was late. Perhaps Grabowski wasn't coming after all.

At first, the news of the archbishop's imminent arrival had delighted Koster. The call had come in over the public phone—his was still broken after the robbery—and the concierge had run the two flights with the message. "An archbishop," he had sputtered at the door. "An archbishop!"

Koster had followed him downstairs only to find that Grabowski was not even there—just a message that he was in Paris and would stop up that afternoon to say hello. But the more time passed, and the more Koster thought about the sudden call, the more he realized that he didn't need Grabowski anymore.

Langelier, the Minister of Culture, had given him full access to the Notre Dame cathedrals, including excavation rights. Koster had only sent those letters to his cousin in case his publisher, Nick Robinson, had failed to win the minister's support, and in order not to alienate the local priests. But now it was too late. Grabowski was on his way.

Koster called for the waiter and a lanky Algerian boy appeared, shuffling his feet. "More coffee, please." The waiter smiled and moved dreamily away. He looked stoned, Koster thought, and he remembered Priscilla's flat expression, the way she had somnambulated through his life for months before he had discovered her addiction. All those colorful little pills at the bottom of her makeup case, like a bag of cat's-eyes. He had never even known. He had always taken her silence as a mark of grief after the accident. But that's when she had changed.

In retrospect, it seemed obvious now that their marriage had been doomed from the very start. Everyone had known it—except for Koster, of course. Nick Robinson had warned him outright. "She's not the one for you," he had told Koster repeatedly, even on the day of his wedding. No matter how much it had hurt back then, he had to respect Nick for speaking his mind. At least he was honest. Nick had always looked after Koster, ever since school. Only the night before he had called again to see how the book was coming.

Koster looked up suddenly. A shadow lay across the table. And at the other end he saw a round face peering through the window, one hand raised up to block the glare. It was Grabowski.

Koster stood automatically. The archbishop walked around the brasserie and in a moment he was by the table, signaling for the waiter. "Sorry I'm late," he said, finally offering his hand.

He was wearing a dark suit and clerical collar. In his left hand he carried an overfull Alitalia bag which made him seem smaller than Koster remembered. Small and tired. "Don't worry. I only just arrived myself," Koster said, suddenly embarrassed by the empty cup of coffee at his elbow. My first words, he thought, and they're a lie. "Listen, I wish I could have caught you on the phone this morning. There was really no need for you to come all the way up here on my account. Everything's been going great. Not that I don't appreciate it. I mean I know you're busy."

Grabowski smiled. "I suppose you look more like your father than your mother. How is he anyway? I haven't seen him in years."

"He's all right."

"Still playing?"

"Semiretired, but you know Dad. He still does guest appearances."

The archbishop nodded and Koster realized just how old he really was. For months his face had appeared in the New York daily papers, always the same photograph, the same defiant eyes. That had been back at the height of the Fabiano scandal. But now he looked as an actor looks after the show is over and he's rubbed away the face paint and the powder. Was this what it meant to be famous, a struggle to resemble some stock photo from the past, a pure moment of dissembling? Perhaps the scandal had humbled him. Perhaps, like Priscilla, he too had changed.

"And the rest of the family?" Grabowski asked, tilting his hand. "How are they?"

"Fine, I guess."

"I heard about you and Priscilla. I'm sorry."

Koster shrugged. Had he seen it in his eyes? "It happens. It's a statistical truth. We were just unlucky."

"Perhaps you should try and reunite. Don't underestimate the value, the importance of a second chance. You are a Catholic, after all. Church doctrine is clear on this."

Koster bristled. "I'd rather not talk about it," he said.

The archbishop laughed, throwing his head back so that the sound rolled over like a wave across the empty brasserie. "Please, Joseph. Don't misunderstand me. It's just that when you get to be my age, you realize that there are only a few things not worthy of a second chance. Even a broken-down marriage. Maybe especially that. When you're young—like you are—you're certain there are some people, some things you simply can't forgive. I remember, believe me. But one day, when you've done something, something you don't know where to put, you'll understand that it's easy to forgive. Except yourself, of course, and that's why we have Christ." He paused, glancing out the window. "I suppose that's why you came to Amiens?"

"In a way," Koster answered vaguely.

Grabowski smiled. "I'm sorry if I seem inquisitive. It's just that I hardly get to see anyone anymore, especially from the American side of the family."

"I came for the book. The one on the cathedrals."

"The book? Of course," he said, waving at the waiter. "Tell me about the book. What's it about? The last I heard, you were working for one of those big architectural firms in New York."

"My publisher suggested the idea. But I guess I needed to get away, after the divorce I mean. Anyway, I went. They were really nice about it at work."

"Really." The waiter set Koster's second cup of coffee on the table. Then he gathered up the first one, stuffing it full of empty sugar wrappings with his thumb. "I'll have the same," Grabowski said.

"It's about the Notre Dame cathedrals," Koster said. "You know—Reims and Chartres as well. An architect's perspective. Form as mathematical construct, as analog."

"Always the mathematician. Oh, I almost forgot. I brought you something." Grabowski reached down and lifted the Alitalia bag onto the table. "What do you know about St. Thomas?"

"St. Thomas?" Koster was startled. "Not much. A few legends. I know he's the patron saint of builders. There's a statue of him in the western portico of the cathedral here. He's even carrying a T square."

"Did you ever hear the story of the Book of Thomas the Contender?"

"And the one about the Persian Cup or Grail or whatever it's meant to be. But there are lots of myths and legends about the cathedrals." Koster watched Grabowski slip a box out of the Alitalia bag. "What's that?" he said.

"When I heard about your project I asked a friend of mine who works at the Vatican library to see if he could come up with anything helpful, for the book." Grabowski ran a thumb nail along the edge of the box, tearing the cellophane tape. Then he lifted the top with his left hand, revealing a sketch of black revolving lines, octagonal, and a weave of calculations on the side. "Recognize this?"

"Sure," said Koster, reaching for the box. "That's the labyrinth, the one at the cathedral."

Grabowski nodded. "According to my friend, this is a copy of a letter sent by a scholar named Thierry of Chartres to one of the original builders of the Amiens cathedral. See for yourself." He lifted a stack of papers from the box. "The letter is actually a kind of dedication written directly into the margin of what appears to be a Gnostic Christian prayer book, a missal apparently given by Thierry as a gift to the builder in Amiens. Because of the legitimacy of the prayer book and its dedication, my friend believes—and I agree with him—that the Book of Thomas the Contender is still hidden somewhere in the Amiens cathedral, just as the old legends describe."

"I don't get it," Koster said. "I mean I'm not saying you're wrong, but what would a medieval architect be doing with a Gnostic prayer book? In those days masons learned from other masons, traveling around the countryside, not from schools. Especially not the school at Chartres." He studied the drawing which Grabowski had placed before him. "These calculations," he said. "They're the measurements of the labyrinth, right?"

Grabowski grinned. "I thought they'd interest you. According to the missal, the location of the Book of Thomas the Contender is somehow tied to the labyrinth itself. Not physically, mind you. It's not just hidden underneath the central plate or something. It's mathematical."

Koster stiffened in his chair.

"What's the matter," Grabowski said. "What is it?"

"These numbers aren't medieval. Look at the way they're shaped. I think your friend at the library is pulling your leg."

"What? What do you mean?" Grabowski turned the sheet around. A moment passed and then he added casually, "Of course. This is a modern sketch. I only brought it along because of the measurements."

"Oh. Well, thanks, but I already have them."

The archbishop's face clouded over. He shrugged his heavy shoulders and began to gather the papers in a pile. Koster watched the way his hands worked. They were the hands of an old man—spotted, worn, and seamed—and he chided his own stony heart. Grabowski had only been trying to help. It had been a gesture. It deserved better.

"You know," he said, "for a while now I've been thinking that the labyrinth could be some kind of mathematical symbol, a numerical metaphor for the cathedral. Like a matrix."

Grabowski smiled wearily. "I thought you might be interested." Then he turned away. "Joseph, what happened between me and your parents was a long time ago."

"I guess so," Koster said. He stared out at the Place Fiquet. A man in an olive-colored raincoat was leaning up against a car, reading a newspaper. The commuters were thinning out. The sun had almost fallen.

"Look, it's probably none of my business," Koster added tightly, "but you could have flown back for Martha's funeral. You knew how Catholic she was. Grandma was always so proud of you. Her nephew the archbishop, the mayor of the Vatican City. She kept asking for you at the hospital. Dad was really upset. He said you were only interested in maintaining your position at the Vatican."

"It was a busy time."

"I guess you had your reasons."

"Please, Joseph, I didn't come here to fight. You may not believe me, but when a pope dies everything comes to a halt at the Vatican. Everything shuts down. I know Aunt Martha asked for me. I'm sorry. I wanted to go. But the Church needed me, Joseph. There had to be some continuity. You must understand that."

Koster tried to find the words with which to frame his anger but there was nothing there. His passion was ungrounded, an echo without source, like the light of a distant star long since extinguished. "I suppose so. I guess you were just doing your job."

It was an argument a quarter century old, and not even his.

"A job I still believe in," Grabowski said. "Despite everything. And it's a job you can help me with."

"Me?" Koster laughed. "Look, I'm not exactly the most diligent Catholic anymore."

"Maybe not, but I'm sure you realize that what

you're doing will be helpful to the Church. The Notre Dame cathedrals are absolutely unique—the way they're built, the way they reflect our love for God."

"For our Lady, really."

"That too. The point is that the more people begin to appreciate the cathedrals, the more they'll try to understand the driving force behind their original construction, the reasons they were built. That's why I brought you these papers. Think what would happen if the Book of Thomas the Contender were actually discovered. Think about it. It would set off an unprecedented wave of interest in all the Notre Dame cathedrals. It would be invaluable, both historically and materially. We would, of course, pay you for thè gospel. That's only fair. And eventually your work might help unearth the Gospel of Thomas as well, the one they say is buried under Chartres Cathedral. Why, the Persian Cup alone is supposed to be worth millions. You'd never have to build another shopping mall again. And best of all, Joseph, think of the challenge. For eight hundred years the labyrinth of Amiens has remained unsolved, a curiosity, a tourist attraction. Eight hundred years! That's six hundred years before Goldbach even stated his conjecture. Isn't that what you were working on before, in college?"

"How did you hear about my work on Goldbach? You're not a mathematician."

Grabowski smiled sadly. "Just because we never talked doesn't mean I never took an interest in you, in all my family." He dropped the papers onto the table. The drawing of the labyrinth seemed to skate across the surface, like the pointer of a Ouija board, a corner coming to rest in front of Koster's cup of coffee.

Koster looked down at the numbers on the drawing, the perfect symmetry of content in the jagged form. Eight hundred years, he thought, glancing back at the archbishop. Then he grinned and said, "How do I get in touch with you?"

Chapter XIII

AMIENS
September 22nd, 1983

AS HE WATCHED THE RIVER SOMME retreat below his feet, Lyman thought that if it hadn't been for Teddy Bashall and that five-pound rainbow they had poached with bread crumbs from the River Itchen, he would never have become a policeman. But they had gone out that day, Lyman from his narrow street lined with low flint walls, the houses rubbing shoulders like gray mares, each one the same save for the vibrant colors of their doors; and Bashall from the padded drawing rooms and studies, through the well-worn corridors and sandstone arches of the college. They'd lived a tie-length's distance, but when they met that day by chance on the balcony of The Review, equally bored by a jungle movie, equally careful with their cigarettes, they both knew with the certainty of children that eventually they would be friends. All that had mattered then was an excuse, a sympathetic interest, and fishing was the natural choice. Already Lyman had known that a man who fishes has no past, no future. There is only the fisherman and his fish, with a moment's lifeline in between.

They had found a cool, moss-covered bank, spotted with a hint of oak roots, where the river was but seven yards across. A field stretched out behind their casting arms and up ahead, along the other bank, a pair of willows and a girdle of impenetrable sedge grass quivered in the breeze, then vanished as the float sank to the center of the earth and stopped.

When the farmer found them they were walking slowly back along the Itchen toward town, in single file between the cow field and the river, their poles dangling from their weary fingertips, the bag round Bashall's neck weighed down with grayling and that one thick rainbow trout, bulging with roe and out of season. They didn't even try to run. They waited for him without speaking and he took them to the college warden who lived—and this was used against them later, as a mark of hubris—within spitting distance of the crime scene. The farmer did not say more than a few words. He didn't need to. With a shake the trout fell from the bag, a sequin flash of scales, and Lyman realized they were finished. The farmer hung his head. The fish lay in the grass, already stiffening, the spine curved in an arc as if she were preparing for a final lunge at life.

Bashall was barred from the College Junior Fishing Club. It was at worst a troublesome affair for him. His family owned a trout beat on the River Test and every other year he visited a great-aunt up in Scotland where he hunted grouse. But Lyman was a different matter. He was a local boy. He needed to be taught a lesson. They planned to cane him, until the warden's wife took pity on his dark requesting face and pointed out the legal complications. So instead they called the Winchester Police and Lyman waited in the warden's study, the wooden shelving stuffed with books and magazines on fishing, with improbable trophies of exotic birds, with hunting scenes and that bay window by the desk through which he watched the back of Teddy Bashall grow smaller as the boy withdrew across the fields.

It was as if the great god of the river had suddenly forgiven him when the police van halted on the shoulder of the road and out stepped Uncle Jack. He looked the model of the English bobby, his back straight as a pikestaff. But when the warden let him in and Lyman saw his uncle's face for the first time, it was obvious he had nothing left to count on. Uncle Jack was using his sergeant's voice. He acted as if they'd never sat across from one another at the kitchen table, never shared a pint in secret or gone to football championships together. The warden relayed the facts once more. The farmer cursed and nodded. Then with a tug at the elbow the apology slipped out. But Lyman talked without conviction. He could not understand the point of an apology when it was the river he and Bashall had offended, when the fish had been avenged by her own beauty.

Uncle Jack led Lyman out into the van. The warden frowned beyond the wire grillwork as they started down the road. The river vanished from the rearview mirror. Lyman pressed himself into the seat, between his uncle and another constable named Peter Partner. A lorry came and went and suddenly the van filled up with laughter and the two men shoved him to the floor with shouts of "criminal" and "thief." Uncle Jack squeezed him like a loaf of bread. "Well, Peter," he added with a grin. "What shall we do with him? Hang him? Cut him up for bait?" The van swerved and they both laughed again. "Christ, what next? You were lucky this time, Nigel, I'll say. What did your friend get?"

"Expulsion from the College Junior Fishing Club."

"Well, isn't that justice." He laughed ironically and it was then, in the space of that one open sound that Lyman knew what he would be, no matter what. Then his life had stretched before him as uncharted as the world beyond the river and the county line, pulsing with possibility, and justice too had seemed a clean and easy thing.

Lyman pulled the collar of his coat up and headed back across the bridge toward the hotel. It was getting late, and he had yet to finish his report to London.

A pair of German tourists bickered in front of the cathedral as he strode past. They were what the French called *routards,* either a decade late or early with their tattered blue jeans patched with peace signs. Perhaps they were pilgrims, Lyman thought, as he watched them counting their centimes.

He hurried on, his head down testing out inventions, trying vainly to fill out the last few days with something they would readily accept at home. The Lemur had been calling every day. Even Cocksedge, in a rare but not unprecedented move, had rung him up the night before. But how much could he tell them, and what did they already know?

The night before, Lyman had received another call from Dotty Taylor. She had taken Hadley's orchids over to Smythe at Scotland Yard, and pharmacology had confirmed Lyman's worst fears. The plant did indeed exude a peculiar alkaloid, one of extraordinary power. The first exam had shown up positive for cocaine, a similar alkaloid, but the second test had come back negative. No one had ever seen anything quite like it.

Lyman had immediately called another friend named Baker who worked at the coroner's office. He asked him to test a sample of Pontevecchio's blood, but Baker refused—at least at first. Where were the official forms? he had asked. Why hadn't protocol been followed? To test the blood would require most of the supply remaining in Pontevecchio's file, and there was no way now to get another sample without an exhumation. But Lyman eventually prevailed. He and Baker had spent many an evening at a certain flat in Soho, just above a Greek café. And Baker was a married man.

Lyman needed to know. He needed to prove to himself that what he feared the most was untrue. But as he waited for the test results, all he could think of were the words which David Ellison had used in describing Pontevecchio's death. "One of them took a box out," the Yorkshire vagabond had said. "It must have been a knife or something because while the other two were holding him, the third one pulled his trousers part way down and stuck it in him, right there, in the groin. Bloody savages."

And then Pontevecchio had died. It was perfect. Where better to inject an alkaloid than in the pubic hair, where the puncture mark would be impossible to see? And what better poison to employ than one no instrument had yet been programmed to detect?

It was the work of a professional. And Hadley had always been professional.

Lyman walked on past the cathedral, back toward the hotel. He was tired and fed up. He had spent the entire afternoon arguing with the Amiens police, trying vainly to elicit some support, some access to intelligence. In the end Musel had refused to even see him, and it was only when the captain's shadow—Corporal Pini—ran into Lyman on the stairs by chance, that he had learned the reason why. They had finally heard from Interpol, it seemed, two days before. The man who had fallen to his death from the Hôtel de la Paix had been identified as Aldo Barbieri, a part-time paid assassin and friend of Marco Scarcella.

Now there were two scenarios, two possibilities to keep time with his footsteps as he walked. Either Hadley and his friends in London had sent a message off to Scarcella with the news of Lyman's imminent arrival, or the former Venerable Master had yet another source of information here in Amiens, set up to watch for strangers with a certain small red key. In either case, the news of Lyman's inquiries, and of Joseph Koster's research, had somehow reached Scarcella. And who better to pass that information on than the captain of police? Lyman shook his head. A car whizzed by before him and he stopped short, just as the pavement dropped into the street. He was seeing faces in the dark. Perhaps Musel was just resentful. Perhaps, like most policemen, he harbored a simple jealous love for his responsibilities, for the town itself.

The light changed and Lyman crossed the Place Gambetta. The street was crowded with umbrellas, spinning. A chemist's light flashed notice of a brand-new pain reliever. At least Musel had helped him with the car, he thought, if only indirectly. The day before, the captain of police had sent him with a tepid telephone recommendation to a Monsieur Poincarré in Traffic Control. Several blue Peugeots, it turned out, had indeed been licensed fairly recently as commercial vehicles. After some cross-checking and a call to the boy at Jacques Tellier's antique shop, Lyman was fairly certain the one he was looking for belonged to a man named Maurice Duval, the president and part owner of a local construction company.

The more Lyman pushed, the more difficult it became. Musel had been right—Amiens was a quiet city, resentful of outsiders. And ironically it was the town's size, the forced familiarity which made gossip such a ready coin to the citizens of Amiens, that also formed the stares and silent shrugs which greeted Lyman's questions. Only a few fell gently to his charm, to his penumbral queries. From them he learned that the Duval Construction Company was owned both by Maurice and by his father, Charles-Philip. A moderately successful venture, the company specialized in renovations and was currently involved in a number of projects, including the renovation of the Bishop's Palace

near the cathedral. But something had happened not
too long ago, something about which no one seemed
quite certain. Perhaps there had been an argument between father and son. Some talked about a robbery,
and some embezzlement. Most talked of missing funds.
Indeed, the only fact that all agreed upon was that
Maurice had finally left Amiens, and more—the knowledge coming like the clicking of a tumbler in a combination safe—that he had gone the very week of
Tellier's own disappearance.

Lyman stopped in front of the hotel and looked up
at the balcony. That was where Barbieri had held on
for his last moments. And that, he thought, looking
down at the battered road, is where his moments had
run out. He frowned and entered the hotel.

There was no doubt about it now, he told himself.
Barbieri had been Scarcella's man. But if Scarcella was
watching him, then it probably meant he hadn't found
Jacques Tellier—at least not yet. Lyman had already
checked that foreign telephone exchange at the bottom
of the note which Tellier had abandoned with the missal in the locker. But it had proved to be a small hotel
in Klagenfurt, Austria, where they—of course—had
never heard of Monsieur Tellier. No, thought Lyman.
The antique dealer had gone underground. And if
Scarcella had not found him, with all his men and resources, it was unlikely Lyman would alone.

He rang the little cowbell on the front desk and the
concierge appeared across the dining room. "Monsieur
Lyman," he said jovially, stepping in behind the desk.
"No messages today, I'm afraid."

"Just as well. How about a telephone book?"

"Of course." The concierge pulled it out from below the desk as if he had been waiting for the question.
"Anything else?"

"No, no thanks," said Lyman. Then, as an afterthought he added, "Actually, you can give me some
change for the phone." He pulled out his wallet and

dropped a fifty-franc note on the counter. The concierge counted out the coins while Lyman looked through the book. There it was: *Duval, C-P, Menuiserie-Charpente.*

Jacques Tellier was underground, that much was certain, but perhaps Maurice Duval was somewhere to be found. "Thanks," he said, taking up the coins.

Lyman did not really like to lie, not because he felt bound by some moral stricture, some pang of conscience, but because he knew he wasn't very good at it. He always preferred to tell the people he questioned exactly who he was. It made things easier that way, and he had long since learned to exploit the natural fear which most feel toward the police, the quiet guilt which comes of countless peccadillos and the superstitious knowledge that the law, like justice, does not always work as it's supposed to. But as the phone rang and the coins fell, he remembered that according to Corporal Pini, Charles-Philip Duval had never filed a notice of complaint about a robbery or missing funds. If a scandal had occurred, it was obvious that the construction company's senior owner didn't want it to be common knowledge. The ringing stopped. "Hello," he said. "My name is Randall, Terry Randall."

"Yes?" a girl replied.

"Hello, hello."

"Yes, I can hear you."

"Sorry. The connection's terrible." He paused, releasing more coins. "I represent a chain of bed-and-breakfasts based here in London." His accent was suddenly grotesque. "We are considering the construction of a new property and, frankly, I'm rather keen on Amiens."

"Oui, monsieur. How can I help you?" she said, and Lyman noticed the change in pitch. So far so good.

"I'll be en route to Paris tomorrow," he continued, "and I was wondering if I might stop by and have a chat with Monsieur Duval on the way."

"Of course," the girl replied, and they set a time.

Lyman hung up. The concierge was eyeing him curiously from across the counter and for a moment Lyman was certain he had overheard his bald impersonation. He started toward the stairs, waiting for the concierge to say something, to call him back.

"Monsieur Lyman."

Lyman stopped. "Yes?"

"Would you come here a moment?"

Lyman turned and approached the front desk. "Yes. What is it?"

"I was wondering," the concierge said, "if you wouldn't mind taking this up to Monsieur Koster. His phone is still broken and, well, I've been up and down these stairs at least a hundred times today. The messenger wanted to deliver it himself, but I told him it was against our new security measures. Did I tell you about them?" He held out what appeared to be a business card.

Lyman smiled and took it. "Yes, this morning," he said. "Good show." He waved the card. "And I wouldn't mind at all."

Lyman waited until he had reached the second landing and was quite alone before he read the message on the card. For some reason it did not surprise him. Each case had its rhythm, he reminded himself again, and he had already sensed that this one was approaching yet another beat, a rising meter. He glanced once more at the card. It looked expensive.

Mr. Koster,
Charles Langelier, our illustrious Minister of Culture and a dear friend, informs me you are working on a book about the Notre Dame cathedrals. I have studied them at length and would be more than happy to assist you in any way I can. Come visit me in Paris, tomorrow

morning at 10:00—51 rue de Varennes, near the
Rodin Museum.

Lyman turned the card over. Embossed in a simple
script were the words *Countess Irene Chantal de
Rochambaud.*

He mounted the last few steps and knocked gently
on Joseph Koster's door. After a moment Koster appeared, his hair standing up at the back, his clothes
crumpled as though he had been sleeping in them.
"Oh, it's you," he said vaguely.

"Sorry to barge in like this." Lyman held out the
note. "The concierge said it was for you."

Koster took the card, and Lyman watched his eyes
carefully. No, there was no doubt. He was genuinely
surprised.

"Listen to this," Koster blurted out. "That countess. You remember. The expert on Gnostics and the
cathedrals."

Lyman nodded. It was incredible, he thought. He
was practically shouting it to the hotel.

"She wants to see me tomorrow."

"Really! How nice. Are you going?"

"Of course I'm going. You heard Guy. She's a real
expert on these things."

"That's right. Well, aren't you lucky."

Koster looked up. "Thanks," he said.

They stood there for a moment without talking,
Lyman waiting for the false bravado, the ingenuous
facade to crumble, but it didn't. He was good, this one,
he thought. Or he was everybody's fool. "How about
dinner tonight, Joseph?"

"Tonight?" Koster looked away. "I don't know
about tonight."

"I've hardly seen you since . . . you know. Since
the robbery. And I'll probably be on to Switzerland
next week."

Koster shifted his weight. "All right," he said.

"Of course, if you already have plans."

"No, not at all," Koster protested. He pushed his hair down in the back. "I'd love to, really. Is Italian okay? I'm fed up with French."

Lyman nodded, and another tumbler fell. "Italian would be fine."

The Café Reggio was tucked away only a few hundred yards from the hotel in the shadows of the rue Lamarck. As they approached through the darkness, Lyman saw a bright pink Citroën poking like a tongue behind the showroom window right next door, and he wondered if it were this which had induced young Koster to first try the restaurant. The entire street might have been lifted up from some American suburban town and dropped in Amiens. It had that quality of newness, like the smell of Styrofoam, the solidity and permanence of tent cloth compared with the cathedral in the distance.

An old Wurlitzer was playing something with a mandolin, something Italian, Lyman supposed. The baritone was eager. There were lines of tables and a bar, and then a young girl with a paisley dress who showed them to their seats. Koster looked quite happy now, Lyman thought, as if he had resigned himself to the notion of this dinner and decided, finally, to make the best of it. He was so young, Lyman thought, so nonchalant about his honesty. All he talked about was Mariane.

A tubby waiter in a cummerbund approached to take their order. "Pardon, pardon!" he said jovially. "Ready?"

Ready for what? Lyman thought.

"Try the osso buco," Koster said. "It's great. I'm having it." He smiled at the waiter. "And a bottle of Amarone."

"Whatever," Lyman said.

The wine came and they chatted, but it was not
until the waiter had brought their antipasto that Koster
finally mentioned the archbishop. Lyman was poking at
a piece of endive, trying to appear casual as the American rattled on about his book, about the world of intricate equations, about the labyrinth. Everyone had been
so helpful, he explained, stuffing a slice of rolled salami
in his mouth. Even his cousin had appeared, the one
whom he had mentioned earlier, the one at the Vatican. Lyman sipped his wine, making it last. And then,
like a confession, all the right words tumbled out: the
Book of Thomas the Contender; the missal and the
scholar Thierry.

Or everybody's fool, Lyman thought. Like me. The
weakness of the logical mind is that the world is so
illogical. Koster was being used by Scarcella and Grabowski. He was being duped. Who better to employ in
such a search than someone versed in mathematics,
than an architect?

Up until now Lyman had pursued the case to
France because he knew that somewhere on the line
which ran from London to the labyrinth, somewhere
along the way the man who had hidden in the shadow
of Blackfriars Bridge would emerge into the light. Perhaps he already had. Grabowski had arrived, and Aldo
Barbieri had been Scarcella's man. Both the archbishop and the former Venerable Master. His two major suspects. Lyman took another sip of wine.

Somewhere in the cathedral Jacques Tellier, the
antique dealer, had found the Book of Thomas the
Contender. With it, and with little more it seemed,
he had left France for the town of Klagenfurt in southern Austria in order to sell it to Pontevecchio. The
Fabiano scandal had just broken like a thunderhead in
Italy. Pontevecchio was finished. The only thing that
could save him now was the Gospel of Thomas, a document so old—and so heretical apparently—that its

publication alone would cause irreparable damage to
the Church.

But Jacques Tellier was a cautious man. He knew
the Book of Thomas the Contender was only valuable
for its hiding place. Whoever knew that secret would
be able to discover its connection to the labyrinth. That
was the real prize. If you knew the answer to the labyrinth, you could find the master builder's hiding place
within. And armed with that knowledge you could use
the same equation to unravel the labyrinth at Chartres,
to finally find the thing for which Scarcella and Grabowski had each been searching for so long—the Gospel of Thomas.

So Tellier had devised a rough insurance plan. He
placed a few clues to the labyrinth inside the locker at
the terminal, and then handed the key to Pontevecchio.
All that the banker had to do was collect the package
from the terminal and call the telephone number at the
bottom of the note for the final phrase in the equation.
But Pontevecchio had never made it. He had gone off
to London, too frightened to make the trip to France.
He had gone off and died.

Now all that remained was the key, the key and that
picnic basket waiting in the locker patiently for Captain
Musel—like those time bombs waking under London
Streets, years after the Blitz. That was probably when
Scarcella had first heard of it. If he had known earlier
it was doubtful he had paid much heed or he would
never have permitted Pontevecchio's death. No, Captain Musel had probably been the messenger, wittingly
or unwittingly, through the City of London Police. And
with that knowledge Scarcella had sent his envoys out
to search for Jacques Tellier, the only man who knew
the gospel's final hiding place and the secret of the
labyrinth. But they had not found him. Or if they had,
Lyman knew, he had not talked. For otherwise they
never would have come for Koster at the Hôtel de la
Paix.

The waiter bounced back into view, his hands alive with steaming plates. A long thin bone wrapped in meat stared up at Lyman, the marrow like a Cyclops's eye.

"Go ahead," Koster said, smiling across the table. "Dig in."

And then, Lyman thought, the American had come. That was the problem. "Tell me, Joseph," he said, carefully inspecting the chunk of meat on the tip of his fork. "How did you first get this idea? The book, I mean. Was it your cousin's influence?"

"Didn't I tell you? A publisher friend of mine suggested it."

"Oh, that's right. What was his name again?"

"Robinson. Nick Robinson. In fact I just talked with him on the phone the other day. Checking up on his investment, I guess." Koster smiled. "He says he envies me, but every time I invite him to come over, he claims he's just too busy."

Lyman chewed steadily. It wasn't bad at all. "I wish I could do that," he said. "I don't mean writing a book." He laughed gruffly. "I could never do that. I mean being able to take all of that time away from work."

"You're not an architect. Besides, I was lucky." He took a sip of wine. "They could have said no. I did before, you know, to Robinson."

"What do you mean?"

"I mean he offered me the book and I said no. I was busy at the time with a condominium project."

"Why did you change your mind?"

Koster shrugged. "I didn't. The project was canceled at the last moment. So I had no reason to stay."

"No, I suppose not. Tell me about your friend Robinson. How long have you known him?"

"We went to college together, before I studied architecture in Switzerland. He was an amazing mathematician in his day, especially when it came to fractals.

Really inspired." Koster took another sip of wine. "You know, it's funny," he said. "I hadn't seen him since my wedding when we suddenly bumped into each other at a party being thrown by *Architectural Review*. He hadn't changed a bit. That's when he asked me about doing the book. He even remembered this paper on the cathedrals that I'd done in college. I'd forgotten all about it, but not Nick. He knew it practically by heart. I was flattered. They were giving him some sort of award, but all he kept talking about was my paper. That's Nick for you."

"Successful, is he?"

"Are you kidding? He made more money trading options in a single year at college than I've made my entire life. Believe me, the calculation was simple. Then he bought this broken-down old publishing house which everyone but his grandfather said would ruin him."

"Did it?"

"Of course not. He made another fortune. And if there's anyone who doesn't need more money, it's Nick Robinson."

"Did you ever think it was odd that he should suddenly turn up that way, after all those years."

"Odd? What do you mean?"

"I don't know. It's just that, well, you were tired with your job. You told me your marriage was finished. You were desperate to make a change, and suddenly this old friend pops back into your life, the answer to all your prayers."

"If you put it that way. But don't forget—I turned his proposition down."

"Yes, you did, didn't you. Until your project was suddenly canceled."

"Frankly, I was lucky Nick never found another writer for the job. If he had, I never would have met Mariane, or you, or Guy, or have had this chance to study the cathedrals." He took another bite and said, "This trip has really changed me, Nigel. And I don't just mean the book."

"I know what you mean."

"Do you? Well, what do you think of her? No, tell me truthfully."

Koster dreamed on about Mariane, breaking the thread. Lyman watched him eat between his sentences, the way he gestured, the way he exchanged his knife and fork at every mouthful.

Perhaps it was just coincidence, Lyman thought. Yet he remembered that the first time they had met, Koster had revealed it had been Robinson who'd written to the Minister of Culture, Charles Langelier, for authorization to excavate the cathedrals of Notre Dame. A good friend, he had called him. Wasn't Langelier the same man mentioned in the Countess de Rochambaud's letter? Were they all good friends? Lyman frowned. Or perhaps Koster had traveled to Amiens simply of his own accord, to escape the failure of his marriage. It was so difficult to set a boundary on conspiracy once you had been betrayed. That was what drew the faces in the dark. That was what made a suspect out of chance. But the fact remained—Koster had arrived. Suddenly Scarcella and Grabowski both had access to a bright, experienced architect. Jacques Tellier was underground but here, like a godsend, was an alternative.

Perhaps it was Grabowski who had found him first, armed with some knowledge of the Gospels which he had gleaned already from Pontevecchio. Perhaps, in order not to be involved directly, the archbishop had seized upon his cousin's interest in the Notre Dame cathedrals and was teasing him with legends, feeding him bits of information with the hope that he would gradually reveal the secret of the labyrinth.

Or perhaps Scarcella had discovered him, by

chance, as Lyman had. Perhaps Barbieri had seen Koster measuring the labyrinth, and followed him back to the Hôtel de la Paix with Lyman on that fateful evening.

In the end it didn't matter. By now Scarcella and Grabowski had doubtless come to some arrangement, as they had done through Pontevecchio so many years before. Lyman looked across the table. Koster was cutting at his osso buco with delicate concentration, and Lyman felt like shouting at him, shaking him awake. *Everybody's using you,* he thought with vicious honesty. And then the final truth—*including me.*

Lyman stabbed at his side order of spaghetti. It was cold already and he realized that they must have cooked it in the morning and used a microwave to heat it up. He began to cut it into pieces anyway, thinking as his hands moved that he had no choice now but to reconfirm his fiction. If he told Koster the truth, if he brought him inside, the American would realize that the man at the hotel had not just been an ordinary thief. And then there was Grabowski, a family member and a priest. Would Koster really help a stranger find the truth about his cousin, or would he simply leave France, out of loyalty, out of fear? It was too late. Lyman had no choice. The vagabond in London had failed to see Pontevecchio's killer and now there was but one solution left. He had to draw them out, both Scarcella and Grabowski, to trip them up by using the American, to buy the truth perhaps with the only thing they both found valuable—the Gospel of Thomas. Lyman looked up from his plate. "What? What did you say?"

"Like a detective."

"What detective?"

"I mean I feel like one with this missal and the Book of Thomas the Contender. All the clues point to the labyrinth, but I just can't seem to find the pattern."

"Oh, I see."

"And another thing. You know that Chaldean Cup I mentioned, the one the missal says is hidden underneath the Chartres cathedral?"

Lyman nodded. "What of it?"

"I swear I've seen that shape before. It's a perfect dodecahedron, a twelve-sided geometrical figure. And according to the missal, each side or pentagonal face is marked with a particular gemstone, six pairs in total, with one member of each pair of faces matched to its counterpart after a rotation of three tenths of a turn about the axis perpendicular to the two faces."

"Never mind," said Lyman.

"Maybe the countess will know. I wonder what she's like."

Indeed, thought Lyman, as he took another bite. Ever since he had telephoned Monsieur Clermont a few days earlier, he had been trying vainly to determine the Countess de Rochambaud's interest in the case. As curator of the Amiens Museum, Clermont had been the one responsible for sending her the missal. This in itself seemed perfectly natural. The countess was a recognized authority in the field. But Lyman found it difficult to understand why Clermont had parted with the document so soon, why he had been so eager to get rid of what was clearly a rare prize. Such magnanimous behavior deserved another look.

Lyman finished the last of his spaghetti. It tasted of wet chalk and he washed his mouth out with a solvent portion of red wine. But did the countess work for Scarcella? Was she with the Church, or was she yet another independent player? "You're so lucky, Joseph," Lyman finally said, wondering if his words seemed as false and obviously duplicitous to Koster as they did to him. "It's like a grand adventure, a treasure hunt." He paused, forcing a smile. "I just want you to know that if there's anything I can do, anything, just give me a shove and watch me go. Really."

"Thank you, Nigel. I appreciate that."

"I think when people face death together, it gives them a special closeness, like soldiers in the field. Perhaps you'll think I'm maudlin, Joseph, but ever since the robbery I've felt, well, almost responsible for you."

"You shouldn't feel that way. I'm the one who owes you."

"Maybe so, but I do, Joseph. I was wondering," he added. "Do you think I could come with you to Paris, to see the Countess? It's a lot to ask, I know, but perhaps I could take notes or something. I've never been to Paris."

Koster stopped eating. "I don't know, Nigel. The invitation's for one. What would I tell her?"

"Tell her I'm your friend. I am, aren't I?"

"Of course you are. That's not the point. Look, you could go to Paris anytime."

Lyman tried to look pathetic. This was wrong, all wrong, he thought. Each lie was like a paper cut. It had never bothered him before, yet he felt that this charade was somehow different. This time he was but one of many using Koster, each for his individual pantomime, each with his own amorphous end. There was the River Itchen stretching far before him, from Winchester to Amiens, but when she finally ran her course and all was said and done, which bank would he be standing on? Which side?

"You're right," Lyman said at last. "I could go later. But to be honest with you, Joseph, it's more than just Paris. My life isn't like yours. You're an international writer. You live in New York." He laughed softly. "I run a fishing tackle shop in a small suburban town."

"Sounds great to me."

"Oh, it is in some ways. I have a lot of things to be thankful for. I realize that. But excitement isn't one of them. That's why I came abroad. And now, ever since I met you, all manner of exciting things have started happening. That robbery. Your book. And now this gospel mystery. I've never met a countess in my life."

"Neither have I. Look, Nigel. I understand how you feel. If it were up to me I would say sure. It's the least I can do. But it isn't up to me. It's her invitation. Maybe if everything goes well, we can both go back there together another time."

Lyman nodded sullenly. "I understand. You're right, it would be senseless to jeopardize it all with me hanging on your shoulder."

Koster pushed his plate away. "Of course," he said. "That doesn't mean that I wouldn't appreciate you helping me out here, in Amiens."

Lyman brightened immediately. "Do you mean that?"

"Sure I do. Your French is pretty good. You could screen some historical documents for me, do measurements. That sort of thing. If you want to, that is."

Lyman nodded and he heard something tear inside him. "I suppose I should see that missal first then, the one your cousin the archbishop gave you. What are you doing after dinner?"

Koster laughed.

It was too late for coffee and neither relished a dessert so they asked the waiter for the bill and started back toward the hotel. A thin mist had rolled in from the river and the street fell in and out of view. The neon hotel sign was like a smear of lipstick on the collar of the night.

The concierge was nowhere to be seen, and Koster joked about the new security measures which had been posted on the bulletin board beside the counter. They climbed the stairs like tardy schoolchildren, laughing behind their hands, threatening to set the concierge's wife on one another at the slightest sound.

Lyman collapsed into a chair without even taking his coat off as soon as they entered Koster's room. Everything was so quiet now. Not a car stirred in the streets. Not a footfall. Only the mist rolled gently by, soundless outside the window. Quiet.

The American approached from across the room. Lyman turned, and there was but a moment's pause, like a single synapse sparking, and the hands of Joseph Koster became the stubby digits of Musel.

Lyman felt a chill run up his back. There was no doubt about it now. Captain Musel had sent a copy of the missal to Superintendent Hadley in London. Hadley, or whoever had killed him, had passed it on to Scarcella. Scarcella had given it to the archbishop, and the archbishop to Joseph Koster.

The American took another step. The stack of papers yawed in his arms, and the black brand shifted into view once more. No doubt at all. It was the same file, the photocopy sent to London by the Amiens Police, with the same three lines bisecting every corner like a growing crack along the edge.

Chapter XIV

KOSTER STOOD IN THE FRONT GAR-
den of the Rodin Museum, staring at the statue of
"The Thinker," wondering at the way in which the
great bronze head tipped forward on his fist, like the
blossom of a week-old rose. How many tourists had
walked by and seen within this touchstone, along this
troubled brow, a symbol of their own uncertainties?
The brochure said it was the face of Dante, pondering
his own inferno just across the garden—another sculpture carved by Rodin called "The Gates of Hell." But
only twelve years earlier a younger Joseph Koster had
stood exactly in this spot, and looked up at a face
which he had sworn then was a model of his own.

He had been studying architecture at the École
Polytechnique Federale in Lausanne. The school had
been his mother's notion, a respite from the termination of his mathematical career, a replacement really.
That had been the idea anyway, and he had worked
hard, trying to readjust to this second adolescence.
Then the school board had announced the yearly com-

petition, the medal with the little bear. The entire
school had spent a sleepless week pursuing what for
Koster was forgetfulness. He handed in his project with
reluctance, only to find—to his surprise—that he was in
the final running for the prize, and according to his
friends and teachers both, the likeliest to win. His entry
was the most inventive they had seen in years. All that
remained was the construction of a model, and the
medal would be his.

Koster looked down across the path. Despite the
daring of his plans, the model had been perfect in its
lifelessness alone, like a beautiful stillborn child with
the suitable number of fingers and toes.

He had left by train for Paris the following day,
without waiting to hear the results of the competition.
It was something he had been planning to do for weeks
in order to complete a paper for another class. And
upon his arrival, as he made his way through the Rodin
Museum, it had finally occurred to him that there was a
price to pay for his love of mathematics. It was like
having an alien god, or a synesthesia. Numbers were an
addiction to him, with their own demands and sacri-
fices, their own aesthetics, their own unfailing truth as
distant to the world as he was.

A sudden gust of wind picked up his reverie and
carried it away. Koster started to walk slowly around
the side of the museum toward the garden at the back.
Beech trees lined the path. Lovers sat on crescent
benches, holding hands. A thin old woman in a plain
black smock pushed a pram along the flagstones. There
was a man with a cherry wood pipe, a hippie and a pair
of young Americans who would never, ever speak to
one another again. Koster sighed. How would he ever
find the countess in this crowd? And what did a countess look like anyway?

That morning he had rushed down from the station
to the rue de Varennes only to discover through a
sharp, metallic intercom that the countess had already

gone out for her morning walk. He was to meet her in the garden of the Rodin Museum, just down that street and to the left. But now that he had finally arrived he realized the absurdity of the task. The garden was packed with people. Koster stopped. There. Over by the entrance to the museum. He craned his neck. Down the path, across the forecourt, a tall dark man was starting up the entrance steps.

Nick! he thought. It looked just like his publisher, Nick Robinson. But what the hell was he doing here?

Koster started back along the flagstone path toward the museum. The man on the steps hesitated for a moment, patting the pockets of his jacket as if he were searching for a key chain or a pack of cigarettes. Koster picked up his pace.

The man seemed to sense his approach. Although he was still a hundred yards away, Koster saw him hesitate at the entrance, and then turn slightly to the side as if he'd heard a sound behind him. There—for a moment—was the thick black hair, the strong nose, the Scottish jaw. Then Robinson turned suddenly away, and vanished through the door.

Koster ran across the forecourt, up the steps and into the museum. A party of Japanese tourists filled the foyer. He looked desperately about, but Robinson, or whoever it had been, was no longer in sight. Koster made his way straight through the crowd and into the next room. A pair of stone lovers embraced forever in one corner. It seemed impossible, Koster thought, but the man had simply disappeared.

He walked over to the window. On a nearby pedestal, a pair of hands reached up into the air. Koster could not help marveling at the delicacy of the arching fingers, the way they came together at the fingertips as if in prayer. The sculpture was called "The Cathedral." He recognized the form immediately. In prayer, the hands were shaped exactly like a Gothic arch. He was moving to examine them more closely, when he noticed the reflection of a man in the window glass. He turned, started to speak, and stopped.

It was that man who looked like Robinson. Or was it? He was wearing the same dark jacket, and from behind he looked a little like the publisher. Koster frowned. Wait a minute, he thought. This wasn't the man he'd spotted earlier. Now he couldn't be sure.

He turned and walked back through the foyer to the front door. It had grown warmer; the sun was trying to find an opening in the clouds. He moved along the path which circumscribed the large rococo museum.

It seemed a little silly now, he thought, to think Nick Robinson was even in Paris. He'd just talked to him on the telephone. And certainly, if Robinson had been planning to fly over, he would have called and let Koster know.

Koster dallied for a moment on the path. Barely fifteen yards away a blue-haired lady in a herringbone suit posed on a granite bench. She had an air about her which repelled intrusion. A brooch gleamed on her thin lapel. A string of pearls hung round her neck. She certainly looked like a countess.

"Excuse me. You," a woman said behind him.

Koster turned. He was blocking the flagstone path and the old woman with the pram was trying vainly to slip by. "Oh, sorry," he said.

"Well, come on," she added, plowing by him. "If we stop now he'll wake up, and that'll be the end of peace for all of us." She paused for barely a moment. "You *are* Joseph Koster, aren't you?"

A muffled cry rose from the pram and she looked down in horror. "You see, I told you." She shook the pram furiously. "My grandson. He spent the first month of his life strapped to a camel hump and now he's never happy." Then they were gone, the thin black back retreating with the pram along the path, like digits down a number line, and Koster in pursuit.

Her dress looked homemade. She had a slight limp in her left leg. Her pointed features jutted from the black scarf covering her head. "Countess de Rochambaud?" he said, as he finally matched her pace.

"Call me Irene. I rarely use the title unless I have to. But perhaps you like formality." She threw him a sidelong glance. Her eyes were shiny as pebbles at the bottom of a brook. "Yes, I'd say you do. No matter. Have you been to Paris before?"

Koster fought to keep up. "Three or four times. My family used to live in Italy. And I went to school in Lausanne for a year."

"Lausanne," the countess repeated. It was clear she found the idea distasteful. "But you're American, aren't you? Why did you travel so much?"

"My father's a cellist. He was with the Roman Philharmonic."

"Oh, I see." She stopped abruptly and pointed to a bench. "I think he's asleep," the countess said. "Let's risk it." She pushed the pram across the sloping lawn and sat down just as the baby began to cry again. In a moment she was on her feet, holding him in her arms, a mass of pastel blankets with a pink and pudgy fist. The baby continued crying. "Here, you try."

"No, really," Koster said, moving to defend himself. She laid the baby in his arms. Koster stepped back and there it was, the tiny face only a foot away, and in his own hands. The baby stopped crying. Koster wrapped his right arm underneath the baby's bottom for support.

"You see," she crooned. "Children know these things. Here. You can sit down now. Let's talk about the Notre Dame cathedrals."

"Was he really strapped to a camel's hump?"

The countess stretched her legs out and began to examine her ankles carefully, turning them. "I'm afraid so. My daughter Louise insisted on continuing the caravan to Ain Salah. She's impetuous that way. Always

has been." She pointed at the bundle in Koster's arms.
"Just like him. But, frankly, I wasn't too worried. I was
born near Tamanrasset myself and the Tuareg have
been delivering their own babies for twenty-five hundred years." She peered over the blanket at the baby's
face and Koster realized that the brusqueness and the
nonchalance disguised a deep abiding love. The smile
transformed her face, the smile of a clown, of a pre-
tender. "We're both a couple of damned Algerians."

The baby squealed halfheartedly and Koster found
himself rocking the bundle without thinking. A triangle
of sunlight rushed like a phalanx through the cool wet
grass, stopping at their feet. Somewhere a car honked.

"Monsieur Koster?"

"Yes."

"What is it you wanted to ask me?"

"Ask you? Oh, I'm sorry," he said. "The
cathedrals." He looked up. They had not spoken for
several minutes but he could not for the life of him
remember where the time had gone. "It was about the
Gnostics."

"The Gnostics," she repeated. "What about them?"

"I mean in relation to the Amiens cathedral."

The countess frowned. "Please, if you're talking
about the legend of the Book of Thomas the Contender, I wish you'd just come out and say it. I don't
have enough time left to waste it anymore." And then
with a lilt of her head she said, "As you can see."

He tried to protest but she raised a bony hand.
"Some people think the Gnostics were simply Christian
heretics—the most dangerous the Church has ever
faced, to be sure—but still an aberration, a splinter
group. They weren't," she said. "They were a grand
mélange. Many of their beliefs were actually Babylo-
nian or Chaldean, and many stem back even further to
the Indian subcontinent, to the Brahmans. It's important to remember that the time of greatest Gnostic de-
velopment coincided with the opening of the trade

routes between the Greco-Roman world and the Far East."

Koster slipped the baby to his other arm. "But what about the cathedrals? What do the Gnostics have to do with them?"

"There is a line of knowledge," she replied, "a tradition if you will, which stretches from the Babylonians to the Hebrews and beyond. Even Genesis fifteen refers to how the Lord brought Abram out of Ur of the Chaldees. This tradition is a system of numbers.

"In ancient Babylon, astronomy was the province of the priests, the magi. They believed that numbers derived from planets and stars were divinely ordained. Because of the seven stars of the Pleiades, for example, the number seven became especially fortuitous. Just as the number forty, which corresponded to the number of days in the rainy season when the Pleiades disappeared, eventually developed into a number symbolizing deprivation."

"Like astrology."

"That's right," the countess said. "It was a way of fixing man in nature, the subjective in the objective. And when it combined later with the number theories of Pythagoras, it had a lasting impression on western numerology. Even the Old Testament is full of number symbols. It's no accident that the feast of Lent is forty days long. So, for that matter, was Christ's journey in the wilderness. And all of the medieval masons were familiar with these number systems. They knew them because of the medieval emphasis on Pythagoras and the Neo-Platonists. And they also knew them because they had their own particular interest in numbers."

"What do you mean?"

"In the Middle Ages masons never stayed in one place for very long. They traveled about from one project to the next, working a few months here, a few there. But the roads were very dangerous. Bandits were everywhere. In the end they learned not to carry money with them on their journeys, but to rely instead on fellow masons for food and shelter. Soon a guild or brotherhood was born. What had been a way of protecting one's person became a means of maintaining trade secrets. Masons only passed their knowledge on to fellow masons. So it was that when the Crusaders brought back new number lore from the East, the masons were quick to absorb it, and to pass it along—in secret. The line of the tradition spanned from the Magian Brotherhood in Babylon, through the Gnostics and the Manicheans, past the Paulicians and Catharists to the Templars and Freemasons of today." The countess seemed to freeze. Her bright brown eyes focused on the museum in the distance. "Did you come here by yourself, Monsieur Koster?" she said tartly.

"What's that?" Koster followed her gaze, half expecting to see Nick Robinson hovering somewhere in the shadows. But all he could see was an elderly gentleman with a handlebar mustache, and a man in an olive-colored raincoat reading a newspaper. "Yes, why do you ask?"

"Oh, blast," she said, rising quickly to her feet. "It's Monsieur Cosell. He's always following me about."

"Who?"

"That old man with the whiskers, in the gray coat. A friend of the admiral, my late husband. We'd better leave." She took the baby from his arms. "Would you like to join me for tea at my house?"

"Thank you." Koster looked back up at the old man across the lawn. He didn't seem very threatening. He wasn't even turned in their direction. "Are you sure—" he began to say when he realized that the countess and the pram had vanished from the path. Koster stood up. There they were, moving behind the brambles toward the brick wall at the back. "Wait for me," he shouted, dashing after them.

There was a kind of outdoor stove and chimney by the brick wall at the rear of the garden. It had probably

been used for burning leaves, Koster thought, back in
the days when the museum had been the Hôtel Biron.
The wall was covered with the season's leftovers, tena-
cious vine and brambles. The countess was standing
beside an old, black iron gate set in the brick wall.
Through it Koster could see a pair of sagging basket-
ball hoops and the glass face of a school. The gate was
chained and padlocked.

"Give me a hand," she ordered as he approached.
"Help me lift it over."

"Surely he can't be that bad. Why don't we just go
out the way we came in? I'll talk to him."

"You don't know him as I do. Ever since Jean died
—my husband, the admiral—he's been after me. First
he wanted to buy that piece of property in Cannes.
Then he wanted to discuss it over lunch. Then it was a
weekend at his home in Brittany. Well, don't just stand
there. Climb over." She pointed at the iron gate.

Koster began to look for a foothold in the wall.
"Couldn't we get arrested for this?"

The countess smiled, thrusting her head forward
like a raven. "You worry a great deal, don't you, Monsieur Koster? This is the Lycée Victor Duruy. The
headmistress and I are old friends. Stop. Right there."

Koster was poised on top of the wall, one leg raised
up to scramble over to the other side. "What is it?"

"Can you see him across the lawn? You should be
high enough."

He stared out through the oak trees toward the rococo museum. The old man was standing with his back
to them, talking to a woman in a yellow dress. "I think
we're safe. He hasn't budged. Wait a minute." Koster
noticed another figure approaching in the shadow of a
hedge. It was the young man in the olive-colored raincoat. "Someone else is coming."

The countess tapped his shoe with her bony fingers.
"Over you go then."

He slipped to the playground on the other side.

The countess lifted the pram and he thrust his hands through the gate to help her swing it up and over the wall. She was remarkably fit for an old woman, Koster thought. He was panting while she seemed spry as ever. As soon as he had lowered the pram in safety she hiked her smock up a little and slipped through the narrow gap between the gate post and the gate. Koster stepped back. The space seemed barely wide enough to admit a child and it was only then that he realized just how thin she really was, the barest edge of a woman.

She pushed the pram furiously across the playground. The baby was laughing. Koster rushed after them, along a gravel path which led between two buildings. One, a hulking mass of brick and concrete, appeared to be a science laboratory. Dozens of teenagers waved at them from behind their Bunsen burners. The countess was obviously a familiar figure. She waved back and Koster felt obliged to follow suit. Suddenly the path came to a halt beside a huge green double door, set in the wall which marked the boundary of the school. The countess unlatched a separate smaller portal and swung it open. The boulevard des Invalides stretched just beyond the opening. Koster could see the crown of the Eglise du Dôme across the rooftops, Napoleon's final conquest of the material world.

"This way," the countess said, pushing the pram through. The boulevard was almost empty. Koster followed close behind. A street sweeper dressed in green work clothes prodded a stream of water through the gutter with his broom, the long brown switches so well bundled, so disguised that even as he passed a yard away Koster could not tell if they were plastic or real wood.

The rain fell onto Lyman's face as he looked up from the drab stone of the storefront to the single bruise blue thundercloud above. The rue Victor Hugo shivered in the sunlight. There seemed to be but one cloud over Amiens, surrounded by a spiteful rim of endless blue, and he wondered what each raindrop had reflected on its journey from the Caribbean to the coast of France, how many miles of ocean, how many other faces looking up. The door opened.

"Yes?" A young girl in a corduroy dress leaned a pointed hip against the door.

"Mr. Randall to see Monsieur Duval."

She smiled, fluttering her hands. "Yes, Mr. Randall. We've been expecting you. Please, come in."

The girl ushered him into a waiting room decorated in a floral wallpaper with the same red pheasant bouncing off each wall. Lyman sat down on a modern metal chair while the girl disappeared to find Duval.

The office appeared to be the first floor of a private house. Lyman could smell the scent of freshly baked croissants. He lit a cigarette and noticed a magazine open beside him on a sidetable. There was a picture of a dam being built in Amazonia, a human anthill, and beside it a list of grim statistics. Forty-nine men had died in the construction of the dam, and of them six had been full-blooded Incan Indians. The caption read: *Sacrificed to the God of Engineering?* Lyman tried to imagine the bodies hidden somewhere in the concrete wall, frozen for all time like a nest of ants in amber. He closed the magazine. The girl had returned. Duval could see him now.

This time she led him down a corridor toward the rear of the house. The walls were lined with drawings of barns and turn-of-the-century farmhouses. The girl knocked on a side door and Lyman heard a voice respond.

Charles-Philip Duval stood like a wrestler on the other side of his desk, his arms thrust out for the embrace, his back hunched over, the bull neck wagging side to side. "Mr. Randall," he said, rushing from behind his desk and dragging Lyman in. "A pleasure. Please, sit down."

Duval's office was spacious and flooded with light, despite the grayness of the day. One wall was covered with more drawings: garages and a row of shops; a stadium roundabout; and even the cathedral and the Bishop's Palace. A draftsman's table tilted in one corner. Monsieur Duval had already sat down behind his desk. He had a wide pleasant face, and a tiny well-clipped mustache which balanced out the tonsure yawning like an overturned sea urchin on his head. Lyman pulled up another chair. "Sorry I'm so late," he said. "The train."

"Think nothing of it, Mr. Randall. So," Duval said, rubbing his hands. "What can Duval Construction do for you?"

"First I must insist that my company's plans be held in the strictest confidence. Property is already dear enough in Amiens."

Duval nodded firmly. "Of course. I'd be more than happy to sign a nondisclosure form."

"That won't be necessary. At least, not yet. I've heard a great deal about your company, Monsieur Duval, and most of it I must say is bloody impressive. However," Lyman added, slapping one hand against the other as he had seen Chief Superintendent Cocksedge do a thousand times, "this particular project is extremely important to my company. Large sums of money are at stake."

"Mr. Randall, I would not be in business today if I failed to protect my clients' interests."

"Of course." Lyman hesitated for a moment, and then said, "Frankly, I'm a little surprised. You see, I thought when I made this appointment that I would be speaking with a Maurice Duval. Perhaps he should be present also."

Duval clasped and unclasped his hands. "I'm afraid my son is no longer with the company."

"Oh, really?"

"Not for some time now."

"I see." Lyman waited but Duval remained impassive. "I heard that he was working on the Bishop's Palace. Our plans require a similar kind of renovation and I was hoping to ask him a few questions. You wouldn't happen to have his number, would you?"

"I'm afraid not."

Lyman nodded slowly. "Of course, the project would remain yours, your company's. I'm only looking for some advice."

"Mr. Randall," Duval said at last, leaning back in his chair. "My son is dead. He was killed in a car accident in Austria seven months ago."

Lyman turned away. He closed his eyes for a moment and suddenly there was George, out of nowhere, his muzzle frothed with blood, falling in slow motion to one side, and then the car with Hadley's broken head against the windshield, the horn blaring. "I'm so sorry," he heard himself reply. "I had no idea."

Duval stood behind his desk, looking down. "But I do have some sketches of our work on the Hôtel Bulot, if they'll be helpful to you. And the Bishop's Palace," he said, pointing at the wall. He hovered for an instant more and then started for the door. "Would you excuse me for a moment? I'll get them."

Lyman rose awkwardly. "Of course," he said, but Duval was already gone. Lyman put his hands in his trouser pockets, feeling—in the space between his fingertips—an accident, a coincidence, an incidental tragedy. These were the names that Chief Inspector Cocksedge had employed to score the ransacking of his flat in London—and the Lemur had agreed, wholeheartedly.

Lyman moved over toward the drawings on the wall. There it was: the Amiens cathedral, with the Winter Chapel and the Bishop's Palace to the side. He studied the plans. Somewhere in those walls lay the

hiding place where Jacques Tellier had found the Book
of Thomas the Contender. A title in block letters swam
across the top: ÉCOLE SUPÉRIEURE DE COMMERCE ET
D'ADMINISTRATION DES ENTERPRISES. So, Lyman realized,
they were turning the Bishop's Palace into a trade
school. The irony warmed him. Guy had told him that
even in the Middle Ages the cathedral had been the
town's commercial center, a gathering place for the
guilds. He smiled and it was then that he first saw
the photograph, off to the side, almost behind another
drawing. Charles-Philip Duval was sitting at the head
of the table wearing a tuxedo. Beside him sat a young
man Lyman knew must be Maurice, his son. He had
the same eyes, the same wrestler's slouch, the same
tuxedo even. And beside him, underneath the arm
which he had thrown so casually across her naked
shoulders, a younger Mariane looked up, the bald surprise apparent in her eyes. The flash caught her mouth
open in the middle of a laugh, and for a moment as the
scene came clear and Lyman recognized the way she
leaned the slightest distance toward Maurice, he was
convinced she laughed at him.

"Mr. Randall."

Lyman turned. Duval stood right behind him with a
mass of blue-lined drawings in his arms. "See anything
which interests you?" he said.

"Your work is clearly very professional, Monsieur
Duval." Lyman shifted his weight uncomfortably. "But
that really isn't the issue, is it? If it were, I wouldn't be
here." He paused again.

"Yes?"

"What I mean is, we know you have the required
technical skills for the job but—and I hope you won't
misunderstand me—we are a little concerned about,
how shall I put it, the finances. You see, we heard a
rumor some time ago that your firm was involved in
some kind of financial impropriety. Now," Lyman
added with a fragile laugh, "I know only too well how

these things start sometimes—the competition and all that. But we would certainly feel more comfortable if we were to hear, directly from you, that all this talk about missing money and such is just an exaggeration, with no basis in fact."

Duval smiled and his mustache narrowed, line-thin. "I'm afraid I don't have any idea what you're talking about."

"Surely you don't deny there was some kind of theft?"

"Mr. Randall. I don't deny anything. Why should I? I have yet to be confronted with anything substantive to deny. Please. You may run your business as you choose. But don't ask me to run mine on innuendo."

"I see. Well, I suppose that's that," Lyman answered wearily. "I'm afraid that until I can report to my superiors that all this talk of missing money is as you say—an innuendo—we will not be able to finalize our plans. I can only add that this particular contract will be worth in excess of eight hundred thousand pounds. Consider that, Monsieur Duval. All we seek is the truth of the matter."

"I'll keep that in mind, Mr. Randall." Duval slipped the plans he had been carrying onto his desk and offered his hand to Lyman. Lyman shook it firmly.

"Good day, Monsieur Duval," Lyman said. "I'll be in touch." Duval's hand was trembling. Lyman wanted to say something, to end the conversation on a different note, to tell him that he understood, but the ordinary symbols seemed so distant, so inadequate. "I was sorry to hear" is such a pale beginning to a consolation. What do you say to a man who has lost his future by accident?

"It's only me," the countess said, as she leaned against the intercom. The door of the apartment building buzzed and she shoved it open with her shoulder, dragging the pram in with a flagging hand. Koster followed close behind. They made their way through the apartment foyer but instead of turning off to take the elevator, the countess pushed the pram right through the hall until they reached a set of white French doors which looked out onto a little lawn and garden in the back. "The city has grown up around us," the countess said. She pulled a key out of her pocket and waved it absently. "Welcome to my little island in the sea."

Koster raised a hand to block the light and peered out through the doors. The house was more an island in an atoll than in the sea, he thought, and it certainly wasn't little. Three stories with a pair of cupolas at each end, it was built as if the architect had only planned one half and put a mirror on the edge to make the rest. Both sides were identical, and yet there was a freedom in its uniformity, a whimsical simplicity: light stone, white paint, clean lines. A gravel path encircled the house, and beyond that a ring of well-clipped lawn. It was a natural border before the apartment buildings which loomed five stories all around.

The countess swung the doors open and a dog came bounding out of nowhere, not quite a Newfoundland but something just as large. A flint of a word from the countess and he withdrew. They crossed the lawn onto the gravel path and Koster noticed an old woman standing in the doorway of the house. She had a shoe in one hand and a brush in the other, and was dressed almost exactly like the countess. They looked like a pair of nuns together, Greek women grieving. At first, as she brushed her shoe and chatted, Koster was certain that the woman was a maid or servant of some kind. She asked about the morning walk and brushed. She commented upon the weather. Then, with a bang, the shoe dropped to the ground and Koster realized it was hers. She slipped her naked foot inside. Finally, the countess turned and said, "My sister, Nicole."

"How do you do," Koster answered with a bow.

The woman laughed, floating back into the house. Koster looked up. Why hadn't he seen it before? There was more than a similarity. The countess was thinner but their faces, that curve of the nose, those penetrating almost amber eyes were badges of a common ancestry. The countess pushed the pram inside. Koster followed with the dog, panting and chomping, close behind.

The corridor wound by a set of stairs into a spacious entrance hall. Nicole pushed the pram into the kitchen and out of sight, while the countess showed Koster into the dining room.

A massive oval table stood at the center of the room. The ceiling was more than thirty feet high and a single painting punctuated the far wall, a field of flowers pieced together by Monet. The countess took Koster by the hand and led him through a curtained entrance on the other side. He could feel her bony fingers in his, fleshless as talons and yet gentle, delicate.

The next room was even larger than the last. The furniture was Louis XV, lithe and light with but a trifle too much ornament. An ice green satin sofa beckoned. She ignored it, moving past a granite fireplace stuffed with white birch and ready for a match. The paintings here were more pastel, the same colors as the Kurdistan below their feet.

The countess continued to a sliding door which opened onto a room almost the mirror image of the last, and Koster realized that the house had really once been two, then joined together later. Here was the same fireplace, the same alcove, the same garden doors. But unlike the last room, this one was decorated as an office or a study.

An imposing desk stood squarely to one side, the top covered with papers like a layer of fresh snow. Oil paintings of stallions leaned from the walls. One was called "Pi," another "Nisaba." There were cut flowers

in the corner and on one side what appeared to be a
water clock, all brass and moving parts. The countess
opened a door beside it and Koster saw a staircase
leading up.

"My daughter Louise and her husband," the countess said, "live in the other wing." She began to climb
the steps. "After Jean died, they asked me to move
back to Paris. They thought it would be safer for me. I
don't know. I used to live here as a young girl." She
turned and winked at Koster. "Paris was fun in those
days. Of course, you're too young to remember all that.
But there were some nights." She paused, listening.
"Now each memory is like a fresh glass of champagne."

The staircase turned. Koster noticed that the steps
here were uncarpeted. A little triangular window
looked out onto the garden. The staircase turned once
more and suddenly they were on another landing. The
countess moved ahead, wrestling with the knot of her
scarf. Then, without warning, she stopped and pushed
against a narrow wooden door just off the hall. It
opened slowly, inch by inch, onto a kind of library.
Koster followed her inside.

Two walls were packed entirely with books. There
must have been at least ten thousand titles, Koster
guessed. A formidable collection. The other two walls
were bare except for a black-and-white photograph of a
young man in uniform, and a tiny watercolor of a des-
ert scene. There were no chairs, only a series of
brightly-colored carpets on the floor, and a few pillows.
A window brought the day in. The countess leaned
against one of the walls and slowly lowered herself to
the floor. "Sit down," she said, still struggling with her
scarf. It had fallen behind her head and Koster could
see her hair for the first time, trimmed short and white
as fog. "Please, sit down, Monsieur Koster," she repeated.

Koster sat. The countess finally undid the knot in

her scarf and began to fold it carefully in her lap. "Have you written other books, Monsieur Koster?"

He shook his head. "No, this is my first. But I've done smaller pieces, articles, that sort of thing."

"Why did you choose to write about the Notre Dame cathedrals?"

"Actually my publisher suggested the idea. I'd just done another piece for an architectural magazine and he liked it."

"You're an architect?"

"That's right."

"Are you familiar with Alberti and his theory of harmonic balance?"

"Sounds familiar," Koster lied.

The countess smiled. "Then I'm sure you know that his entire aesthetic construct was based on Vitruvius. And Vitruvius," she added, "on the geometry of the Neo-Platonists, on Pythagoras's system of musical harmony. Proportion and balance. Leonardo's man in the circle and the square."

"The Renaissance was never my strong suit."

"Well, it doesn't matter," she said. "It's the tradition that's important. Numbers meant more to the cathedral builders of the Middle Ages than they do to us today."

"What do you mean?"

"The cathedral builders, that brotherhood of master masons I told you about at the park, did not remain a business fraternity very long, Monsieur Koster. Over time they became concerned with the more metaphysical aspects of their trade. They developed rituals and regalia. As more members of the middle class became involved, there came to be a new kind of mason—a Speculative Mason, instead of an operative mason or journeyman who worked with his hands.

"Eventually the fraternity began to attract some notable members. Your first President, Washington, is reported to have been a Mason. Jefferson and Benjamin

Franklin were. Many lodges grew to be extremely political and wealthy, the founders of democracy. That was
why the Church considered them such a threat to the
pope in Rome." She smiled wryly. "In truth, they were
never at odds with Christianity. All Masons are deist,
believing in one God. But to them it doesn't matter
what you call Him. Buddhists can be Masons, and they
are. So can Moslems. In some lodges the Koran is used
as frequently as the Christian Bible. Yet many Masons
harbor special feelings for the Gnostics because they
share a common heritage."

"Are these the same Masons I've been reading
about in the press?"

"I beg your pardon?"

"The I Four, that scandal in Italy with the Vatican
Bank."

The countess drew her legs together at her side.
"I'm afraid that each thing has its shadow, Monsieur
Koster. Rome had its Carthage. Your country has the
Soviets. And Freemasonry has its I Four. But please
don't look on Scarcella and his pseudolodge as exam-
ples of real Masonry." She paused and began to rub
her ankle absentmindedly. "Of course, this is all a bit
of a diversion from my normal studies, but I know that
there are some who still observe the fundamental rules
of Masonry."

"Well, that's what the papers said."

"You have a remarkable memory, Monsieur Koster.
That incident occurred a long time ago."

Koster shrugged. "Maybe, but I still don't see how
it applies. The legend says the gospel's hiding place is
somehow linked up with the labyrinth."

"Numerically."

"Right, numerically. But what does that mean?"

The countess shifted slowly to her feet. "The Masons used numbers in a variety of ways during the Middle Ages," she said, "all of which were based on
Pythagoras's system and the one developed in Chal-

dea." She pulled a volume from a pile of books on the floor. "I put these aside this morning when I knew you were coming. Let's see now." She began flipping pages. "According to Emile Mâle here, the Masons considered twelve the number of the universal Church. Three was the number of the Trinity, and therefore, of the soul. Four, on the other hand, was the number of the elements and the four corners of the earth. It symbolized the body of the material world." She paused for a moment.

"Here it is. He says, 'To multiply three by four is in the mystic sense to infuse matter with spirit, to proclaim the truths of the faith to the world, to establish the universal Church of which the apostles are the symbol.' You see? It was no accident that the apostles picked another man to maintain the body of twelve after Judas Iscariot died. It was preordained." She closed the book.

"So the number twelve could mean the gospel's hidden under a statue of the twelve apostles. Is that it?"

The countess smiled. "I suppose it's possible," she said. "But frankly it could point to any number of things. The apostles are represented throughout the Amiens cathedral, in both stone and glass. It might as easily be a form of *gematria.*"

"*Gematria?* What's that?"

"It's an ancient system of transforming numbers into letters, and vice versa. Like a code." She replaced the first book and pulled another volume from the pile. "The Gnostics were especially fond of using it in spiritual exegesis. Here." She pointed to a page. "Casper Lewis says the word *gematria* first appeared around A.D. 200. But Farbridge claims that even earlier, Sargon of Babylon ordered that the wall of Khorsabad be made equivalent to the value of his name. Christ was known among the Gnostics as eight-oh-one from the word dove, or as eight-eight-eight from Jesus."

"Hold it a minute," Koster said. "Go back a page. What's that?"

The countess turned the pages one by one. "What's what?"

"That," he said, pointing at a drawing in the book. "Right there."

"Oh, that's another example of *gematria*. It's called an *abraxas*. They're the work of Basilidian Gnostics. Quite valuable. Here," she said, handing him the book. She walked across the room and knelt down beside a small wooden box on the floor. "I have a few here in my collection. They're found all over the Mediterranean world, especially in Egypt and Italy. *Abraxas* stands for God, you see, because the letters of the word in Greek notation make up the number three hundred sixty-five—the days in a year. I suppose it's a remnant of Zoroastrianism. Anyway," she said, "they used to carve the word *abraxas* on stones and other objects and then hang them around their necks as talismans."

Her hand dipped in the box and Koster saw the stone medallion suspended from her fingers, spinning on its leather thong.

"What's the matter, Monsieur Koster? What's wrong?"

He shook his head. "I've seen one of those things before. In Amiens."

"An *abraxas?*" The countess looked shocked.

"I think it was the same." He pulled it gently from her hand.

"Who had it?"

"A friend of mine. It was a present from her boyfriend. Her ex-boyfriend."

"Well, perhaps it was just a curio. Perhaps he bought it for her somewhere else."

"Yeah, maybe," Koster said as the night returned and Mariane stood before him once again, naked with her arms across her breasts, smoking her cigarette by the window so that her brother wouldn't smell the smoke, tossing the burning butt into the street when she had finished. Had that one act of guile been just a symbol too, the number of betrayal? Koster shook his head, trying vainly to dislodge the thought. It was just a gift, he told himself. And yet, what did he know about this other man, Maurice, except what little Guy had told him? Mariane had never talked about her past affairs and Koster had always assumed that her silence was just a matter of tact, of shyness even.

The countess took the *abraxas* from his hand. "It's certainly worth investigating, if you have the time."

They sat back down on the pillows and she continued talking about the Gnostics and cathedrals. Koster listened patiently, trying to remember all she said, but the image of that small medallion would not go away— hard stone and strangely carved, pressed deep within the softness of Mariane's breasts.

In half an hour Nicole appeared at the door with a message that the minister of culture, Charles Langelier, was on the telephone. Koster saw his opportunity. Despite the protests of the two sisters, he insisted he was anxious to return to Amiens, to apply the knowledge he had obtained. The countess led him down the stairs and out through the entrance hall.

"The minister," he said.

"Oh, he can wait," she answered with a sour pinching of her lips. "Please come and see me again. Any time."

Koster hesitated in the doorway. Down the hall, Nicole stood with the telephone receiver dangling like a hanged man from her fingertips. The countess leaned a little closer, and took his hand up in an awkward grasp, their fingers overlapping. "And please be careful," she said with a smile. Their hands unlocked, and she was gone.

Chapter XV

AMIENS
September 23rd, 1983

CHEZ MARIUS WAS A BEER HALL ON rue Ernest Cauvin, just across the way from the Amiens Cinéma II. A few desultory parasols sprouted along the street but it was still too early for the dinner crowd, and the rain had driven everyone inside. The jukebox blared a Benny Goodman medley. The orange candle-light slipped through the windows on the sliding sound of trombones, clarinets and trumpets. Koster hovered in the doorway, taking in the mock Bavaria, the bar and countless beer mugs hanging, the posters of the same Germanic girls with the same come-hither smiles he had seen already in a thousand New York bars.

"Joseph! Joseph, up here."

He looked up. Mariane was leaning over a wooden railing, waving at him from the second landing. He waved back and started up the steps.

There were only three tables on the second landing, and Mariane stood alone beside the railing, wearing a pair of blue jeans and a baggy white wool sweater. Koster kissed her on both cheeks. "You look great," he said.

She sat down and he knew immediately that something was amiss. She wrapped her fingers round the beer mug on the table and began to turn it slowly, without speaking.

"What's the matter, Mariane?"

She shrugged. "I don't know."

Then she looked up and there it was—the lie.

This is how it starts, he thought. From white to black and all that grayness in between. "Something's bothering you," he said, sitting down beside her.

"It's probably nothing, Joseph. Really." She took a sip of her beer. "Don't you want a drink?"

"It can wait."

Mariane frowned. "All right, it's about Nigel Lyman."

"What about him?"

"He's been asking a lot of questions around town."

"Of course he has. He's helping me research my book."

A young waiter in a black vest appeared at the top of the stairs. He was carrying a tray full of foaming steins. Koster called him over. The waiter approached and immediately began to set two beers on the table before them. "Wait a minute," Koster said. He turned to Mariane. "Did you order these?"

"Compliments of the gentleman at the bar," the waiter said.

Koster looked down across the railing to the main floor below. "Talk of the devil," he said. Nigel Lyman was leaning up against the bar, his hand aloft and toasting. Koster toasted back. "Come on up, Nigel," he shouted.

"No, Joseph, wait." Mariane grabbed him firmly by the wrist.

"No what? What's wrong with you today, Mariane?"

"There's nothing wrong with me," she said defensively. "It's him."

"Who, Nigel?"

"If that's his real name. Be careful, Joseph. You shouldn't trust him."

Koster looked deep into her eyes, searching for an answer, a temporary truth. "Why not?" he said. "What's he going to do, steal my book idea? He saved my life, didn't he?"

"I hope I'm not barging in on you two lovebirds." Nigel Lyman climbed the last few steps and paused to catch his breath.

"Not at all," Koster said. "Have a seat."

"The concierge at the hotel said I might find you here. Hello, Mariane. Don't you look wintry in that pullover."

"Monsieur Lyman."

"I don't mind telling you," Lyman said. "I've been on pins and needles all day long waiting for you to come back from Paris. How did it go? How was the countess?" He pulled out a chair and settled down.

Koster described his journey into town. He told them how he thought he'd seen Nick Robinson at the Rodin Museum. He talked about the countess and their quick escape across the garden gate. Lyman peppered him with questions. What had made him think it was his publisher? Who was Cosell, the man with the whiskers? Who was the fellow in the raincoat? Even the consulates, which he had passed along the rue Varennes, intrigued the Englishman. He asked the oddest questions.

As Koster recounted his conversation with the countess, he kept trying to catch Mariane's attention, but she would not meet his eyes. She was looking at Lyman. Then, as she took her beer up for another sip, Koster finally said the word *abraxas*. It acted on her like an incantation. She blanched and stiffened in her seat. She put her glass down and began to rifle through her purse, hunting for a cigarette.

"Mariane."

"Yes, Joseph."

Even Lyman seemed to sense that there was something wrong. "Don't you wear a pendant like that around your neck?"

"You know," she answered with a bubble of a laugh. "I was just thinking the same thing. But I'm sure mine's different. I mean, where would Maurice get the money?" She turned away, caught on the barb of her own words. "Would anyone like another beer?"

"Why don't you let me see it for a second? Maybe he picked up a bargain."

She looked at Lyman. Then she ran her hands around her neck, under her long brown hair, and dexterously unclasped the chain. For a moment, as she slipped it through, the pendant caught on the collar of her sweater and Koster could see the small medallion like a stain against the wool.

"Is it an *abraxas?*" Lyman said.

Koster picked it up. It looked so simple in his hand. A small ridge about the edge, and a string of rough Greek letters running through. Less than an inch across. "Yes," he said. "Just like the one the countess had." He gave it back to Mariane. "Why don't you tell us about it?"

She clutched the small medallion in her hand. "Maurice gave it to me."

"Where did he get it?" Lyman asked.

She glanced at him for a moment and then turned back to Koster. "Joseph. I don't want to talk about it."

"Why not?"

"I just don't."

"Mariane, this could be very important," Lyman said. "This could be the clue we've been looking for."

"Important to whom, Monsieur Lyman?"

"What do you mean? For the book. For Joseph."

"I'd still rather not talk about it."

Koster took her by the same hand in which she held the medallion. "What's the matter with you, Mariane? Don't you care?"

"Please, Joseph."

"No, answer me."

"I promised."

"Promised who? Maurice? What did you promise him?"

"Joseph, don't!"

"Is he more important then? Is that it?"

"He found it," she said at last. "There." She took another sip of beer. "Are you happy now?" She looked at Lyman. "One of his men found it. Is that a crime?"

Lyman shrugged. Then he leaned back slowly in his chair. "Perhaps."

"He's right," Koster said. "You may be at risk just wearing that thing if it was stolen."

"It wasn't stolen. It was found. How many times do I have to tell you?"

"Just once," said Lyman.

Mariane sighed. She dropped a crumpled pack of Marlboros on the table. There was only one cigarette left. She pulled it out of the pack, straightened it carefully, and slipped the filter into a corner of her mouth. Lyman offered her a light. "It was during Christmas," she said. "Two years ago. That's when they started turning up—the *abraxas.*"

"Where?" Lyman put in.

"At the Bishop's Palace. Maurice was doing the renovation. First it was one, then three, then a whole pile of them. The *abraxas,* I mean. But Maurice didn't hear about them until later. His men found them digging in the basement of the south wing."

She took another drag off her cigarette. Then she reached out and crushed the empty pack of Marlboros in her hand. "One of the workers—Pierre, I think— went to an antique dealer on the rue Dupuis. Jacques

Tellier. That was the dealer's name. Tellier told him that the *abraxas* were worth some money and suddenly everybody started going crazy looking for them. No one would do their work. They were all treasure hunting.

"It didn't take long before Maurice heard about it. He went to see Tellier himself." She shook her head. "That was the biggest mistake of his life. I never liked that man. There was something about him. I don't know. Like those fishes at the bottom of the sea, the ones without color, the ones that never see the light . . ."

"What happened then?" said Koster.

Mariane unclasped her hand and the pack of Marlboros rolled out onto the table, opening like the blossom of a paper rose. "Tellier had already been to jail. At least, that's what they said. It's hard to keep secrets in a town this small. Anyway, he told Maurice the *abraxas* were worth as much as fifteen thousand francs."

"How much?" Lyman asked.

"Fifteen thousand. He also told him that they could lead to a much greater treasure, something worth millions." Mariane smiled. "Maurice was always talking about leaving Amiens and moving to Paris. He kept saying how he wanted to marry me, but that we had to wait until he'd made enough money." She looked up suddenly at Koster and said, "That was a long time ago."

Koster nodded. "Go on."

"Then something happened. He and Tellier had a falling out. I don't know what started it. Maurice suspected Tellier was cheating him, I know that. One night Maurice came over while Guy was out. He told me that he'd had it with his father and the company. He'd been drinking. I tried to calm him down but it was like the world was riding on his heels. He started complaining

about Tellier again, about the money." She took a final
drag off her cigarette and stamped it out.

"Even now, after all this time, I don't know what I
said. It's funny, but I just can't remember. I'm sure it
was about Tellier. I'm sure I asked him to forget about
the money, the *abraxas*. I'm sure I did." She looked at
Koster and he felt his ribs give way. "I never saw him
again," she said.

"What happened to him?" asked Lyman.

"He went to Charles-Philip's and took some money,
some checks out of the safe. Not very much." She
shrugged. "Enough to get him out of town, I guess."

"What kind of safe?" said Lyman.

"I'm sorry?"

"Was it a combination safe, or did it require a
key?"

"I don't know. Key, I think. Why?"

"Was anything else taken?"

"No, that was it. Except for his passport of course. I
didn't hear from him for months. Not a word. Then I
got a telegram from Kitzbühel, in Austria. Actually it
was sent to Charles-Philip, his father, but all it said was
'I'm sorry. All is well.' He never wrote to me." She
lifted the *abraxas* and fastened it about her neck. "The
Amiens police were the ones who told us about the
accident. It was in March, earlier this year. It happened
in a town called Lech. He was hit by a car. The report
said he'd been drinking." Another laugh slipped out,
brittle. "I suppose that you could say he liked to drink.
It helped him relax. But he was never nasty to anyone.
And he loved my brother. He really did. He was always
kind to Guy."

Koster nodded and took her by the hand.

"They sent his body back, what was left of it. We
buried him at the chapel of St. Roch. It was really a
very nice service." She looked up. Her eyes were filled
with tears. "You're not going to talk about this to anyone, are you? I promised Charles-Philip. He was al-

ways so afraid of a scandal, of people talking." She laughed. "Isn't that funny? The real scandal was that they never did. Just a few of the right words and Maurice might have never left."

"I'm sure it wasn't your fault," Koster said.

Lyman coughed. "Were you the last to see him before he left Amiens?"

"No, I don't think so. Charles-Philip said he stopped off at the Bishop's Palace. The night watchman saw him leave."

"What does that have to do with anything?" Koster said.

Lyman shrugged. "I don't know. Perhaps nothing." Then he added, "Let me fetch you a glass of water, Mariane?" He leaned forward and a white handkerchief appeared, like a prop in a magic trick.

She took it reluctantly from his fingers. "I'll be all right," she said.

Lyman frowned. "Oh, one more thing, before I forget. Do the initials G.L.F. mean anything to you?"

"G.L.F.? I don't think so."

"Are you sure?"

"Nothing special."

"Well, in that case, I think I'll be on my way. I'm sure you two would rather be alone anyway." He stood awkwardly. "I'm sorry if I said anything to offend you, Mariane. Really. I didn't want to."

She did not answer. She did not even look at him.

Koster shrugged. "Good luck getting through," he said.

"Through where?"

"Didn't you see the boy scouts in the square?"

"I didn't come that way."

"I think it's some kind of pilgrimage. There were thousands of them on the train."

"Thanks for the tip. I guess I'll see you back at the hotel." Lyman hesitated at the table for a moment more and then started down the stairs.

As soon as he had disappeared, Koster turned to Mariane and kissed her gently on the cheek. She only pulled away. He started to say something but she hushed him with a glance and Koster realized she was watching Lyman as he crossed the floor below and headed out the door.

"Why did you do that?" she said, finally.

"Do what?"

"Force me to tell you all of that in front of him."

"What do you mean?"

"About Maurice."

"I didn't force you. I was just curious. It could be useful for the book. What's the big deal, anyway. It's only Nigel."

"Only Nigel!" She shook her head. "You don't understand, do you? You didn't let me finish. I just got a call from Charles-Philip. He told me some Englishman came by his office this morning to ask about a building project."

"So?"

"That's what I said. But Charles-Philip was worried he would find me. You know, upset me by dredging up the past, by asking a lot of questions about Maurice. So I asked him what the stranger looked like, and well," she said, "I didn't know what to think. It was Lyman. He was even wearing the same green coat and everything."

"Maybe he was just trying to get some information for the book."

"Joseph, he was using a false name. He said he worked for a hotel chain."

"Oh." Koster slumped against the table.

"And another thing. Since when do shop owners carry guns about, especially when they're on holiday? And why did he want to know about Maurice in the first place? Maybe he's one of Tellier's friends. Or a treasure hunter."

"Oh, come on, Mariane. I'm sure there's a perfectly logical explanation. The guy saved my life."

"Of course he did. You couldn't help him find the gospel if you were dead. I'm telling you, Joseph, that man is lying to you. He's hiding something."

"How can you be so sure?"

"I don't know. I can feel it."

"Feel it. With what? Your feminine intuition?"

"Don't patronize me, Joseph."

"I'm not. I just find it hard to believe."

"Why? Because it doesn't fit your formula of Nigel Lyman, because it isn't laid out in front of you like a column of numbers? You can't prove I love you either. Does that mean I don't?"

"Of course not. That's completely different."

"Is it?" She leaned forward suddenly and kissed him forcefully on the lips. "You were jealous, weren't you?"

"Jealous?"

"About Maurice. Don't lie to me. That's why you wanted me to talk about him, isn't it?" She slipped a hand behind his neck and drew him close to her. "You don't have to be jealous," she said. "That was a long, long time ago. And I never loved him like I love you."

He did not answer her. She was right. He did feel jealous of Maurice, of all the time they'd spent together, of all the memories she kept of him inside her.

They kissed again, and he felt her words undo him. But he could not prove she loved him.

Lyman ducked into the twilight, weaving through the wayward crowd, trailing after the day. It was almost half past five. There was a line outside the bakery. A pair of boys took up the rear. They were wearing brown uniforms, well-pressed and striped with ensigns, like miniature soldiers out on leave. Koster's boy scouts, Lyman thought. One of them was holding a

piece of waxed paper covered in red preserves. They
were going back for seconds.

The street unfurled and there was the cathedral.
Lines of buses leaned against the pavement. Lyman
pushed on and as he walked the scouts became more
frequent. First another pair. Then a group of five or
six. A few flashed golden braids or colorful insignias.
Some looked to be nine or ten years old, while others
seemed too big to wear their uniforms, too much like
the real thing. He turned the corner and the main
square of the cathedral stretched before him. Koster
had been right. There must have been at least two
thousand scouts, talking, running, jabbering in groups.
Each one appeared the replica of yet another still, the
same cut of clothes and color, like the reflections of a
single schoolboy in a fun house hall of mirrors. Lyman
moved between them feeling much too tall, too broad,
too old.

The Bishop's Palace was connected by a low iron
fence to the Winter Chapel, which in turn jutted like a
crooked thumb directly from the northern flank of the
cathedral. The walls of the palace were spattered with
graffiti. One scrawl read *Vicious Drugs,* another *Devo.*
Someone had even drawn a swastika on a shutter. The
shape was identical to the ones scored by the flagstones
on the floor of the cathedral itself. And yet the symbols
were an age apart. Lyman turned his back on the
crowd and started toward the gate between the palace
and the Winter Chapel.

The palace was U-shaped, with off-white window
frames and a gray slate roof. A square of lawn lined
with giant oak trees stretched from the main entrance
to a distant wall. There was an old red Ford parked
beside the steps leading up into the palace. A bell
chimed suddenly, followed by a great cheer from across
the palace walls. Lyman looked up. The scouts were on
the move. He could hear the sound of feet slapping on
stone.

He mounted the steps of the palace. As he entered the main door, it became clear that the building was still in the process of being renovated. The vestibule was empty. The rooms he passed along the way were devoid of furniture, covered in plaster dust, made various only by the odd wood box or pile of lumber.

He reached the main hall of the palace and spied an old man wearing a pair of baggy trousers and a blue cap sitting on the central stairs. The man was asleep, his cap drawn low across his eyes.

Lyman started toward him up the stairs. The old man stirred without waking. There was a bottle of Fanta by his feet but it was filled with a liquid that was clear instead of the normal orange color. Lyman bent down and picked it up. It smelled of raspberries. Probably homemade, he thought. He replaced the bottle on the stair. "Excuse me," Lyman said. "Hello."

The man shuddered to his senses. "Yes, I saw you," he said blearily. "Don't worry about that. This is state property. What do you want?"

Lyman smiled. "Just a curious tourist," he replied. He looked around. "A bit cold, isn't it?" he said.

"The cathedral's next door." The old man pointed over Lyman's shoulder. Lyman turned around and noticed a window that overlooked the square. The crowd of boy scouts was beginning to thin out. They were entering the cathedral for the twilight mass.

"I know," said Lyman. "And this is the Bishop's Palace."

"Sounds like you don't need a guide."

"And you're the night watchman."

The old man leaned forward. His eyes were glazed a royal blue, his thick skin chapped and red. His broken frown caught Lyman by surprise. It was such a pale mask of hostility. It looked so tired, so artificial, so damned familiar.

"That's right," the old man said. "What's it to you?"

"I just want to ask you a few questions."

"What kind of questions?"

"Questions about Maurice Duval, about the *abraxas*."

"You're a cop, aren't you?"

Lyman sat down on the step next to the old man. "That's right," he said. Then he leaned over and picked up the soda bottle. "May I?"

The night watchman started to reach for the bottle himself, but then thought better of it. He folded his arms and shrugged. "Help yourself."

Lyman sniffed the bottle. "Smells good," he said. "Make it yourself?"

"My sister does. Look," he added, "I've never seen you around here before. You're no French policeman, if you're a policeman at all."

"Well," Lyman said, as he sniffed the bottle again. "I suppose we could walk over to Captain Musel's house and ask him, couldn't we? And then we could visit Monsieur Duval, and I could tell him what a nasty disposition you have right after you just wake up." Lyman smiled. "I bet the liquor helps. Against the cold, I mean."

"Yeah, I guess so." The night watchman glared at Lyman without speaking.

Lyman ignored his frank appraisal. He didn't care. He had all the time in the world.

"So what do you want to know?" the old man said at last.

Lyman considered the question carefully, like an unopened present. "Tell me about the last time you saw Maurice Duval."

"It was the night he left town."

"What happened?"

"That was a long time ago. It's hard to remember." He pursed his lips. "I think I came on about seven o'clock. Maybe later. Anyway, I must have been on my rounds because I didn't hear him drive in. Usually I could hear his car on the gravel." He drifted on the memory. "But I saw it when I got back. It was parked near the south wing."

"The blue Peugeot."

"Right. So I went outside but Maurice wasn't there. The car was empty."

"Was it usual for Maurice to come by so late at night?"

The old man shrugged. "Once in a while. We'd had some things stolen. Tools. You know."

"I see." Lyman paused. "So you noticed the car was empty. Then what?"

"I checked the outer door to the basement of the south wing. The lock had been jammed open with a piece of paper."

"Maurice had the key though."

"Of course. He had the master key."

"Go on."

"I checked the basement but it was empty. So I decided to go back and wait for Maurice inside."

"Here, you mean?"

"Yeah, here. But he never showed up. I waited and waited and then I went to the window upstairs to see if the car was still there. That's when I saw him."

"Would you mind showing me exactly?"

The old man scowled. "I knew you'd ask me that." He tipped slowly to his feet and started up the stairs. Lyman followed. They made their way to the second landing where the night watchman paused beside a window. "There," he said, pointing.

The window faced the front court of the palace and Lyman could see the lawn which stretched out eastward to the rue Dupuis, the great cathedral to his right, and below it the south wing of the palace. "What do you mean?" said Lyman. "Where?"

"There. I saw a light go on in the basement. Then it moved to the outside door. It was Maurice."

"You're sure of that? It's a long way off."

"Of course I'm sure. He was wearing his porkpie hat and everything. Then he got into his car and drove away."

"Where exactly did you first see the light?"

"Right over there," he answered, pointing once again. "Through that second window. I was watching and it just came on."

"Like a torch, a flashlight?"

"Right. The room wasn't wired yet."

"I don't understand. Why would someone turn a torch on in the middle of a room? Why not at the entrance?"

"Don't ask me. Look, is that it?" the old man said impatiently. "I've got to make my rounds." He turned and started down the stairs. Lyman shuffled after him until they reached the step where the night watchman had been sleeping earlier.

"You never saw him after that?" Lyman insisted.

"Look, I told you. I was the last one to see him before he disappeared. At least according to Charles-Philip." He reached down for the soda bottle.

Lyman watched him unscrew the cap carefully. He watched the way he pursed his lips around the opening, the way his Adam's apple bobbed as he drank.

When he was finished the night watchman wiped his mouth and offered the bottle to Lyman.

"Thanks," Lyman said. He clasped it in his hand, feeling the shape, the hardness of the glass. He lifted it to his mouth. The raspberry smell blossomed about his face. He turned his wrist to drink, and as he did so his eyes fell for a moment on the window overlooking the cathedral square. The crowd of scouts had grown smaller. Only a few hundred remained. Lyman leaned against the banister. He craned his neck. He strained his eyes, and in a rush the words returned. *The bloke in the shadows did all the talking back. He had a deep voice, I remember. The voice of a big man.* Lyman moved swiftly down the steps. His hand reached out to keep him from the window. *All I can say is that he wore a long black coat, and a white shirt.* The boy scouts fell away again. A hole appeared within the crowd. Lyman felt himself drawn into it, enveloped, and at the center there he was, a lone black shape against the uniforms, a rose on his lapel, staring at the Bishop's Palace, balding and with his Father Christmas eyes—Scarcella.

Lyman was down the hall and out the door before he even realized that he was still carrying the soda bottle. He placed it gently on the cobblestones but it tipped over anyway, the liquor spilling out, breaking his heart. He rounded the iron gate, his footsteps slapping on the cobblestones, clapping up against the wall of the cathedral. Suddenly the square appeared before him. A few scouts dawdled here and there, but most had finally entered the cathedral for the service, the culmination of their pilgrimage. Lyman turned round and around, panting, sweating at the neck. Scarcella was gone. He felt the shadow of the night descend. The wind lashed at his face. He turned once more and saw the tail end of a black coat scurrying down the hill.

Lyman ran after him. The street curved down around the edge of the cathedral grounds. On one side stretched a park, and on the other a parking lot for tourists. The figure vanished between two cars. Lyman stopped to catch his breath. He was too old for this, he thought. Too tired. He straightened up and there he was again, the man in the black coat, struggling across a narrow bridge where the cobbled street crossed over a canal beyond the parking lot. Lyman cursed and started after him.

Though no more than ten feet across, the water of the canal looked swift and deep. Lyman bolted across the bridge. He had lost the figure once again. The street curved sharply and continued down one side of the canal. On the left, a line of brick row houses stretched as far as the eye could see. And on the right, across the cobbled street and the canal, another row of battered houses stood right on the water's edge.

Most were in disrepair or crumbling at the joints, beyond salvation. A series of planks spanned the canal, from the street directly to their entrances. Swallows with blue backs weaved the night air. They were harvesting insects off the water. Lyman could hear their wings beat like the pounding of a thousand hearts, close to him, right above his head. One wheeled and almost smashed into the bridge before veering off into the darkness.

Lyman started down the deserted cobbled street. The houses to his left were occupied, and he could see lights shining from the upper landings, hear television sets. But on the other side, across the water, the houses were abandoned. Most had neither doors nor windows. Some were fenced off, the little plank bridges leading to their entrances tangled with barbed wire. Lyman looked into each one as he passed by, hoping to spy Scarcella in the shadows. Nothing. Only the swallows moved about the silence, flying through the shattered windows, circling through the darkness and then reappearing out of breaches in the walls. Lyman couldn't see a bloody thing from the street. He would have to pick a plank and try the other side.

He lifted a leg over the knotted strands of wire guarding the nearest plank bridge. The canal churned by before him, black and forbidding in the waning light. He tested the plank. It seemed strong enough. Bloody hell, he thought, and started across, slowly, carefully. The water sighed beneath him. A swallow darted past his head and he almost lost his balance, straightening at the last moment, his arms extended as though to grasp the air. The door to the house across the canal was only a few more yards away. He took another step. The plank groaned and he felt his foot catch on a streamer of barbed wire. Not now, he thought with desperation. His trouser leg was hooked about the cuff.

He lifted it again and the material came free. One step,
then two and he was on the other side.

Lyman paused in the doorway of the house. His
breath burned in his chest. A stairway leading nowhere
hung from the roof above. The window frames had
been removed. Brick ends poked through. Holes
opened on the rib cage of the house, revealing beams,
gray stone supports. He turned. There, in the distance,
like the sound of brick on brick. What was that sound?

He started up the side of the canal, pressing his
back against the house fronts to keep from slipping
down into the water. It was coming from up ahead. He
reached inside his coat and pulled out his Walther
PPK. The sound was almost regular now, almost the
beating of a drum. He paused beside another doorway
and then the pistol was inside. Darkness. Emptiness.
Lyman lowered his weapon and took a long, deep
breath. Then he was past the door and moving on the
edge of the canal once more, pausing only as he neared
another door. Up went the gun, the step, the turn, the
moment in the empty doorway with his shadow up
against the light and all that bloody time to aim. He
lowered his weapon and breathed. *Clack. Clack.* He
slipped out the door. Another plank went by, another
doorway and he realized with relief that the row of
houses was a temporary fear. There was only one door
left, and then the street turned and a wall took over.
He waited for the moment. *Clack. Clack.* The noise
began to blend into his heartbeat. *Clack.* He pushed his
back against the wall, facing the canal, his pistol poised
before his chin. He sighed and in the turn the gun fell
and the eye lined up the barrel and the sight, the bullet
and the frightened grimace of the boy who sat before
him on the ground. Lyman lowered his pistol, breathing hard. The boy did not even blink. He was sitting
with his feet hanging out through a hole in the wall
overlooking the canal. A bamboo fishing pole jutted
out into the void. There was a net and bucket beside

him, and in his left hand, within his tiny fist, a piece of
rose red masonry. Lyman slipped his gun into his holster. All he could think of was that raspberry liqueur,
spilling from that soda bottle on the ground, sliding
through the cool glass neck and down into the earth.

Chapter XVI

AMIENS
September 24th, 1983

"THE CAPTAIN IS VERY BUSY," COR-poral Pini said, stretching to his full height before the door.

Lyman folded his arms. He wore his green wool coat with the plastic bone toggles and hood. His hair was wet from the rain, his cheeks red from rushing up the stairs. "I don't care if he's busy," he said. "I tried to reach him all last night. Tell him that he's going to be a damn sight busier if he doesn't see me now."

"I'm sorry, Inspector Lyman. He left orders not to be disturbed."

"Don't you understand? This is bloody serious." He laid a hand on Pini's shoulder for emphasis but the corporal shook it off.

"Just who the hell do you think you are?" the Frenchman hissed. "You're not in England anymore. As if that would make a difference, the way your own department talks about you. Face it, Lyman. You're not anybody's favorite."

Lyman grabbed the corporal by the lapels of his

uniform and pulled him close. "Now you listen to me, you little bastard. One man's already died in this town. You were lucky with him. He was a little bastard, too. But he won't be the last one unless you get off your prissy little ass and do something about it."

The door swung open behind Corporal Pini. Captain Musel stood in the doorway dressed in a white undershirt with a hand towel draped across one shoulder. "Bravo, Inspector Lyman. Very dramatic. Yes, very theatrical. A second career, perhaps, when this one's over."

Lyman pushed by Corporal Pini and entered the captain's office. Musel closed the door behind him. "Sit down?" he said, pointing at his desk. "Or perhaps you'd like to smash something up first. Maybe a bit of furniture."

Lyman dropped onto the chair before the captain's desk. Musel shook his head. Then with a smile he walked back into the little bathroom just behind the file cabinets.

Lyman watched him wash his hands. "I want to know about Maurice Duval," Lyman said, finally. "About his accident in Austria."

Musel bent down to rinse his face and Lyman noticed rolls of fat rippling the undershirt around his waist. "What about Duval?" he said, tamping his face with the towel.

"He and Jacques Tellier were partners. Your own man, Poincarré, identified his car."

"Yes, so I heard. So they knew each other. Is that a crime?" The captain hung the towel on a hook behind the bathroom door.

"Of course not. But what about Maurice's death in Austria, and that robbery at his father's office?"

"What the hell do you want from me, Lyman?" Musel said. He slipped a shirt across his shoulders. "Charles-Philip Duval never reported a robbery. Never. He denied it ever happened. And as far as

Maurice is concerned, his death was declared an accident months ago. There were dozens of witnesses. He was drunk. He ran out into the street without looking. It happens. Look, without some evidence of a crime, I don't initiate a case. I've got too many other things to do, too many real crimes, with real criminals and real victims to contend with. It was his own damned fault. He brought it on himself. He had absolutely no respect for Charles-Philip, none whatsoever."

"Just how well exactly do you know Monsieur Duval?"

Musel stepped forward menacingly. "What did you say?"

"You heard me."

"I know him. So what? Amiens is a small city. He runs an important business here in town."

"Just wondering."

"Yeah, well you can stop fucking wondering." The captain pointed his finger at Lyman's face. "What do you get out of this? That's what I'd like to know. It sounds to me like you have a lot of nasty little suspicions and not much else. Why are you pushing so hard? I've tried to be patient with you, Lyman. I really have. I asked you to be careful. I told you I didn't want any trouble, and the first night you're in town one man is almost strangled and another falls to his death after you take a shot at him." The words caught in his throat and he turned swiftly on his heels. For a moment he stood there without speaking, his back to Lyman, simply buttoning his shirt. Then, when he had tucked it in, he moved back behind his desk and sat down, his chair creaking underneath him. "I've done everything that Paris and your own department's asked of me. I've extended every courtesy. What else can I do?"

"You can show me your file on Duval."

"Oh, for God's sake." Musel reached over for his telephone. "Get me what you have on Maurice Duval," he barked into the receiver. "There," he said, hanging up. "Are you satisfied?"

Lyman frowned. "Look, Captain. I know that it doesn't seem like much," he said. "Just a lot of loose ends. I know that's how it must appear to you. But the case is really there now. I know it is." He paused. "Otherwise Scarcella wouldn't be here."

"Scarcella! Here, now?" Musel looked horrified. "Are you sure?"

"I'm almost certain."

Lyman described the incident at the Bishop's Palace, the solitary figure in the crowd, the chase by the canal. When he had finished, Musel leaned back in his chair and looked up at the ceiling for several seconds without speaking. "Scarcella," he said finally, the second syllable receding, falling off into another pause. "Yes, well, that would be wonderful, but 'almost' is a funny little word. Once again you have no evidence, nothing concrete."

"How can you say that, especially after your own people opened that picnic basket? You read Jacques Tellier's letter. You saw what he told Pontevecchio."

"If Tellier is meant to add credibility to your story, then you might as well start packing, Inspector Lyman. You're living in a house of cards. Anyone could claim what Tellier claimed. Does that mean that I should pull my men out of the streets to chase him down?"

The door opened behind Lyman and Corporal Pini strode in. "The Duval file, sir," he said.

"Very good." Musel held out his hand and Pini gave it to him. "That will be all, Corporal. Thank you."

The young policeman tossed a scowl at Lyman as he turned to leave.

"Look here, Pini, sorry about before," Lyman said. Each word was like a pebble in his throat. "I guess I lost my temper a bit."

The corporal nodded and continued out the door. "Inspector Lyman?"

Lyman turned. Musel was holding the folder out across the desk.

"Oh, sorry."

A single sheet of paper slipped out of the file. Lyman tried to catch it but it wafted in between his hands and landed on the floor. "This is it?" he said, incredulously. He picked the paper up between two fingers. "This is the whole file?"

"I'm afraid so."

Lyman dropped the sheet onto his lap. Three paragraphs. Single-spaced. That was all.

"As you can see," Musel said, "it was a party that went too far, that simply got out of hand and ended in tragedy. Duval was staying at the Hotel International in Lech, Austria. It's a ski town, one of those jet set playgrounds full of chalets and teahouses.

"On February twenty-seventh, he and some other men were having a party in his room. Apparently the party got a little loud. Some people complained. I think it was only eleven or so in the morning. Well, as it turned out, one of the maids came in to clean the room and when she did Duval jumped up out of nowhere, thrust her aside, and stumbled out into the corridor." Musel threw his hands up in the air.

"The place was a shambles. There were broken glasses and tipped ashtrays everywhere. And a lot of liquor. Dozens of bottles, according to the maid. Even the bed had been stripped down," he said. "The other two men were surprised at first. Then apparently they just shoved her onto the bed, laughing the whole time, and followed after Duval. They were drunk too, it seemed. Anyway, there was a big scene on the stairs and the lot of them ended up down in the lobby. Someone called security but by the time they arrived it was all over. They say Duval walked out into the street. He was killed almost instantly."

Lyman scanned the document. It was incomprehensible. There were sentences without verbs, pronouns without definition.

"He was struck by a car," Musel continued, "a Volkswagen, driven by a couple of American girls who claimed they had come to Lech on holiday. Which they probably had, since the back of their car was full of ski equipment. They were just frightened tourists. Unfortunately the body then bounced into a truck going the other way. Duval never had a chance. If the first blow didn't kill him, the second one surely did. He was dragged eleven meters before the driver—a local man —finally managed to bring the truck to a halt against a snow bank. The body was thrown up by the rear tires over an embankment, and down into the river below. That's where it finally came to rest. The officer in charge said you could follow the trail in the snow, there was so much blood."

Musel sighed. Lyman closed the file and tossed it back onto the captain's desk.

"He had identified himself," Musel concluded, "as Maurice Duval when he checked into the hotel, and the police later found his passport confirming his identity. The other two men disappeared. Duval had been at the hotel nine days, but no one claimed to have seen him much because he didn't ski. He kept to himself in his room." Musel shrugged. "That's about it. The autopsy revealed that there was a large amount of alcohol in his bloodstream. Nothing much else, I'm afraid."

Lyman shook his head. "Naturally," he said sarcastically. "Musel, you know as well as I do that this report is bloody rubbish. Of course they didn't find anything. They didn't want to. You said it yourself: Lech is a tourist town. The last thing they need is some scandal, even the hint of a scandal. I want to talk to that maid myself."

"You want to call Austria?"

"I'll pay for it, if that's what's worrying you. In cash."

"That would be greatly appreciated, Inspector, but that wasn't my concern. I simply don't see the point. After all, the accident occurred months ago. I'm sure the maid's forgotten everything by now."

"Maybe." Lyman leaned forward in his chair. "May I?" He reached for the phone.

Musel shrugged.

It took Lyman several minutes to find the number and get through to the Hotel International. At first he was afraid that the maid might have been a seasonal employee, a French or Austrian student looking for a free pass to the ski lifts. But when he finally heard her voice he knew his fears had been unfounded. Christina Kung was going nowhere. She answered his questions in French as if she had answered them a hundred times before, and indeed, Lyman realized, she probably had. Her story was almost identical to the captain's. Yet something in it nagged at Lyman.

"Excuse me, Mademoiselle Kung?"

"Madame Kung."

"Yes, Madame Kung. Just one more question if you don't mind."

"Yes."

"If you say he didn't like to be disturbed, it must have been a nuisance getting in to clean his room."

"It certainly was. He never left it."

"Then why did you decide to clean it then, especially when you heard there was a party going on?"

The telephone lay dead in Lyman's hand. Only a distant crackling marked the open line. "You know," she said at last. "Now that I think about it, I guess I was a bit surprised myself."

"What do you mean?"

"Well, the first time that I passed the room there was a DO NOT DISTURB sign on the door. He always had it out. Then, oh, about twenty minutes later, as I was pushing my bin along the corridor to get to the laundry chute, I noticed it had been turned. Now it said ROOM

SERVICE REQUESTED. I'd already done the rest of that
corridor so I thought I might as well do his room too.
Sometimes when people have parties, they like to have
extra ice, that sort of thing."

"And that's when the man pushed by you? Duval, I
mean."

"Exactly."

"What did the other two look like?"

"They were South American, I think. Maybe Ira-
nian. I'm not sure. One of them at least. Dark. You
know the type. They threw me on the bed."

"Yes, I heard. Dreadful. Did they ever discover
their names?"

"I wouldn't know that. They left before the police
could question them."

"Didn't the police check the register?"

"You'd have to talk to the manager about that."

Lyman waited as Madame Kung passed the telephone. "Yes?" a man's voice echoed down the line.
"Zimmer, here. Hello?"

"Ah, Monsieur Zimmer. First, let me thank you for
all of Madame Kung's assistance. Very helpful. She's a
credit to your hotel. Really."

"Yes, well, you're quite welcome. Is that it?"

Lyman moved the receiver away from his ear. "Not
quite," he said. "Would you mind terribly going back
over your register to the time just before Duval's accident. Around February the twenty-seventh, I think."

There was another long pause. Lyman raised his
eyebrows and Musel frowned back. "Hello," Lyman
said. "Hello, are you still there?"

"Just a minute," came the reply. "Right. I have the
pages here."

"Who were the two men with Duval, the ones who
left without checking out, without paying? You should
have that on record."

"What about them?"

"What were their names?"

"Let's see. Yes, here they are. One was called Ian McKenzie, and the other," he said, pausing once more, "Aldo Barbarosso. Yes, that's it."

Lyman froze. "What was that last name again? Did you say Barbarosso?"

"That's right."

"Thank you, Monsieur Zimmer. Thank you very much." Lyman hung up. "Aldo Barbarosso. Ring a bell, Musel? Sound familiar?"

Musel dropped his head so that his chin disappeared, layer by layer, into his open collar. He closed his eyes.

"Come on, Musel. What are you going to tell me now? That it's just coincidence. Aldo Barbarosso. Aldo Barbieri. They're almost identical. I'll wager anything you like that it was Scarcella's man having cocktails with Duval. My friend with the wing-tipped shoes." Lyman smiled. "Anything at all."

"This is ridiculous. I don't go about accusing people just because their names sound suspicious." Musel shot a hand into the air. "And what could Scarcella's men have possibly wanted with Duval?"

"Perhaps he'd learned something about the labyrinth, or the gospel itself."

"Which gospel? Enough!" The captain straightened in his chair. His hands fell against the armrests with a thud. The coils of fat around his neck extended as he stretched to his full height. "You're peddling in sauerkraut, Inspector. Perhaps will never get you closer to the truth."

Lyman nodded. He crossed his legs. He ran a hand through his hair and said, "I suppose you're right. Of course you are." Then he sat back in his chair and pulled his coat together at the front. One of the plastic bone toggles was loose, he observed. He played with it delicately, turning it in his fingers. "But there's one thing I do know," he said finally, looking up. "The mis-

sal which you found in that picnic basket is the key to
this mystery. That and Thierry's letter."

"So you keep saying."

"What did Clermont tell you about them?"

"He sent them on to Paris for analysis."

"But that was months ago. Surely there's been
some word by now."

"Inspector Lyman, unbelievable as it may seem to
you, I have other matters to attend to. Other cases. If
you're so convinced of their importance, why don't you
call Clermont?"

Lyman frowned. "I have. He never rings me back."

"No doubt he's busy too."

"No doubt," said Lyman tightly, as he stood.
"Thanks for your time." He started for the door.

"Inspector."

Lyman hesitated. "Yes, Captain."

"I suppose if I sent you packing, you'd just come
back again, wouldn't you?"

Lyman frowned. His hand hovered near the doorknob. "You don't understand," he answered quietly.
"It's not just Pontevecchio anymore. I don't know."

It was as if he bore the weight of a hundred fath-
oms on his back. No matter how he tried, Lyman could
not shake the image of his son, floating in some dark
compartment at the bottom of the South Atlantic. He
shook his head.

"It's me," he said. "It's Scarcella. Every time he
breathes I feel it. Every time he takes a step I can feel
it rubbing at me."

There was that little girl in Terracina, cowering on
the bed. There was George. He looked up.

"I don't want any executions in my town," Musel
said flatly. "Is that clear? I don't care who he is or what
he's done. I will not permit it."

Lyman opened the door but the captain called him
back. "And Lyman," he said.

"Yes, Captain?" Musel began to fiddle with the pa-

pers on his desk. Lyman waited in the open doorway.
"Yes, Captain," he repeated.

"Good luck."

Lyman pulled his collar up against the cold as he descended the steps of the Musée de Picardie and headed
for the street. Clermont, the director, wasn't in. He was
somewhere in the public library next door. He was
bloody out.

Lyman kicked a chestnut off the path before him
and it spun along the grass and down into the rue de la
République. A hole opened in the clouds above and he
felt himself lean without design into a solitary patch of
sunlight on the far side of the pavement, out of the
shadow and the cold, into a memory of Brighton and a
high moor just above the cliffs near Roedean, just he
and Jackie and the open sky, where he had told her for
the first time of his love. Then it had seemed the kind
of stark confession that one should only have to make
one time for it to live up to its promise. He hadn't
known then it was but a single phrase of a continuous
exchange, a daily test and confirmation of their marriage, a litany so regular that in the end it was the only
thing that didn't change.

Lyman rounded the hedge beside the street and the
public library came into view. There was a little garden
in the front with pale September flowers and a well-
trimmed lawn. Lyman strode up the path. A granite
doorway opened onto an expansive corridor with a
white marble floor and sinister, gilt-edged oils. To his
right a sign with an enormous arrow announced the
Maison de la Culture. Lyman wondered if he should try
that corridor first or head into the library itself, but it
was the sound of voices which eventually enticed him
past a stairwell into the reference section. Drawers
lined the walls to his left. Ahead, a gray-haired woman

with a pink sweater sat at a desk checking what appeared to be validation cards.

"Excuse me," Lyman said. "Do you know Monsieur Clermont, of the museum?"

The woman looked up with one eye. "Audio room B," she answered, pointing lethargically.

"Thanks." He crossed the room toward a series of bookshelves which jutted from the opposite wall. A few children leaned against them, chatting quietly. Rooms A and B were set right next to one another. He knocked three times and entered.

Clermont was sitting alone in the corner of the windowless room with a pair of headphones on his head, listening with his eyes closed, playing with a pencil. Lyman shut the door. The curator remained motionless, so Lyman sat down quietly beside his cubicle and waited. He noted the drooping mustache, the heavy round earlobes hanging just below the hairline, the eyebrows forging an alliance. Clermont must have been fifty or so, Lyman thought, somewhere in the middle. His clothes were younger. He had a blue silk kerchief up his sleeve. One hand reached up to snatch the headphones and the other to straighten his tie.

"Oh, sorry," Lyman said. "I didn't mean to startle you."

Clermont regained his dignity. He reached over and switched off the cassette recorder in the cubicle.

"Excuse me, but is your name Clermont by any chance?"

Clermont sat up in his chair. "Yes. Why? Do I know you?"

"No, we've never met. Although I've tried to reach you several times by telephone. The name's Nigel Lyman. It was about that Masonic missal which you gave to the Countess de Rochambaud."

The curator looked at his watch. "Yes, I got your messages. I'm sorry," he said. "I've been very busy. We're mounting a new exhibit." He started to rise but

Lyman dropped a heavy hand across his shoulders and the man sank back in his chair.

"I was wondering if you wouldn't mind answering just a few more questions."

Clermont's back went limp. "Look, what do you people want from me? I told you. I don't know anything."

"I'm sorry?"

Clermont glanced up. He looked desperate, Lyman thought. He looked bloody terrified.

"What are you talking about?" Lyman said. "What people?"

Clermont stood up and laughed, a shy laugh, slate thin. "It's getting late. I have an appointment."

"What people?"

The curator began to move across the room. "I don't know anything," he repeated. Then, without warning, he made a quick dash for the door.

Lyman grabbed him by the shoulders and pushed him up against the wall. "What people?" he repeated.

"You're not the only one around here asking questions."

"What do you mean? Who? Who else?" Lyman said. "When?"

"Just a few weeks ago."

"What did they look like?"

The curator struggled in Lyman's grip. "I don't know."

Lyman leaned against him harder, bringing his face close. "Well bloody remember."

"He was dark. He was tall and dark. Dark eyes. Dark hair, combed back. Spanish or Italian."

"What did he say?"

"He asked me about the missal. Just like you."

"And what did you tell him?"

"Nothing. I told him that I didn't have it. I didn't. I'd already sent it to the countess."

"Was he surprised?"

"Surprised! He threatened to kill me."

Lyman smiled. Clermont's feelings were so transparent, so immediate. Nature had given him a victim's face. He was the one with the weak knee, the one cut leg out of all the thousands on the jostling African plain.

"Why exactly did you send the missal to the countess?"

"Please, I've already told you everything I know."

Lyman tightened his grip. "It's a simple question," he said. "You had this remarkable document in your possession, obviously a rare prize, a once-in-a-lifetime find, and you decided to give it away. Why?"

"I didn't want to get involved. I didn't want that missal here. I had a pretty good idea what it meant and I didn't want any part of it."

"So you sent it to the countess."

"Yes, why not? She's the expert. I thought, let them fight it out if they want to. It was none of my business. That's what I told him."

Lyman felt his heart jump. Let them fight it out, he thought. But who? The countess and the stranger, the man with the dark hair and Latin voice? Two fronts, two sides, he thought, remembering what Koster had told him of his meeting with the countess in Paris. *Each thing has its shadow,* she had said. Something like that. *Rome had its Carthage, and Freemasonry its I 4.*

"Let them fight it out," Lyman repeated slowly.

So perhaps there were two forms of Masonry after all. Two sides. Yes, he thought. It had all seemed so perfectly timed. The *abraxas* in the book. The way the countess had turned to that particular page, at that particular moment. And hadn't Mariane said the *abraxas* were worth as much as fifteen thousand francs? The same amount as in Jacques Tellier's passbook. The very same.

"I understand. You didn't want to get between them, is that it?"

"That's right."

"Between the stranger and the G.L.F."

"Of course. That's why I sent it to her. I knew it would make her happy. And besides, she's been supporting the museum for years."

Lyman nodded. Now it began to fit. It was the countess who had bought the *abraxas* from Tellier. She was the mysterious G.L.F. who had paid that fifteen thousand francs.

"Listen to me, Clermont," he said, poking the curator in the chest. "I want to know about the G.L.F."

"What about it?"

"What do they do exactly? Who are they?"

"But I don't understand. I thought you said . . ."

Clermont began to struggle once again. Lyman spun him round. He wrenched the curator's left arm up in a half nelson and pushed his face against the wall. "Never mind what you don't understand," Lyman said. "Just tell me about the G.L.F."

"Okay, okay. It's no big secret anyway. It's the Grande Loge Féminin. They're based in Paris. The countess is a kind of matriarch to the lodge."

"You mean they're Masons too?"

"Yes, dammit, let me go."

"What kind of Masons?"

"You're breaking my arm."

"Tell me."

"They're Speculative Masons, that's all I know. A women's lodge. The Countess de Rochambaud's their leader. She promised to protect me. That's why I gave her the missal."

So there were two fronts, thought Lyman. Or three, if you counted the archbishop as an outside player. Yet something still bothered him, something which Madame Kung had said about Maurice's death in Austria.

Who could have turned that sign around on the hotel door in Lech, and why? Who could have known what they were doing to Maurice in that room other

than Barbieri and McKenzie? And if one of them had
turned the sign, one of Scarcella's own men, it could
only mean that he had wanted someone to walk in on
the interrogation, that he had welcomed an intrusion.
Then he was more than Scarcella's man. He was working with his own agenda, or one belonging to another
of the players. But who? The G.L.F.? Did the countess
have a mole in Scarcella's camp?

Lyman sighed. Perhaps he was just peddling in
sauerkraut, as Captain Musel had said.

He released Clermont and stepped away. "I found
you once," he said. "Remember that. I can always do it
again."

Clermont began to rub his arm. He didn't say anything. He simply stood there glowering at Lyman.

Without another word, Lyman turned and headed
out the door. He walked back through the library with
his chin down, watching the floor, trying to piece together what he'd learned, trying to find a pattern.
When he reached the entrance he stood for a moment
on the steps of the library and looked up at the sky. A
pavilion of ominous clouds had gathered to the west,
but at least it wasn't raining. Not for two days now. He
pulled his hood up just a little at the back and started
down the steps.

Scarcella, he thought. Grabowski. The Countess de
Rochambaud. Yet there was a difference, he knew. The
countess was manipulating Koster—that much was
clear now—but it was doubtful she had been involved
in the Pontevecchio incident. After all, Clermont
hadn't sent her the Masonic missal until three or four
months *after* the hanging in London. Lyman smiled. It
seemed the man in the wing-tipped shoes had left a
modest legacy. Based on Clermont's description, it was
clear that the curator's foreign visitor and Barbieri
were the same. Barbarosso. Barbieri. The man with the
wing-tipped shoes. How strange, Lyman thought. He
had collected all his names, yet the man who had fallen

from the balcony of the Hôtel de la Paix remained a
stranger.

He crossed the street and headed back toward the
hotel. A vegetable shop with an outdoor stand caught
his eye as he walked by. Lyman had never seen such
monstrous squash, bloated and oddly colored, fuchsia
and olive green. The peas were expensive. He leaned
across and squeezed a melon.

It was odd, he thought, how in the end we all remained unknown to one another, like legendary islands
always distant but a few more leagues, always just
across the horizon. He had never really known Jackie.
He had never understood her hunger for the city, but
he had used it to his own advantage. She had nursed
her cool ambition and he had listened, late at night,
over a few biscuits and a glass of milk, as her dreams
grew one upon the other, like crystals, planning the
next decade of advancement, planning his life, as if
somewhere in the glint, in the gestures of her hands or
the way she'd always end her paragraphs with "then
they'll see," he would finally unmask her.

It was like his own son, Peter, who had always
meant one thing to him, and something altogether different to his friends, to the boys at school, to his
mother. It was as if there had been many Peter
Lymans, each one discrete and separate, a digit in the
sum of who he was, never complete until that final instant in that sinking battleship when they had all
rushed in together at the end, all those countless Peter
Lymans crying out in one unanswered voice. We were
all strangers in the end, he thought, always unknown to
one another. He stopped. A car honked at his heels. A
pair of schoolgirls giggled.

It took him only a few more minutes at a desperate
run to reach the Hôtel de la Paix. He barreled through
the door and up into the open phone booth before the
concierge could even say hello. Coins spilled every-

where as he emptied out his pockets. Come on, he told himself. Keep calm now. He picked up the phone and dialed.

This time Monsieur Zimmer wasn't quite so nice, not quite so deferential. Lyman turned and smiled at the concierge as he waited for Madame Kung. Then, growing louder by the second, it seemed as though he could hear her footsteps sounding on the lobby floor before she finally picked up the receiver. "Hello," Lyman said. "Hello, Madame Kung?"

"Yes?"

"Listen, I'm sorry to bother you like this. It's just that I forgot to ask you something before."

"Yes? What is it?"

"I was just wondering. Would you mind describing the gentleman in the room?"

"What, again?"

"No, I mean Duval. The man who was killed. Maurice Duval."

"Oh. Not at all. Well, how do I begin? He was not too tall, I suppose. But he wasn't short either. He had dark brown hair. With some gray in it, I think."

"Yes. What else?"

"To be honest, I never much cared for him. There was something, I don't know, colorless about him. Maybe because he never went outside. He was always so pale, so thin, as if he were sick, as if he never saw the light."

Lyman spun about. "Thank you, Madame Kung." He dropped a hand over the mouthpiece. "Excuse me," he shouted at the concierge. "Is Monsieur Koster in?"

"Hello. Hello." Madame Kung's voice echoed tinnily through the receiver.

"Yes, I'm sorry, Madame Kung." Lyman slipped the phone between his ear and shoulder and began to search for another coin. "Thank you," he continued. "You've been very helpful."

"He's over at the cathedral, Monsieur Lyman," the concierge replied. Lyman nodded furiously.

"You're welcome too, Madame Kung. Yes, good-bye." He broke the connection and then turned back to the concierge. "Quick," he said. "Get me the number for the Cartier Photo Shop, the one next to the cathedral."

"Of course." The concierge reached for the phone book behind the front desk and began to flip through the pages. "Here," he said. "Ninety-three, fifty-seven, thirty-four. And by the way, your office called again. A man named Cocksedge. That's the second time today."

Lyman ignored him and dialed the numbers. A voice responded and he dropped his coin into the booth. "Hello. Hello?" he said.

"Cartier Photo."

"Is Mariane Soury-Fontaine there?" he asked as calmly as he could.

"One moment."

An eternity passed, and then he heard a rustle at the other end.

"Hello, this is Mariane."

Lyman leaned against the phone booth, drawing the receiver close. "Mariane. Mariane, listen to me. It's Nigel Lyman."

"Oh, Monsieur Lyman. What a surprise." Mariane's voice was cool.

"Look, I don't have time to explain. I want you to go next door to the cathedral and find Joseph."

"Why?"

"Please, don't argue with me. Just tell him to meet me in the basement of the Bishop's Palace in about twenty minutes."

"Look, Monsieur Lyman. I don't know exactly what you have in mind, but as far as I'm concerned . . ."

"Tell him to bring a spade and a pick. Oh, yes. And some lamps. Maybe Guy can help him there. In twenty minutes. And tell him to be discreet about it."

There was a long pause. "For God's sake, Mariane," Lyman continued. "This is important. I'd do it
myself if I thought I could. But I need his help, Mariane. I need him."

"So do I, Monsieur Lyman." "Yes," Lyman said.
"The labyrinth, the Book of Thomas the Contender."
He hesitated. "But it's more than just that." He closed
his eyes and pressed his forehead up against the wall.
"It's about Maurice as well. It's about the accident in
Austria."

"Damn you," she said suddenly. He heard her catch
her breath, and then the words came out just as he
knew they would, each one a knife stroke deep inside
him. "All right," she added, calmly now. "I'll tell him."

Chapter XVII

AMIENS
September 24th, 1983

IN THE SLANTED AUTUMN LIGHT, IN the basement of the Bishop's Palace, Koster remembered that it had taken mankind five millennia to think of a symbol for nothing. Then in some unknown Indian village a nameless Brahman had drawn a sign called *sunya*, meaning empty, and out of the void, the darkness, the zero was carried on the backs of camels, like the grandchild of the Countess de Rochambaud, through the deserts of the Middle East, from the Levant to the West. He turned and looked up at Mariane. "How long did he say?"

"I told you, twenty minutes."

Koster sighed. "Right. Sorry." He shifted on his seat. The basement was half full of metal folding chairs, stacked back to back in rows. Mariane stood with her brother by the door leading up into the courtyard of the Winter Chapel. A single light bulb hung from the low ceiling casting a dusky orange glow. "Well, it's been at least half an hour now. What's keeping him?"

"I don't know, Joseph." Mariane walked over and stood beside him. "I just wish . . ."

"Wish what?"

"I wish he'd just get it over with. I'm frightened, Joseph. I don't know why, but I am."

"I like Nigel," Guy cut in.

"We all like him," Koster said. "That's not the point."

"Why isn't it?"

Just then, as if on cue, the basement door swung open and Lyman appeared under the lintel. "Sorry I'm late," he said. "I had to see the watchman." He turned to Guy. "Did you find a spade?"

Guy smiled. "Of course," he answered, pointing at a pair of grub-axes leaning against the wall.

"Good."

"Just a minute, Nigel," Koster said. "What's this all about? We can't just start digging up the place."

"I thought you told me Langelier gave you excavation rights."

"He did, but there are certain formalities. I can't just do it willy-nilly." He put his hands in his pockets. "And besides, what's the point? The labyrinth is the answer. You said so yourself, remember?"

Lyman ignored him and continued through the basement. When he had reached the farthest window facing up into the courtyard, he began to move about in circles, keeping his eyes on the window the whole time.

"What are you doing?" Koster asked.

"I'm sighting off against that room on the second floor. That's where the watchman told me he was standing when he saw the light go on the night of Duval's disappearance." Lyman stopped. "Here," he said, looking down at the dirt floor. "Fetch me one of those picks, will you?"

Guy carried one over to him. Lyman hefted the grub-ax in his hands, testing the weight, and then swung it upward through the air, over his right shoulder and down into the earth. The blade vanished with a thud. Lyman heaved and the ground began to crack and loosen at his feet. He worked the dirt apart into a shallow trench. Guy ambled over to help. Mariane sighed and Koster watched, following each swing, thinking that each arc the ax described was like the curve between his apprehension and curiosity, and somewhere on that line he had to place his trust.

Minutes passed. The hole deepened and suddenly the rhythm of the digging stopped midbeat. The Englishman fell to his knees. Koster could not help himself. He sidled over toward the hole and looked inside. Lyman was dragging his fingers through the earth.

"Get one of those lights," he said. "I can't see a bloody thing."

Guy lit one of the oil lamps and in seconds the room was filled with a cheery yellow light. Lyman's fingers settled on a stone. He brought it up and without even looking Koster realized what it was—another *abraxas,* like the one around Mariane's neck. "The same," Lyman said.

Koster reached for a grub-ax of his own.

They dug side by side for another fifteen minutes when suddenly Lyman's blade struck something that sounded like metal and the earth shuddered at the bottom of the trench. Lyman kicked the dirt aside, revealing a long section of corrugated iron still half buried in the ground. A few more strokes and they could bend it over without difficulty. It was brittle and mottled with rust. A draft of wind whistled through the basement. The lamplight flickered.

"What is it?" Mariane said, trying to look over their shoulders.

"A passage," Koster said.

"More like a grave," Guy added with a shudder.

Lyman scowled. "Pass that light over. Mariane, you'd better stay here."

"Why?" she said. And then more firmly, "I want to come too."

Lyman swung his feet over and down into the hole. It was about three feet wide and appeared to run parallel to the floor. "I don't think you should."

"Why not?" said Koster. "If she wants to go, why shouldn't she? She's as much a part of this as you are. Maybe more."

"That's not the point."

"We'll go first."

Lyman frowned and pulled his legs up out of the ground. "Have it your own way."

Koster took Mariane by the hand. "You follow her," he said to Lyman. "Guy can take the rear." Then, without pausing for an answer, he lifted one of the lamps down into the opening and slipped within the narrow breach.

Once in the tunnel itself, Koster dropped to his knees and crawled forward, holding the lamp up before him in his left hand. The dirt gave way to blocks of stone, well-hewn and snugly laid without a trace of mortar. Mariane tugged at his trouser leg. He turned to see her close behind, rocking on her elbows. "Are you okay?" he said. She nodded without speaking.

After several minutes, Koster noticed that the shaft was starting to decline and suddenly, only a few yards distant, the passage ended abruptly, falling off to emptiness. He was perspiring heavily. Crawling with only one arm had tired him and he put the lamp down for a moment and rested. A fine veil of dust descended through the light. Koster looked up. There was a crack in the block of stone directly above his head. The dust was slipping through it into the light and for a moment he understood the terror of the sailor in the belly of a sinking submarine, the miner's fear as he sees the final wood support give way. He took another breath. Nothing happened. Get a grip on yourself, he thought. Mariane was tapping his left ankle. He started toward the edge of the tunnel, holding the lamp out before him, cautious, prickly with fear.

The shaft opened onto the heart of another corridor, several feet below. Koster brought his legs up and dangled them over the edge so that he could slip to the floor of the new passageway with ease. As he did so he noticed a small room to his right. It was only about eight or nine feet deep, surrounded on all sides by a low stone bench. Mariane called his name and he turned to see her head appear through the breach in the corridor wall. He put the lamp on the ground and helped her down. In the distance, at the end of the long dark shaft, he could see Lyman and Guy crawling forward end to end, palled by a firefly glow. "Come on," he said. Then he realized he was whispering.

Mariane took the lamp up from the floor and started down the corridor. Koster hurried after her. They made their way through the damp darkness, hand in hand, scanning the ceiling and walls for other passages. Suddenly Mariane stopped and pointed. Just ahead, a shiny object lay at the foot of the right wall. They moved upon it cautiously, Mariane holding the lamp up high, until in a rush they realized what it was —a cross of some kind, an altarpiece. Koster reached over to pick it up. But this was no ordinary cross. Even in the dim lamplight he could see that it was oddly shaped, golden, and covered with glittering stones.

"Wait!"

Koster paused. It was Lyman who had spoken.

"Don't touch anything," the Englishman continued.

"Why not?"

"Let's just go on for a bit first. We can always come back for it later."

"Joseph, look."

Koster glanced around. Mariane was standing further up the corridor. The torch glowed high above her head and she was poised midstride, her legs apart, her right hand pointing. Koster scowled at Lyman. Then he turned to follow Mariane.

On the lip of the lamplight he could see that the corridor dissolved into a void of darkness, marking a new chamber. He took the lamp from her hand and lifted it higher. First there was a pedestal and chair to his right. Then a wooden rostrum. The floor appeared to be identical to the one in the cathedral above, a mosaic of black and white tiles, like a chessboard with a tessellated border. Koster walked slowly forward, shining the light about the room. There was a golden star etched in the center of the tiled floor. Within it glowed a single Hebrew letter.

"What is this place?" Mariane said, her voice echoing through the darkness.

"I don't know. A temple of some sort." He swung the light around. Across the way, set directly within the stone wall itself, Koster saw a spiral staircase leading upward through the ceiling. He moved closer, wondering if he had finally found the entrance, when he noticed that the staircase was blocked with boulders from above. Even more interesting was the way in which it had been constructed, with stone supports located underneath the individual stairs instead of at the center of the spiral. Then he realized why. Climbing the first few steps, he leaned across the inside banister and glimpsed the playful winking of his own lamp far below, like the moon in a puddle of water. The newel revolved around a well.

"Look, Joseph. Over here."

He turned away from the stairs. Mariane was walking at the very edge of the lamplight toward the wooden rostrum. Koster crossed the tiles uneasily. As he approached he saw the rostrum was topped with a kind of compass and a builder's square, leaning together, one against the other, and that they appeared to be made of solid gold. What did it all mean? he thought. He was about to pick the compass up when Mariane began to scream.

He whirled about. She stood but a dozen yards away, a little mound by her feet. "What is it?" he said, moving toward her. "Jesus Christ! You scared me."

"It's Maurice Duval," said Lyman. He stepped from the shadows.

Koster looked down and suddenly the mound in front of Mariane took shape, the broken torso gathered up its errant ribs, the ragged shirt, the jawbone, and the skull assembling, the leathery hands uniting once again as if in prayer. "My God," he said, bringing his own hand to his mouth. The bile crawled in his throat. "Mariane."

He took her in his arms. "Are you all right?"

She could not answer. She buried her face against his chest and he could feel her shuddering as she gasped for air. Koster looked up. Both Lyman and Guy were advancing from across the room. "How do you know it's him?" Koster said.

"I didn't until just now," said Lyman. "But it is him, isn't it, Mariane? Go on, tell him. It is Maurice, isn't it?"

Mariane nodded without turning. "Yes," she said finally. "Yes, it's Maurice. The shirt." She suddenly released her grip and turned to face the Englishman. "You knew all the time, didn't you?" She took another step. "Didn't you? Answer me." She struck Lyman on the chest, first one blow and then another. "Didn't you!"

Koster reached out to pull her back but Mariane was already spent. Her hands hung at her sides like two stones. Lyman had not even tried to defend himself. He just stood there with a dull, confused expression on his face.

"Call the police, Guy," Koster said.

Lyman took a step away. "I wouldn't do that if I were you."

"Call the police, Guy," he repeated, the words edged slightly sharper. Guy started for the corridor but Lyman pulled him back.

"Just one moment. Let's not be hasty here."

Koster planted himself before the Englishman, his chest out, drawing himself up, trying to look bigger. "Get the damn police," he said gruffly. "Now."

Guy started for the corridor again. This time Lyman let him pass. "You don't understand," he said.

"Save it for Captain Musel, Lyman. Or is it Terry Randall now? I can barely keep up."

Lyman sighed. "I am the bloody police," he said flatly.

"What?"

Lyman reached into an inside pocket and pulled his wallet out. "Here," he said, tossing it to Koster. "Go ahead. Take a peek. Detective Inspector Nigel Lyman. City of London Police."

Koster opened the wallet and the ID stood straight up, like a flag. It was Lyman all right. A little younger but the same.

"Give me five minutes," Lyman said. "Ten at the most. That's all. Then, if you're still not satisfied, I'll go with you to Musel. Ten minutes. It's all I'm asking."

"Why are you so afraid of Musel if you're a cop?" Koster tossed the wallet back to Lyman.

"It's not that I'm afraid of him. I just don't trust him very much."

"But we should trust you, right?"

"Come on, Joseph. Ten minutes. Is it so much to ask? And besides, you have to trust me now. You don't have any choice. We have to have faith in each other." He looked desperately at Mariane. "Don't you see?"

They stood for a moment in silence at the side of the checkerboard floor. Koster had wrapped his arm around Mariane to support her. At their feet lay the grim mound of dried skin and bone which was all that remained of Maurice Duval. Lyman shifted his weight from one foot to the other, attending the response, the pause. The lamplight flickered.

"Ten minutes?" Mariane said.

"Fifteen, at the very most."

She nodded almost imperceptibly. "Let's just get the hell out of here."

Chapter XVIII

AMIENS
September 24th, 1983

THEY SAT IN THE BASEMENT OF THE Bishop's Palace in metal folding chairs, all save Lyman who was pacing like a lecturer, fearful of their glances, worried by the patch of mud across his chest as he began to gather up his story. No one believes a man with muck on his shirt, he thought. And they had to believe him. This time it was all or naught. He had faced that boy by the river with his gun and something had happened in the space between the gun sight and the boy's unscored and open face. It had brought him back to Crosley once again, to that look of horrible surprise as the knife slipped through its mark, to the man with the wing-tipped shoes, to the fear which Lyman felt each time his pistol cleared the holster. Either he solved the case or it was over. There was no return now to the drab stairs and the steampipes by the door.

"I know what you're probably thinking," he said, raising his forearm smoothly, the presentment of a fly. "It's a question of trust, isn't it?" He found his left hand in his pocket and pulled it out. "It's a question of beliefs. The things we believe. The beliefs we fight for. Ends and means." Lyman sighed. This was all wrong. He was starting all wrong and for an instant he resented Koster with a lightning passion, for making him save his life, for making him run through this pointless game.

Lyman gathered himself up and there it was, at the baseboard of his memory, that book of discount coupons he had scooped out of the dustbin after Koster had tossed it away. The simplest show of human weakness, Lyman thought. That was the key to Koster.

"Let's stick to the facts," he said. "Much of this you know—the *abraxas* and the man at the antique shop. You were right to distrust Tellier, Mariane. He'd already spent six years in jail for smuggling before he moved to Amiens."

"I knew it," Mariane cut in. "I knew there was something about him."

"Yes," he said. "And it was the words you used to describe him which helped me unravel the line. The *abraxas* were found beneath the Bishop's Palace, and Maurice confronted Tellier. The antique dealer told him what the talismans were worth and Maurice became a part of the conspiracy. Then something happened between them.

"We may never know what it was. Perhaps it was greed, or fear. Whatever the reason, Tellier double-crossed Maurice and began to investigate the *abraxas* and their history on his own." Lyman smiled. "But Maurice didn't trust the antique dealer, and on the night of your argument, Mariane, perhaps the very night that Tellier first discovered the entrance to the temple, Maurice came to the Bishop's Palace to see what Tellier was up to. Tellier was caught. There was a struggle, and somehow Maurice was killed.

"Imagine it for a moment. Tellier is standing where

we stood, in that darkened corridor below. His weapon
is in his hands and Maurice is lying at his feet."

Lyman sighed as he caught sight of Mariane's face.
It was pale as a lily in the feeble light. "Tellier had
already been to jail," he added quickly. "He knew what
would happen to him if he were caught, so he decided
to make a run for it. But he needed money, papers. He
was too frightened to travel under his own name, and
he had no time to buy a new identity. Maurice was
killed on a Saturday and the banks were closed the
following day. In all likelihood Tellier didn't keep much
money at his house. The Amiens police said he was a
timid man, with a history of complaints about robbers
in the night. And so," Lyman continued, looking down,
his hands palm up before him, "having killed him, Tellier decided to become Maurice. He put his hat and
coat on, he took his car, and he drove off through the
night."

Lyman paused for a moment and scanned the faces
of the three before him. They were his tribunal, he
thought glumly. Koster had moved a trifle closer to
Mariane. His arm was about her shoulders but she
hardly seemed to notice him. Her attention was focused on Lyman. Her chin was raised, her hands folded
in her lap, her white skin glazed by the light like a
porcelain figurine.

Guy sat on Koster's other side. He also looked en-
raptured by the tale, leaning forward with his elbows
on his knees, his stubby fingers playing with his beard.
He could have been watching television, Lyman
thought. Perhaps this was a good sign.

"As he drove home," Lyman continued, "Tellier realized that no one would look for Maurice Duval in
Amiens if he had already left the country, the gendarmerie on his heels. So he went to Duval's office,
opened the safe with the keys he had found on Maurice's body, and stole the money and passport. It would
have been easy for someone familiar with forgery and

smuggling, as Tellier was, to doctor the passport and then slip across the border. He probably knew the friendliest checkpoints, the softest guards."

"You're running out of time," Koster said abruptly.

Lyman planted his feet. "Give me half a chance, for Christ's sake. You said ten minutes."

"This is absurd. Even if you're telling the truth about Maurice, that doesn't explain what you're doing here. A British detective. A local French crime."

"I didn't come here because of Maurice. I knew nothing about him when I arrived." He shook his head. "I was assigned to the Pontevecchio case, in London."

"Pontevecchio? You mean the banker?"

"That's exactly what I mean. When Pontevecchio left Italy last year, just before the collapse of his bank, he was assisted by a fellow named Balducci who was milking him for protection money. Somehow or other Balducci heard about Jacques Tellier and the things he'd unearthed here in Amiens. Both of them were Masons, and both had been involved in smuggling."

"What do you mean unearthed? The *abraxas*? The Contender?"

"Yes, both. But even more important, Tellier had found the missal with its reference to the Gospel of Thomas at Chartres."

A hush swept over them. Lyman took a step away. First there would be duty, he thought, and then the mystery of numbers. And if that failed there would always be something else, some show of human weakness to recline on.

"You mean the one my cousin gave me," Koster said. "You mean the Gnostic missal?"

"The Masonic missal."

"But why? What does Grabowski have to do with this?"

Lyman paused. "I'm not sure, at least not yet. But I know the Book of Thomas the Contender isn't important. The real prize is the Gospel of Thomas at

Chartres. At first I didn't understand. After all," he
said to Guy, "you had told us there were several other
copies of the gospel already in existence. But then I
realized that it's the age of this particular version that
makes it so important, the fact that the sayings could
be Christ's own words, and Gnostic words at that. Heresy, Joseph."

He nodded. "Yes, Jacques Tellier realized that. I'm
sure he was desperate to go to Chartres. To actually
have the Gospel of Thomas in his hands would have
given him more power—the treasure is better than the
map. But the journey was impossible. He had killed
Maurice, you see. The only place where he could go
was out of France.

"So he searched for another way to sell the information and the missal. I doubt that Balducci himself
really believed Tellier's story about the gospels. If he
had, he probably would have bought the information
himself. But he knew Pontevecchio would. He knew
Pontevecchio was desperate enough to believe anything
that would save his bank. His life was in ruins. His
Banco Fabiano was on the verge of collapse. Warrants
had been issued for his arrest. Archbishop Grabowski
and the IOR would no longer cover his debts. They
had disowned him. But here," he said, snatching the air
with his fist, "here, at last, was the wonderful thing he
needed to make your cousin—and the powerful ma-
chinery of the Vatican—come to his rescue."

Lyman clasped his hands together. A stillness had
settled on the room. Mariane and Guy continued to
stare at him raptly. Even Koster had uncrossed his legs.
He was leaning closer, listening.

"But Jacques Tellier was a timid man. He knew that
there was nothing to prevent Pontevecchio and
Balducci from killing him once they knew the secret of
the labyrinth at Amiens. So he devised an insurance
policy. He went to the meeting in Austria armed with
only enough information to persuade Pontevecchio

that his story was legitimate. The rest he placed in a locker at the Amiens coach terminal. All Pontevecchio had to do was give him a down payment on the final price, and Tellier would hand over the key to the locker in Amiens. Armed with that information, and after one final phone call for the last phrase in the equation, Pontevecchio could then go to Chartres and unearth the Gospel of Thomas.

"Even the choice of lockers was designed to thwart some attempt by Balducci or Pontevecchio to dispense with Tellier. Any package left over a week at the coach terminal is brought directly to the Amiens police. That's where it stays for sixty days until it's finally opened. In theory at least. As it turned out the police were a little lax this time. Tellier's picnic basket arrived on May twenty-eighth, 1982, but it wasn't opened until September twentieth. By then, Pontevecchio had flown to London to try to sell his knowledge of the Gospel of Thomas to the Opus Dei, a wealthy right-wing Catholic group. But his guide, Balducci, betrayed him. Despite all of his schemes, despite the millions of pounds he had squirreled away in Switzerland and the Caribbean, Pontevecchio ended up being hanged under Blackfriars Bridge."

"I thought they said he committed suicide," Koster cut in. "That's what I read. That's what they said in the papers."

"You're right. That's what the inquest ruled the first time. A trifle too quickly, it turned out. You see, the Amiens police saw Pontevecchio's name in a letter which Jacques Tellier had left in the locker as a final safeguard, to protect himself against betrayal. They alerted the City of London Police. The case was reopened," Lyman said, trying to sound convincing. What was the point of telling him the truth? What would he gain if Koster knew that he himself had only been assigned to fail?

"Somewhere along the way Marco Scarcella got involved. He was the head of the I Four, a secret Masonic Lodge to which Pontevecchio also belonged."

"Are you saying Scarcella killed Pontevecchio?"

Lyman smiled, cherishing the question. It was the first. The words wound to the heart of Koster's curiosity. "Perhaps," he said. "Only, if he did, and if Scarcella first found out about the Gospel of Thomas in London, why did he wait to investigate? Of course he might not have had enough information. Or perhaps, like Pontevecchio's guide—Balducci—he didn't really believe the story. It is fantastic, even for a Freemason, I imagine. But in September, when the Amiens police opened the picnic basket, it was already too late for Scarcella. He was in jail at Champ Dollon, in Switzerland, caught while trying to transfer millions from a Geneva bank account."

Lyman laughed. "You can imagine his mood when he first heard about the picnic basket. I'm sure he sent word out immediately that he wanted Jacques Tellier found. The antique dealer had gone underground, you see, after his meeting with Pontevecchio. Somehow, probably through the telephone number in the picnic basket, Scarcella's men tracked Tellier to a tourist town in Austria. There they tried to make him talk. But, fortunately for us, they bungled the job, and drugged and beaten though he was, he managed to escape, only to be struck by a car in the chase."

"Maurice," said Mariane. "After all these months of grieving . . . and it was a stranger." She shook her head. Tears began to well up in her eyes. Koster reached out to comfort her again.

"I'm afraid so," Lyman said. "They sent back 'what was left of him,' you told us. But the real Maurice remained here, buried underneath the cathedral."

Mariane wiped her face with her hand. "All this time," she said, trying to catch her breath. "All this time, and he was only a few hundred yards away."

Lyman pulled a folding chair out and sat down facing them. It was a time for greater intimacy, he thought. He had to bring them in.

"So Scarcella was left with the drawing, the letter, and the missal," he said, "but with Tellier dead he had no way to interpret them, no access to the temple here at Amiens, and no numerical key to unravel the labyrinth at Chartres, to finally unearth the Gospel of Thomas. He must have been mad with frustration." He smiled grimly, relishing the thought.

"Here was this treasure of historic proportions, capable of toppling the Church, a lever of unspeakable power, a document for which countless men had already killed and died, and it was just beyond his reach, just out of sight . . . until you arrived." Lyman looked pointedly at Koster.

The American was sitting with his legs crossed, his arms akimbo. He was waiting too, and then the words began to settle, one after another, and with them his expression. He brought a hand up to his neck. His eyes widened. He straightened in his chair. "The thief at the hotel," he said.

Lyman nodded. "The thief was Scarcella's man. And he wasn't alone that night. I might as well tell you now. You should know it all before you commit yourself anyway. There was another man on my balcony that night, only he didn't fall. He made it to the roof. I was about to follow him when I heard you calling out next door." Lyman looked down at his hands. They were filthy but oddly still. "Who else knew about your book besides Nick Robinson, your publisher, and Archbishop Grabowski?"

"You can't be serious. Look, I'm not exactly fond of him, but you don't really think my cousin had anything to do with that guy in my room."

Lyman shrugged. "Perhaps not. But he had plenty of motives to silence Pontevecchio: one, in case Pontevecchio revealed what he knew about Banco Fabiano and the IOR; and two, because of the Gospel of Thomas. And he also had the time. Pontevecchio was last seen alive at eleven o'clock on the evening of June seventeenth. But he wasn't found until half past ten the following day. That's eleven and a half hours, more than enough time to fly from London to Rome to receive the shocking news."

"Now you think Grabowski got the missal from Pontevecchio," Koster said. "Before you told us it was in that locker."

"A copy was sent to the City of London Police, and the original to the Countess de Rochambaud in Paris."

"She never mentioned that."

"Of course she didn't. It was she who bought the original *abraxas* from Jacques Tellier for fifteen thousand francs. They were the ones you saw in her collection. She's a member of the G.L.F., another Masonic group. But she didn't kill Pontevecchio. The missal didn't reach her until *after* his death. No. It was Scarcella who gave the missal to Grabowski."

"But why would he do that? Why would he even tell him?"

"In order to reach you."

"Me? I don't know anything. I didn't even know you were a cop."

"Don't you see? It's obvious. Scarcella was warned that I was coming to investigate. So he sent his men out here to Amiens to meet me. They were the ones we saw at the cathedral on the first day that we met, the day you were measuring out the labyrinth. They followed us both back to the hotel. But they failed to frighten us away. And when Scarcella learned that you were now involved, he naturally assumed Grabowski was behind it."

"But I came here because of the book. My cousin had nothing to do with it."

Lyman nodded. "You and I know that. But Scarcella didn't. Tellier was dead, and Scarcella needed someone else. You were the logical choice. You know

mathematics and architecture. You're familiar with the
cathedrals, with their history and legends. Scarcella's
hoodlum tactics have failed him, so he's decided to
have you find the answer for him, at a distance, in
safety." Lyman smiled ironically. "Like a missile."

"Well, he can forget it," Koster said. "I'm getting
out of here. Why didn't you tell me, Nigel?" He shook
his head. "And to think I trusted you. I thought you
saved my life. I thought you were my fucking friend."

He stood quickly and began to walk toward
the door, slowing with each step, his momentum gradually receding, and suddenly the chairs filled up with
children and Lyman saw himself, a striped cap on his
head and ink stains on his elbows, the maths don dron-
ing far away: If you travel half the distance in between
two points, then half again and half again forever,
you'll never reach the other side.

"If I had told you," Lyman said, "would you have
stayed?"

"Sure I would." Koster turned around. "Probably."
He slipped his hands into his pockets. "That's irrelevant anyway. The point is that you didn't tell me."

"And what about now?" Lyman looked at each of
their faces in turn. Guy was stroking his beard meditatively. Mariane had stopped crying. She was staring at
the window facing out onto the courtyard of the
Bishop's Palace. Koster simply glowered at him openly.

"What about it?" he said. "You're the one with all
the answers, Nigel. You're the one manipulating everybody. Congratulations. You found the temple. You
found Maurice. Great fucking job."

Lyman stood slowly. "But it isn't over," he said.
"You're the only one who can understand the labyrinth. You know that."

"Why should I do anything? Why should I help
you?" Koster laughed bitterly. "You've got a lot of
nerve. You set me up and then you ask me to help you.
What about this?" he said, pulling at his collar. The

blue line wriggled round his neck. "Do you think I enjoyed being strangled by a total stranger?"

First duty, then the mystery of numbers, Lyman thought. "You can't give up now," he said. "You know who Scarcella is. You know what he's done. He's here, right now, in Amiens. I've seen him."

"Good for you."

"Look, Joseph. Without you I don't have the labyrinth. And without that I have nothing. We have to keep feeding them. We have to draw them in. Then, when we're good and ready, when we have the Gospel of Thomas ourselves, we can tell Grabowski everything. Don't worry. He'll pass it on to Scarcella. That's when I'll set the hook."

"You're crazy, Nigel. I don't care who he is, or what he's done. It's not worth dying just to see him busted."

"You won't be safe in New York now, Joseph. You know too much."

"I'll take my chances."

"So that's it, is it? You just give up and run back to America, to your safe little job, is that it?"

"That's a pretty fair description."

"And what about the labyrinth? After all these centuries the answer is in your hands and you're just going to throw it away, you're just going to forget it. Do you really believe that? Or at night, Joseph, when you're lying in bed and you can't sleep, won't the image keep you wondering, the numbers swimming about, looking for a pattern? And what about the Gospel of Thomas? If it's as old as it appears, it could topple the Church."

"I got over my work on the Goldbach Conjecture. I'll get over this too." He shook his head. "You don't get over death, Nigel. If you want to be a hero, you go ahead. You lure Scarcella in. You trap Grabowski."

"I don't want to be a hero, Joseph. Don't you understand? I don't give a damn about Pontevecchio." Lyman took another step. "You don't see it, do you? You've made a symbol of your life and now you've forgotten what it means. I've already been a hero. Once, long ago. Yes, I didn't tell you that, did I? It wasn't part of the disguise." He laughed privately, a soft dry sound. "Well, I can tell you now. It was sheer heaven for a year and hell forever since. You remember, don't you? You know exactly what I'm talking about. All those prizes at the start and then what, Joseph? Then where do you go?"

"Listen, if you want to prove something to yourself, don't do it at my expense."

"I'm not talking about me," Lyman shouted back. He had not meant to raise his voice. "I'm not holding myself up against Scarcella as some moral beacon. It's not a question of pride. My God, look at me. Do I look proud? You think everyone is as innocent as you are, Joseph. I'm not innocent. There are no innocents. We caused that silly little war as much as they did."

"What war?"

"The Falklands' war. The war with bloody Argentina. The war Scarcella helped supply with missiles."

"He's talking about his son." Guy's voice was like the wind, the sound of snow falling.

"The one who died in the war," Mariane said from the other side.

"And Scarcella supplied the missiles," Lyman added flatly, in the simplest show of human weakness.

He had won.

Part III

Jesus said to them, "When you make the two one, and when you make the inside like the outside and the outside like the inside, and the above like the below . . . then you will enter the kingdom."

The Secret Sayings of Christ
The Gospel of Thomas

Chapter XIX

CHARTRES
September 25th, 1983

THE CLOUD HOVERED OVER THE HO-
rizon like a smoke ring, pearl gray and ominous. The
flat land rippled as the train screamed by, sheep
scattering in fields, hedges running. Lyman thought he
heard the train wheels clicking but it was only the knitting needles of a woman across the aisle. She was fash-
ioning what appeared to be the sleeve of a sweater,
bright blue with cherry-colored anchors. It looked so
strange without the rest—disjointed, the last part of a
body found. He shifted uncomfortably. The seat was
new. The whole train was new, decompartmentalized.
Only the people were old. "Look here, Joseph," he
said, leaning forward suddenly. "Can't you go over it
once more?"

Koster sat across from him, rolling his eyes. "Just
forget about it, okay? It's something you either have
the knack for, or you don't. Like police work."

"But I have to understand."

"It has to do with group theory, with relationships

described by roots which exclude transcendental numbers. It has to do with symmetry. Okay?"

"Can't you explain it without numbers?"

"That's like asking me to speak French without using words. Here," he said, "imagine my fist represents the dominant sequence equivalent to the symmetry of the labyrinth at Amiens." He thrust it out. "And here," he added, circling the fist with his other hand, one finger jauntily extended, "here is the other sequence I discovered, like a minor in music, circling about. You see? Like the rings around Saturn."

"Right," said Lyman, desperate. Old man, new maths. The woman with the knitting needles was eyeing him oddly. She wrenched at her yarn and a fresh blue length appeared, as if by magic, out of the bag by her feet. Lyman sighed. "Like Saturn."

"That's right. So I transmuted the second sequence with *gematria*, and it turned out that the numbers are equivalent to a word which Guy says was the phrase for 'spirit' or 'engineer' back in the Middle Ages. Like the modern French word *génie*. But the last few letters made no sense. Then I realized it was a hybrid: GN thirty-seven twenty-four. You see? Letters and numbers. That was the final reference.

"Even in the Middle Ages the Bible was organized in the same numerical sequence. Genesis, chapter thirty-seven, verse twenty-four. 'And they took him,' meaning the dreamer Joseph, 'and cast him into a pit: and the pit was empty, there was no water in it.' It's an obvious reference to the well which I saw in the temple, the one with the spiral staircase wrapped around it. In the old days, the well extended all the way up to the cathedral. The priests and deacons used to draw their water from it for their services, for cleaning and that sort of thing. The well was the main entrance. What we crawled through was intended as a ventilation shaft."

Obvious, Lyman thought derisively. If it were so obvious, why had it taken him so long? "Child's play," he said tightly.

Lyman suddenly felt tired. He looked out the window and noticed that the flat gray fields of corn and winter grain had been replaced by trees. The train rode on an embankment at least fifty feet from the forest floor, and the fecund thickness of the branches put him in mind of South America. The rains had swelled the leaves, the tree roots, the bogs which glittered periodically through the green. Only the occasional stone house—passing in a wink's time—only the periodic village brought him back to France. Is this what Argentina looked like? he wondered. Surely they had jungles there, or was it all just plains and archipelagos, buckled by mountains, circled by condors? "I want to thank you," he said suddenly. "For going along with all of this, Joseph."

Koster gazed out of the window. His hair was getting long and it hung across his forehead, covering one eye. He started to speak, then stopped. "Forget it," he said finally. "We're even now, that's all." He tried to smile. "What about Grabowski though? What do I tell him?"

"Tell him you were finished with your work at Amiens, and that you decided to go to Chartres. Don't tell him about the temple or the labyrinth. And for God's sake, don't tell him the sequence."

"What if he asks about you?"

"As far as anyone else is concerned, I'm just a tourist you met on the way."

"He won't believe that. If Scarcella's on to you, then Grabowski must be too."

"Perhaps. But as long as he thinks you don't know, we'll be safe. Trust me."

"What about Mariane?"

"Listen, Joseph. Scarcella has no reason to harm anyone, least of all Mariane. He has to play this very carefully now, especially after the hotel. Why should he try and force the information out of you when you're about to give it to him through Grabowski? Really. There's nothing to worry about," he lied. "All you have to do is unravel the second labyrinth and I'll handle the rest. Then you can go back to New York."

Another town flashed by. Gazeran. Epernon. Maintenon. They were approaching Chartres and Lyman could see more houses through the trees. Fields skipped about, slate gray like chips of water, like ponds furrowed by the wind.

"That's not what I meant," Koster said quietly. "I want to help. I do, really. I understand exactly what you're feeling."

Oh, God, Lyman thought. Here it comes—the American capacity for empathy. Or maybe it was just Koster's Catholic demeanor, his desire to confess.

"I had a son once too," Koster said evenly. "But there was an accident. He died soon after he was born."

"I'm sorry," Lyman said.

The American shrugged, the knitting needles clacked, and the window darkened without warning. There was a muffled press of air and Lyman realized they had gone underground. A tunnel or a bridge. The countryside had been replaced by darkness and the pale lines of his own face in the glass. Then they were free again.

Lyman tried to think of something to say. People had begun to gather up their belongings. A man in a black coat and heavy grease-stained boots stood right beside him in the aisle. He was carrying a suitcase marked with a stamp from the Republic of Togo.

Always distant but a few more leagues, thought Lyman. Always unknown to one another. "We must be getting close," he said. Koster nodded.

The train began to turn, tilting to one side, the houses stretching into streets and other houses still, into a warehouse and a water tower through the trees, only a cartoon shadow to the spires rising of a sudden up ahead, two towers like two hands about to clasp. "I can see the cathedral," Lyman said.

Koster leaned forward, craning his neck to see out the window. "Where? Oh, yeah," he said. "It looks so small from here." Then he added, "Can you imagine walking toward it through the fields, Nigel? I mean back in the Middle Ages. Can you imagine seeing it like this on the horizon for the first time? The Cult of Relics and all that. Like a pilgrim."

Lyman nodded and the cathedral vanished behind trees. Like a pair of pilgrims, he thought.

They checked into a little hotel near the Place Drouaise, due north of the cathedral near the convent of the Soeurs du Bon-Secours. The Métropole stood parallel to the road to Rouen. It was an agreeable one-star establishment, clean and moderately priced, and Lyman was delighted to discover a real bathtub in his room.

After unpacking they had coffee in the dining room downstairs and then headed directly for the cathedral. Lyman wanted to get an early start. He reasoned that if they could discover the location of the gospel by the end of the day, they might return to Amiens as early as the following evening. All that remained then was the rendezvous with Scarcella, the final confrontation.

They were discussing the details when the street curved suddenly. Beyond the circle of the Place Drouaise, rising high above the rooftops and the trees, poised on a hill at the very center of the town, stood the cathedral. For a moment neither of them spoke. They moved together silently through the street, form-ing a memory. A stone walk extended from the road between a line of trees, beside the rampart of the old medieval town, up, up and around the hill, into the dark entanglement of streets before the western square, the woodwork and the stone, the towers racing one another to the sky. "The roof looks so green," said Lyman.

"That's the oxidization," Koster answered automatically.

What did he see, thought Lyman, with his architect's perspective? Oxidization over green?

The Promenade des Charbonniers circled the walls of the old city. It would have required a formidable force, thought Lyman, to breech those ramparts in the Middle Ages. They shot straight up above the path, fifty feet of grim uncompromising stone. And then a path above, and then another wall before the town itself. No wonder the towers could be seen so far away. The cathedral rose like a lighthouse from the open plain.

It took them fifteen minutes to climb the walk, and they found themselves, tired and winded, at a gate which opened onto a narrow cobbled street within the walls of the old city. The pavement led them on, past alleys and a garage now and then, past other crooked streets. Chartres was completely different from Amiens. These buildings had been standing for six hundred years. No bombs had fallen here. There were no shrapnel marks, no sudden stands of 1950s brick within circles of old stone.

As they walked they followed the cathedral towers high above the rooftops. Koster had begun a monologue about the history of Chartres but Lyman kept it at a distance. He didn't care to know the facts, not this time anyway. He preferred his own interpretation. Then, suddenly, the street simply gave up. They slipped inside another gate and discovered they were standing at the northern flank of the cathedral. Lyman shaded his eyes, blocking his own horizon, taking in the stonework a single section at a time. The flying buttresses unrolled against the walls like miller's wheels and he thought that the cathedral appeared not like a lighthouse now, a beacon at the center of a plain, but like an engine churning, static in our time but relentless, grinding with the force and patience of tectonic plates, a God machine.

"It looks like we missed the morning service," Koster said beside him.

"Good. Less of a crowd."

They entered the cathedral through one of the side doors and the first thing Lyman noticed was the darkness. At Amiens, the majority of the cathedral's original windows had been broken over the centuries, and then replaced by white translucent glass. But here the windows were the same as they had been since the Crusades, from ruby to cobalt blue, each pane a phrase, each lancet a whole story. They moved slowly toward the central aisle, wary of their footsteps. Lyman glimpsed a little room just off the western entrance where slides and photographs were on sale. Spiritual memorabilia, the Cult of Relics, he thought, remembering Christ's words within the Temple. *But you have made it a den of thieves.* Or was that only Luke's interpretation, just one more gospel truth?

"Anyone here to speak in English?"

Lyman tugged at Koster's sleeve. A tall, almost emaciated Englishman with a seedy tweed jacket stood by the bulletin board beside the souvenir room. He had salt-and-pepper hair, pushed back with abandon, and a long red woolen scarf about his neck. "Anyone here for the lecture in English?" he repeated, cocking his head.

Koster planted himself before the guide. "Excuse me," he began.

"Yes, all in order now. All in good time. Gather round."

A group of what Lyman took to be Americans sidled by.

"I was wondering," Koster added, "if I could talk to you about the labyrinth."

The guide winced. "The labyrinth," he repeated.

"That's right. The legend of the Gospel of Thomas."

"Oh, that! You're not going to start dancing about the labyrinth, are you?" He turned and smiled at the impending crowd.

"What are you talking about?"

"Every year we get a few odd pilgrims who run through the labyrinth in their stocking feet. Spiritual vibrations and all that."

A woman tittered. The guide smiled back. "And Thomas doesn't play much of a role in this cathedral," he continued. "This is the cathedral of Our Lady. Anyone here from Los Angeles? That belongs to Our Lady too, as the full name of the city implies."

The guide turned and began to chatter on about the history of names. Lyman grabbed Koster by his anorak. "Never mind," he said, pulling him away. The crowd was getting out of hand.

"Do join if you want to, the morning lecture in English."

Lyman and Koster wandered over to the center of the cathedral. Most of the flagstones were covered by chairs but the shape of the labyrinth was clearly visible beneath them—a white path in black boundaries, four quadrants once again, but this time truly round instead of octagonal like the labyrinth at Amiens.

"The trick is to let yourself go," Koster said, pulling out a tape measure. "Once you have the numbers, finding the pattern means falling into it. That's the hardest part."

Lyman reached for the tape. "I'll hold this end. You take the other side."

Several hours passed before they had gathered enough information for Koster to begin his calculations. He sat in a chair by the center of the labyrinth, punching at his calculator and scribbling numbers in his notebook.

Lyman waited patiently at his side. The darkness of the cathedral lent it privacy. He could watch the faithful pray, listen to the same gasp at the same Madonna in a dozen different languages, listen for the whir of film.

Lyman closed his eyes. He thought about buying Jackie a card. Something suitable. A snapshot of a gargoyle from the air. A demon in stained glass. A postcard of his own soul. He opened his eyes. "How much longer, Joseph?"

Koster looked up. "I don't know." Then he sighed. "It's just not working out. I don't know."

"What do you mean, you don't know? I thought you said this would be easy."

"According to my calculations, both Amiens and Chartres share a basic pattern, with seven bays in the nave, four in the choir and three in each arm of the transept. Seven is also the number of chapels they have in common, again in a three-four pattern."

"Stop me if I'm wrong, but if the two labyrinths share a basic pattern, shouldn't that be good? I mean, doesn't it make it easier?"

"Of course it should. That's just it. But the numbers don't make sense. The *gematria* doesn't work."

Lyman sighed. He had wanted it all to be over. He had wanted it all to end. Now with each passing moment, and each passing day, he could feel Scarcella slipping away. Grabowski would return to the Vatican. Koster would go back to New York. But when the game was up, when all was said and done, where would he go? Where could he go?

"Listen to me, Joseph," he said. "The longer we stay here, the greater the chances that Scarcella will either leave France or discover the Gospel of Thomas himself. He could be here in Chartres already."

"Great."

"What I mean is, I was hoping to bring the gospel back to England, to set up the trap there. Now that's out of the question. We'll have to do it here. And that means we'll need help, local help."

"You mean the police."

"I'm afraid it means Captain Musel. I can't try and persuade the Chartres gendarmerie, not at this stage of the game. It would take forever, and time is something we don't have, even if they did believe us." He paused and looked down at the floor. "I'm going back to Amiens."

"Why don't you just call Musel?"

"This isn't something I can ring him up about. I'll have to show him the temple. I know it's dangerous, but it's the only way. And it won't be easy. Even if he agrees, he'll be working in another jurisdiction."

"Maybe I should come too."

"No, you stay here. It's better you spend your time on the labyrinth. I'll be back tomorrow." He stood slowly. "Call me at the Hôtel de la Paix if anything happens."

"What do you mean, happens?"

"I don't know. Anything. Look, stop worrying. We were very careful at the station. I'll see you tomorrow night." They shook hands. "Good luck."

With that he turned and headed for the entrance. The guide was back again for his last tour of the day, repeating the same words, the same speech as in the morning. "Please join if you want to." Lyman hesitated in the doorway. Something was wrong. He spun about, trying vainly to spot Koster in the crowd. There he was, chatting with another man.

For a moment Lyman considered rushing back. Then he noticed the American glance at his watch and speak a few words, and the stranger in the olive-colored raincoat moved away.

I'm getting tired, Lyman thought. I'm losing touch. He cocked the collar of his coat and shuffled out the door.

Chapter XX

CHARTRES
September 26th, 1983

KOSTER KNEW HE WAS ABOUT TO DIE when he first saw the gun. It came out of the darkness, out of the corridor ahead, the muzzle only, powder-flash red and pointing. He crouched against the wall, for the first time understanding the real character of stone, its intricate compactness. Then he heard the cry, and turned to follow Lyman to the ground. There was a dull thud as the body settled on its side, the slightest tremor, and even in the darkness he could see the tributary spreading through the Englishman's shirt, the jagged hole like an open can of soup.

Koster woke. The room was dark, his sheets and blankets soaked with perspiration. A truck groaned down the street. He turned on the light by his head. The clock on the nightstand read seven.

Seven, three, four, twelve. He repeated the numbers again, like a litany, over and over, trying to lean on them for balance. Numbers had always invoked a sense of security in Koster, and yet now they computed his failure. He had spent half the night at the Chartres cathedral trying to unravel the labyrinth. Half the night and for nothing. He was no closer to the truth, no nearer to the Gospel of Thomas. He sat up in the bed and rubbed his eyes. It was time for a shower, he thought, and then back to the labyrinth again.

It took him forty minutes to wash and dress. He was just slipping his shoes on when Jean-Luc Agay, the owner of the Hôtel Métropole, knocked on the door and told him that he had a visitor. Koster asked him who it was, but the innkeeper only shrugged. The stranger had not volunteered his name. He was a big man, in his sixties. He was wearing a suit, and glasses. That was all he knew.

Koster followed the innkeeper down the stairs. His visitor was sitting at a table in the dining room. He was facing the other way, reading a newspaper, drinking a cup of coffee with his left hand.

It was Grabowski.

"Joseph," the archbishop said when he saw him. He tossed his newspaper on the table and stood up. "It's good to see you again."

"What are you doing here?"

"Taking in the country. And I wanted to see how you were getting along."

Koster turned for a moment to the innkeeper. "Another café au lait, please," he said.

Agay vanished with a nod.

"How did you find me?" Koster said.

"I asked the concierge at the Hôtel de la Paix."

"Of course."

"Are you all right, Joseph?"

"Why? What do you mean?"

Grabowski sat down once again at the table. "You just seem a little nervous," he said.

"Must be the work."

"How's it going? Any luck with that missal?"

Koster sat down beside the archbishop. "Actually, I

wasn't getting very far with the labyrinth at Amiens, so I thought I'd try this one instead."

The innkeeper returned with a pair of coffeepots and a small plate of croissants. Koster thanked him. Then he began to measure out equal portions of coffee and hot milk, pouring them one on top of the other in his cup. When he had finished, he pushed the service over to Grabowski.

Where were the signs of guilt? he thought, watching the archbishop's hands. Where were the nervous glances? Had Lyman been dreadfully wrong? "How long do you plan to stay?" he said, finally.

"Oh, I don't know. A few days, I suppose. I haven't seen this part of France in years. It's quite charming."

"Yes, it is, isn't it. You know, sometimes I think about getting out of New York. Going out to the country. Away from the crime and the pollution."

"I don't blame you. It must be hard to live in New York."

"Unless you have a lot of money."

"I suppose."

"But you know, even the suburbs aren't safe these days. Even places like Amiens."

Grabowski frowned. "What do you mean?" he said.

"Didn't I tell you what happened?"

The archbishop shook his head.

"At the hotel. They said it was attempted robbery, but I don't know." Koster pulled the collar of his shirt down, exposing the blue slash line around his neck.

"Mother of Christ! When did that happen?"

"My first week. I'm surprised you didn't hear about it. It was all over the local papers."

"No," Grabowski answered quietly. "I had no idea."

"You're not safe anywhere these days. Except perhaps at the Vatican. But I guess that even there you have crime. I bet you get a lot of pickpockets for those Papal balcony scenes."

"I wouldn't know."

"I thought you were the mayor or something."

"It's strictly a ceremonial title. My work at the IOR takes up most of my time."

"I bet it does. How is it these days, anyway? Are they still hounding you?"

"Who?"

"The press, the paparazzi. I would have thought they'd given up by now, after all this time."

"I'd rather not discuss it."

"Oh, come on, why not? It's been years."

"I'd simply rather not."

"Some people would consider that a sign of guilt."

For a few seconds neither of them spoke. Then Grabowski leaned forward slowly, resting the tips of his elbows on the white tablecloth. "What do you want from me, Joseph? A confession? Is that what you expect?"

"That's not up to me."

"You're damned right, it's not." Grabowski pushed his coffee cup away. "What do you know about Fabiano, anyway?"

"I've read a few things."

"You've read!" The archbishop laughed flatly and dropped back in his chair.

He wasn't wearing a priest's collar, Koster noticed for the first time. He was wearing a dark blue tie with little yellow squares.

"Well, I lived it," Grabowski continued. "All those years with Pontevecchio. You were only a kid then. You were barely born. They were hard years for the Church. Spiritually, politically. There was Vatican Two."

"Financially."

"Yes, financially. What's wrong with that? You make it sound as if banking and the Church are mutually exclusive. It's okay these days when a priest acts like a politician, but if he's a businessman, God help him. Everyone gets offended. Well, I ask you, Joseph.

What's wrong with business? How do you think we pay for all the hospitals we run, for all the schools, the soup kitchens? This is the real world. It costs money to help people."

"It wasn't always that way. Not in the beginning, anyway."

"When? In some pristine, imaginary age?"

"You know what I mean. In Christ's day."

"Don't be naive, Joseph. Even Christ had a bureaucracy. Someone took care of the transportation. Someone took care of the money."

"Who, Kazimierz?"

"That's not the point. The point is that without a defined hierarchy, without the proper finances, the Church could never have survived. It would have been crushed, persecuted out of existence."

"Like the Gnostics. They didn't believe in a hierarchy. They didn't require money."

Grabowski shook his head sadly. "I wish I could afford your simplistic view of the world, Joseph. I really do. But the sad truth of it is, to succeed a Church requires a structure, an organization. And an organization requires money. Not only to feed the poor, but to finance missionaries. To pay for the heat in day care centers." He pointed out the window. "To build cathedrals, Joseph."

"I'm not talking about that. I'm talking about Fabiano."

The archbishop sighed. "Look, I don't have to defend myself to you. The courts exonerated me. You can believe what you want. That's your prerogative. But I never benefited personally from any one of those transactions, if that's what you're thinking. I live a simple life." He paused. "I came here to help you, Joseph. That's why I brought you those papers. And as far as my past is concerned, if I ever made some mistakes in judgment, if I ever got blinded in some small way by the monies generated by Pontevecchio, it was only because of my love for the Church."

Koster dropped his napkin on the table. The archbishop glanced back for an instant, and in that moment, as their eyes met just before he turned away again, Koster knew—with the certainty of numbers—that Lyman had spoken the truth.

"I'm sorry, it's none of my business," Koster said. "Of course the Church needs money, operating expenses." He tried to smile. "And I don't want you to think that I'm not grateful for your help. I'm glad you came. Really I am. Have you checked in yet?"

Grabowski shook his head. "Not yet."

"Well, why not? I'm in room thirty-six. There's an empty one right next door."

"You mean you want me to stay?"

"Of course I do."

Grabowski turned toward Koster slowly, his eyes downcast, his mouth half open. "I don't know what to say." Then he looked up. "Thank you, Joseph," he added gently, without inflection.

"Thank you for what?"

"For believing in me. For taking me on faith."

The cathedral square was empty, except for a beggar by the western door, and a watchful tourist left over from the weekend. Koster and Grabowski walked along the northern wall of the Chartres Elementary School. Koster was talking, but Grabowski only heard the sounds of children playing on the other side, the swells of laughter, of footfalls running toward the future.

For the Church, he thought. It was always for the Church.

They crossed the street and stopped by the cathedral gate. Koster said something about a meeting later on, at the hotel, with his tourist friend from England. Grabowski tried to look agreeable. He shook his cousin's hand as warmly as he could. He watched his back retreat along the path. He even waved as Koster finally slipped into the entrance to the cathedral. Then his whole demeanor changed. He turned briskly on his heels and headed back across the street, into the narrow garden at the center of the square, along the well-clipped lawn until he stood before the watchful tourist who was sitting with his camera on a bench.

"Tell him it's off," he said contemptuously. "Tell him he made a mistake when he sent that man to the Hôtel de la Paix in Amiens."

"Sorry?" The dark young man in the olive-colored raincoat looked at him and smiled. "My English is not good."

"It's good enough."

The young man shrugged. Then his smile collapsed, his eyes narrowed, and he started to his feet. Grabowski struck him squarely on the shoulder with his open palm. For a moment the young man struggled to keep upright. He reached for the archbishop, but Grabowski pushed him down again and he fell across the bench.

"Just so you realize my conviction," the archbishop said. He dropped a hand on the young man's shoulder and squeezed the nerves and muscles at the base of his neck. "Tell him that we had a bargain. He said no more bloodshed. That's what he told me. That was the condition."

Suddenly the young man in the olive-colored raincoat laughed, a deep spontaneous frothy laugh. "It's a little late now, isn't it, to be concerned about your morals? Eventually, Your Excellency, we will have to come to terms. It is unavoidable. You are the only buyer."

"Never," Grabowski said. "Not anymore."

The young man brushed off his clothes with an air of casual resignation. "Never," he repeated, playing with the word, "is what you told Pontevecchio."

Chapter XXI

AMIENS
September 26th, 1983

IT HAD BEEN A LONG AND ARDUOUS
afternoon, and the cold was creeping through his joints
as Guy wound up his final lecture of the day. He stood
on the western steps of the Amiens cathedral, running
down the list of stone apostles in the porch, trying to
gather up the strength to fashion a pretense of noble
curiosity, if only at the end. He had said these words so
many times that they had taken on the resonance of
prayer, and each day, each rendition was a struggle to
give meaning to the same inflected hum, to find something nameless and sublime in the commonest of
sounds. "That's John," he said, "with the poisoned cup
which Aristodemus gave him." He pulled his sweater
down in back. "And look, there's James," he added
sprightfully. "Like a pilgrim from Compastella. You see
his traveler's cloak covered with shells?"

There was a uniform nod from the crowd. Cameras
clicked. A pair of men at the back grew impatient. Guy
hurried through the final sentences. He knew the telltale rolling of the eyes, the awkward glances, the shuf-

fling of the feet. "And here of course is Thomas," he said. "Here, perhaps for the first time, we see him carrying the architect's square, a reference to the legend in which he was commissioned to build a palace for Gondoforus, the mysterious king of the East."

"What legend was that?"

Guy turned around. He could not tell who had spoken. "According to the story," he said, "King Gondoforus invited Thomas to come to his kingdom in India, and to build him a palace as beautiful as the ones in Rome. When Thomas arrived, Gondoforus gave him a plan for the palace he wanted, and left him with a key to the royal treasury. Then he went off into another province. In his absence, Thomas set about preaching the gospel, and distributing the king's wealth to the poor.

"When Gondoforus returned and learned what the apostle had done, he ordered that Thomas be flayed alive. But just before the execution, the king's brother recovered from a long illness and said, 'Brother, I have seen the palace of gold and silver and precious stones which this man has built. It is in paradise, and it is thine if thou wilt.' When Gondoforus heard this, he begged the apostle's forgiveness and was baptized on the spot."

Guy looked out through the crowd, hoping that the man who had spoken earlier would ask another question. Had it been the American, the one with the tortoise-shell glasses? Or one of those two at the back?

"Of course," he continued, "the palace is only a symbol. The apostles, you see, were the architects of the edifice of faith—the Church."

He lingered on the silence. The questions had run their course. It was cold now. It was growing dark. They wanted to scramble back home, back to their buses and Paris for that prearranged meal. He finished with a flurry of laughter, a joke about priests, a poke at himself. Then he held out his hands and they filed past before him with their thank-yous and coins, with occasional smiles. He searched their faces, trying to recall the ones who had spoken most often. It was not that he thought they were any more likely to give. But Guy harbored a hope that of them he might recognize one with the same frantic longing that had sprung up in him so spontaneously, so unexpectedly twenty years earlier, when he too had been a face in the crowd.

He covered his money. The crowd fell away, all save the two at the foot of the steps.

"Are you Soury-Fontaine?" one of them asked. His accent was Italian or Spanish. He was wearing a hat with a medallion on the band. The other man had a mustache. He looked paler, more pleasant. British perhaps.

"Yes, that's right," Guy replied.

They started toward him slowly. "And you have a sister," the man in the hat said. "Her name is Mariane?"

Guy was startled. This was the voice, the man who had asked about St. Thomas. "What about Mariane?" he replied.

The two men came to a stop. "I'm afraid there's been an accident. Now don't worry. She'll be all right. But I suggest you come with us immediately. We have a car. We can take you right to her."

The stranger grasped Guy by the wrist, pulling him gently away.

Father Marchelidon closed the confessional window and sighed. They were such little sins, he thought, and yet the people of Amiens could not bear them.

He leaned back and closed his eyes, waiting for the sound of footsteps to recede. He was so tired. He felt that if he were to hear the story of another lie, another duplicitous spouse, another petty hurt, he would lose control and scream at the darkness. People were killing each other across the world, and here they just squandered their love like loose change.

He slipped out of the confessional and headed for the western portico. It was getting late, he thought. The sisters from Brazil would be arriving any minute. He pushed his way through the doors and out onto the steps.

Guy stood on the far side of the portico, flanked by two men.

"Guy!" the priest said. He started across the steps. "Do you know what time it is? You promised you'd be ready."

The two men took a step away. One was holding Guy by the elbows.

"I'm sorry, Xavier," Guy answered sadly. "You'll have to tell the sisters I can't make it."

"What do you mean, you can't make it? Are you serious? They've traveled thousands of miles. What am I supposed to tell them? Sister Theresa will be furious."

Guy tried to shrug. "It's Mariane. She's had an accident."

"What accident?"

"Isn't that so?" Guy said, looking at the man in the hat.

"I don't understand. I just saw her at the photo shop before confession. She looked perfectly fine."

"He's busy," the man in the hat replied.

Father Marchelidon looked at the stranger for the first time, and his stomach curled into a ball. He had seen this man before. Perhaps the face was a little different, but he wore the same expression. He had seen him in Buenos Aires, stepping out of unmarked cars at night, knocking on apartment doors, ushering people away. He had seen him on the far side of a light in San Luis. In the end, of course, the city and the country didn't matter. Men like this always spoke the same language. They always said the same thing.

"Father Marchelidon," someone called out behind him. The priest turned around. A nun stood by the main door of the cathedral. She was wearing a traditional habit and her face looked unnaturally small in the folds of her veil. "Father, I hate to be rude, but we have to make the station by seven."

"Sister Theresa, I'm sorry. I was just telling Guy here."

As he spoke another nun appeared at the entrance, and then another still. Soon they were joined by a dozen more who followed Sister Theresa across the steps. "So this is Guy," she said. "We've heard so much about you in San Luis. It's a pleasure to meet you after all this time." She offered him her hand.

The man in the hat stepped away. "How do you do," Guy replied.

"And these men," Father Marchelidon broke in. "These men are . . . these men." He floundered desperately. "These men heard about your school in San Luis, and they're thinking about making a donation. Yes, that's right," he continued, trying to catch up with the lie. "They were very impressed with what they heard from Guy. Isn't that right?"

"They were?" said Guy.

"Yes, of course."

Sister Theresa sighed. "Oh, thank you," she said, grabbing the stranger by the hand. She began pumping it wildly. The other nuns gathered nearby, cooing. One had translated into Portuguese and the rest were pressing closer, mumbling *"Obrigada, obrigada,"* over and over.

Father Marchelidon grabbed Guy by the sleeve and pulled him away from the crowd. "Go on," he said.

"What about Mariane?"

"I'll take care of her. Go on, get out of here." The priest gave Guy another push. Then he turned to face the strangers. The man in the hat was trapped in the black-and-white whirl. Sister Theresa had withdrawn a wallet from her inside pocket and was holding it up before him. A plastic line of photographs dangled like a kite string from her hand.

"Here it is from the south," she said proudly. "You see the bougainvillea. Some day we'd like to build a kindergarten there, something for the unwed mothers." She sighed again. "Some day."

The stranger in the hat brushed the wallet to the side. Then he barreled through the crowd and up the steps, taking them two at a time. Father Marchelidon tried to block his path. He held his hands out but the stranger struck him on the neck and he fell back, stunned, ears ringing.

"Well, I never," Sister Theresa said, trying to buoy him. "They can keep their money, as far as I'm concerned."

Father Marchelidon looked up across the steps and smiled. The two men had finally reached the entrance but he knew they were too late. Guy had already vanished through the door, into the twisting passageways and hidden corridors within, into the dark and sanctuary.

Mariane had been worried all day. First the shock of seeing poor Maurice, broken and scattered in that room beneath the cathedral. Then to find out someone had tried to kill both Joseph and the Englishman. And now, to make it all worse, Joseph had gone off to Chartres.

She finished unpacking a carton of Kodak film and stacked the little yellow boxes onto a tray. Then she carried them from the storeroom, down the long corridor, and through the curtain to the front of the shop. There was hardly anyone about. The weather had been bad and most of the tourists had decided to forgo this side trip in their journeys. She started to drop the boxes of film into the display behind the counter. 1000

ASA. 100. Now, if the tourists went anywhere, she thought, they would go to Chartres, to Joseph. Where she should be.

"Mariane." It was the owner of the store, André Cartier. He was motioning to her.

"What is it?" she said.

Monsieur Cartier was a large man, like a well-filled pastry, topped with a dollop of gray hair and foamy white sideburns. He wore a long black apron to protect him from the chemicals, twill trousers, and a pair of pointed shoes. "You see that man," he said, and then, "Don't turn around!"

"How can I see him if I don't turn around?"

"Well, turn slowly then. Discreetly."

She glanced casually about. The far wall was covered with posters of the cathedral. A man stood just below them, peering at a row of slides in a luminous glass stand. "What about him?" she said.

"Keep an eye on his hands. He's been here for fifteen minutes, but he doesn't need any help, and he isn't looking for anything."

"Maybe he's just cold."

Cartier frowned. "Maybe, maybe," he said, his head wobbling indecisively. "But keep an eye on him anyway." Then he snorted, like the sound of a breaching whale, and darted back behind the curtain.

Mariane returned to her stacking. She dropped the boxes of film one at a time into the display case behind the counter, counting them off. He certainly didn't look like a shoplifter, she thought, glancing around. He was just an old tourist with glasses. And his eyes were friendly and bright, twinkling, like a pair of morning stars. Then, as if he had felt her watching him, he looked up with a smile. Mariane took the last box of film from the tray and let it slide through the top of the display, down the long glass chute. Like the eyes of Père Noël, she thought.

The tourist disappeared and suddenly there he was, right there, beside the counter. "Mariane," he said soothingly, almost in a whisper. "Mariane Soury-Fontaine."

"Yes," she answered. "May I help you?"

Chapter XXII

CHARTRES
September 26th, 1983

FOR THE FIRST FEW SECONDS KOSTER was convinced the sound was just an echo of his own imagination, another bad dream. He had not been able to sleep. The numbers had been biting at him from the darkness just beyond the bed. He had walked the labyrinth in his mind a thousand times and it always brought him back to the same spot, to this lumpy pillow, to the blankets at his ear, to sleeplessness. Then the sound had slipped him from his reverie. First a creaking of the floorboards, and then a padded step. He pulled the blankets down so he could hear more easily. There was a scratching at the door, a knock, a voice.

Koster was up and armed with a coat hanger in ten beats of his heart. He moved cautiously toward the door, holding his breath, trying to remember the position of that one squeaky floorboard which he had noticed when the light was on. Steady, he told himself. He put a hand out before him. Someone was there, on the far side of the door. He could practically feel them. He turned the knob as quietly as he could, and snatched the door wide open.

"Oh, Joseph," Mariane said, as she slipped into his arms.

Koster brought the hanger down, trying to free himself. "Mariane, what are you doing here?"

She stepped into the room and he closed the door behind her, turning the light on at the same time. "What is it? What happened?" he said.

Mariane walked slowly across the room without speaking. The window shutters were closed but she did not seem to notice. She simply stared at the darkened glass. Koster could see her face in the reflection. It looked haggard and pale. Her hair was tangled. Her eyes were puffy and raw.

"You've been crying," he said. He put his arms around her but she pulled herself away. "What is it?" he repeated.

"They tried to kidnap Guy," she said, finally.

"Who did? When?"

"Scarcella's men. At the cathedral, when he was finishing up his last tour. Oh, Joseph." She turned away, bringing her hand to her mouth. "They wanted me to help them find the gospel. It *was* Scarcella, I'm sure of it. He came to the shop. He told me they had my brother, that I had to do exactly what he said. Then, right afterwards, I got a telephone call from Guy. I don't know how he did it, but he managed to escape. He was hiding in the rectory. He was terrified, Joseph. You know how he is. He's like a child sometimes."

"I'd better get Nigel," Koster said.

"No!" Mariane's voice was desperate. "It's his fault we got into this."

"He has to know, Mariane." Koster guided her to the bed. "Go on. Sit down," he said. "I'll be right back."

Lyman's room was just a few yards down the hall and it was only a matter of seconds before he emerged from behind his door, dressed only in a vest and pants. Koster told him briefly what had happened and the Englishman sighed. "Give me a minute," he said.

Mariane was still sitting on the bed when they returned. Her face was hidden by her hair, but Koster could hear that she was crying and his heart went out to her.

"Now then," Lyman began, sitting in the armchair by the window. "Tell me precisely what happened."

"They tried to kidnap Guy."

"You're sure it was Scarcella."

She described the man in the photo shop, the way he had lingered, the way he had approached her after Cartier had left the room. Lyman nodded somberly. "All right, let's not start worrying now," he said. "No sense in that. At least Guy managed to escape."

"He said something about Father Marchelidon," Mariane continued. "He was there, at the cathedral. I think he was." She whimpered. "I'm not sure. They wanted me to help them find the gospel. They threatened to kill Guy if I didn't, Joseph. That's what they said."

"It's okay, don't worry about it." Koster sat down beside her on the bed. "It's okay."

"Where's your brother now?"

"We have some family in Brittany. He said that he was going to go and hide there for a week or so, until everything quiets down. He wanted me to go, too."

"Why didn't you?" Lyman said.

Mariane looked up, her eyes wide with surprise. "Because I wanted to come here. I wanted to be with Joseph."

Koster put his arm around her shoulder. "And you said she'd be safe, Nigel. You said Scarcella had Grabowski in his pocket, that everything would be fine."

"Something must have happened. A change of heart, perhaps."

"You mean another mistake. Just like that old woman with the knitting needles on the train."

"We don't know it was her. It could have been anyone. At least I persuaded Musel."

"What happened on the train?" asked Mariane.

"We were followed, that's what," Koster said. "Grabowski showed up this morning. Right out of the blue. He said the concierge at the Hôtel de la Paix had told him where I was. But I never told the concierge. No one knew, except Lyman and me. And you, of course."

"And the labyrinth?"

Koster shrugged. "The numerical relationships are incompatible. They operate under completely different systems."

"In other words," Lyman explained, "he doesn't know what it means."

"That's what I said."

"Oh, Christ!" Lyman stood up. "This is pointless. Come on, Mariane," he said, offering her his hand. "Let's see if we can find you a room."

"No, I don't want to be alone." She looked over at Koster. "Let me stay with you. Please."

Koster patted her on the back.

"As you wish," Lyman said. "I'll see you in the morning. Try to get some sleep." Then with a final wave, he left and closed the door.

As soon as he had gone, Mariane disappeared into the little bathroom near the window, and Koster sat back on the bed. He could hear the water running in the sink. He could hear the sound of the soap in her hands. He pictured her looking at herself in the mirror, poking at the bags below her eyes, blowing her nose and dropping the tissue in the toilet. Then he heard it flush and she reappeared in the doorway. She had borrowed his brush, he noticed. She had taken her sweater off. It dangled from her fingertips, dragging on the floor. She was wearing a dark blue dress, buttoned at the back, tight at the hips with a slight flare below the knees.

"You don't mind, do you?" she said.

"No, not at all. Of course not."

She moved toward him from across the room, her chin up, the white skin of her neck exposed. She had taken the *abraxas* off, he realized, and he was about to say something when she sat down beside him on the bed, resting her head against his shoulder.

"I can sleep on the floor if you like," he said.

"No, Joseph. Not tonight." Then she shrugged. "Whatever you want, Joseph. I must look a frightful mess."

She turned toward him suddenly. Her eyes were moist with tears. Koster felt himself drawn down. He felt her kisses covering his face. They fell back slowly on the bed and her body pressed against him, the humid softness of her thighs, her hand between his legs.

"What's the matter?"

Koster sat up, trying to look calm. "Nothing," he said.

Mariane reached out for him again but he did not move. "What is it, Joseph? I thought that's what you wanted."

"So did I." He looked away. The faucet was still dripping in the bathroom. A car swished closer to Rouen.

"Is it Priscilla? Is that it?"

"No, it has nothing to do with her." He shrugged helplessly. "I don't know."

"You don't want me anymore. That's it, isn't it? I wouldn't blame you if you didn't."

"Don't be silly. I'm crazy about you, Mariane. Maybe that's why."

Mariane sat up. She glanced at Koster for a moment and then slid off the bed, crossing the room to the armchair. Her purse lay on its side beneath the window. She reached down and took out a pack of cigarettes. "What does that mean?" she said.

He watched her tear off a match. "I don't know, it's just that this time I want it to be different."

Mariane lit a cigarette and the smoke spilled from her open mouth.

"I want to give us a chance," he said, "a real chance. I don't want to force myself on you in some moment of weakness."

"I wish you would."

"No, you don't. Don't be ridiculous."

Mariane took another drag off her cigarette. "What happened between you and her?"

"You mean Priscilla?"

She nodded. "You told me once that there were other men. That she betrayed you?"

"No, it wasn't that. It wasn't the drugs either. All of that came later. She just used them to forget."

"Forget what?"

Koster shrugged. "We had a baby, you see. But he died when he was only a few weeks old." He closed his eyes. "It's called SID Syndrome."

Mariane stubbed her cigarette out in the ashtray by the bed. "I'm sorry, Joseph," she said. "I had no idea." She moved a step closer, raising a hand toward him, but he turned away. "I'm sure it wasn't your fault."

"I know that," he said reproachfully. "Don't you think I know that?" Then he added, "It's funny but I can still remember standing over him in the middle of the night, just looking down and seeing him there, not moving, just lying there in his crib. Cold. Like a doll in a sleeping suit. No one really knows what causes it. The doctors said he just stopped breathing."

Mariane placed a hand on his head. "These things happen, Joseph," she said. "It just happened."

"Yeah, to me. To Priscilla and me. Ten thousand to one. That's what the odds were. That's what I kept thinking as they lowered him into the ground. I worked it out. Statistically, you see. Statistically, it should never have happened." He looked up.

"The problem was, I didn't miss the baby, and Priscilla knew it. I could barely remember what he looked like. I don't know. It's hard to explain. It's as if there hadn't been enough time for the image to develop, to come together in my head. I wanted to remember him." He laughed flatly. "When he died I felt like the world had taken off its mask for the first time and I could see it, right there, in front of me, right there. Do you understand? Ten thousand to one. That was the real betrayal." He shook his head. "Nigel was right. I've made a symbol of my life. That's why Priscilla could never forgive me. I even made a symbol of my son."

Mariane cradled his head against her breast.

"Look at me," he said, after a moment. "I should be comforting you and here you are. I'm making a fool of myself."

"I love this fool," she said.

He looked up. "I love you too, Mariane."

"Joseph."

"Yes?"

"I have to tell you something." She stepped back, looking down at him.

"Yes," he said. "What is it?"

She tried to speak but the words seemed to harden in her mouth. Then she shuddered. "Just hold me, Joseph," she said. "We don't know what's going to happen. Anything could. And now that Scarcella's here, something could go wrong. Something could happen to us."

Koster pulled her down beside him on the bed. "Nothing's going to happen to us," he said. "You have to believe that. I won't let it. We're going to be all right."

"But what if it did?" she said. She looked down at the floor. Her mouth was trembling. "I just want you to know that whatever happens, I love you, Joseph. That's all. Do you believe me? No matter what."

"No matter what," he said. He took her in his arms and they fell back against the blankets, their fingers slipping down, desperate for a handhold on the moment.

He watched her for a long time without moving, without saying a word. She sat on the arm of the armchair, wearing her panties and bra. She was smoking a cigarette. She was turned away so that he could only see one corner of her face, layered by the light and shadows from the shutters. She brought the cigarette to her mouth. She took a drag. She opened her mouth and just as the smoke began to slip between her lips, she drew it in, deep into her lungs, and blew it out again. Wave upon iron blue wave billowed across the room, trapped by intermittent bands of light, vanishing in the dark.

"What time is it?" he asked.

Mariane jumped, startled by the sound. Then she turned her head and said, "I don't know. Early, I guess."

Koster smiled. He licked the sleep from his mouth. "It's freezing in here," he said. "Why don't you open the shutters?"

"No, I like it like this."

Koster slipped out of the bed and kissed her on the back of the neck before ducking into the bathroom. "Want some breakfast?" he said, peeing. It seemed so loud, frothy and thunderous.

"No, thanks. I'll get some coffee if you like, if you're going to work up here."

"Work?"

"On the labyrinth. Your calculations."

"Oh, right." He poked his head out the door. Mariane had lit another cigarette. "Aren't you cold?"

"A little."

He crossed the room and took her in his arms. "How's that?"

She jumped to her feet. "I'm sorry," she said, trying to smile. "Your hands are like ice."

"They are?"

She turned and put her cigarette out in the ashtray. Then she looked up at him again, her hair partly covering her face, her mouth half open. "Joseph," she said. "What do you think's going to happen?"

"What do you mean?"

"Guy says that if the Gospel of Thomas is as old as Nigel thinks it is, it could change the Church forever."

"I guess so," he answered vaguely.

"Don't you care?"

"Sure I care. It's just that I've been so busy with the labyrinth." He shrugged. "Besides, I don't go to Mass much anymore. You know that."

"Why don't you go, Joseph?"

"I don't know. I guess I got too old. I really don't know. Maybe it's because religion's based on faith, and faith always seemed like the opposite of proof to me, of truth even."

"I've always believed," said Mariane. "That's the problem. I mean, what if Nigel is right? What if I've spent my whole life believing a lie? All of those prayers, Joseph. Where did they go?"

"I'm sure they weren't wasted, Mariane."

"But how do I know that? And what about all those nuns and priests in the world. All those missionaries. What are they really preaching? Whose words? I don't know what's right anymore."

"Listen, Mariane. If the gospel is genuine, if it really contains the words of Christ, then it deserves to come out. And if it's a fake, it will probably be forgotten. Besides, we have to solve the labyrinth first. Then we can worry about the gospel, okay?"

Mariane nodded. "I suppose you're right." She

reached down and picked her dress up off the floor. "Joseph," she said, "what do you think about when you're working?"

"What do you mean?"

She slid one foot and then the other into the dress and pulled it up, swiveling the fabric over her hips. "I mean, you have all these numbers before you and they all have to make sense. They all have to mean something."

"It's not like that. I don't think, oh, this number means this or that. They're not just symbols. They're relationships."

"Is that what the labyrinth is?"

Koster shook his head. "I wish I knew."

She straightened her hem. "I don't understand how you do it. All this geometry means nothing to me. Shapes and numbers."

"It's not that difficult. Geometry's just common sense. Here," he said. Mariane was trying to reach the buttons at the back of her dress. "Let me help."

"Thanks."

She turned away and Koster did them up one at a time. They looked like flattened pearls.

"It may be common sense to you," she said. "But it's nonsense to me."

"No, it's not." He turned her around in his arms. "Take this dress," he said.

"What about it?"

"You know how to sew, don't you?"

"A little."

"Then you know something about geometry. It's like when you have to fit a piece of cloth to a convex shape, like the front of your dress here at the bust. How do you do it?"

"You cut a pointed section, a dart from the material, and sew the two pieces together."

"Exactly. And you can do the reverse by cutting the fabric and sewing a pointed patch into the slit."

"A *godet,*" she said. "So what?"

Koster laughed. "Well, I don't know how to sew," he said, "but all of these characteristics—whether a piece of fabric splits, overlaps, or conforms to a surface —are reflective of the fabric's geometry. You see? Without even realizing it, you already know most of the tenets of topology, a kind of mathematics that's much more complicated than geometry."

There had been moments like this before. Koster remembered each one with a punishing clarity. But they had come to him so many years before that he had thought they would never come again. And now it all seemed obvious. Now the strange twelve-sided shape took its place in line. The dodecahedron. The drawing in the missal.

"What is it, Joseph?" Mariane said. "What's wrong?"

Koster snatched her by the shoulders. "Topology," he answered breathlessly. "Not group theory. Topology. My God. What an idiot I've been. It's been staring me right in the face." He dashed across the room. There was a stack of papers near the armchair and he wrestled with it for a moment before pulling out a tattered pad. "My pencil," he said, looking desperately about. "Where's my pencil?"

Mariane pointed at his feet.

"Thanks."

"Joseph?"

Koster leaned back in the armchair. He began to scribble madly on the paper.

"Joseph?"

"Yes." He looked up. "I'm sorry, Mariane."

"Do you have it? Do you know where the gospel is?"

"Not yet," he answered, playing with the pencil. He took a step inside, and turned. The labyrinth unfurled like a medieval pennant, one step at a time, one flagstone. Around he went, one quadrant to the next, as if the winding trail were just a twisted number line within a spinning wheel, the mainspring of some great machine. "But give me ten more minutes and I'll tell you."

"I'll get some coffee."

In the end it took him over an hour, but Koster did not notice. Dimensions, sides, and edges too: These were the properties that mattered. Homeomorphs. Edge to edge. Fear to fear. Side to side. Emotion to emotion. The things which made us human. The things we shared. The touchstones. "You'd better get Nigel," Koster said. He looked up and there was Lyman, sitting on the bed. "When did you come in?"

"Just now. Five, ten minutes ago."

"I didn't see you."

"So I noticed," Lyman said. "Well? Do you have it?"

Mariane came over and offered Koster some coffee. He shook his head. "No, thanks." Then he looked at Lyman and his face broadened into a smile, a grin, stretching. "Topology," he said.

"Topology—what's that?"

"It's a kind of mathematics. It deals with the fundamental characteristics of objects, the properties which make a thing what it is, properties which can't be destroyed by stretching, bending or twisting."

Lyman looked disgusted. "Like your theory group," he said.

"Group theory. No, that's different. Look, imagine a soccer ball. It has two dimensions, no edges, and two sides. In fact it retains these same basic characteristics even if you let the air out and twist it all around. Get it? Topology studies these kinds of invariant properties. Objects that are topologically equivalent are called homeomorphs." He tore a piece of paper from his pad. "Haven't you ever seen a Möbius strip? Here," he said. "A piece of paper has two dimensions—length and width. It has one edge all the way around. And it has two sides, top and bottom. You see?"

"So?"

"Now imagine if you glued the ends together. It looks like a ring. I've changed it topologically. It still has two dimensions and two sides, but now it has two edges instead of one." He gave the strip of paper a half twist and brought the edges together to form a loop. "And this," he continued, "is a Möbius strip. It's really unusual topologically, because unlike most imaginable surfaces, it doesn't have two sides. It has one. You see? If you run a finger along the outside, you'll eventually end up on the inside of the paper, without ever taking your finger off. One side."

"Fascinating," Lyman said. "But what does this have to do with the labyrinth?"

Koster dropped the papers on the floor. "That twelve-sided shape which Thierry drew into the margin of the missal. The Chaldean Cup. I told you I'd seen it before. Well, now I remember. It looks exactly like the three-manifold which Seifert and Weber discovered at the University of Geneva, back in 1932."

"The what?"

"Three-manifold. It's a kind of topological space. Of course, it can't really be depicted from the outside. To do so you'd have to view it from a higher dimension. But it can be visualized," Koster said, "as a dodecahedron."

"Like the one Thierry drew," Lyman volunteered. "The Chaldean Cup."

"Exactly. The different colors of the precious stones indicate how the identification, how the gluing of the opposite sides should be carried out: each member of each pair of faces is matched to its counterpart after a three-tenths turn about the axis perpendicular to the two faces."

"Well, you've lost me," Lyman said. "What's this manifold do anyway?"

"Manifolds don't do anything. They're models for the structure of the universe."

"But if it was discovered back in 1932," Lyman said, "why does it look like the Chaldean Cup? What did the Babylonians know about topology?"

"I'm not sure. I know it seems strange, but I can't believe it's just a coincidence. The Chaldeans were the most sophisticated mathematicians of their day."

Lyman scowled. "Look, I'm not interested in the bloody cup. I want to know about the Gospel of Thomas. What the hell does this topology have to do with the gospel?"

"It's the answer, don't you see? I was looking at the labyrinth in strictly Euclidian terms. I was looking at symmetry and numerical measurements instead of topological invariants. It's a totally different perspective."

"And."

"And by using topology it becomes clear that the labyrinth is a kind of numerical pointer. By following the white path to the center of the labyrinth, you run a kind of topological journey. And if you apply that same topological journey or transformation to the basic numerical structure of the cathedral, it brings you to a specific point at the heart of the crypt below."

"Where? What point?"

Koster paused. "You have to promise me something first."

"What do you mean? Promise you what? What are you talking about?"

"That I'll be in on it. Remember what you said, Nigel. You can't dig it up all by yourself. It's too late for that now anyway. I'm sure they're watching every move we make."

"For God's sake, Joseph, you've already done your job. Now let me do mine. Please try to understand," he said. "I don't want any unnecessary casualties. Not at this stage of the game. Not again."

Mariane gathered up the dirty coffee cups and

placed them on a tray. Her face was very pale. "I'll let you settle this alone," she said.

"Don't go too far," said Lyman. "I want everyone to keep together, just in case Scarcella tries another move."

"I'll be right back."

Lyman opened and shut the door behind her. Then he turned to Koster with a frown and said, "Tell me where it is, Joseph."

"Not until you promise. You know I'm right. It would look pretty weird if Mariane and I suddenly disappeared. Scarcella might get suspicious. He might send a messenger instead of coming himself. You know I'm right."

"Where's the gospel, Joseph?"

"Promise."

"Oh, for Christ's sake." Lyman turned away. "If I do," he added crisply, "will you do everything I tell you, down to the last detail, without any questions?"

"Of course. You're in charge. You and Musel."

"And if something happens and I ask you to leave? You promise to go?"

"Nigel, I'm not stupid. I don't want to die. But I can't just walk away from this. Not now."

"I thought you wanted to leave. You were the one complaining about the risks."

"That was before."

"Before what?"

"Before everything. Before you told me the truth about yourself. Before I knew you. It was just different then."

"Where's the Gospel of Thomas, Joseph?"

"You agree then?"

"Yes, I bloody agree. There. I said it. All right? I agree. Are you satisfied?"

Koster smiled. He picked up a drawing of the Chartres cathedral. "Here," he said, pointing at it with his finger.

Lyman gathered near. "Where?"

"In that window space at the eastern end of the old Carolingian crypt. According to the records I've been reading, there was a great fire on the morning of September seventh, 1020, in which the Carolingian cathedral was destroyed. Guy mentioned it once back in Amiens, remember? St. Fulbert was the chancellor at the time, and he wrote to King Robert, William the Fifth, and several other noblemen for money to rebuild it.

"Eventually they kept the original Carolingian crypt underneath the choir, and built a much greater one around it. Then either Fulbert or a guy named Bernard of Chartres had the windows of the old crypt covered up. There was no point to them anymore, since they now faced the Romanesque ambulatory instead of the outdoors. It's there, Nigel. And the Chaldean Cup as well. Thierry was Bernard's brother. That's how he knew about it."

"Are you absolutely sure?"

"It all fits, Nigel. It all works perfectly."

Lyman sighed. "Thank God," he said.

Just then there was a loud knock on the door. Koster held his breath while Lyman moved behind the bed. "Who is it?" the Englishman said.

"It's me," said Mariane.

Koster exhaled. "Come on in."

The door opened and Mariane took a step into the room, rolling her eyes. A figure loomed behind her. "Look who's here," she said uncertainly. "We met in the dining room downstairs. He just insisted on coming up."

"It's all right, Mariane. Isn't it, Nigel?"

"Yes, do come in. Please." Lyman stepped forward from around the bed. "How do you do? It's a pleasure to meet you finally."

Archbishop Grabowski pressed through the doorway with a smile. "Just fine. You must be Joseph's English friend. I'm sorry I missed you last night."

"I see my reputation precedes me." Lyman shook his hand. "Well, well. We've got good news for you."

Grabowski looked surprised. "You do? What? What have you got?"

Your downfall, Koster thought. Then he glanced away. Despite his size Grabowski looked so frail now, like an old oak hollowed by the wind, scooped out by the ice and the rain.

"The labyrinth, Kazimierz," Koster said. "The Gospel of Thomas." He tried to smile. "Everything we've all been looking for."

Chapter XXIII

CHARTRES
September 27th, 1983

THERE MIGHT HAVE BEEN A TIME once, Lyman thought, when what he knew he had to do now would have seemed a kind of cowardice, the hollowest revenge. But as he walked across the open square, through the windless twilight thick with fog, he realized that the world and he had changed, and that the ends and means had grown entangled, indistinct, irrelevant. There would not be a Champ Dollon this time, no fast escape across the moors, no rotors of a helicopter turning, warming up. This time Scarcella would not get away. He would feel the world slide out from underneath him, hear the sounds of life grow distant in his ears, slip at an angle into darkness through the waves, and sleep.

It had just started to rain when they finally reached the entrance to the crypt. The archbishop held his black umbrella open over them, trying to protect them from the rain as they struggled with the lock. Mariane kept close to the American. There was a small sign posted on the door, Lyman noticed, which said the crypt was closed for renovations, and he reminded himself to congratulate Koster on his foresight. The lock tumbled, the door swung open, and Grabowski turned a torch on, illuminating the corridor within. "All clear," said Koster forcefully.

They filed in through the entrance, one by one. Lyman lingered in the doorway, staring at the ancient houses as they drifted on the fog across the square. He carried a pick in one hand and a chisel in the other. His long green coat hung heavily from his shoulders, the hood slightly askew, the plastic bone toggles dangling down. He wore his piebald Irish fishing hat, tilted, so that a fine line of rain spilled off the rim at the back.

"Nigel?" Koster stood in the doorway with a quizzical expression on his face.

"Here," Lyman said, and offered him the pick and chisel. "I'm going to stay outside for a while. Go ahead. You can start without me. I get a little claustrophobic anyway."

The light in the corridor flicked on. Mariane had found the switch. "Are you sure?" said Koster.

"Yes, of course. I'll be down in a few minutes."

The American took the tools. The trio disappeared around the corner, and Lyman leaned against the door frame with a sigh. He could hear their footsteps echo off the thick walls as they moved deeper and deeper into the heart of the crypt. Then there was nothing but the rain, the gentle tapping on the surface of the square. It was hardly more than a mist really, but puddles had already formed between the cobblestones, along the pavement and the ribbed depressions of the street, spilling together to the north, a trickle to a puddle to a stream, and somewhere in the valley was the River Eure, turning waterwheels, carrying boats, tying the earth.

Lyman took a step into the rain and there they were: the warden and his uncle Jack; the farmer cursing; the open empty bag; that thick trout falling once again, spilling her scales, turning as she tumbled end to end, and down into the grass beside his feet. Lyman reached into his coat.

"Hello," he said, feeling like a fool. "Come in. Hello." The radio crackled in his hand.

"We have you," came the reply. It was the high-pitched voice of the Amiens police captain, Musel.

"Is everybody ready?"

"Of course we're ready. We've been ready for hours. I don't know how you talked me into this, Lyman, but it better pay off."

There was a silence. Lyman stared across the square. Damn this fog, he thought. He could barely see a thing. The medieval houses appeared disjointed and half built, stenciled by dark beams of wood, spotted with windows. "It'll pay off," he said.

"But Grabowski never called. I'm telling you, my men followed him all day. He didn't take a shit without them giving him the paper."

"They must have missed the call," Lyman said. "Don't get cold feet on me now, Musel. Grabowski is Scarcella's man. I know he is."

"One hour," Musel said. "You hear me? And I do it only out of courtesy. If my own men tell me that there wasn't any contact, I believe them. One hour. Then we go back to Amiens."

The radio died in his hand. Lyman stuffed it back into his coat and leaned against the door frame. The mist was lifting slightly. The houses were more visible across the square. He could see a television flickering in the dark, magnesium bright, shaking out a story. He reached into his coat and pulled out a pack of cigarettes. Then he ducked back into the corridor.

The Romanesque crypt curved out of sight before him, a wide stone ambulatory, a few mosaics, and a chapel to the side. The corridor must have been fifteen feet across. The stone looked cold, ice gray, and ancient. Lyman struck a match and lit one of his Players,

inhaling deeply. A small piece of tobacco fastened itself to his lower lip, bitter and delicious. He pulled it
off. The smoke made the world seem clearer, he
thought, but he knew it was just the nicotine. An illu-
sion of clarity. A myth. A footstep echoed down the
corridor, and then another, and Lyman realized someone was approaching. He moved against the wall. It
was Mariane.

"Oh, hello," he said. "Any luck?"

"We were worried about you."

Lyman smiled. "I'm flattered. How's the digging?"
He might have been querying a fisherman about his
catch. His voice had the same quality of false indiffer-
ence.

"Nothing yet. They've gone about a meter and a
half, a little less. Joseph says the mortar's surprisingly
soft. He wants to know if you're coming down."

"I don't think so. I'd better stay here."

Mariane shrugged. "Whatever you say." She looked
out into the courtyard. "It's already dark."

"Yes," Lyman said.

"Foggy too."

"Yes, no wind." Lyman smoked his cigarette quietly, watching Mariane. She seemed frightened and he
cursed himself for allowing Koster to persuade him to
give in to this ridiculous charade. She had no business
being there. It was his war, not theirs. He had manipu-
lated them, as certainly as Scarcella, as certainly as the
Countess de Rochambaud. And suddenly he remembered the daughter of that Italian magistrate, that
twelve-year-old girl in Terracina, bloody and dying in
that little bed, staring wide-eyed at the rose and
straight pin in Scarcella's hands. It had been his fault
Mariane had been approached by Scarcella. They had
stood front to front across the counter of the photo
shop, only a foot away. Scarcella had looked deep into
her eyes.

"I'm sorry," Mariane said quietly.

"Sorry? What do you have to be sorry for?"

"For the way I treated you before. I didn't know. You were just doing your job."

"Forget it. I'm sorry that I had to lie to you."

"Sometimes you have to. Anyway, I was wrong about you. I should have listened to Joseph." She shivered in the open doorway. "Well, I'll tell them what you said." She turned and started down the corridor.

Lyman waited for her to disappear around the corner before he stepped back through the open door. The rain had stopped. The fog was curling, rolling on, retreating across the square. He took up his position. Time passed. The fog came and went, billowing. The rain came and eased and grew intense, only to ease again. Lyman did not know how long he had been waiting when he saw a figure scurrying across the square. It was only as the face grew clear that he realized his hour was up. It was Captain Musel. The French policeman's clothes were wet from the rain and he looked anything but happy.

"What's the matter?" Lyman said. "You're compromising the whole operation."

Musel ducked into the doorway. "It's over," he said. "We're rolling it up. Scarcella's not coming."

"You can't be serious."

"Look at my face," he said. "Do I look as if I'm joking? We've been waiting all day, for God's sake. I tell you, Grabowski never called. He never talked to Scarcella."

"You don't know that for a fact."

"Come on, Lyman. Give it up. Let go. If Scarcella were ever here, he's long gone now. And he's not coming back." He shook his head. "Neither are we. You'd better tell your people we're leaving."

"All we need is a little more time."

"I'm sorry, Inspector. I really am," Musel said. "But it's over. You did your best. I'll put that in my report. You did all you humanly could. Now you have to think of those people downstairs. You have to think of their safety. I'm sorry. I shouldn't even be here. It's not even my jurisdiction." He held out his hand. Lyman looked at it for a moment and then shook it reluctantly.

What was the point of arguing? Try as he might, he could not shake the truth. Something had gone wrong, dreadfully wrong. "Thanks for trying," Lyman said. "I understand." He paused. "Captain, can you do me just one more favor?"

Musel sighed. "What now?"

"Can you at least post a man by the door for the night? You're going to have to stay in town now anyway. I'm sure you've missed the last train back to Amiens."

"There's another one in twenty minutes."

"One man, Musel. That's all I'm asking. Just in case Scarcella shows up. Just tonight. Then, if he doesn't, well, then I'll know that it's really over."

"I don't think so."

"I'll pay for his hotel room."

"That's not the point."

"One night."

The captain shook his head. "I shouldn't do this, you know. God damn you, Lyman. Why did you have to come here? You're asking me to put my pension on the line. I don't owe you anything. You're just a stranger."

"That's exactly right."

"I'm going to regret this, I know it." Then he laughed tightly. "All right, you win, Lyman. One man. I'll post him under the southern porch where he can watch the door. But remember," he continued, raising a finger and pointing. "It's only for tonight. It's over, Lyman. Finished."

Musel turned and headed out the door. Lyman watched the fat man walk across the square, watched him disappear into the fog. Then he thrust his hands into his trouser pockets and closed his eyes, listening to the random raindrops, listening to his heart. Over, he told himself. How could it ever be over? He shook his head, moving slowly back into the corridor.

A small apsidal chapel appeared to his right, shallow and full of broken artifacts, nameless, indistinct. What could have happened? he wondered. Scarcella had tried to kidnap Guy. He had threatened Mariane. And yet now, for some strange reason, the archbishop and Scarcella had had a falling out, a change of heart. Musel was right. Grabowski had not called anyone. Lyman had given him a thousand opportunities, but they had waited out the day together at the Hôtel Métropole. Lyman. Grabowski. Koster. Mariane. All of them. Never apart, not for a moment even. Lyman froze. He could hear the sound of pounding in the distance. It was Koster in the crypt, armed with his chisel and pick. He spun about. Except for that one time, Lyman thought. Right at the very start, when Mariane had gone downstairs to put the coffee tray away.

The fog had lifted slightly by the time he reached the door. The rain had started again. The cobblestones glistened, dipped in the milky wetness of the sky. Lyman looked up at the cathedral's southern porch. Musel's guard stood off to one side, wearing a hat, smoking a cigarette. Lyman waved and he waved back. Perhaps he was wrong, Lyman thought. Perhaps he was just jumping to conclusions.

He looked across the open square and as he did so, as the fog receded slowly down the street, the figure of another man came into view. At first Lyman thought it was Musel. He was about to shout a greeting, hoping the captain had changed his mind, when he realized with a chilling certainty that it was not the French policeman. The fog licked at the stranger's feet. His glasses caught the soft light of a passing streetlamp, his face came into view.

Lyman fell back. He felt his hands freeze at his sides, the cold begin to creep along his spine, clawing

at the nape of his neck. Then he let go, breathing. He
took a step forward, and peered up at the southern
porch. The guard was lying at the base of the stone
apostles. His hat had tumbled down the steps. Another
man leaned over him.

Lyman darted back through the door. The ambulatory was brightly lit and he struggled for a hiding place,
turning round and around, until he suddenly remembered the chapel down the corridor. It was shallow, but
at least it would hide him from the entrance.

A minute passed, two minutes, and he heard a footfall on the stone. He reached into his coat and pulled
his gun out slowly, reluctantly. It felt odd in his hands,
huge and bulky. He loaded a bullet into the chamber,
and saw the face of Crosley in the darkness down the
corridor, the look of bald surprise as the knife slipped
into him. *Shoot, Nigel! Bloody shoot!* And then the
quiet countenance of that boy beside the river back in
Amiens, with that piece of rose-red masonry in his
hand, staring open-faced into the barrel of his gun.
This gun.

"I can hear them," someone said.

"They're in the Carolingian crypt."

Lyman held his breath. Then he breathed. Then he
held his breath. A shadow wavered on the wall and a
young man in an olive-colored raincoat ambled by.

"That's far enough," Lyman said, stepping forward
into view.

During that first moment, as the thread unwound, it
was almost unavoidable that he should feel some sense
of disappointment. There was George in London.
There was the Hôtel de la Paix. There was his son
Peter. But against the horror of those memories,
Scarcella looked piteous and pale, dwarfed by his own
actions, only a symbol of who he really was.

He was a big man, but his size was insincere. He
was dressed in an ivory raincoat. Beneath it Lyman
could see a charcoal suit, a red rose pinned to his lapel.

He wore thick black plastic spectacles. His bald pate was flecked with rain. His puffy round face shifted from expression to expression, holding one and then another up against the moment, trying them on. "Well," he said at last, in perfect, well-clipped English. "Inspector Lyman."

"Signor Scarcella."

The young man in the olive-colored raincoat began to tip his body slightly to the side, cutting down the target.

"Don't even think about it," Lyman said. He pushed the young man with such brute strength against the wall that the sound of the air being forced from his lungs resounded down the corridor. Lyman searched him carefully, holding the muzzle of his gun against his neck, puckering the skin. He was carrying an American 357., a Python. Lyman tossed it to the ground behind him. "You too, Scarcella," he said.

"I never touch them."

Lyman laughed. It felt good to laugh. It made him feel strong. "You too," he repeated.

Scarcella shrugged and slowly, deliberately, he reached into his coat and pulled out a small Beretta. The butt was covered with malachite and ivory. Lyman snatched it from his hands and threw it to the floor. "This was a special occasion," Scarcella said.

"Right. Now, turn around. Slowly." Lyman stepped back, his gun still aimed at Scarcella's belly. "Put your hands on your neck, behind your head. Both of you."

They did so.

"I've waited a long time for this," Lyman said.

"So have I," Scarcella said. "Of course," he added whimsically, "I didn't visualize it quite this way."

"I bet you didn't."

"But I wanted to meet you."

"Here I am. And here's my gun."

"So I see. Yes." Scarcella laughed. It was a young man's laugh, spontaneous, sporty even.

In the distance, Lyman could hear a steady, rhythmic pounding. They were still digging in the crypt, hacking at the mortar.

"You're an intelligent man," Scarcella said. "You know who I am, what I can do."

"You're not doing very much at the moment, are you?"

"I could make you wealthier than you've ever imagined. Pick an island, Lyman."

"Go ahead," Lyman said. "Make it easier."

Scarcella smiled. "You're not going to do anything silly, are you?"

"I don't know. That depends on your answers now, doesn't it."

"Still trying to solve the puzzle. You're as bad as Koster. How admirable. Always the inspector."

"You murdered Pontevecchio, didn't you? You'd better tell me, Scarcella, or I swear I'll put a hole in you. Who's your man at the City of London Police? It wasn't just Hadley, was it?"

"Oh, this is so tiring. Really, Lyman. You're not going to kill me." He took off his glasses and began to rub one of his eyes. "I know who you are, you see. I know all about you. I know about Jackie and your son, Peter. I know about the College Killer. I know about George. I even know about poor young Geoffrey Crosley. You see?" He put his glasses back on.

"Your hands, Scarcella. I'm warning you." Lyman took a step back.

"It's no use warning me. I already know what's going to happen. But you," he said, gazing deep into his eyes. "You're the one who needs a different future. Let me make one for you."

Lyman pointed the gun at Scarcella's face. "If you don't answer my bloody questions, I'm going to put a bullet in you. God help me but I will."

"And then what? What are you going to do then? Go back to England, back to your little metal desk with the bottle in the second drawer? Back to Dotty Taylor? I'm offering you another door. When you've already stepped through so many, Lyman, what is another door?"

Lyman tried to pull the trigger. He tried with all the power of a thousand nightmares. He tried to picture Peter's frantic struggle in the dark as the cold Atlantic drew him to the ceiling. He envisioned little George, still panting in his lap, still trying to lick the blood back. And then the sun shone through the clouds between the three trees by the river, and they gathered in a circle, their heads bowed, the two boys watching, following the rainbow flashes as the trout fell to the ground.

Lyman brought the gun round with a vicious snap. It struck Scarcella on the cheekbone and he stumbled, first one knee bending, then the other, crashing to the floor.

"You're a bloody fool. You don't see it, do you?" Lyman said. "You don't understand at all. Criminals don't win, Scarcella. In the end, it's only crime that wins. That's all. Only the ugliness." He waved the gun. "Now get cracking. We're going for a little walk to police headquarters."

"Don't turn around," a voice said, out of nowhere.

Lyman felt the power rush from his arms.

"Lower the gun. That's right."

His fingers turned to stone. The gun dangled at his side. One second it was there, and then it vanished from his grasp.

Lyman turned around. A pale man with a thin mustache stood in the open doorway.

"Where have you been?" Scarcella said. He leaned awkwardly against the wall and struggled to his feet. His cheek was bleeding where Lyman had struck him with his pistol. "That's the second time today, Mr. McCoy. You're making a habit of being late."

"I'm sorry, Signor Scarcella."

Scarcella walked across the corridor, picked up his Beretta, and slipped it inside his raincoat. Then he turned and looked at Lyman with a smile. "Too bad," he said. "You had your chance, Inspector." He took another step. "They were right about you. You don't have it in you anymore. No wonder you let Crosley die. You're all washed up."

"If I don't have what you have, Scarcella, I'm a lucky man. There was a time I thought I did."

Scarcella nodded and the young man in the olive-colored raincoat struck Lyman in the face with his gun. A flashing light exploded in Lyman's head. Then came the pain, the rush of blood inside his mouth. He stumbled to his knees. His entire head throbbed with the pounding of his heart.

Scarcella walked over to him casually, his hands on his hips. He shook his head, and with a sigh of exasperation, reached underneath his coat. Lyman shrunk back reflexively, expecting to see the Beretta. But with a simple movement of the wrist, Scarcella pulled the pin out of the rose on his lapel, removed the flower, and held it up before him. A trickle of icy water seemed to crawl down Lyman's spine. Scarcella took a step closer, the pin in one hand and the flower in the other. Lyman could not take his eyes off the pin. He felt the presence of Scarcella rise up all around him. He heard him breathing in his ears.

Lyman shook his head, trying to tear his eyes away. Scarcella stepped closer.

Suddenly, Lyman lashed out at the rose. Thorns tore at his skin. He threw the flower to the ground. Petals scattered.

Scarcella cursed under his breath and stepped away. He shook his hand. Then he glanced down at his fingers. They were scratched and stained with blood. The thorns had cut him too. He looked up.

Lyman could feel the hatred in the old man's eyes. It was palpable. It radiated from him with a power and virility that belied his age. "You're dead," Scarcella said. He reached into his raincoat and pulled out the Beretta.

Lyman shrugged. "Go ahead. It's easy to pull the trigger. It's the easiest thing in the world." He laughed scornfully. "Go ahead. Do it. I'm not afraid. I don't give a bloody damn."

"Wait!" The pale man with the thin mustache rushed forward. "They'll hear the shot in Paris. We can take care of him outside."

The man in the olive-colored raincoat smiled. He reached into his coat to put his gun away. Then Lyman saw the cool glint of a blade.

"All right, but hurry," said Scarcella. "We've wasted enough time." With that he turned and headed down the corridor, into the heart of the crypt.

Lyman found himself staring at the young man in the olive-colored raincoat as he struggled to his feet. The blade caressed the air before him, cutting it open, and Lyman remembered one of his old instructors at the academy back in England.

They call it cut to ribbons, he had said the first day of their self-defense class, *because if your knife's sharp and you're good, you can slice a forearm like a joint, and the skin will hang down from the bone in strips like crimson ribbons.*

"Come on," McCoy said flatly. He motioned to the young man with the knife. "Let's get it over with."

There was a single naked lightbulb in the ceiling of the crypt which cast a snowy afternoon glare about the room. Nearly forty feet across, the crypt was roughly semicircular, punctuated by a pair of massive pillars near the center. A large, stone altar stood by the wall where Koster and Grabowski were digging. Mariane hovered nearby, trying to shine a flashlight over their shoulders and down into the opening in the wall.

Koster slipped the chisel into another crack, and began to hammer at it steadily. More masonry gave way. It was difficult to maneuver his arms in the narrow shaft, and the hammer kept slipping off the chisel. He rested for a moment, scraped some of the loose stone back behind him, and then took aim and struck again.

The more Koster worked, the more uncomfortable he felt to be digging so far inside the crypt, to be scraping right at the heart of the cathedral. Somewhere at the root of this great edifice was a tiny spring which was said to have magical curative powers. For centuries before anyone had even built a structure here, the mound and grove around it had been worshiped as a holy site, a place where farmers made their offerings to the earth—the Great Mother. The Virgin. The Cult of Relics. He smashed his hammer desperately against the chisel.

It was as if the cathedral were alive around him, breathing and sentient, as if it knew exactly what he was doing.

More masonry gave way. Dust choked the cavity. He waved at the air before his face.

Then, suddenly, there was a glint of gold, the hint of something to the side, a surface winking from the mortar. Koster dropped the chisel and reached deeper into the hole. It was there, he thought. After all this time and speculation, after all the calculations, it was there.

He began to shovel the mortar back behind him like a badger. First gold and then a glassy nub, an edge, a side. Grabowski was the next to see it. He joined Koster in the opening and they began to work the object from the wall together, pulling and pushing at it like the loose tooth of a child.

"Give me some room," Koster said excitedly. "I've almost got it."

The cup was still half buried in the mortar, but he could see the workmanship. It appeared to be a clear dodecahedron, at least twenty inches in diameter. The gold was covered with impressions, shapes like half moons, stars, planets. The precious stones were primitively carved and coated with dust. There was a hinge on one side. There was a latch.

"I'll take that, if you don't mind."

Koster shifted around in the opening, and noticed a pair of legs standing in the doorway to the crypt.

He slipped out of the hole to his feet. A large man wearing an ivory raincoat and glasses was walking down the steps. Koster had never seen him before but he recognized the balding head, the jolly round features. There was a bloody line across his face, a gun in his right hand. As he approached the altar, Grabowski moved to cut him off.

"Scarcella! What are you doing here?" he said.

The man looked coldly at Grabowski. "I found myself another invitation." He looked at Mariane and bowed.

Mariane stepped back.

"I was going to call you," the archbishop said. "I was making sure it was all here."

"Lying is a sin, Your Excellency."

"Wait a minute," Koster said. "What's going on? What's he saying, Mariane?"

Mariane turned away. She shook her head and said, "I'm sorry, Joseph."

"What do you mean, you're sorry? What are you saying? You told him?"

"I had to, Joseph. He's got my brother. Please don't hate me. He threatened to kill Guy if I didn't help. I had to tell him."

Koster felt as if someone had kicked him in the stomach. "Why didn't you tell me? What about last night?"

"Touching," said Scarcella. "It's a pity I can't stay, but I have a plane to catch. The cup, please, Mr. Koster."

Koster turned suddenly on Scarcella. "Is that all you care about? Well, fuck you," he said. "What about us? What are you going to do now, have us commit suicide?"

Scarcella laughed. "What are you talking about?"

"You know damn well what I'm talking about. I'm talking about that guy in London. About Pontevecchio." Koster moved in front of Mariane, covering her body with his own. Scarcella's gun looked so unreal, a prop, like something on TV.

"Are you really that fond of your cousin? I'm amazed. And after everything that's happened. Such devotion deserves something. I know," Scarcella said playfully, "I'll give you a choice. You see. No one can accuse me of being an unreasonable man. If I lie to you, you can live. But if you force me to tell you the truth, well—then I'll have to kill you."

"That sounds like a confession to me."

"Does it?" Scarcella smiled. "In that case," he said, pointing his gun at Koster's face, "I'm afraid you don't have a choice after all."

There was a shout off to the side. Koster waited for the charge, the flash, the instant when the light would gather up its source—one hundred and eighty-six thousand miles per second—and then the bullet in its wake, ponderous in comparison, crude, deadly. But the moment never came. Scarcella turned, Grabowski struck him with the full force of his massive shoulders, and the two went down.

Koster grabbed Mariane and pulled the girl away. The two men were rolling about on the floor, over and over one another. Scarcella cursed. The gun came up, held by two hands. Grabowski was the bigger of the two, but Scarcella fought with the viciousness and fury of a cornered beast, clawing, scratching, gouging at the eyes with his free hand.

Grabowski swung his legs around, balancing himself on Scarcella's body, pinning him to the stone. He forced the gun down slowly. The muzzle turned until it pointed at Scarcella's face. Scarcella looked at it and smiled, hysterical. Gritting his teeth, he said, "Forgive me, Father."

The archbishop's hand gave way. Scarcella heaved and Grabowski rolled off to the side.

Koster saw the gun. He saw it tilt, come down, the muzzle brushing the archbishop's cheek. He saw it catch against his chin.

Scarcella laughed and it was then that Koster finally saw his opening.

He took a step, reached down and punched Scarcella in the face twice, hard, so that the skull bounced off the stone floor of the crypt . . . and was still.

The gun dropped to the ground. Grabowski struggled out of Scarcella's limp embrace.

"Is he dead?" Koster said. "Jesus, I didn't mean to kill him."

"He's alive," Grabowski answered wearily. He picked up Scarcella's gun and pointed it at Koster's chest. Then he scrambled to his feet.

"What are you doing?"

"I'm sorry, Joseph."

The archbishop was breathing hard. The fight had winded him badly. He was an old man, Koster thought. He was spent. "Put that down, Kazimierz."

"I'm sorry," Grabowski repeated. "But the gospel is just too important."

Koster moved back toward the altar. "Are you crazy?" he said.

"I'm taking it with me, Joseph. It has to be studied. It has to be analyzed." He pointed the gun at the opening. "Now dig it out."

Koster shook his head. "Dig it out yourself."

Grabowski frowned. "All right. Get back over there by Scarcella. Both of you."

Mariane and Koster moved away. Grabowski

reached into the wall and began to clear the last few pieces of mortar from the cup. He scooped and pulled, he heaved, and Koster saw the golden object fall into his hand.

It radiated with light, as if it were on fire, the twelve sides glimmering, the precious stones like flames.

"Are *you* going to kill us, Kazimierz?" Koster said. "Is it really worth that much to you?"

"Not unless you make me." The archbishop tucked the cup against his chest and started toward the door.

Koster took another step. "You're not going to get away with this. You know you aren't."

"Keep back, Joseph." Grabowski aimed the gun at Koster's face. "I'm warning you. Don't make me kill you."

"You're not going to kill me. You couldn't."

"I mean it, Joseph."

Koster watched the gun shake as he moved. "No, you don't," he said. His voice was calm now, clear. He no longer felt afraid. "You couldn't kill me. You couldn't kill anyone. No matter what's happened, you're still a priest, Kazimierz."

Another step, another beat of his heart, and Koster saw the gun bear down. Grabowski widened his eyes. His mouth fell open in a cry as he turned and pulled the trigger.

It was still raining. Lyman could feel the water running down his neck. His hat had fallen off when Scarcella had struck him with the gun. He closed his eyes and turned his face to the sky. He had never felt a rain like this. It was cold and raw. It was alive.

"That's far enough."

Lyman turned to the side. The man in the olive-colored raincoat stood with his knife out before him. He began to move about in a half crouch, wiggling and wagging the naked blade as if he were charming a snake.

Lyman reached down and slipped his belt off. The man with the knife drew closer.

Lyman whirled the belt around his head. The buckle gleamed in the light. There was a thrust. Lyman stepped back, whipping the belt before him, but the young man pulled away at the last moment. There was another thrust, a parry, and Lyman found himself pressed up against the wall of the cathedral. Nowhere to run. Nowhere to hide. This is it, he thought.

The young man smiled. He faked once to the left and thrust. Lyman felt the smooth blade cut across his ribs as he brought his knee up suddenly. He felt the knee connect. The young man groaned. Lyman grabbed him by the arm and swung him round so that the young man struck the wall with a frightful thud. The wind rushed from his lungs. Lyman grabbed him by the wrist, to keep the blade away. Then he shot a palm thrust to his face and punched him once below the Adam's apple. The young man's head cracked up against the stone. He crumpled into Lyman's arms like a bag of dirty laundry.

Lyman pulled the knife out of the young man's hand and turned to face McCoy. McCoy stood motionless. He looked transfixed, like an animal in the headlights of a car. Then he said, "No, wait," and held his hands up.

Lyman only laughed. The knife felt good in his hands. The rain washed his face. He could still taste blood in his mouth. He took a step forward.

"Wait, you're making a mistake. I'm not who you think I am."

Lyman ignored him. He took another step, turned the blade in his hand, and handed it to McCoy.

"Don't worry," Lyman said, trying to smile. "McCoy, McKenzie, right? You're the one who turned that sign around, on that hotel door in Austria? No wonder the countess knew so much. You were working for her all along."

McCoy looked surprised. "How did you know?" he said.

"I knew there was an inside man. You were the only one left."

With that, the sharp report of a revolver echoed from the crypt. They looked at one another for an instant, frozen by the sound. Then Lyman said, "Come on," and started down the ambulatory at a run.

It took him only a minute to reach the entrance to the crypt. Even without turning the corner, Lyman could smell the acrid stench of gunpowder in the air. He looked inside and saw the archbishop in one corner, the Beretta in his hand. There was an expression of unspeakable horror on his face. His eyes looked glazed, unfocused, dead.

On the other side of the crypt, Mariane stood with her hands covering her mouth. Koster had his arms around her. Scarcella was curled in a ball at their feet. There was a pulsing hole where the side of his face had been. The pistol he'd taken from Lyman lay inches from his hand.

"Nigel," Koster said, breaking the spell. "Thank God you're all right."

Lyman began to walk toward the archbishop. "The gun, Grabowski," he said, stretching out his hand. "Give it to me."

"It was self-defense," said Koster. "Kazimierz had to do it."

"Give me the gun," Lyman repeated.

Grabowski did not even seem to hear him. Lyman pulled the weapon gently from his fingers, and in that moment the Chaldean Cup slipped out of the archbishop's other hand and tumbled to the floor. There was a dull crack as the golden vessel struck the stone. It wobbled for a foot or so, and suddenly the catch gave way and the two sides fell apart like a cut melon. The cup was hollow. It lay on the floor, six facets on each side, exposed and empty.

Grabowski brushed by Lyman and knelt down on the floor beside Scarcella's head.

"He's dead," said Lyman, wondering at the words. And now they seemed to mean so little.

The archbishop did not turn around. He closed what was left of Scarcella's left eye, wiping the blood from his fingers on Scarcella's ivory raincoat. Then he crossed himself and silently began to pray.

Mariane and Koster moved back toward the center of the crypt. She looked up at Lyman for a moment and it was only then that he recalled the blow he had taken to his face. He could see the pain in her eyes.

"What happened?" she said.

Lyman poked at the swelling underneath his right cheek. "I ran into Scarcella's gun."

"I'm sorry, it's all my fault," she said. She shook her head helplessly. "I had to tell him. He's got my brother."

"I know you did. It doesn't matter, Mariane. Scarcella would have found out anyway."

Koster put his arm around her shoulders. "Nigel's right. It's not your fault."

"You mean you're not angry?" She glanced back up at Koster.

Her face looked so pale, Lyman thought, in the white light of the crypt.

"Of course not," Koster said.

"I was afraid you'd think I was like her, like Priscilla."

"Oh, no," he answered gently, cupping her face in his hands. "That was a long, long time ago. Before I met you. Another lifetime. Another Joseph Koster." He shook his head. "And don't worry about Guy. We'll find him."

"He's in a warehouse across town near the Gare St. Roch, on the road to the Hippodrome."

Everyone looked up. The pale man with the thin mustache was walking down the steps, his eyes on Scarcella's bloody face. "Number twenty-seven rue Lucien," he said.

"Oh, Mr. McCoy. Forgive me," Lyman said. "This is Joseph Koster and Mariane Soury-Fontaine." They nodded at one another. "But I'm afraid you're a little late," he added, pointing at the golden cup on the floor. "By about six centuries. Of course the cup itself must be worth something."

McCoy smiled back with an air of quiet resignation. "The money means nothing to us," he said. "Why don't you keep it?"

Lyman reached down and picked the cup up in his hands. It was heavier than it looked. The stones glittered. Diamonds, he thought. Rubies and emeralds too. There was a piece of mortar caught in the hinge. He pulled it out and it crumbled between his fingers. He looked up, sensing someone staring at him. It was Koster.

"You're right," the American said. "It's soft. It looks brand new. Like it was set this morning." He shrugged. "It looks like someone beat us to it, Nigel."

Lyman glanced over at McCoy. The man with the thin mustache was watching him closely.

Topology, Lyman thought, trying to remember. Topology. That was all that Koster had revealed before Mariane disappeared downstairs and placed her call to Scarcella. But who, beside Koster, knew enough about numerology and mathematics to take advantage of the clue?

McCoy met his gaze, and Lyman suddenly remembered what Scarcella had said by the entrance to the crypt. *That's the second time today, Mr. McCoy. You're making a habit of being late.* The second time today, thought Lyman. He looked at the mortar in his hand. After all this time. Brand-new. And in that instant

Lyman understood. No wonder McCoy didn't seem to care the cup was empty.

He turned suddenly and handed the cup to Koster.

"What are you doing?" the American said.

"Consider it an early wedding gift. Not that I'm trying to interfere, or anything like that. I'm just old-fashioned." It smarted when he smiled, but even the pain was comforting. It meant he was alive.

"We can't just keep it. It belongs to the Church. It's a kind of relic."

"In that case," Lyman said, "I'm sure that Father Marchelidon knows a certain school in Brazil where they could use some help. Some divine intervention." He laughed.

Koster smiled at Mariane. Then he turned to Grabowski and said, "What do you think, Kazimierz?"

Grabowski remained silent.

"Kazimierz?"

The archbishop did not even turn around. Koster shrugged. "You didn't hear, did you, Nigel?" he said. "You were still outside."

"What's that?"

"Scarcella finally admitted it. He killed Pontevecchio. He hanged him from that bridge in London. I told you, didn't I? You've solved your case. I knew that Kazimierz couldn't have done it."

Lyman shrugged. He looked down at the archbishop, who was still kneeling at Scarcella's side, praying silently. Only his lips moved. "Yes," he replied. "I suppose so. I suppose you were right all along."

Half an hour later, as they were walking back across the square toward the police station, Lyman stopped for a moment and stared back up at the cathedral. The rain had tapered off. An ambulance was parked beside the entrance to the crypt. They were carrying Scarcella's body out on a stretcher. The red light of the

ambulance reflected off the wet cathedral walls. It glittered in the thousand puddles littering the square.

Suddenly Koster was beside him. "Nigel," he said
breathlessly. "They just announced it over the police
radio. Guy's okay. They found him. Scarcella's men
gave up without a fight, as soon as they knew the warehouse was surrounded."

Lyman smiled. "I'm glad," he said.

"I want to thank you too, Mr. McCoy," Koster continued.

The man with the thin mustache simply nodded.

"Aren't you coming? They're bringing Kazimierz
back to the station. He's got to fill out a report."

"I don't think so, Joseph," Lyman said.

Koster looked back at Mariane who was standing
near the open door of a police car by the curb. "Well, I
guess I'll see you later," he said.

Lyman nodded. "Good luck with your book, Joseph. And say hello to your publisher, Nick Robinson,
for me." He turned and looked at McCoy.

Koster smiled sadly. "That sounds like a good-bye
to me."

"You've got other things to do now," Lyman said.
"And I'm tired of good-byes. Let's just say *au revoir.*"

They shook hands. Lyman reached out and patted
him once on the shoulder. Then Koster turned and
headed back toward Mariane.

Lyman watched them get into the police car. It
started noisily and began to move away. He could see
them through the rear window leaning together, and he
felt his heart reach out to England and to Dotty Taylor.
It had been so long since he had felt the warm touch of
her hand, since he had woken next to something other
than his anger. But it was not quite over yet. He still
had one more thing to settle.

"McCoy," he said. "Before you wander off."

The ambulance followed the police car across the
square, red light spinning.

McCoy stood with his hands in his coat pockets. "Don't forget who helped you find that girl's brother."

"I know that," Lyman said. "And I'm not interested in what you did earlier today. You were the one who put that renovations sign on the ambulatory door. Don't bother to deny it. That mortar was only a few hours old. You took the manuscript this morning. You know it and I know it."

"I've no idea what you mean."

Lyman took a step closer. "Don't lie to me. I'm in no mood. I've been killing myself with this thing for months. Unless you want me to hang you out to dry here with the Chartres police, you'd better learn to be more agreeable."

"I'm telling you, I don't know anything."

Lyman grabbed him by the collar. "That's the wrong answer, McCoy. I could make it my business to prove where you were this morning. You wouldn't want that, would you?" He brought his face close to McCoy's. "I could make it pretty uncomfortable for your countess and the G.L.F."

McCoy looked frightened. "What do you want then?"

"You know what I want. Scarcella's man. The one at the City of London Police. It wasn't just Hadley, was it?"

McCoy turned away. "You won't like it," he replied.

"I'll be the judge of that."

"All right then, Lyman, if that's what you want." He looked Lyman straight in the face.

"It was Cocksedge, Lyman. Are you happy now? Does the truth make you happy, Lyman? He and Hadley worked together. They were even in the same lodge." He paused. "That's how Scarcella met them. That's how he managed to bribe and blackmail them to help him."

Lyman nodded grimly and released McCoy. He closed his eyes, remembering the day of his assignment to the case, so many weeks before in London. *I'm trying to help you, Lyman,* Cocksedge had assured him. *I'm on your side.*

And indeed, thought Lyman, that was the worst part of it all. For it had been Cocksedge who had first accepted him into the ranks after he had left Winchester. That was the irony. As a favor to his dear old uncle Jack. One Freemason to another. And Chief Inspector Hadley too. All in the family. One for all and all for one. Lyman would never have become a City of London policeman if it had not been for Cocksedge, and now he would have to destroy him.

He looked up at the great cathedral across the open square. The flying buttresses were lit like Ferris wheels by bright lights hidden in the grass. Lyman shook his head. No, he thought. Cocksedge had destroyed himself, like Pontevecchio and Grabowski, like all the men who had come into contact with Scarcella. He could see that now. It had been obvious for a long time. He had simply kept it hidden from himself, afraid perhaps of what he might find in the crypt of his own heart, afraid that he was just like them.

He looked up at McCoy. "Thanks," he said quietly.

"Does that mean I can go?"

Lyman nodded. "Tell the countess, good luck."

The man with the thin mustache smiled and said, "I will."

"Oh, one more thing," Lyman added. "Just out of curiosity."

"Yes?"

"Where exactly is she taking the gospel?"

McCoy looked away. "Don't worry, Mr. Lyman. It's long gone now."

"But where?"

The man with the thin mustache looked back at Lyman and frowned. Then he raised his right hand slightly and pointed at the sky.

Lyman turned. He looked across the square at the

cathedral where McCoy had pointed, high above the great walls rising, the gargoyles and the copper roof, the spires reaching for the sky. The clouds had drifted and the backdrop of the night revealed a string of lights way in the distance, far above. It was an airplane winging west from Paris, chasing the sun across the North Atlantic to America. Lyman laughed quietly to himself.

"I hope the world is ready for it," he said finally.

He followed the flight of the airplane above the cathedral and felt himself pulled skyward by the buttresses and walls, buoyed by the bright lights in the grass. He imagined rising past the gargoyles, past the spires and copper cross. He saw the silver outline of the airplane hovering against the darkness, the portholes glowing warmly, the sound of knitting needles and the small shape of the woman sitting with her seatbelt fastened, pulling at the blue yarn in the large bag by her feet.

It had stopped raining, Lyman realized, as the airplane moved away. The sky loomed black and infinite above the great cathedral, empty, except for a few blue stars just coming into view, the clear clean fire of the Pleiades.

Chapter XXIV

THE BOX LAY ON THE MARBLE DESK. He removed the remainder of the wrapping, cutting the string carefully. The box was green. It was labeled Au Printemps. It was made of cardboard.

There was a note inside. At first he almost missed it as he pulled the top away. It was hidden in a clot of tissue paper. He picked it up. It was a business card.

From all of us, to all of you, it read. *Twin spirits. Congratulations.* That was all. He turned it over. At the center of the card, embossed in a simple script, was the name Countess Irene Chantal de Rochambaud.

He smiled. Underneath the tissue paper was another box, much smaller, made of wood. There was an odd little window in it at the very top, which he realized was some kind of electronic gauge to monitor humidity. He reached down and lifted it onto his desk. The latch was on the side. No, there were two, he noticed. He opened them and took a long, deep breath. Then he lifted the top of the wooden box and the air around him seemed to fill with gold dust, floating, spinning, pinpricks of light. He put the top down on the desk and the gold dust settled into paper motes, fragments of parchment from the ancient weathered text within.

A buzzer sounded and he reached across his desk.

"What is it, Denise?"

"It's that editor from *PW* again. You promised him an interview."

"Tell him I'll have to call him back. And hold my calls, please. I don't want to be disturbed."

"Yes, Mr. Robinson."

Epilogue

THE RIVER WOUND ITS WAY ALONG the valley floor, across the open fields and hedgerows, heavy with rain, wavering the weeds and willow branches. Lyman stood in the center of the chalk stream breaking in a brand-new pair of Orvis waders, air mail from America. He wore his old felt Irish fishing hat and a wool sweater. A landing net hung at his side. The sun was starting to descend and he could see the last ring of a rise against it.

A hatch of flies had just exploded on the water. After weeks of hanging on to weeds and river bottom, the insect larvae had finally made it to the surface. Lyman watched the profusion of flight with one eye as he tied an olive dun to the tippet of his line. The artificial fly looked tiny in his hand. He blew on the hackles carefully to straighten them.

The trout rose with the understated swelling of a heavy fish. Lyman barely heard the surface of the river breaking. He looked up and saw the circles rolling toward him from upstream. Then the river settled once again. He waited and waited and the shadow rose. The brass plane broke and in a second it was over. The insect was sucked down. The river closed around it. The strong jaws of the trout slipped back and disappeared.

Lyman heard his name called out long before he saw the boy. It was the warden's son, John. He was hurtling along the footpath on the far side of the river, running full out, ignoring the weeds, the holes of water rats, running for the hell of it.

Lyman flung the fly up in the air, whipping his arm back simultaneously, letting the weight of the line shoot the olive dun back through the air behind him. Then forward, then back, building momentum. The fishing line curved perfectly.

"Nigel. Nigel," the boy shouted from the bank. His voice vanished across the open fields. "London's on the phone. Mr. Randall got a call from Interpol. They say that everything's a mess since they took Cocksedge out. They want you back there right away."

Lyman stripped a few more yards of line from his reel and let it slip through his fingers slowly. His cast extended across the surface of the river, inching closer toward the rise.

"Nigel, answer me! They say it's an important case. Nigel!"

Lyman felt the power in his arm as he brought the rod back once again. He counted as the line extended far behind him. Two. Three. And then he leaned a little forward in a grim determined way. His right arm fell, the rod curved and the line unrolled itself. He felt it slipping through the fingers of his left hand, rushing off the water through the air, above the trout rise, straight, straight, straight down the center of the river as if it would go on forever.

ABOUT THE AUTHOR

Born in Chicago, J. G. Sandom was raised and educated in Italy, France, and England. Winner of the 1978 Academy of American Poets Prize, Mr. Sandom resides in New York where he is the founder and creative director of the nation's leading interactive multimedia advertising agency. He is currently working on a new novel, *The Hunting Club*, recently optioned by Warner Brothers.

If you enjoyed *Gospel Truths*, you will want
to read
J. G. Sandom's newest work,

The Hunting Club

coming soon in Doubleday hardcover.
Look for it at your local bookseller.

Here is a special preview of *The Hunting
Club*.

**The Hunting Club
by J. G. Sandom**

Thump. Thump. Thump. Across the wetlands of New Jersey, the two Bell helicopters fly, across the Hudson River to the city. Manhattan claws the morning sky, the ethereal blueness of another day thrown up by the Atlantic. The helicopters swoop, Glen Morrow in the lead, with John Payne riding on his heels across the leaden winter water, across the broken wooden docks, the shattered warehouses and empty lots. *Thump, thump,* the rotors spin, each set with the cadence of a beating heart and the gush of unseen thermals. Morrow swings his craft across the silver skyline, skidding on the air. The two ships tilt and slide. Payne feels the blood rush to his head as he strains against the force of gravity, his body pressed to the door, against the Plexiglas and steel, a thousand feet of air and then the distant city streets below.

"How'm I doing?" Morrow says into his headset microphone.

"Okay, but don't get too close to the buildings, or they'll pull your license, Glen. I mean it. And keep your damn tail steady."

Glen Morrow's helicopter falls, swoops down along the West Side Highway by the river. "Jesus Christ," says Payne. He trims his cyclic stick and follows. They skirt the river at a hundred knots, past Houston and TriBeCa, skimming the patchwork quilt of brownstone roofs, riding the shimmer of a thousand cars, the glimmer of Christmas lights and neon to the south. The financial district looms ahead, a stand of crystals, black on blue, with the spires of the World Trade Towers propping up the morning sun.

"I told you not to get so close," says Payne, but Morrow does not hear him. He is trying out his brand new speaker airphone. His helicopter pulls up to a hover, against the black face of a skyscraper. Payne shimmies in beside him.

"Pull back," says Payne. "You're still within five hundred feet." He can clearly see a line of curious faces staring out at him from windows in the building. "Stop showing off."

"Are you ready, John?" says Morrow on the radio.

The words reverberate inside Payne's headset. He turns the volume down. "For what?"

Thump. Thump. "Tonight. Tom's bachelor party."

"I guess so," Payne replies, but Morrow is already on the phone with someone else. The bachelor party. It's all they'd talked about all week.

Payne shakes his head. He pulls up his collective and the helicopter rises slowly. Morrow is talking to a woman. The voice seems familiar, but Payne can barely hear her. Then the knowledge comes to him from nowhere and he understands why Glen is hovering so close. This is Bob Litchfield's building.

"What do you mean he's on the line," says Morrow with disgust. "Tell him it's me, Jill. And look out the window, behind you."

"I'm sorry, Mr. Morrow. I can't hear you. There's a . . ."

"Just turn around," says Morrow. "That's right. Hello."

Payne sees the telltale hourglass shape of Litchfield's secretary behind the tinted glass, can almost feel her catch her breath and pull away.

"Is that you, Mr. Morrow? You're awful close," she says.

"Tell Bobby I'm on the line, Jill."

There is a click and Payne can hear Bobby's high-pitched nasal voice. "I've got Rick on hold, Glen. Let me call you back."

"Did you confirm the reservation?"

"That's what we're talking about. The Quonset Hut, right? Tom said he'd meet us there at eight."

"Look out your window, Bobby."

There is a gasp, and arms swing wildly in the window next to Jill's.

"You're nuts, Glen," Litchfield says.

"Pull up, Glen, dammit," Payne says, but his words just

echo in his head. Morrow is talking to the Teterboro tower. Someone has lodged a complaint.

The helicopters drop away, across the pyramids of glass, across the West Side Highway and out into the bay. The Statue of Liberty glows green against the inky water. Morrow is still talking to Mildred in the Teterboro tower. He is explaining that he pulled in close to Litchfield's building because he thought he saw a jumper on the roof, and for some strange reason she believes him, for some uncanny reason she accepts each word without a moment's hesitation, as if there is something in Glen's voice so genuine and clear, so naturally persuasive that to dispute it would seem petty, insincere.

How does he always do it? wonders Payne. Mildred signs off with a word of thanks, and Morrow's laugh resounds across the airwaves.

"I'm telling you, Glen. They're going to pull your license." Payne tries to sound responsible, but he knows that chiding Morrow is useless. It is so hard to be mad at him. It is like being mad at a tree, or the tide.

"They can try," says Morrow. His ship dives forward suddenly, banking toward the Statue of Liberty, cutting at the air. *Thump. Thump.* Payne starts to follow, but Morrow's A-Star is too fast. Payne pulls up his collective. He flares his ship into a hover, and strains to watch as Morrow's helicopter hurtles toward the sea like Icarus descending. A laugh rolls through his headset. The distant ship banks steeply around the statue, almost crashing through the giant torch. Payne holds his breath. The helicopter falls and falls, disappears behind the crown—a single rotor disk from Liberty—only to reappear unscathed, skimming the waves across the bay like a bird of prey, churning up whitecaps, trailing the sound of laughter.

He can't hear what the world is saying with the water rushing around his ears; only the music pounding through the white enamel and the rumble of a distant subway, timed to the pulsing of his heart. Payne lifts his face out of the sink and blows a pearl of water from his lips.

His eyes are half closed. He reaches for a paper towel and rips it from the gleaming chrome dispenser on the wall. He wipes his face, and there he is in the mirror the hair disheveled, dark, and wet along the brow. There is the thin peak of a nose, the hazel deep-set eyes, the wide mouth and high forehead. He crumples the paper towel in his fist and runs a hand back through his dark brown hair. Then he straightens his tie. He is prepared now. He is ready for the world, he tells himself. He spins about on his heel and heads out through the men's room door.

A jumble of round tables, orange birds of paradise in square terra-cotta pots, a waiter with a tray of sky-blue frozen daiquiris—Payne visually gathers up the restaurant. The Quonset Hut is packed tonight, the tables dressed in starched white tablecloths, resplendent with heaped plates of fish and fowl, blackened Cajun blues and Cornish hen, the telling curve of ribs, radiccio salad, crab, and shrimp, with countless fluted glasses spilling their light across the eager faces of the crowd. I have to pace myself. It's early still, Payne thinks as he looks down at his watch. Across the room, the background hum of conversation is punctured by Glen Morrow's laugh. There, past the tall blonde with the cinder-colored cocktail dress, beyond her Afro-American companion in the double-breasted navy suit, there's Morrow with his Caribbean tan and wide disarming smile, faithful Bobby Litchfield at his side. And there's Tom Demarest. Poor Demarest. Trying to make a go of it, trying to forget the seconds ticking, ticking slowly toward the moment when he'd finally turn and say, "I do." Somewhere there is the sound of breaking glass. Somewhere a knife slips on a plate and a woman in a chartreuse mini-skirt picks up her napkin from the floor, her silver earrings dangling. Payne weaves his way between the tables, drawing the bands of conversation to him, a disappointment here, a compliment, a curse. He ambles casually around a wide stone pillar and skillfully avoids the waitress—*Hi, I'm Tiffany*—porting yet another bottle of champagne to table twenty-seven.

"What happened? You get lost?" says Avery, as Payne sits down beside him.

"The place is packed. For a Wednesday."

Rick Avery grins and looks around. "The Babylon of our millennium. The overfed and undernourished flotsam of our self-indulgent culture."

"You should have been a copywriter instead of an art

director," Payne replies. The waitress pops the cork on the champagne.

"A morass of mindless mediocrity, mooning mawkishly," adds Avery.

"Malcontents."

"Misfits."

"Misanthropes."

"Plenty of babes, though," Avery says.

"That too."

Rick Avery is dressed in a pair of black jeans, a black turtleneck and umber jacket. His dark brown hair is long and straight and falls constantly across his bright black, plastic-rimmed glasses. He smiles and says, "Speaking only as a disinterested observer, I'm sure, Mr. Payne. How is Jan, anyway? Still vomiting when she sees you in the morning? Not that I blame her, mind you."

"She's home," Payne says, lifting his glass toward the waitress. "Weaving a tapestry."

"Oh, you guys," says Bobby Litchfield. "You ought to be setting an example for Demarest here."

"Don't look at me," says Avery. "I have yet to fall. I'm the last of the Watusi, the only warrior left."

"The only one not guaranteed to get laid on a Friday night," says Morrow. He looks up at the waitress. "Right, Tiffany?" Glen's tanned face lights up with a smile. He has just returned from another weekend in the Caribbean and his skin is cocoa brown.

"Hey, you missed me," Tom Demarest complains, pointing to his empty glass.

The waitress frowns and pulls the bottle of champagne out of the standing wine bucket. "He thirsts for you," adds Morrow. "In seventy-two hours he'll be a married man."

Tiffany is a gaunt, red-haired giant from Michigan, looking for a speaking part. "My heartiest congratulations," she says flatly.

She is wearing false eyelashes, Payne notices. Her pink taffeta dress is tight across the chest. "You mean condolences?" he says.

"What's that?" says Morrow. "Trouble in paradise?"

Tiffany empties the champagne bottle into Demarest's glass, and slips it back into the silver wine bucket, neck down through the ice.

"Take it from me, Tom," Morrow adds, "marriage is a

wondrous, sacred act. The union of two people. The sharing of two lives, ideas, ambitions. I should know," he says to Tiffany. "I'm on my third." He reaches out and takes her by the hand. "Pay no attention to these barbarians."

"Let go of me, mister."

"How about another bottle?" Morrow says, releasing her.

She pulls her arm away. "Haven't you guys had enough?"

"Enough!" says Avery indignantly. "Have we had enough, boys?"

"No!" they answer uniformly.

Tiffany shakes her head and walks away. They all stare at her as she wiggles in between the tables.

Demarest sighs. "I've never had a redhead," he admits. He is a large man, with the rounded shoulders of a former weight lifter, with light brown thinning hair, combed with aplomb across his bald spot. His eyes are a gravy brown, oxlike, set close together, linked by a tuft of light brown hair at the bridge of his short, flat nose.

"What about that girl, Beth Cohen, from Mount Holyoke? She had red hair," says Payne.

"Oh, sure! That was only for a month, fifteen years ago. And it came out of a bottle, so it doesn't count."

"You should see this redhead we just cast for Jackson's Wax," says Avery. "Unbelievable. She plays the girlfriend of a guy who wakes up from a nap in a complete panic when he realizes that he's only got"—his face contorts in horror—"ten minutes to clean up his apartment before this heavy date. We see the redhead walking down the city streets, dressed in her office clothes, stepping out of a florist with a huge bouquet, thoughtfully examining the label of a California cabernet in a dusty wine store, waving at the old *guido* who works at the corner newsstand. Meanwhile, as she strolls, we keep cutting back to the apartment where this guy is running around like a wild man, spraying and polishing everything in sight with his Original Jackson's Wax. You know. He sprays the kitchen counter and a roast chicken—no red meat, of course—appears out of nowhere, steaming with baby carrots. Spray and puff . . . like magic. The redhead arrives at the front door and we get her view of things: the perfect living room with everything agleam; the seductive music; the table set for dinner in the background, candlelit; and our handsome hero, twitching his tail like a hungry cat."

"A true man of the eighties," Payne says.

"Right. Sensitive yet strong."

"Breadwinner *and* bread baker."

"You taking notes?" says Morrow, jabbing Demarest in the ribs. "We're warning you. It's not too late."

"Prepare to dive," cries Avery. "Whoop, whoop. Dive! Dive!"

"Oh, come on, you guys." Bobby Litchfield takes his wire-rimmed glasses off and begins to wipe them with his kerchief. His eyes are large and wet, the corners red from drinking. His thin receding hair is short and curly. He is wearing a red silk bowtie and a russet Gieves tweed jacket. "Don't let them kid you, Tom. I've been married for twelve years and I've never regretted it. Well, practically never." He smiles.

"That's because she doesn't give you enough free time for you to realize you regret it," Morrow says.

"And before you know it you'll have kids. Right, John?" adds Litchfield, with a wink at Payne. He replaces his glasses and pushes them deftly up the snub curve of his nose. "Don't listen to these jerks. Having a kid is really great. It's why we're on this planet in the first place. It's what really counts."

"Tick, tick, tick," says Avery. "Each second brings you closer to the altar." He spreads his hands out on the table-cloth. "Well I'm happy being free. And I'm the only member of The Hunting Club who can say that now, and really mean it." He lifts his champagne glass. "To Tom and Anna Demarest. May they rest in peace."

Demarest smiles. It is the smile of an idiot, thinks Payne, the smile of a man who hasn't got a clue.

He remembers the day of his own wedding four years earlier. He had worn the same flat open face. The world had been so full of promise then, of things to come, of possibility. Except the possibility of failure, failure by forgetfulness, dissolution by neglect. It wasn't that he didn't love Jan anymore. Love itself seemed to have changed. It had been homogenized by time, made dull by repetition, until the feelings had retreated into background hum, like the constant scratching of cicadas, the drumming of chopper blades.

"I thought you guys might like to order now." Tiffany has returned, Payne notices, with a handful of menus and another bottle of champagne. She slips the fresh champagne into the wine bucket, and hands the menus to them one by one. "We also have some specials. For appetizers we have fresh chanterelle mushrooms cooked in olive oil with a hint of garlic . . ." Payne watches her mouth as she drones on, the way her lips come together in the corners, the slight overbite, the curve of her nostrils, the pink tenderness where her bright red plastic earrings hang. He takes his menu and drops it on the table. She delivers her lines precisely, smiles, and glides away.

They study their menus for a moment without speaking. Then Avery turns to Morrow. "I have a bone to pick with you," he says.

"Pick away, lad."

"It's about that gaming stock."

"Which one?"

"The one you told me about. The Shangri-la Casino. The one with all the bowling lanes."

"No, that's the Showboat."

"You know the one I mean. In Atlantic City. I did exactly what you told me. I bought the stock at seventeen."

"And?"

"And disaster, man. It dropped to fourteen when I finally sold."

"That was yesterday. I told everyone to see last week. If you'd come out with us last Wednesday . . ."

"I did," says Litchfield. "At nineteen fifty. Two thousand shares. Let's see, that's five K if you don't count taxes or commissions." He grins at Morrow. "Thanks, Glen."

"Yeah, thanks a lot," says Avery bitterly.

Morrow hunches over the table. "How many times do I have to tell you guys? If you're going to play this game, you have to have the stomach for it. You have to be able to lose. If you can't afford it, don't take the risk." He fixes a cold stare on Avery. "And the next time I say sell, Rick, sell. Don't fuck around. Don't go up to Vermont for the weekend and forget about it. Don't wait until after lunch. If I tell you to do something, do it." He smiles and his face abruptly changes. The blue eyes soften. The lines about his mouth relax. It is the face of a petulant god, thinks Payne. One minute it holds the wrath of thunder under a dark and furrowed brow, the next it lights up like a fissure in the clouds. The deepset ice blue eyes grow bright. The golden head tilts back. The famous Morrow smile expands across the tanned and noble face, at once both artfully bemused and natural: the proud grin of an older brother watching you at the plate; a father looking through a lighted doorway at his sleeping child.

"Ready to order?" Tiffany's Midwestern accent lifts a corner of the conversation.

"Yeah, we're ready," Morrow says.

Payne settles on Atlantic salmon broiled with dill, served with asparagus and new potatoes. He can see the woman at the next table chewing contentedly on the light pink flesh.

As soon as Tiffany departs, the conversation turns to Anna, Tom Demarest's fiancée. Demarest sings her praises. She is the most beautiful, the most understanding, the most impeccable family . . .

Payne finds himself staring at the woman at the next table. She is eating asparagus with her fingers, gliding the green buds through Hollandaise, biting off the dark tips with white teeth. The woman is about Jan's age, with the same brown hair, the same highlights of red copper even, spilling over her bare shoulder. Her skin is very fair, her features delicate and small. So much like his wife, except, of course, without the bold bow of Jan's pregnant stomach.

The food comes and Payne finds himself drawn into conversation with Avery about his search for an apartment in New York. Now that Demarest is getting married and moving out, Avery can no longer afford the house that they've been sharing in Connecticut. It's time to find a loft, or a one-bedroom in the city. "It's got to have a lot of light," he says, chewing his mushroom ravioli. "Big windows. I've got to get back to my work. You know I haven't painted in six months."

"I haven't had sex in two."

Avery snorts and turns away. Then he glances back at Payne and says, "You're kidding, right?"

"I wish I were."

"What are you two talking about?" Morrow leans across the table for the bottle of champagne.

"Nothing."

"About my apartment. Or lack thereof," says Avery.

"How about it, Bobby? I thought you said you knew a lot of landlords."

"If you want to spend two hundred thousand, I can get you a place on Park."

"Actually, I was thinking about Soho or TriBeCa."

"Who wants more wine?" says Morrow, waving the bottle in the air. "It's still half full."

Payne offers up his glass. "Thanks."

"So, what did you think, John? How'd I do? Today, I mean," says Morrow casually.

"Fine. Just fine," says Payne.

Litchfield knocks Payne's glass out of the way, and replaces it with his own. Morrow keeps pouring the champagne.

"You know you gave Jill a heart attack this morning," adds Litchfield with a giggle. "When your helicopter came whipping up like that, I swear, she almost had a cow."

"Trying to get me fired," Payne replies. "You're crazy, Glen."

"Was that your final class?" says Litchfield.

Morrow nods. He is gazing into space, absent.

"It was with me," says Payne. "I'm a traffic reporter, not a fucking stunt pilot."

"You see. And you were so reluctant to give lessons. I told you so."

"Was I?" Payne says. "I don't remember that."

"I do," Morrow says.

Payne sips his champagne. "You did all right today," he says. "You're a very capable pilot, Glen."

The words have their desired effect. Morrow smiles privately and leans back in his chair.

Why had it been so hard to say? Payne wonders. Morrow *was* a good pilot. More than that, he was a natural. Perhaps that was the reason. Morrow was a natural at so many things. He always had been.

Payne feels the champagne bubbles sting his tongue. Morrow already had so much. Did he really need to fly down to his farm in Pennsylvania? Why couldn't he drive, or take a train like everybody else? When the engine caught and the helicopter shuddered into life, when the steel blades pulled him from the power of the earth, Payne wished to be there by himself. It was his world. It was his city from the air, the towering stone, the metal and the glass, the mile on mile of highway, street, and road. He closes his eyes and rises higher, above the silver Hudson River, above the urban lots, the oily stream of traffic, trimming the bottom of the clouds, suspended, like the baby in Jan's uterus, curled up and all alone in his Plexiglas balloon.

Somewhere a woman laughs. He turns to see if he can spot her in the crowd. Hands rise to gesture or to eat. Someone is pointing. Someone waves over at the door. Payne sees the crowd reflected in the mirror behind the bar. It shifts and undulates. It seethes and eddies. The woman laughs again but he can't see her.

He turns back to the table. Avery is telling a story about a junior account executive at McQuaid, Delaway, and Scoosi, the ad agency where he works. "I've fallen in love," he admits. "She has the face of a Venus. Long blond hair. Green eyes. Curves that don't quit. I'm talking parabolic."

"Why don't you ask her out?" says Morrow.

"I did."

"And?"

"She told me she doesn't date guys she's working with. It's against her code."

"She couldn't say it was your hairy nostrils. Dear John," says Payne, falling in.

"Wait, it gets worse. About two weeks ago I'm working late on the Goldcrest account when I realize I need confirmation on a board change. So I take the stairs up to the A.E.'s office to see if he has sign-off from the client. There's nobody around. It must be nearly nine o'clock. I hear Michael—that's the account executive's name—in his office. It sounds like he's on the phone, because I can only hear one voice. So I knock on the door and poke my head in." Avery pauses for effect. "There's Michael behind his desk, leaning back in his chair, his eyes closed and his hands locked together behind his head. He hears me coming in. 'Yeah, what's up?' he asks me, casual-like. I tell him what I need. He thinks about it for a moment, and then says, 'Go ahead.' So I split."

"That's it?" says Demarest. "What about the blonde?"

Avery smiles. "At first I didn't see them."

"What?"

"Her shoes, man. I was looking up at Michael. He sat

there so nonchalant. It was only when I was about to leave that I looked down and saw the bottom of these green pumps poking out from under the desk."

"You gotta be kidding," Payne says.

"An hour later, I'm standing by the elevator to leave when the door opens and there's Michael and the junior A.E. They're all bundled up in their coats. I look down and, sure enough, there are the green pumps."

"So much for her code," says Morrow. He pushes his empty plate away.

"Are we finished here?" Tiffany has returned. "How about some dessert?" She waves at a Puerto Rican busboy with a tray, and he starts to take their plates away.

Payne reaches into his jacket and fishes out his Marlboros.

"Are you on the menu too?" says Demarest.

The waitress straightens, arms akimbo, one fist on her hip. "What's that?"

"You heard him," Morrow says. "He's getting desperate as the hour draws near."

"With whipped cream," Demarest says. "I like whipped cream."

"Now, now, boys, simmer down." She wags a finger at them. "You want dessert, or not?"

"And hot fudge topping," Demarest says, "dripping down the side."

"You're terrible," she says and laughs. "Well, here, if you don't want anything else." She drops their tab on the table. Litchfield picks it up. He glances at it for a second and hands her his American Express card.

"What about my dessert?" says Demarest.

"Now look what you've done," says Morrow. "He's heartbroken."

The waitress smiles uncertainly.

"Cold, heartless woman, you've destroyed him," Morrow says. Demarest looks crushed. He takes his napkin and dabs the corners of his oxlike eyes.

"Oh, poor baby," she replies. Demarest reaches out for her but she slips gingerly away. "Okay, that's it," she says, no longer smiling. "I don't want to have to call the manager."

"Oohh," says Demarest, with mock terror. "Not the manager. Please, God, not him!"

"Come on, you guys," says Payne. "Cut it out. Thanks for your help, miss."

Everyone laughs. Tiffany shakes her head and strides away.

"No sense of humor," Morrow says.

"Uptight," says Demarest. "Frigid."

"This is an outrage to The Hunting Club," says Morrow. "Our guest of honor has been slighted."

"Insulted," Avery says.

"Spurned, I would say."

"Is it my nose, my breath?" says Demarest.

"Or both," says Payne. He plucks a book of matches from the ashtray and lights his cigarette.

"I move we adjourn immediately . . ." says Morrow.

"Seconded," Demarest says.

". . . and reconvene in more suitable surroundings."

"Where to?" says Litchfield, perking up.

"Where the women are easy and the drinks flow free."

"A land just beyond the horizon, a fat country," adds Avery. "Where the deer and the antelope play."

"The Party Girl Lounge," says Morrow. "Six blocks up."

"What's that, a strip joint?" Litchfield crinkles his nose.

"I believe the correct term is exotic dancers," Morrow says.

"I'm game," says Demarest. "But only if we take the cars. It's fucking cold out there." He pushes his chair back from the table. "What's the matter, BB? Got something against naked women?"

"Very funny." The busboy returns with Litchfield's credit card. "If you guys want to," he says absently, adding up the figures. "I guess one drink won't kill me."

"No, but the view might," Avery says.

Demarest laughs. It is a forced and stuttering laugh, choked off by a cough. The laugh of a drunk, Payne thinks.

"Give her a fat tip," says Avery.

Payne stares at Demarest struggling with his coat. She earned it, he thinks. And then he wonders, do I look like that? A red-eyed, pale accountant. Once tall and trim, now bulging at the middle. A bald spot yawning on my head. Not as bad, perhaps, but close to it. The same theme. Two thirty-six-year olds rushing headlong into middle age. And he remembers Demarest from another time, another winter day, his long legs pounding down the football field, the Hadley–Williams game, his arms outstretched, and Morrow's perfect pass descending. They had been 13 and 0 that year, 13 and 0 thanks to Tom Demarest and Morrow. And to think the coach had almost cut Tom from the team, until Glen had intervened.

"Here, Tom," Payne says, stepping in. He slips the coat over Demarest's broad sloping shoulders. Until Glen had practiced with him every day, every rainy afternoon for hours, pass and receive, pass and receive, until Tom could catch them in his sleep, and Morrow pleaded with Coach Dunbar, and Demarest was lifted from the fire, like a moth on Morrow's fingers.

"Thanks, buddy."

They file out through the narrow central aisle between the dining tables. Morrow nods at the maitre d', drives through the brass revolving door and they gather in the silent street, the night wind nibbling at their skin.

"Nervous, Tom?" says Payne. Demarest shudders from the cold. They both look up, up past the outline of the art gallery across the street, beyond the World Trade Towers, where a distant 747 slips into view and is gone.

"I guess a little," Demarest says.

Payne clasps him by the shoulder. Avery and Morrow are walking up the block, with Litchfield clipping at their heels. "That's only natural," Payne says quietly. "Don't worry about it."

"But are you happy, John? In your marriage, I mean. I guess you must be since you're having a kid."

What could he say? "Of course I am, Tom. You will be too. Anna's a fine girl. I mean that."

They turn quickly from the Quonset Hut and make their way up the street. Payne lifts the collar of his leather jacket up against the cold wind gusting from the river. His words have fallen to the ground, it seems, blown off into the night. They mingle with the echoes of footsteps, rise up against the brick walls lining the street, and disappear. What business did he have to give advice? He'd known Demarest for fifteen years. Payne flicks his cigarette into the gutter. Too long to tell him the truth.

ELIZABETH GEORGE

"A spectacular new voice in mystery writing..."
—*Los Angeles Times*

"George is a master...an outstanding practitioner of the modern English mystery."—*Chicago Tribune*

❏ A GREAT DELIVERANCE

27802-9 $4.99/$5.99 in Canada

Winner of the 1988 Anthony and Agatha awards for best first novel

"Spellbinding...A truly fascinating story that is part psychological suspense and part detective story." —*Chicago Sun-Times*

"Exceptionally assured and impressive...highly entertaining."
—*Newsweek*

❏ PAYMENT IN BLOOD

28436-3 $4.99/$5.99 in Canada

"Satisfying indeed. George has another hit on her hands."
—*The Washington Post*

"Complex, rich, and accomplished enough to elbow the author between P.D. James and Ruth Rendell." —*Kirkus Reviews*

❏ WELL-SCHOOLED IN MURDER

28734-6 $4.99/$5.99 in Canada

"Like P.D. James, George knows the imports of the smallest human gesture: [This book] puts the author in the running with the genre's master."—*People*

❏ A SUITABLE VENGEANCE

29560-8 $4.99/$5.99 in Canada

"The book is both unusual and extremely satisfying and proves once again that George belongs in a very small field at the top of English murder mystery writing."—*The Toronto Sun*

❏ FOR THE SAKE OF ELENA

08118-7 $20.00/$23.50 in Canada

"George is...a born storyteller who spins a web of enchantment that captures the reader and will not let him go."—*The San Diego Union*

Available at your local bookstore or use this page to order.

Send to: Bantam Books, Dept. EG
   2451 S. Wolf Road
   Des Plaines, IL 60018

Please send me the items I have checked above. I am enclosing $_____ (please add $2.50 to cover postage and handling). Send check or money order, no cash or C.O.D.'s, please.

Mr./Ms._____

Address_____

City/State_____ Zip_____

Please allow four to six weeks for delivery.

Prices and availability subject to change without notice.   EG 10/92

From *The New York Times* bestselling author
THOMAS GIFFORD

THE
ASSASSINI

❑ 28740-0 $5.99/$6.99 in Canada

When lawyer Ben Driskill's sister is murdered, he sets out to find the murderer himself—and uncovers an explosive secret. For his sister is an outspoken nun who had been on the trail of the assassini, an age-old brotherhood of killers once hired by the Church to protect it in dangerous times. But whose orders do they now obey?

"Masterfully plotted and brilliantly told, *The Assassini's* suspense is unrelenting and its satisfaction is guaranteed."
—Ross Thomas, author of *The Fourth Durango*

"A monumental thriller, Gifford's masterpiece."
—Ira Levin, author of *The Boys from Brazil*

THE
WIND CHILL FACTOR

❑ 29752-X $5.99/$6.99 in Canada

Hitler lost the war. But some Nazi survivors view this defeat as merely a temporary setback. Their key personnel are now in place inside the corporations and capitals of every major nation. John Cooper is an heir to this evil and as he races against time a figure from his past is revealed and for a single electrifying moment Cooper's fate, and the fate of billions, will hang in the terrifying balance.

"Thunders along at breakneck speed...a blistering novel of suspense."—*Hartford Courant*

"The flair of a new Len Deighton."—*Detroit Free Press*

Available at your local bookstore or use this page to order.

Send to: **Bantam Books, Dept. FL 36**
2451 S. Wolf Road
Des Plaines, IL 60018

Please send me the items I have checked above. I am enclosing
$_____ (please add $2.50 to cover postage and handling). Send check or money order, no cash or C.O.D.'s, please.

Mr./Ms._____

Address_____

City/State_____Zip_____

Please allow four to six weeks for delivery.
Prices and availability subject to change without notice.   FL 36 6/92